PRAISE FOR BESTSELLING AUTHOR
STEPHEN LEATHER

'A writer at the top of his game . . . The sheer impetus
of his story-telling is damned hard to resist'
Sunday Express

'An aggressively topical novel but a genuinely
thrilling one, too'
Daily Telegraph

'As tough as British thrillers get . . . gripping'
Irish Independent

'Explores complex contemporary issues while
keeping the action fast and bloody'
Economist

'A master of the thriller genre'
Irish Times

'Fast-moving, lots of atmosphere'
Mail on Sunday

'Masterful plotting . . . rapid-fire prose'
Sunday Express

'Action and scalpel-sharp suspense'
Daily Telegraph

'Leather is an intelligent thriller writer'

STEPHEN LEATHER

TALL ORDER

HODDER

First published in Great Britain in 2018 by Hodder & Stoughton
An Hachette UK company

This paperback edition published in 2019

1

A CIP catalogue record for this title is available from the British Library

A format ISBN 978 1 473 60419 3
B format ISBN 978 1 473 60420 9

Typeset in Plantin Light by Palimpsest Book Production Limited,
Falkirk, Stirlingshire

Printed and bound in Great Britain by Clays Ltd, Elcograf S.p.A.

Hodder & Stoughton policy is to use papers that are natural,
renewable and recyclable products and made from wood grown in sustainable
forests. The logging and manufacturing processes are expected to conform
to the environmental regulations of the country of origin.

Hodder & Stoughton Ltd
Carmelite House
50 Victoria Embankment
London EC4Y 0DZ

www.hodder.co.uk

For Skye

Chapter 1

Ten Years Ago, New York

The boy was only nine years old but he was a seasoned traveller and as soon as he was in his first-class seat he picked up the in-flight magazine to see what movies would be showing. 'Seen it, seen it, seen it,' he muttered to himself, but loud enough for his mother to hear.

'Would you like a drink?' asked a stewardess with dyed blond hair and a toothpaste commercial smile. 'I have water and orange juice.'

'Is it freshly squeezed?' he asked.

The smile tightened a fraction. 'I'm sure it was before it went into the carton,' said the stewardess.

'Do you have Coke?'

'I have Pepsi.'

'I don't like Pepsi,' said the boy. He pouted and folded his arms.

The boy's mother smiled at the stewardess. 'He'll be fine with water,' she said.

'He's probably had all the sugar he needs already,' muttered the stewardess, placing a glass of water next to the boy. 'I'll be back with a play pack for him. Would you care for champagne?'

'Water for me, too,' said the boy's mother. She opened her purse and took out a pack of aspirin, popped a tablet into her mouth and washed it down with her glass of water.

'Do you have a headache?' asked the boy.

'It helps my circulation while we're flying,' she said.

'Shouldn't I have one?'

'You're nine. You don't need it.'

The boy put down the magazine. 'I wish Dad was with us.'

'He's busy, honey. He'll join us in Paris next week.'

'But I want to see him in London.'

'Your father's a busy man, honey. He has a lot to do in Washington. You know that. Now fasten your seat belt.'

The boy smiled sarcastically and lifted his magazine to show that he already had his belt on. Then he twisted around to look at the two men in dark suits who were sitting at the back of the cabin. One of them waved. He was the nice one. His name was Tom and he said he had a son who was the same age as he was. The boy waved back.

The engines kicked into life. 'Why do we always have to fly?' asked the boy.

The boy's mother frowned. 'What do you mean?'

'Flying's boring. There's nothing to see. Why can't we go on the train?'

'We're going to London, honey. We have to fly. You can't go to London from New York on a train. But we can get a train from London to Paris.'

'We could go on a boat to London. Boats are fun.'

The woman laughed. 'Honey, it would take for ever. This way we'll be in London in seven hours.'

'But flying is boring.'

'There are some children who never get to fly first class their whole lives.'

'They're welcome to my seat if they want it.' He folded his arms and scowled. 'I'm bored.'

'You can watch a movie. Or play on your Nintendo DS.'

The stewardesses moved through the cabin collecting glasses and making sure that seat belts were fastened and tray tables were up. The plane reversed away from the terminal and headed down the taxiway. Ten minutes later they were airborne. The boy leaned across to the window and looked out. He saw water far below, and boats so small that they seemed like toys. He saw a ferry and three yachts sailing in a line and a huge ship that was loaded with containers. In the distance were the skyscrapers of Manhattan. The boy tried to find the one that King Kong had climbed but there were too many. Then the boy saw something small streaking through the sky. It looked like a rocket, with a plume of smoke behind it. He could see small fins on the back, where the smoke was. The boy frowned. He'd been at a space shuttle launch once with his dad but this wasn't anything like that. The shuttle went straight up into the sky but this rocket wasn't going straight up, it was curving through the air, heading towards the plane.

'Mum, look at this,' he said.

'Look at what, honey?' said his mother, her face buried in a magazine.

'There, outside the plane.'

His mother sighed and put down the magazine. 'Honey, I'm reading.'

The boy turned back to the window. The rocket was moving faster now. And it was a lot closer. He opened his mouth to tell his mother but the rocket seemed to accelerate and then it slammed into the wing and erupted in a ball of flame. The plane lurched to the left and then began to spin. The boy screamed. He turned to look at his mother and she was screaming too. Everybody was screaming. Even the two men in dark suits at the back of the cabin were screaming.

The plane was spinning faster, pushing the boy against the fuselage. He tried to reach for his mother but she was too far away. There was a ripping sound and then the back of the cabin broke off and there was a wind so strong that it tore at the boy's hair and he saw the two men in dark suits spin out into the sky, still strapped into their seats. The stewardess with the blond hair was flattened against the ceiling, screaming in terror, then the wind whipped her away and she was gone. Those passengers who were still conscious were screaming at the tops of their voices but the sound was lost in the roar of the slipstream. Then everything went black.

Chapter 2

Ten Years Ago, New York

From where they were standing, the three men could see the burning wreckage of the jet streaking across the darkening sky. One of the men was holding a digital video camera, and he was muttering to himself as he tracked the main fuselage as it spiralled down towards the sea.

'*Allahu Akbar, Allahu Akbar,*' shouted the one named Hamid. He was from Dubai in the United Arab Emirates.

'*Allahu Akbar,*' echoed Saeed, the man standing to his left. He was holding the Stinger missile launcher unit on his shoulder as he stared up at the carnage in the sky. A black and white checked scarf was wrapped around the lower part of his face. Saeed was an Iraqi, though he had entered the United States with a French passport that showed his place of birth as Algeria.

The third man, Rashid, also had his face covered with a scarf, and he was wearing wraparound sunglasses. 'This is what happens to the infidel dogs who kill our Muslim brothers around the world!' he shouted. He had the dark skin and glossy black hair of a Pakistani but he spoke with the flat vowels of a north of England accent.

The man with the video camera turned the lens on him.

Rashid clenched his fist and punched the air. 'We are bringing the war to your country, where it belongs!' he shouted. 'What we have done today we will do again and again until we bring your country to its knees. *Allahu Akbar! Allahu Akbar!*'

Hamid finished filming. He clicked the camera shut. 'Put the launcher in the truck,' he said. 'And let's get out of here. Hakeem will be waiting and I want to see this on the Internet.'

The final pieces of the plane hit the water and the remaining flames flickered out. The three men climbed into their black SUV. Hamid got into the back with his camera. Saeed put the launcher on the back seat, slammed the door and got behind the wheel. Rashid took the passenger seat. 'Come on, let's go,' he said. 'We need to get away from here. They'll set up cordons as soon as they realise what's happened.'

Saeed started the engine and hit the accelerator. They were on a narrow track that ran by a small industrial park, a dozen or so warehouses with empty car parks. There were no street lights but Saeed kept the headlights off until they joined the main road.

There wasn't much traffic around and he kept to just below the speed limit. 'Did you see the way it fell apart when the missile hit?' said Saeed. He drummed his hands on the steering wheel. 'It must have been in a hundred pieces. More.'

'Keep your eyes on the road,' said Rashid. 'And keep your speed down.'

'You worry too much,' said Saeed.

Hamid opened the video camera and pressed the play button. He grinned as he watched the screen. 'I should be in Hollywood,' he said. 'The focus is perfect. And the way I follow the missile, Spielberg couldn't have done better.'

'Let me see, let me see,' said Saeed.

'Keep your eyes on the road!' Rashid shouted.

Saeed twisted around in his seat. 'Show me,' he said.

Hamid held out the video camera.

Rashid's eyes widened in horror as he saw the traffic lights ahead turn red. 'Saeed!' he screamed.

The SUV roared through the red light. A truck coming at them from the left sounded its horn and Hamid threw himself across the back seat. Its lights burst through the side windows. 'Sorry, sorry, sorry!' shouted Saeed, wrenching the wheel to the right and stamping on the accelerator. The truck missed them by inches, its horn still blaring.

'Fucking hell!' shouted Rashid. 'What the fuck are you doing?'

'I'm sorry,' said Saeed, applying the brakes.

'We could have fucking died!'

'Well we didn't, Allah be praised.'

'Keep your eyes on the fucking road.'

'I will, I will.'

Rashid sat back in his seat and looked at his watch. The plan was to drive to a shopping mall and transfer to another vehicle. They would torch the SUV to destroy any forensics, and then drive west. There was a good chance that all the airports would be closed in the wake of the attack but that wasn't a problem; they weren't going anywhere. They would hole up in a motel and wait until the hue and cry had died down.

Chapter 3

Ten Years Ago, New York

'Now they're saying maybe it was struck by lightning,' said Ricky Sanchez. He was watching CNN on his mobile phone, propped up against a ceramic mug containing a dozen or so ballpoint pens, most of which he had chewed on. The screen was showing two coastguard vessels on the ocean as a headline ran across the bottom: MORE THAN 300 FEARED DEAD AS PLANE CRASHES INTO ATLANTIC. Sanchez was in his early forties and so wide that he had trouble getting in and out of his chair. There was a small, framed photograph of his pretty wife and four young sons on the table in front of the bank of CCTV monitors covering the shopping mall above them. Sanchez was cracking peanut shells and washing the nuts down with a Dr Pepper.

'It's too early to tell,' said his colleague. Dean Martin was ten years younger than Sanchez, and about half his weight. Both men were wearing dark blue uniforms, though Martin had hung his jacket over the back of his chair.

'You think the A-Rabs did it?' asked Sanchez, reaching into the bag of peanuts.

Martin shrugged. 'Too early to tell,' he repeated.

'Fucking A-Rabs. What is it with them blowing themselves up all the time?' He cracked a shell and popped the nuts in his mouth.

'Could have been a missile,' said Martin.

'A missile? Like a rocket? Where would the A-Rabs get a rocket from?'

'Surface-to-air missiles are easy to buy these days,' said Martin. 'Plenty of arms dealers out there who'll sell anything to anybody.'

'You're shitting me? And they could shoot down a plane?'

'Sure. They call them man-portable air-defense systems. MANPADS. Lots of companies make them. The missiles can be up to six feet long and engage targets up to four miles away. That means a plane above twenty thousand feet is pretty much safe, but they're obviously vulnerable at take-off and landing.'

Sanchez looked over at him. 'How come you know so much about shit like that?'

Martin shrugged. 'I watch a lot of Discovery Channel.' He stood up and picked up his jacket. 'I'll do a walk-around before I head off,' he said. His shift had finished ten minutes earlier but he had wanted to watch the news reports. Two more men were due to work the graveyard shift with Sanchez but one had phoned in to say that he would be half an hour late and the other had gone straight to the men's room with a newspaper.

'You mean a run-around,' said Sanchez. He weighed close to four hundred pounds, and spent most of his shift sitting in his high-backed chair watching the bank of monitors that took feeds from the fifty or so CCTV cameras around the mall. All the shops and restaurants had closed for the night but they were still supposed to do a walk-around every hour. Sanchez rarely did and wasn't bothered whether or not his colleagues did either.

'See you tomorrow,' said Martin, fastening his jacket and checking his baton and handcuffs. They weren't allowed firearms, which was fair enough because the mall was in a nice suburban area and the only problems they had to deal with were the occasional misbehaving schoolchild and the odd shoplifter.

The security office was in the basement, adjacent to the underground car park, and Martin took the stairs to the ground floor. The elevators and escalators had all been switched off and with no muzak playing, Martin's footsteps echoed as he walked through the deserted mall. He took off his belt and placed it on a bench by the fish pool along with his holdall. He removed his jacket, then jogged up one of the escalators and did a quick run around the upper floor. It was close to half a mile all the way around and took him just under three minutes. Once he'd done his circuit he dropped and did twenty-five press-ups, fifty sit-ups, and then ran down the escalator and repeated the session on the lower level. He was breathing heavily but not sweating by the time he'd finished.

He put his jacket back on, refastened his belt and carried his holdall along to the side entrance. He had to swipe his keycard through a reader to open the door that led to the main car park at the rear of the mall. He had left his car in the employees' car park, the furthest away from the main building.

A black SUV drove off the main road and into the parking lot. Martin frowned as he watched the vehicle drive slowly through the empty lot. His frown deepened as he realised it was heading towards another car, a white sedan parked in front of the Sears entrance. He hadn't noticed the white sedan; it was empty and in an area not well lit, close to a bank of bushes.

The SUV switched off its headlights as it pulled up next to the white sedan. Martin started walking towards it but he kept close to the mall building. Doors opened and three men got out. Arabs, by the look of them. Two of them bearded. Wearing casual clothing. Martin stopped in the shadows, wondering what the hell was going on.

Another vehicle appeared, a large red Chevrolet Silverado truck. It growled across the parking lot, its lights off, and parked some distance away from the SUV and the sedan.

Another Arab got out of the passenger side of the truck. The driver stayed where he was. The guy who had been in the truck was overweight and in his fifties with a long, grey beard. He was wearing blue jeans and a long grey coat that flapped around his ankles as he walked towards the three men standing by the SUV. One by one he embraced them and kissed them on the cheeks. He seemed elated, and kept patting the men on the shoulders as if praising them.

Martin stopped. It was a strange place for a meeting: the mall was shut and the nearest open premises were the 24-hour

McDonalds and KFC and they were a couple of hundred yards away.

One of the men went back to the SUV and took out something. He took it over to the older man and showed it to him. It was a camcorder, Martin realised. They were showing him something they had filmed. The man pumped his fist in the air and shouted something. All four men were clearly excited.

Martin walked closer, sticking to the shadows. He heard one of them shout something and the older man made a patting motion with his hand, obviously telling him to calm down.

Another went over to the SUV and pulled out a piece of equipment. The breath caught in Martin's throat as he realised what it was: an FIM-92 Stinger surface-to-air missile launcher.

Martin moved closer to the wall. It was too much of a coincidence – a plane had blown up just half an hour earlier and now four Arab men were moving a missile launcher less than twenty miles from the airport.

The man with the launcher headed towards the sedan. Another man had taken a can of petrol from the rear of the SUV and was sloshing it over the roof.

Martin knew he had to act quickly. There was no point in calling 911 – the nearest police station was a ten-minute drive away and by the time a patrol car turned up the SUV would be in flames and the Arabs long gone. He started to run. The two cars were about a hundred feet away, the truck maybe a hundred and fifty.

He was up on the balls of his feet and wearing rubber-soled boots but even so the men heard him almost immediately. The one by the SUV turned, his mouth open in surprise.

Martin increased his pace, his arms pumping at his side. Sixty feet. The man dropped the petrol can and pulled open the door to the SUV. Martin knew he was going for a weapon. He ran faster. Forty feet.

The man with the launcher dropped it and reached inside his jacket. Martin ran faster. Twenty feet. The baton was banging against his hip but he ignored it. He wasn't planning to use a baton.

The older man had the quickest reactions; as soon as he heard Martin's rapid footsteps he had started running to the truck, which was already moving.

The man at the SUV was holding a large gun, an Uzi or an Ingram. Multiple shots exploded from both but they were notoriously difficult to aim. Spray and pray. But with a fire rate of five or six hundred rounds a minute they were very effective at short range. Martin figured that the safety was still on and he was close enough to see the uncertainty in the man's face, so he carried on running, his boots slapping against the tarmac.

The older Arab reached the truck and ran alongside it, grasping for the door handle. He pulled it open. The driver shouted something at him and the man climbed in.

The man at the SUV fumbled with the safety catch, then swung the weapon towards Martin, but he was way too slow and Martin knocked the gun to the side with his left hand and punched the man under the chin, snapping his neck back. He heard the bang of a gun off to his left and a bullet thwacked into the side of the SUV. He grabbed the Uzi with his left hand and slammed his right hand against the stock. He turned and dropped into a crouch as his finger slid over the trigger.

The red truck was driving away, tyres screaming. The bearded Arab by the sedan had a large handgun in his right hand. He fired again but the shot also went wide. Firing one-handed was never a good idea. It was difficult to aim, difficult to track and difficult to deal with the recoil. Martin fired once and his round hit the Arab in the chest, but the man didn't go down. The Uzi was firing 9mm rounds and they weren't manstoppers. Martin fired again. And again. The third shot caught the man in the throat and he staggered back, fell against the car and slid to the ground.

Martin kept low and cradled the Uzi to his chest as he ran to the third man. He had turned and was rushing towards the driver's side door. Martin reached him just as he was pulling the door open and slammed the side of the gun against the man's head. He went down without a sound.

Martin looked around. He was breathing slowly and evenly and hadn't even broken a sweat. The Arab he'd shot wasn't dead but death was only a minute or so away. His eyes were wide open but flat and lifeless and blood was frothing from the wound in his throat. His chest moved slowly and as Martin watched, blood trickled from between his lips. The gun was still in the man's right hand. A Glock. Martin went over, picked it up and tucked it into his belt as he considered his options. The obvious thing to do would be to call the police. But Martin had something else in mind – something that might work to his advantage. He walked quickly to the trunk, put the launcher in and slammed it shut, then put the Uzi on the roof, opened the rear door of the sedan and lifted the dying man in.

The Arab by the driver's door was still unconscious. Martin rolled him over and fastened his handcuffs on his wrists before opening the door and heaving the man inside. He shut the door, picked up the Uzi and jogged over to the SUV.

The first man he'd hit was still out for the count. Martin had used his only pair of handcuffs but he took off his tie and used that to bind the unconscious Arab's hands behind his back, then bundled him into the rear seat of the SUV. He slammed the door and looked around, reassuring himself that no one had reacted to the shots. All was silent. He peered at the road but the red truck had gone. The camcorder was lying on the ground where it had been dropped. Martin picked it up.

He pulled out his wallet and took out a business card. At the top was the logo of Homeland Security and underneath it a name and several phone numbers. He took out his phone and tapped in the cell-phone number. The man he was calling answered the phone and Martin took a deep breath. This was going to take some explaining.

Chapter 4

Present Day, London

Dan 'Spider' Shepherd sipped his coffee as he stared at the bank of CCTV monitors in front of him. Outside in the stadium some forty thousand people were watching the game, but Shepherd was only concerned with the people in the stands. MI5 had received intel that half a dozen known jihadists from the north of England were going to meet at the stadium. Under normal circumstances finding them would be akin to locating the proverbial needle in a haystack, but Shepherd's near-perfect memory gave him an edge, which is why he had been assigned to the stadium's security centre an hour before the game was due to start. He was in radio contact with a dozen MI5 surveillance experts scattered throughout the stadium and had already spotted two of the jihadists and called in their location.

Shepherd's near-perfect photographic memory meant that he was better at spotting faces than the most sophisticated facial recognition programs available. Shepherd didn't just recognise faces; he remembered body shapes, clothing, even the way a person walked. It was a skill he'd been born with, a skill that had saved his life on more than one occasion. Not that his life was at risk as he sat in the high-backed orthopaedic chair and sipped his coffee. He hadn't been in harm's way for months. His career with MI5 had apparently been put on hold and he had been attached to the Metropolitan Police's Super-Recogniser Unit indefinitely. There were a dozen police officers working full time in the unit, based on the third floor of a grey stone building in Lambeth, south London. There were another hundred and fifty or so officers in stations around London who had proven their ability to recognise faces and who could be drawn on when needed.

The unit had been set up in 2015 after it became clear that identifying suspects from CCTV images was a specialised skill and one that couldn't be done by computers, and it now accounted for a quarter of all the identifications made by the police in London. Most of the unit's work involved chasing down petty criminals – thieves, muggers, carjackers. Shepherd's brief had been to use the unit to pursue terrorists, specifically Islamic jihadists. There were now believed to be more than a thousand ISIS fighters in the UK – many were British-born men who had returned home after fighting in Syria, but hundreds had slipped into the country under the guise of asylum seekers. Shepherd had been through American and British databases of surveillance photographs taken in Syria and spent his days reviewing CCTV footage from the four hundred thousand CCTV cameras around the city. He had personally identified a dozen ISIS fighters, three of whom had already been picked up by the authorities. When any member of the unit had any spare time they would help Shepherd, but the workload was mainly his. And that was his job. Eight hours a day. Five days a week. The visit to the stadium was the first time he'd worked away from the Lambeth office in three months.

The job was as boring as hell and he had asked several times to be moved back to operational duties but his requests were ignored. He was either being sidelined or punished, and there was nothing he could do about it. The transfer had happened after his former boss Jeremy Willoughby-Brown had been found shot dead in the garden of his home. No one had ever been arrested for the shooting and the fact that Shepherd had been in the vicinity of the man's house at the time of the murder meant that he had to undergo hours of interviews that bordered on interrogation before his version of events was accepted. He had been en route to Willoughby-Brown's house for a mission debrief, and he had heard two shots. By the time he reached the garden

Willoughby-Brown was dead. What Shepherd could never admit to was that he had seen the killer, Matt Standing of the SAS, or that he had spoken to him after the killing. Standing wanted revenge for the death of his sister and had shot Willoughby-Brown twice in the chest. Standing had left the gun at the scene and swabs taken from Shepherd's hands proved that he hadn't fired the weapon, but he had been under a cloud ever since and had been kept off active operations.

He took another sip of his coffee. Two Asian men were sitting together close to the halfway line. Both were wearing United scarfs. He zoomed in on their faces. Both in their twenties, both with beards and both clearly enjoying the game. Their faces weren't known to him. He took another sip of coffee and used his mouse to click to another camera. This one was inside the stadium, near the toilets. More Asians, but none that he recognised. There was a clock on the wall facing him, slowly ticking off the seconds. The match would be over in an hour and he'd be home forty-five minutes after that. Katra had promised him a steak with his favourite red wine sauce and he was looking forward to it.

Chapter 5

Present Day, London

Sarah had been a United fan since she was six years old. Her bedroom was festooned with photographs of the team, she had half a dozen scarfs and her quilt cover was in the team's colours. She watched every one of the games on TV and whenever they played in London, no matter who their opponents were, she'd beg and plead to be allowed to go. Usually either her mother or father would give in and take her, even though they had no interest in the game. But that night her mother wasn't feeling well and her father – an accountant – was tied up with a last-minute audit. But the tickets for the match had been purchased, so Sarah had turned on the charm with her sister and Eleanor had been easy enough to persuade. Unlike their parents, Eleanor was a big fan of the beautiful game and had agreed to take her. It was a school night but Sarah was top of her class and her parents agreed that a few hours away from her books wouldn't do her any harm.

The score was one–all at half time and they went to the concessions area in search of refreshments. Sarah looked over at a stall selling team shirts and practically salivated. Eleanor touched her lightly on the shoulder. 'Do you want one?'

Sarah looked up with wide eyes. 'Do I want one? Are you serious? I'd sell my soul for one.' She had long blond hair and was wearing a long pink quilted coat and a United bobble hat and scarf.

Eleanor laughed and opened her bag. Unlike her younger sister, Eleanor had chestnut hair, cut short, but she was also wearing a

United scarf. 'Well there's no need for anything that drastic,' she said. She opened her purse and handed Sarah the money. 'You go get yourself one,' she said. 'Think of it as an early Christmas present.' Sarah hugged her and took the notes and then ran to the concession stand, where there were four lines of at least a dozen people queueing to buy shirts. Eleanor couldn't help but smile at her sister's enthusiasm. She looked around for somewhere to buy a coffee but the area was crowded so she decided to stay where she was so that she could keep an eye on Sarah. Sarah joined one of the lines, clutching the notes.

An Asian man in a black puffa jacket walked by Eleanor. She thought he was talking into a phone but as he drew away from her she realised he was muttering to himself. She frowned. It was too easy to jump to conclusions when you saw a brown-skinned man with a beard acting suspiciously but no one wanted to be seen to be racist. But there was something about the man that seemed off and she continued to watch him. He wasn't carrying anything but even if he'd had a rucksack or backpack she probably wouldn't have reacted any differently. Despite the recent terrorist attacks, London was still one of the safest cities in the world and you couldn't live your life jumping at shadows. Besides, it was a football match. Terrorists didn't target football matches; they blew themselves up on Tube trains or brought down planes or shot tourists. The man walked away, and was soon out of sight.

A bald fan in a United shirt with tattoos all over his arms bumped into her but immediately apologised and wouldn't leave her until she had promised that she was okay. When she looked over at Sarah again, she was only one customer away from being served. Sarah waved at Eleanor and Eleanor waved back, then Sarah blew her a kiss and Eleanor laughed. She stopped laughing when she saw the Asian man walking towards her. The man was still muttering to himself and looking around as if searching for something. For a brief moment Eleanor had eye contact with him and her breath caught in her throat. His eyes were dead. Lifeless. A feeling of dread washed over her. The man stopped walking and raised his right hand. It was clenched into a fist. He was holding something. Something metallic. Eleanor looked over at Sarah again. Time seemed to have frozen. Sarah was pointing at a shirt, and smiling. The middle-aged woman behind the counter was smiling back. Eleanor opened her mouth to shout at Sarah. Then she looked at the Asian man. He too was opening his mouth. He was quicker than her, by a fraction of a second, and the last thing she heard was him screaming '*Allahu Akbar!*' at the top of his voice before there was a blinding flash and a thump, and everything went black.

Chapter 6

Present Day, London

Shepherd stared at the blank CCTV screen in disbelief. 'What the fuck just happened?' said the stadium's head of security, who was standing behind Shepherd's chair.

They had all heard a dull thud off in the distance and even though they were in the bowels of the stadium they could hear the screams of terror from outside. There were scenes of panic on several of the CCTV monitors as spectators rushed for the exits.

One of the screens had gone blank. It covered the concession area. On a screen showing the view from a camera close to the one that had died, spectators were screaming in panic.

Shepherd scanned the screens in front of him. Scenes of chaos and terror, but no indication of what had happened.

There were cameras covering the pitch and the referee had blown his whistle and called the game to a halt. The players were running off the pitch.

On one of the screens a paramedic in a yellow and green tunic was running against the tide of spectators, rushing to get out.

Shepherd thought that a bomb had gone off in the concessions area but he didn't want to say anything until he was sure. The radio on his desk crackled and one of the surveillance team called in. That was when he was sure.

Chapter 7

Richard Yokely wasn't a fan of the Pentagon, but when the Secretary of Defense personally called him and told him to report to his office and to be quick about it, he did as he was told. It was the sheer size of the place that Yokely always found intimidating. The Pentagon was one of the world's largest office buildings, covering six and a half million square feet. It was so big it had six ZIP codes, all Washington DC codes despite the fact the building was actually in Virginia. The man Yokely was there to see had his own personal ZIP code, to make mail delivery that much more efficient.

Yokely was wearing a dark blue blazer, a crisp white shirt and a dark blue tie with pale blue stripes. His shoes were tasselled, the black leather gleaming as if they had been freshly polished. He had a chunky gold ring on his right ring finger and a Rolex Submariner watch on his left wrist. He was in his late forties and had spent almost half his life working for government departments that were almost always known by their initials.

More than twenty-five thousand people worked on the seven levels of the Pentagon, two of which were below ground. Despite its size, the five-sided building had been designed so that a person would never take more than seven minutes to walk between any two points. Yokely strode along the corridor towards the Defense Secretary's office. A PFPA guard was murmuring into his radio but he stopped long enough to open the door so that Yokely could go inside. The Pentagon Force Protection Agency had been set up not long after the September 11, 2001 terrorist attacks, the clearest case of locking the stable door after the horse had bolted that Yokely had ever seen. American Airlines Flight 77 had slammed into the west side of the building, killing one hundred and twenty-five military personnel and Pentagon workers plus the sixty-four people on the plane.

Christopher Mullins was sitting at his desk and he made no move to get up. There was a bottle of Scotch and a half-empty glass close to his right hand. 'Sit down, Richard,' he said, waving at a chair. Yokely sat down. The Defense Secretary looked like shit. He was in his early sixties but looked a decade older. What was left of his receding hair was flecked with dandruff and there were dark bags under his eyes. He had loosened his tie but was still wearing his jacket. He wiped his chin with his hand, reached for the glass and then appeared to have a change of heart and sat back in his chair. 'Have you heard about the plane that went down out of JFK?'

Yokely nodded. 'Only what was on CNN.'

'CNN doesn't know shit,' said the Defense Secretary. 'It was shot down by terrorists and we've got them under wraps. And by "we", I mean me. They're not in the system.'

Yokely raised an eyebrow but didn't comment.

'So there are several ways the scenario can play out. I can put them in the system, which means we get them to trial in months or years and all the time they sit in their cells we'll have kidnappings and hostage-taking and hijacking and who knows what else as their terrorist buddies do all they can to get them released. Then when we do eventually strap them down and inject them with whatever it is we inject them with these days we'll be creating martyrs to inspire a whole new generation of terrorists.'

'I'm assuming you have a Plan B?' said Yokely.

'Like I said, they're not in the system. And they can stay that way. So Plan B would be that we interrogate them, find out what they know, and then we dispose of them.'

This time Yokely raised both eyebrows.

'Don't look at me like that, Richard. I'm not suggesting anything that you haven't done before. That is the whole point of Grey Fox.'

'Grey Fox tends to get involved when all other options have been tried,' said Yokely. 'This sounds like we're going straight to Plan B.'

'It has to be that way,' said Mullins. 'GITMO showed us what happens when we go the interrogation route. The whole world bitches and moans and we get all that crap about human rights. You and I know both know that anyone who ended up in Guantanamo Bay deserved to be there. But listening to the *Times* and the *Post*, you'd think we were the fucking enemy, not al-fucking-Qaeda.' He shook his head in contempt, then reached for his glass again. This time he drained it. 'Sometimes you wonder whose side the fucking media are on. It sometimes feels to me that half the journalists in this country would be happier under Sharia law.' He refilled his glass. 'We have to move now and we have to move quickly. We have what we might call a window of opportunity. There is a brief period of time available to us in which we can strike back at the terrorists in such a way that they will never, ever, repeat their actions of today.' He sniffed. 'Have you got a cigarette?'

'Cigars,' said Yokely.

'I hate cigars,' said Mullins. 'I'd given up cigarettes.' He shrugged. 'But at times like this . . .' He motioned for Yokely to give him a cigar. Yokely fished out his cigar case and gave one to the man, then looked at him expectantly. 'Of course, you too,' said Mullins.

Yokely slid one of his small cigars between his lips, then leaned over and lit the Secretary's with a battered Zippo before lighting his own.

The Defense Secretary blew smoke up at the ceiling. 'The Israelis had the right idea, after Munich,' he said.

'The Wrath of God?' said Yokely.

'Exactly.'

The Wrath Of God was Israel's response to the massacre at the 1972 Olympics in Munich where eleven Israeli Olympic athletes were taken hostage and eventually killed by the Palestinian terrorist group Black September. Over the following twenty years, Mossad assassins tracked down and killed more than twenty-five people involved in the terrorist outrage. No trials, no interrogations, just retribution. Revenge.

'I heard from a Mossad contact that before each assassination they sent flowers to the next of kin, with a message – "a reminder that we do not forget and we do not forgive". I always thought that was a nice touch.'

The Defense Secretary nodded. 'That's the route we're going to take, Richard. But without the fucking flowers. These people, they don't care about the country they live in. Family, clan, tribe, that's all they care about. The problem is they think they can carry out acts like this without there being repercussions to the things they care about. So that's going to change. We're going to hit their families, Richard. And we're going to hit them hard.'

Yokely nodded slowly. The group he worked for – Grey Fox – was often tasked with assassinations, but usually they were the result of considerable deliberations in the White House and came after all other avenues had been at least considered. On this occasion it felt that the retribution was a knee-jerk reaction and he had learned from experience that the old adage 'revenge is a dish best served cold' was true. But he wasn't being asked his opinion, he was being tasked with an assignment and he would do it to the best of his ability. Come what may. 'These terrorists, how many are there?'

'Three,' said Mullins. 'One's dead already.'

'And where are they exactly?'

'They're in a disused warehouse in Queens. It was the closest place we could find at short notice.'

Yokely frowned. 'And why haven't the cops got them?'

'Blind luck,' said Mullins. 'They were changing vehicles and a guy spotted them and was smart enough to know what he'd got.'

'But he didn't call the cops?'

'He's got a pretty low opinion of law enforcement at the local and state level. They've turned him down in the past and he's been trying to get a job with Homeland Security. He called the last guy who'd interviewed him and he called his boss and his boss called me. So as things stand right now there's just a handful of people who know that we have these men.'

'Including the President?'

'Of course. I'd hardly be running this by you without the President's approval. But he's in Japan and won't be back until tomorrow. Richard, I want you to find out who put this together and I want them dead. No trials, no appeals, just do what has to be done. I want these bastards to know that if they fuck with the US of A the US of A will fuck with them.'

'Do we leave the bodies where they fall?'

The Defense Secretary shrugged. 'I don't care. Just make sure you leave no trails. So long as they're dead, we're good.'

'Not a problem,' said Yokely. There were three ways of carrying out an assassination: a straightforward hit where the body was left in open view; a killing made to look like an accident; or a disappearance, where the body was never found. Yokely was proficient at all three.

'So, this guy that found them. What can you tell me about him?'

'Former army. Served in Iraq. Name's Dean Martin. That's all I know. He's got the terrorists under wraps with a Homeland Security agent called Tommy Garcia. Garcia reports to the head of Homeland Security so the loop is pretty tight.' Mullins flashed Yokely a tight smile. 'I've had Garcia checked out, he's dependable so you can use him for any Homeland Security intel you need.'

'Does he know what I'll be doing?'

'No, just that he'll be assisting with the initial investigation. Cut him loose as soon as possible, and obviously tell him to keep mum. I want you only using personnel that you've used before. I don't need to tell you how sensitive this is, Richard. And if anything goes wrong there must be total deniability. Total and absolute.'

'I understand that,' said Yokely. 'And so far as the operation goes, how far do I take it?'

'As far as it goes,' said Mullins. 'Everyone involved, everyone who helped them, everyone who supplied equipment, paperwork. And their families. Their wives, their husbands, their parents.'

'And their children?'

'We wipe out their genes, Richard. We show them that if they attack us, everything they ever were, everything they might be, everything they think they will be leaving behind, it all goes. If we do this one time, it'll stand as a warning for ever. And after this, no one will fuck with Americans. Even suicide bombers will think twice about blowing themselves to Kingdom Come if they know it'd mean the death of their loved ones.'

'Maybe not if they thought they'd be joining them in paradise,' said Yokely. 'This was the President's idea? I wouldn't have thought he'd have the imagination.'

The Defense Secretary chuckled. 'The concept is based on a CIA paper I submitted after Nine Eleven,' he said. 'I put forward the proposition that if we couldn't get our hands on Bin Laden then we should hold his gene pool responsible for his actions; that we should round up every human being who shared his DNA and lock them up on the understanding that they would be freed only when he gave himself up or died.'

'How was it received?'

'With a lot of head shaking and political correctness bullshit, of course,' said Mullins. 'But that's changed now. If we let the bastards get away with this it'll be open season on our airlines forever more. So it stops now. Here and now.'

'Has this been cleared by the White House?'

'It's sanctioned, we have the President's blessing, but the fewer people who know what's happening, the better.'

'And funding?'

'You already have access to the Grey Fox black accounts. Use what you need. I'll make sure that more is made available before the end of the week.'

'And manpower?'

'The usual suspects, obviously, but pull in whoever you need. But again, the fewer in the loop, the better.'

'And if anything goes wrong?'

'I'm assuming it won't be an issue, Richard. But depending on the circumstances, we should be able to pull you out of any shit you fall into. Just don't fall.'

'I don't plan to,' said Yokely. 'But I'm always happier performing with a safety net.'

'We'll take care of you, Richard,' said Mullins. 'You have my word.'

'And when do I stop? At what point will I have done enough?'

'I'll contact you through the usual channels,' said Mullins. 'Other than that there is to be no communication. I don't need reports from you and you don't need my clearance for any actions. You have carte blanche to do whatever needs doing.' He held out his hand. 'You're going to be changing the world for the better,' he said.

They shook hands. Mullins had a firm grip and he put his left hand on top of Yokely's hand, the way an undertaker might console a grieving relative.

'I hope it works out that way,' said Yokely. 'One more thing. What about the King of Cool?'

The Defense Secretary frowned. 'The King Of Cool?'

'Dean Martin. What do we do with him?'

Mullins tightened his grip on Yokely's hand. 'That's your call,' he said.

Chapter 8

Charlotte Button walked slowly up to the front door and rang the bell. She took a deep breath and tried to steady herself, wondering what the hell she could possibly say. There were no words. There just weren't. The door opened. It was Tony. Patsy's husband. His eyes were red and he was holding a bottle of wine in one hand and an empty glass in the other.

'She's in the garden,' he said, his voice a dull monotone.

Button's phone buzzed in her raincoat pocket and she took it out. It was a text message from Ellis: *Where the hell are you?*

Button put the phone away. Tony was still standing there, a faraway look in his eyes.

'Tony, I'm so sorry,' she said, but even as the words left her mouth she realised how pointless the sentiment was. Sorry wouldn't solve anything. Sorry wouldn't make it better. Sorry wouldn't bring Eleanor back.

Tony blinked, then seemed to see her for the first time. He forced a smile.

'Thanks for coming, Charlie,' he said.

Button hugged him tearfully. He sniffed and wiped his nose with the back of his hand. 'This is just . . .'

'I know, I know.'

'Come on through. Please. She's in the garden. Oh, I said that didn't I?' He pushed the door closed with his shoulder.

'Here, let me take them off you.' She relieved him of the bottle and the glass and followed him through to the kitchen.

He picked up another glass and then opened the kitchen door.

The sky had darkened and the first stars were appearing overhead. Patsy Ellis was sitting on a bench overlooking a small rock pool, her head in her hands. Tony stood looking at her. 'I feel so bloody useless,' he said. 'What am I supposed to do, Charlie?'

'Just be here for her,' said Button. She handed him the bottle and glass, walked over to the bench and sat down. Ellis looked up and smiled through her tears. 'What took you so fucking long?' she whispered.

Button put her arm around her. 'I'm sorry.' She kissed Ellis on the cheek and tasted salt. 'I'm so, so sorry.'

'I can't believe it,' said Tony behind them. 'It was a football match. A bloody football match.'

Button shook her head. 'Awful,' she said.

'Eleanor was taking her sister to the match,' he said. 'Sarah's a huge United fan.' He shook his head. 'Was a fan. She was a United fan. I have to get used to using the past tense. Who does that, Charlie? What sort of person bombs a football match?'

'You know who does that!' Ellis hissed at him. 'We all know.'

Tony took an involuntary step back and almost stumbled into the pool.

'And they'll keep doing it until someone stops them,' said Ellis, louder this time.

'It's okay,' said Button, and gave Ellis a hug.

'No, it's not okay,' mumbled Ellis, and she began to sob. Her husband looked at Button helplessly.

'Just put the wine down and go,' said Button quietly. 'Let me talk to her.'

'I should stay,' he protested.

'No, I'm okay,' said Ellis, blinking away her tears. 'I'm okay. I just need to talk to Charlie.'

'Patsy . . .'

'I'm okay, really. I won't be long.' She stared at him. 'Please. Just do this for me.'

He sniffed. 'Okay.' He looked at Button, and his lip trembled. 'Take care of her.' He put the bottle and glasses on the bench and stood there, still not sure if he should go or stay.

'I will,' said Button. She put her arm around Ellis and hugged her. 'We'll be okay. Just give us a few minutes.'

He nodded sadly and walked slowly back to the house.

'Tell me this is just a dream,' whispered Ellis. 'Tell me everything is okay and Eleanor's not dead and the world is just the way it was two hours ago.'

'I'm sorry, Patsy.'

'Tony said I should ask my doctor to give me some tablets. Tablets? What the fuck are tablets going to do? Are tablets going to bring Eleanor back?'

Button shook her head.

'I said I wanted a drink and everyone is like, "You shouldn't drink, darling, drinking won't help." What the fuck, Charlie, drugs will help but alcohol is some sort of mortal sin? Where's the logic in that?'

'Nothing wrong with wine in my experience,' said Button. She took her arm away, reached for the bottle and poured wine into one of the glasses. She gave it to Ellis and she took a couple of gulps. Button opened her mouth to tell her to slow down but then decided against it. She was entitled to drink any way she wanted to. She poured wine for herself and sipped it.

'Remember when you and I took Eleanor riding, that first time?' said Ellis. 'She loved it so much. We agreed to pay for her lessons after that and it cost us thousands. She could have ridden for England if she'd kept at it. Then she discovered boys.' She shook her head and took another gulp of wine. 'She wanted kids, too. That's what she wanted more than anything; she just had to find the right man. And now she'll never get the chance.' She wiped away her tears, then put down her glass and dabbed at her face with a handkerchief. 'I can't believe I'm never going to see her again. Never going to talk to her. Never going to hold her. Eleanor was my goddaughter, but she was as close to me as Hannah. Closer in some ways. Hannah has always been so bloody independent, ever since she was tiny. Once she went to university we barely saw her. But Eleanor was here all the time. She was always the first to call on my birthday.' She wiped her eyes. 'This is so unfair, Charlie.'

'How are Eleanor and Sarah's parents?'

'How do you think?' said Ellis bitterly. 'They've lost both of their daughters. They're devastated. We said we'd go but they said not now, they don't want to see anybody. We'll go around tomorrow.' Tears were running down her face.

Button put down her own glass and reached for Ellis. Ellis sobbed and buried her face against Button's shoulder. Then she took a slow, deep breath and straightened up. She swallowed, then looked into her eyes. 'I need you to do something for me, Charlie.'

Button stared back at her. 'Anything,' she said, and she knew the moment the words left her mouth that she meant it. 'What do you want me to do?'

'We know who the bomber was. ISIS have already released a video with the usual sort of anti-West shit. Ali Naveed. A Syrian. Came over here as a supposed child refugee. The council put him with a foster family in Ealing.' Ellis smiled but her eyes were dull and lifeless. 'I want you to kill anyone and everyone close to him,' she said flatly. 'Anyone who helped him, anyone who loved him, anyone he loved. I want every one of the fuckers dead.'

'Patsy—'

'Don't try to talk me out of this, Charlie,' she said. 'I'm done with the lot of them. They took Eleanor from me and I want them dead. All of them. If anyone knows how I feel, it's you. I want it done, and there's nothing you can say that will make me change my mind.'

Button smiled tightly. 'I'm not going to talk you out of anything,' she said.

'You'll do it?'

Button nodded. 'I'll get it done. If that's what you want, what you really want. But you need to think it through. If people start to die, won't you be the first person they'd look at?'

Ellis shook her head. 'I'm Eleanor's godmother; she's not a blood relative. Her mum and I were friends at university. Best friends. But no one is going to connect Eleanor to me. And even if someone at Five spots the connection, what then? No one's going to go public with the information. Who wants to hand a propaganda coup like that to the enemy? You think they'll let ISIS know that they killed the goddaughter of the acting head of MI5?'

'My worry is that someone might put two and two together. It could end your career.'

'Like it did yours? Let's face it, Charlie, you're doing very nicely in the private sector.'

Button held Ellis's hands. 'I'm not saying no, Patsy. I'm just saying you need to think it through. You need to be sure.'

'I have done, and I am,' she said, nodding earnestly. 'You think I care about my career? About this country? The powers that be have allowed this to happen. They let scum like Naveed into this country. We let British-born Muslims pop over to the Middle East to fight for ISIS and then we welcome them back with open arms. Enough's enough, Charlie. If it means the end of my career, fine. And if there are consequences down the line, I'll face them, and I'll face them gladly.'

'Okay,' said Button. 'I hear you. And yes, I understand exactly. There are times when revenge is the only option.'

'I owe it to Eleanor,' said Ellis. 'I will not allow her death to go unpunished. Whatever it costs, Charlie. I'll pay. I'll happily pay. Just have the fuckers killed.'

Button shook her head. 'It won't cost you a thing,' she said. 'It's on me.'

Ellis hugged Button hard. 'Thank you. Thank you so much.'

'It's the least I can do, Patsy. But I'm going to need help. The sort of intel I'll need isn't available to the private sector, not in the time frame I'll need.'

Ellis forced a smile. 'Don't worry about that,' she said. 'I have a plan.'

Chapter 9

Present Day, London

D an Shepherd stared at the screen in front of him and tried to concentrate. It was recorded CCTV footage taken outside a mosque in South London, two weeks earlier. It was just after early morning prayers and there were hundreds of Muslim men, most of them wearing Islamic clothing and skullcaps, milling around and chatting in small groups. Shepherd was scanning faces, looking for anyone he recognised from MI5's database of suspected and wanted jihadists. As he forced himself to work, his mind was still in turmoil from the previous day's stadium bombing. He had raced to the scene and it had been carnage. There were bodies everywhere and the injured were screaming and begging for help. He saw at least a dozen dead and many more injured. One of the first casualties he had seen was a teenage boy, his arm a bloody mess. Shepherd had used the boy's scarf as a compress and tried to stem the bleeding until a paramedic had arrived and taken over.

Half a dozen paramedics were on the scene within minutes but they were faced with an impossible task. Most of the spectators had fled but some stayed to help. Those with medical training did what they could, others just offered comfort. It was as bad as any war zone Shepherd had ever been in.

From the injured boy he had moved to help a middle-aged man who had lost most of his right hand, his face slashed by dozens of pieces of shrapnel. He was slumped against a wall. Again Shepherd used the man's scarf, this time to fashion a tourniquet.

'My boy, where's my boy?' the man kept mumbling. 'Where's Alex?'

There was a youngster on the ground, not far away, and Shepherd didn't have to go over to see the boy was dead. He had ignored the man's questions but stayed with him until a paramedic was able to take over.

The media was now saying that twenty-two had died in the bombing and that many more were badly injured and the death toll was expected to rise over the next few days. A video had been released on social media of the suicide bomber launching a rambling tirade against the West and how the British were persecuting Muslims at home and in the Middle East. Most news outlets were refusing to show it. Messages of condolences were coming in from around the world, and a group of eighties pop stars were planning to record a single to raise funds for the injured.

Shepherd's thoughts were interrupted by a loud 'Yes!' He turned to look at the woman sitting at the workstation next to his. She was a relatively new member of the unit, Sally Anne McLachlan, a former family liaison officer whose recognition abilities were noticed after she arrested two wanted paedophiles she had spotted in a cinema while out with her kids. She had recognised them from photographs the paedophile unit had sent out six months earlier. She had only glanced at the pictures but a glance was all she needed. The Super-Recogniser Unit heard about the arrests and called her in for a test that she passed with flying colours.

Shepherd went over and stood behind her. 'What have you got?' he asked.

She pointed at the screen. It was CCTV footage of a group of Asians gathered in the street. She had paused the image. It was black and white but quite clear.

'This is one of the cameras outside the mosque in Stoke Newington you wanted me to keep an eye on. See the guy on the left with the white skullcap?'

She pointed and Shepherd immediately recognised the man.

He was a former sociology student from Westminster University who a year earlier had gone to fight with ISIS in Syria. His name was Tahir Rahman and voice recognition experts at MI5 were sure that he was the masked man seen in ISIS videos decapitating a French journalist with a machete. He was one of several hundred home-grown jihadists that MI5 suspected had slipped back into the UK. Border Force were supposed to be watching for the returnees but their record was patchy at best. McLachlan pressed a button to restart the video. Rahman was in deep conversation with the other men and had his head to the side but as he turned, Shepherd got a full-on view. There was no question it was him. Shepherd grinned. Rahman was the third jihadist she had spotted.

'Well done,' he said. 'I'll pass on the intel. He's close to the top of MI5's most wanted.'

'Do you want me to work backwards, see if I can get an address?'

Usually that was too much trouble and would take up too much time but Rahman was a high-value target. 'Go for it,' said Shepherd. He went back to his station and fired off an email to his boss at MI5, updating him on Rahman's identification. Just as he pressed 'send' Shepherd's phone vibrated in his pocket and he took it out. It was a landline calling. 'Yes?' he said.

'Mr Shepherd?' It was a man. Upper-class accent with a slow drawl that made Shepherd think of wood-panelled boardrooms and grouse-shooting weekends.

'Yes?'

'Mrs Ellis would like to see you in her office. Can you make a two o'clock appointment?'

'Sure,' said Shepherd.

'Excellent,' said the man. 'We shall see you at two.'

The line went dead and Shepherd stared at the screen of his phone. Patsy Ellis was the acting head of MI5 and had been since the untimely death of Jeremy Willoughby-Brown a year earlier. Her appointment was supposed to have been temporary but there had been no sign of a permanent replacement being found. Shepherd had never met Ellis but knew of her. She had

spent much of her career with MI5 but had left to join the Joint
Intelligence Organisation, the agency that was responsible for
assessment and forward planning. JIO offered advice and support
to the Joint Intelligence Committee that oversaw the work of MI5,
MI6 and GCHQ. She was close to sixty and the office gossip
was that she had requested retirement so that she could pursue
her dream of writing crime thrillers. But no one knew more about
the workings of the British intelligence agencies than Patsy Ellis
and the powers that be were reluctant to let her off the leash.

Shepherd was reasonably sure that it was Ellis who had sidelined him with the Super-Recognisers. The summons from Ellis
meant one of two things – either he was being brought in from
the cold, or his career was over.

Chapter 10

Present Day, Pattaya, Thailand

Lex Harper's phone buzzed and he opened his eyes. He groped to his left but instead of his phone, on the bedside table he found only air. He opened his eyes. The lamp was missing. And his clock radio. He groaned as he realised he wasn't in his own bedroom. His phone was in the pocket of his jeans and his jeans were on the floor by the bed. He rolled over and pulled out the phone. The message was from Charlie Button and as usual it was short and to the point: *You have mail.* He groaned. It was five o'clock in the morning, which meant it was eleven at night in the UK.

A soft hand brushed against his chest and slowly moved down between his legs. 'You horny?' asked the girl sleepily.

'I've got to go,' said Harper, sitting up.

'Okay,' said the girl, turning away from him and curling up into a ball, her long black hair covering the pillow. Within seconds she was snoring again.

Harper pulled on his boxers and jeans. He found his shirt on the back of a chair and his socks on the dressing table. He took out his wallet, trying to remember whether he was supposed to pay the girl or if it had been a freebie, and decided that either way she wouldn't complain if he left her a couple of thousand baht. He took out the notes and placed them on the pillow, pulled on his shoes and headed out. He went along a corridor to a lift and as he waited for it to haul itself up to the seventh floor, fragments of the previous night began to return. He'd been playing pool in a bar by the beach and Mickey and Mark Moore had turned up, two London criminals who had made Pattaya their home, and after a couple of games they had led him astray. At some point they were in an ice bar, shivering and drinking shots as their breath feathered around them, and in the early hours they had headed for Lucifer's disco in Walking Street. The Moore brothers were regulars and were ushered to a table in a corner. The brothers always preferred to drink with their backs to the wall.

Harper had spotted the girl almost immediately. Or she had spotted him. Their eyes had met and he'd smiled and she'd smiled back and within seconds she was by his side. She had waist-length glossy black hair and a tiny silver dress and impossibly high heels. Her name was Noy or Poy or Doy and she had latched on to him as if her life depended on it. He remembered buying several bottles of champagne and at some point he might have been sitting on a motorcycle with his hands around her waist as she drove at breakneck speed, her hair blowing across his face. Other than that, the night was pretty much a blur.

The lift arrived and he took it down to the ground floor, hoping that he wasn't in the middle of nowhere. He walked out of the building and smiled as he saw the beach. Joy her name was, and he remembered her telling him that she had three overseas sponsors, men who sent her money every month so that she could live in the style to which she had become accustomed. One was from Holland, another from Germany and the third was the most generous, a fifty-five-year-old car salesman in Glasgow who was sending her thirty thousand baht a month with the promise that he would marry her and retire to Thailand. All three were going to end up disappointed because Joy was planning to marry an American so that she could live in New York, a city she had only ever seen in the movies but which she had set her heart on.

He flagged down a yellow and blue taxi and had it take him to an Internet café on Beach Road that was open twenty-four-seven. It was owned and run by a former go-go dancer called Rose. Harper had known her, and her brother Kung, for more than five years, and they had never questioned why he popped in to use their computers at all hours of the day or night. Most of their customers were bargirls who would use Kung to help them draft emails to their sponsors, offering a range of reasons why they needed money – sick family members was a common one – and tourists wanting to keep in touch with home. Rose was behind the counter and she flashed him a beaming smile. She was in her forties and her dancing days were long behind her, but even after three children she still had a figure that turned heads.

'Hi Lek,' she said. 'Are you up early, or late?'

Like most Thais, Rose usually mispronounced Alex or Lex as 'Lek', which meant small and was a common Thai nickname. He'd long since given up trying to get them to not call him Lek.

Harper laughed. 'Late, I'm afraid,' he said. 'Can I have a coffee?'

'Of course.'

She made him a cup of instant coffee and he grabbed a pack of crisps. He paid her and sat down at a free terminal. He sipped his coffee and then went through to the Yahoo Mail account that he used to communicate with Charlotte Button. He clicked in the draft file and there was one message there, short and to the point: *I need you in the UK now. Under the radar.* At the end of the message was a mobile phone number, presumably a throwaway.

Harper logged off the account and started popping crisps into his mouth as he considered his options. A pretty girl next to him with dyed blond hair was on Skype tearfully telling a guy in Norway that she was pregnant and needed money for an abortion. She was in her late teens but her English was surprisingly good, with a slight Australian accent that suggested either she watched a lot of Australian television or had shacked up with an Australian for several months at least. When Lex had walked in she had been telling the same sob story to a guy in Dubai who had promised to transfer fifty thousand baht to her bank account. She seemed to be able to cry on cue and dabbed at her eyes with a tissue as the Norwegian guy told her not to worry and that he would help her. He asked her if she was sure the baby was his and she burst into tears again. He apologised quickly and asked how much she needed. 'Sixty thousand baht,' she sobbed. Lex figured she had upped the price for daring to question her integrity.

He finished off the pack of crisps, screwed up the bag and tossed it into a wastepaper bin.

'More coffee, Lek?' asked Rose. She had recently taken up vaping and blew a cloud of whatever it was up at the ceiling.

'I'm good, Rose, thanks.'

He ran his hands through his hair. Button had said 'Now' whereas usually she'd say 'Soonest' or 'Urgently', so she meant he had to be on the next flight out. And the 'under the radar' was new. She knew that he was always careful about flying in and out of the UK, so the fact that she mentioned that she didn't want anyone to know he was there was significant. The lowest of low profiles. He had to be the invisible man and that meant the job she had for him was big. He could buy his ticket at the airport, that wouldn't be a problem. But first he had to go home and pick up one of several bug-out bags that he kept for those occasions when he had to move fast. He had three, each with different passports and driving licences, money and clothes, depending on where he planned to be. His European bug-out bag had a UK passport and an Irish passport, wads of sterling and euros, a washbag and shaving kit and a pair of black Levi jeans and a Ted Baker shirt. The clothing and toiletries he could buy anywhere but the UK passport was genuine, albeit not in his name. He looked at his watch. He might have time for a shower but if not he could do it at the airport. The fact she wanted him there immediately meant money would be no object, which meant he'd be flying first or business class.

Chapter 11

Ten Years Ago, New York

It took Yokely just under four hours to drive from Washington to Queens. A helicopter would have been quicker but would have attracted attention, and it gave him the opportunity of making a number of phone calls. The first was to Gerry McNee, whose ancestors had fled the Irish famine and repaid their adopted country by supplying generations of men for the American armed forces. McNee was a former Green Beret who had moved to Military Intelligence, where he had shown a talent for interrogation. He had spent two years at Guantanamo Bay and had been a frequent visitor to Abu Ghraib prison in Baghdad before control had been handed over to the Iraqi authorities in the spring of 2006. These days he was pretty much on full-time attachment to Grey Fox.

McNee answered as he always did with a curt 'Yeah?'

'Gerry, please tell me you're in Manhattan,' said Yokely.

'Heading out for dinner as we speak,' said McNee.

'Cancel that, I need you in Queens, ASAP,' said Yokely. 'I'll text you the location. I'm en route from DC so you'll probably get there before me. Keep a lid on whatever you find there and wait for me.'

He cut the connection and phoned Peter Leclerc. Leclerc was a Canadian by birth but had moved with his parents to live in Detroit when he was a toddler. He had joined the Coastguard after leaving university but had soon tired of searching vessels for contraband and refugees and had switched to the Drug Enforcement Administration. Yokely had met Leclerc there during an operation against the Medellin cartel there and had been so impressed with the man's attention to detail and complete lack of emotions that shortly afterwards he'd invited Leclerc to work with him at Grey Fox.

'Peter, where are you?'

'I'm stuck at Newark en route to Manila,' said Leclerc. 'There's been a plane crash at JFK so air traffic control's in a mess and I'm not sure when I'll be leaving.'

'I need you in Queens,' said Yokely. 'What's Manila, business or pleasure?'

'Offering advisory services to the new government,' said Leclerc. 'Nothing I can't duck out of.'

'I'll text you the location. Gerry's on his way but you'll probably get there before him. I need you to bring full disposal equipment. There's a guy from Homeland Security called Garcia holding the fort and a security guard by the name of Dean Martin. Be nice to them, but make sure they don't go anywhere.'

'Got you,' said Leclerc.

Yokely made two more calls.

The first was to the cell phone of Karl Traynor, a senior analyst with the Financial Crimes Enforcement Network. Traynor was based in Washington and spent most of his time sifting through financial transactions around the world looking for sources of terrorist funding. He asked Traynor to see if there had been any short selling of US airlines over the last few weeks. In the days before the 9/11 attacks, there were four times as many put options against British Airways as usual, and six times as many put options on United Airlines. Shares in both airlines plummeted after the planes hit the twin towers. The betting against American Airlines was even more severe with more than four thousand five hundred put options signed – almost three hundred times normal volumes. Whoever placed those bets made tens of millions of dollars. Financial services company Morgan Stanley, who occupied twenty-two floors of the World Trade Center, also saw a huge jump in put options between 6 and 10 September that netted the 'investors' more than one million dollars when the shares tumbled after the twin towers collapsed. Yokely wanted to know if something similar had happened prior to the JFK attack. Traynor promised to call him back if he found anything.

His next call was to David Dalton, a disposal expert with a penchant for using wildlife to get rid of bodies. He was still officially employed by the CIA in their Seattle office, but more often than not he was on attachment to Grey Fox. Like many of the Grey Fox team, Dalton was former Special Forces, a Green Beret who had been attached to the CIA while based in Afghanistan. Dalton said he wouldn't be able to get to New York that night but would be there first thing in the morning. Yokely ended the call and turned on the radio. It was tuned to a rock 'n' roll station and he tapped the steering wheel in time with the music as he drove at precisely the speed limit, running through a mental checklist of everything he had to do.

Chapter 12

Present Day, London

Lex Harper almost never flew directly into the UK. The days of fobbing off a bored immigration officer with a fake passport were long gone. The automated system used facial recognition tied in with the picture stored on the passport's chip, but even going for a face to face involved swiping the passport. Passports had become too complicated to forge, and stolen passports were quickly red-flagged. Harper actually had three UK passports, all genuine and with his photograph in all of them, albeit with different names and dates of birth. One was in his bug-out bag, the other two were in a safety deposit box at a bank in Bangkok. They cost five thousand pounds each and were supplied by a contact in Liverpool who arranged for homeless people to apply for passports they would never use. The homeless person was paid a thousand pounds spread over two years, and the middleman took the rest. It was pretty much a faultless system, even if the homeless person died, as passports weren't checked against death certificates.

Harper used a passport in the name of Roger Norrie. He didn't care if Norrie was alive or dead; all that mattered was that the passport was good. And it was. It was perfect. He flew EVA Air direct to London Heathrow and used the automatic passport reader to pass through immigration. He took the Heathrow Express to Paddington and checked into a cheap bed and breakfast a short walk from Hyde Park, chosen because it didn't insist on payment with a credit card. They did want to see his passport, but he had no problem checking in as Roger Norrie after handing over two fifty-pound notes to the receptionist, who had a chemistry textbook open on the counter. The room was on the second floor at the rear of the building. There was a single bed, a flimsy wardrobe and a tiny windowless shower room with a noisy extractor fan that ground into life when he pulled a greasy cord to switch on the light. He dropped his bag on the bed, grabbed a handful of money and headed out.

Bayswater was as crowded as usual, reflecting the true ethnic mix of London – he heard six different languages being spoken within a hundred yards. He bought three pay-as-you-go mobiles from three different phone shops on Queensway, then bought a coffee and a couple of plastic-wrapped sandwiches and went back to the hotel. The receptionist looked up from his textbook and smiled as Harper went by. Harper smiled back, then headed up the stairs. There were framed prints of flowers on the wall, complete with Latin names. The frames were dusty, the prints mouldy at the edges and the glass on one was cracked. The stair carpet was threadbare and stained and the flock wallpaper was peeling away in places. At the top of the stairs the carpet had been nibbled away by rats or mice and there were droppings in the corners, but Harper wasn't planning on writing a scathing review on TripAdvisor. The hotel was perfect for what he needed: they took cash, there was no CCTV and the receptionists were generally transient and paid little attention to who came and went.

He let himself into the room, sat down on his bed and used one of the throwaway phones to send a text message to the number that Button had given him: *The eagle has landed.*

He sipped his coffee and ate an egg and cress sandwich as he waited for her to get back to him. The phone rang within minutes.

'Eagle?' she said. 'I always had you in mind as a jackdaw. Or a crow.'

'That's racist, Charlie. Or at the very least, birdist.'

She ignored his attempt at humour. 'What's your hotel like?'

'Not salubrious,' said Harper. 'But there's no CCTV and the receptionist usually has his head buried in a book.'

'Even so, I think I'd rather be outside,' she said. 'Are you near the park we met last time?'

She was being more careful than usual, Harper realised. 'Sure.'

'See you there in an hour,' she said.

'I'll carry a red rose and a copy of the *Financial Times*.'

'A Mars bar and a copy of the *Sun*, more like.'

She ended the call and he had a quick shave and showered before eating another sandwich and finishing his coffee.

Chapter 13

Present Day, London

Patsy Ellis kept Shepherd waiting for more than an hour in her outer office. The longer he waited, the more convinced he became that she was going to fire him, but when her male secretary eventually said he could go through he opened the door to find her walking towards him, hand outstretched, all sweetness and light.

'So glad to finally meet you,' she said. She shook his hand and waved him to a straight-backed chair. 'And so sorry to have kept you waiting. It's all hands to the pumps, obviously.'

Shepherd took his seat as she walked back behind her desk. She was tall, even in flat shoes, wearing a dark blue skirt suit, a white blouse and a pale blue loosely tied scarf. She looked tired. There were dark patches under her eyes and her skin was dull and lifeless. She had tied her greying hair back, which emphasised the lines around her eyes, and she sighed as she dropped down on to her chair. She forced a smile. 'So, Charlotte always speaks highly of you,' she said.

Charlotte Button was Shepherd's former boss at MI5. She had left under a cloud after Jeremy Willoughby-Brown had exposed her for using government resources to wreak revenge on the men who had killed her husband. It was a messy business, but at least she was still alive and well and working in the private sector.

'It's been a while since I've seen her,' said Shepherd, choosing his words carefully.

'That's understandable, considering the circumstances under which she left,' said Ellis. 'But I know she always regarded you as a valuable member of her team.'

'Good to know,' said Shepherd.

'And I know you've been doing sterling work at the facial recognition unit,' she said. 'Your memory is a definite asset. You're picking up jihadists at a very impressive rate.'

Shepherd shrugged. 'I think I could be better used,' he said.

'Undercover work, you mean?' She flashed him a tight smile. 'I understand that there isn't much in the way of an adrenaline kick sitting in front of a computer all day, but results-wise, it's time well spent.'

'I'd rather be out and about,' he said. 'Given the choice. I was never one for desk work.'

'Duly noted,' said Ellis. 'But at the moment, it's your memory and recognition skills that we need to make use of. I'm aware that you were at the stadium yesterday when the bomb went off. I gather you did what you could to help?'

'It wasn't much.' He shuddered at the memory of the carnage he had witnessed. There were times when his near-perfect memory was as much a curse as a blessing. For the rest of his life he would have to live with the image of the dead boy lying on the ground while his father cried out for him. 'I was looking at the feed from the concession area not long before it exploded and I didn't see anything remotely suspicious.'

'You weren't there to spot potential suicide bombers,' said Ellis. 'The intel we had was that jihadists were getting together for a meet, nothing more. What happened took everyone by surprise. I'm putting you on the stadium bombing. We don't believe for one minute that Ali Naveed was a lone wolf. The device he used was very sophisticated and placed for maximum impact. A lot of thought and planning went into that attack. We need to find out who was helping him, and we need to move quickly.' There was a cup of tea on her desk and she reached for it and took a sip. 'Everyone who entered the stadium that evening had to go through a metal detector. There was no way he got in wearing a suicide vest. Someone had to have given him the vest once he was inside. We've got all the CCTV footage inside and outside the stadium and it all has to be gone through. The Met has agreed to put the Super-Recogniser Unit on it full time for the next week, and we've agreed to fund whatever overtime is necessary. We have photographs of every member of the stadium staff and we need to see if Naveed met anyone outside the ground, or inside.' She passed him a thumb drive. 'All the photographs are on there and we're arranging for the CCTV feeds to be available in Lambeth.'

Shepherd took the thumb drive. 'How many cameras inside the stadium?'

'Thirty-two,' said Ellis. 'Plus ten covering the outside. And we're getting council feeds from the area.'

Shepherd forced a smile. Assuming they looked at the four hours leading up to the explosion, that meant almost a hundred and seventy hours of footage. Assuming the whole unit piled in, it would take them a couple of days to review it all.

'Locating the person who gave him the vest is our first priority,' said Ellis. 'But we need to know who else was working with him. We need to start looking at CCTV footage from all the mosques in the Ealing area. In fact we need to be looking at pretty much every CCTV camera within a mile of where he lived. Your team needs to nail down where he went and who he met for at least the last month.'

Shepherd's smile tightened. What Ellis was asking made perfect sense, but it was a huge job. Thousands and thousands of hours of video would have to be looked at. But if it got them closer to the bastard who had caused the carnage, he'd do whatever it took.

'The Met has agreed to draft in some of the Super-Recognisers based at stations around London, which probably means you'll have another dozen or so at your disposal. The Met was already understaffed and with the threat level raised to critical every available officer has been called in. If the threat level drops we might be able to get you more manpower at the unit but at the moment the Met is stretched as far as it can go. Believe me, Dan, I do appreciate the magnitude of the task.'

'It's a grind, but it's doable,' said Shepherd.

'Excellent,' said Ellis. 'Now, as this is being run out of the Met's Lambeth base, it is being seen as a police operation. They'll obviously have first sight of anything you find, but I need you to stay in close personal contact with me on this, Dan. I don't want any surprises. Anything the Met knows, I want to know.' She gave him a business card. 'My mobile number is on the back. Any hour, night or day. Text or call.'

Shepherd took the card. 'Will do,' he said.

'Do you know anything at all about this Ali Naveed?'

'It's not a name I've come across.'

'No one has,' said Ellis. 'Though we're not even sure if it's his real name. He entered the country six months ago as an un-accompanied minor, claiming to be fifteen years old and a refugee from Syria. He was put with a foster family in Ealing and was apparently a problem from day one. One of the first things he asked for was a razor, and his foster parents expressed their concern that he was considerably older than he claimed to be. His teachers also spoke to social services querying his age.'

'And nobody did anything?'

'It's difficult, Dan. What is happening in Syria is truly awful, and when a child arrives in this country claiming that his parents have been killed, what can we do? He was treated as if he was a fifteen-year-old but yes, we can assume he was considerably older. Early twenties, perhaps. Certainly, he gave his foster parents all sorts of problems. He was out all hours of the night, he stopped going to school and he was always telling his foster mother to cover her head when she went out.'

'They were Muslims, the foster parents?'

Ellis shook her head. 'No. Non-denominational. They're long-standing foster parents and have looked after more than a hundred children over the years. Anyway, they weren't able to cope with him. They were looking after another child, a ten-year-old boy, and they complained to social services that Ali was bothering him.'

'Bothering?'

'Going into his room at night, watching him take a shower.'

'Bloody hell!' groaned Shepherd. 'And that didn't set alarm bells ringing?'

Ellis shrugged. 'Hindsight is a wonderful thing.'

'No one saw the warning signs, and two dozen people are dead,' said Shepherd. 'We should be finding out who let him into this country and putting them behind bars for a few years. If we started holding people responsible for their actions, they might start paying more attention.' He shook his head. 'So the thinking is that he came into this country deliberately to launch a terrorist attack?'

'It seems unlikely that he was radicalised in just a few months. So yes, we think he was sent here. We need the unit to start going through all the CCTV footage in the area around the foster house. We need to know where he went in London, and who he met.' She saw the look of disbelief flash across Shepherd's face. 'I know, I know, it's a mammoth undertaking. Thousands of hours, tens of thousands of hours. But it's the key to finding out who is really behind this. I know you can do this, Dan.'

Shepherd nodded. 'I'll give it my best shot.'

She nodded at the business card. 'Do that,' she said. 'And stay in touch. Anything you get, no matter how small, I need to know about it.'

Chapter 14

It was dark when Yokely eventually pulled up in front of the warehouse in Queens. There were several cars already there. A black SUV, a white sedan and a large van with the name of a courier company on the side. He switched off the engine and climbed out. The warehouse was metal-sided with a sloping roof, a delivery ramp to the right and a door to the left with a sign over it saying APEX IMPORT-EXPORT. He walked around to the back of his SUV and took out an aluminium briefcase.

As Yokely walked over to the entrance, the door opened. His hand moved automatically to the Glock in its underarm holster but he relaxed when he saw it was Leclerc. He was dressed for the tropics, sporting a cream linen jacket and light cotton trousers. He was a decade younger than Yokely with close-cropped hair and a broken nose.

'No need to shoot your way in, Richard,' he said. 'It's all under control.'

Yokely chuckled and shook Leclerc's hand. 'Sorry to ruin your trip, Peter.'

'I'm not a big fan of the Philippines,' said Leclerc. 'Too many distractions.'

Yokely looked up at the building. 'What's the story with this place?'

'Homeland Security use it for short-term storage. We can have it as long as we want. The Homeland Security guy arranged it. His name's Garcia. Tommy Garcia. He's inside.'

'Just so you know, Gerry McNee is driving in from Manhattan and David Dalton will be flying in first thing.'

'I'm in good company, then,' said Leclerc. He stepped aside and followed Yokely into the warehouse.

'You got the gear?'

'In the van,' said Leclerc.

There were several pallets piled high with boxes and wreathed in polythene off to the right, close to the metal shutter at the delivery ramp. Beyond the pallets was a glass-sided office. There were two men sitting either side of a desk.

'That's Garcia, with Martin, the security guard who set all this off. I've asked them both to stay there until we know where we stand.'

'What's your impression of Garcia?' asked Yokely, setting the briefcase on the floor by the wall.

'Solid guy. Understands what's going on and I think just wants to get out of here and leave us to it.'

'And Martin?'

'I haven't really spoken to him. In effect he's a civilian so I'm keeping my distance.'

'Probably best,' said Yokely.

Leclerc pointed at three bodies, face down on the concrete. One was handcuffed behind his back and the second had his wrists bound with what looked like a necktie. The third was clearly dead.

'So, we've got three bad guys,' said Leclerc. 'One dead, two alive. The dead one is Hamid bin Faisal – we've got a Saudi passport for him. Arrived in the country ten days ago.'

He handed Yokely a Saudi passport. There were a dozen or so visa stamps, the most recent showing that he had flown into Miami Airport.

Leclerc gave Yokely a second passport. This one from the United Kingdom. 'We've got a Pakistani with a British passport. Rashid Makhdoom. Born in Karachi but he's a British citizen. And last but not least, Omar Ibrahimi, born in Algeria but now a French citizen.'

Yokely took the French passport and flicked through it. Ibrahimi had arrived in the US just a week earlier, at Boston Airport. He checked the British passport. Makhdoom had also arrived a week earlier, but he had flown into Baltimore.

'The launcher is over here,' said Leclerc, walking to the far left-hand corner of the warehouse. 'It's an FIM-92 Stinger and the serial number is on it so there shouldn't be any problem tracing it.'

Yokely looked down at the launch pack and nodded. Next to the gun were an Uzi and two semi-automatics. A Glock and a Beretta. He frowned. 'This security guard, he took them down himself?'

Leclerc nodded. 'Yes he did.'

Yokely looked over at the glass-sided office and raised his eyebrows. One of the men was wearing a dark blue uniform and a peaked cap so Yokely assumed that was Martin.

Yokely used his cell phone to call an old friend, Sam Hepburn. Hepburn was a senior analyst with the National Security Agency based at the NSA's headquarters in Forte Meade, Maryland. Yokely gave him the serial number of the missile launcher and asked him to check its history. Hepburn didn't ask any questions, just said he'd get right on it.

'They recorded the whole thing on a video camera,' said Leclerc as Yokely ended his call. He handed him a Sony camcorder. Yokely flipped out the screen and rewound the DV tape. He pressed the play button. Three men in ski masks were standing in front of a banner with Arabic writing on it. One of them was holding the Stinger launcher. He spoke in Arabic as the other two posed. The next shot was the Stinger being taken out of an SUV. Behind them was the skyline of Manhattan. The ski masks had been replaced with black and white checked scarfs tied across their faces. The man with the Stinger was aiming it. Then there was a voice. An English accent. 'Okay, okay, there's a plane taking off now. American. This is it guys. This is it. *Allahu Akbar*.' That must have been Makhdoom. The Brit. It was Bin Faisal holding the video and Ibrahimi holding the missile.

'*Allahu Akbar*!' screamed Ibrahimi and he launched the missile. It streaked up into the air and for a moment it disappeared from view, then Bin Faisal caught up with it, high in the air, a vapour trail streaming from behind it. There was a plane in the distance, still climbing. Yokely's stomach lurched. Three hundred and twelve men, women and children preparing for a flight across the Atlantic. Settling down in their seats, checking the in-flight magazine, flicking through the movies on offer.

The missile curved through the sky and smacked into the mid-section. There was a yellow flash, the plane split into two and then the two pieces fractured into more than a dozen. The three jihadists were screaming and shouting and praising Allah. Yokely switched off the camcorder, shaking his head. He took out the tape, slipped it into his pocket and gave the camcorder back to Leclerc.

'Okay, do me a favour and send Garcia over. Stay with Martin, I'll talk to them separately.'

Leclerc nodded and headed to the office. A few seconds later, Garcia walked over. He was wearing a dark grey suit and a red tie. He was in his mid-thirties with jet-black glossy hair and olive skin and there was a stars and stripes pin in his lapel. He didn't seem to be carrying a weapon. Yokely offered his hand.

'Tommy Garcia?' said Yokely. 'I'm Richard Yokely. Hopefully you've been expecting me. Thanks for your help with this.'

'Not a problem,' said Garcia.

Yokely smiled. 'You're not related to the actor, are you? Andy Garcia?'

'It's a common name,' said Garcia.

'Yeah, but you look a lot like him. He's not a cousin or anything?'

Garcia smiled, obviously pleased at the comparison. 'Not that I know.'

Yokely gestured at the office. 'So this guy Martin, you interviewed him at Homeland Security, right?'

'I did his secondary evaluation,' said Garcia. 'We decided to pass but I gave him my card and told him to keep in touch.' Garcia smiled thinly. 'The last thing I expected was for him to turn up with three terrorists.'

'And why did you pass?'

Garcia shrugged. 'Our work these days is more cerebral than physical. We sift data, assess risks, set up systems to anticipate problems before they happen. Martin's skills lean more to the physical. If you wanted someone to jump out of a plane, abseil down a building or go in with guns blazing, then he'd be the perfect candidate.'

Yokely nodded. 'Any other reasons?'

Garcia looked pained. 'I like the guy, that's why I gave him my card. He's done a hell of a lot for this country and he deserves better than guarding a shopping mall . . .'

'But . . .?'

'As part of our recruitment process, we run applicants through a battery of psychological tests and they have a sit-down with a psychologist. Martin didn't exactly fit the profile we're looking for.'

'Because?'

'He went through a lot in Iraq and Afghanistan. Most of what he did is classified but you can see from that thousand-yard stare of his that he's walked the walk. And that changes a man.'

Yokely nodded. 'Look, I think you're pretty much done here, Tommy. We can handle it from now on. I don't know what your boss told you, but I don't expect you'll be asked to file a report on this. It never happened.'

'That's my understanding.'

'You did good work today. It won't be forgotten.'

'So I just go?'

Yokely nodded.

Garcia grimaced. 'Bit of a problem,' he said. 'My car's back at the mall. Dean and I drove over in the two vehicles the suspects were using, the SUV and the sedan.'

'Not a problem. I'll get one of my colleagues to run you back,' said Yokely. 'Just give me a few minutes with Martin.'

Yokely walked over to the office. Martin stood up and removed his cap as Yokely entered, showing his military background.

Yokely smiled and held out his hand. 'You did your country a great service today, Mr Martin,' he said.

Leclerc was standing by the door, his hands in his pockets.

Martin had a firm handshake, and his pale blue eyes stared

into Yokely's as they shook. He wasn't a big man, a couple of inches below six foot, but he had a powerful build and the look of a boxer.

'Just doing my duty, sir,' said Martin. He was smiling, but Yokely could feel himself being measured up as Martin's eyes flicked down, taking in Yokely's tasselled loafers, his class ring, the scar on his thumb, and then he looked into Yokely's eyes again.

Yokely waved at one of the chairs. 'Please, sit,' he said. There was another chair on the opposite side of the desk but Yokely stayed standing.

'I'll give the vehicles a quick check over,' said Leclerc. He headed towards the exit.

Yokely smiled at Martin. 'So, can you tell me in your own words what happened this evening?'

Martin nodded. 'I'd just finished my shift. I was on my way out when I saw these three guys drive up in an SUV. They parked near a car. A white Ford Fusion. A few minutes later a red truck arrived. A Chevrolet Silverado. There were two more Arabs in the truck and one of them got out. They were celebrating something, and they were looking at a camcorder. All pumped up. Then one of them pulled a Stinger launcher from the SUV. I think they were planning on moving it to the Ford and torching the car.'

'You knew what it was?'

'The Stinger? Sure. That was when I went over to them. They pulled guns but I took them down.'

'You weren't armed?'

Martin shook his head. 'They won't let us have guns. Bad for the mall's image, they say.'

'And the men. They had what?'

'One of them had an Uzi and one pulled a Glock. I think the other one had a gun too but he didn't have time to use it.'

'You took out three men, two of them armed, with what?' He nodded at the baton in Martin's holster. 'With that?'

'I didn't get time to draw my baton,' said Martin. 'To be fair,

I had the element of surprise on my side. They weren't expecting me.'

'What about the red truck? I don't see it outside.'

'It drove off. The older man, he ran like the wind and jumped in. It sped off before I could do anything.'

'Did you get the plate?'

Martin shook his head. 'Too far away, and the lights were off.'

'What about the one that got away?'

'He was fifty, maybe a bit older. Overweight. Grey beard, all straggly. Blue jeans and a long coat. He was wearing glasses, round with metal frames.'

'You'd recognise him again?'

'Hell, yeah. I got a real good look. He could run too, for an old guy. Like a fox after a chicken.'

Yokely nodded thoughtfully. 'Okay, so you take down three armed men, killing one of them. You're not just a security guard, are you, Mr Martin?'

Martin grinned. 'Former Navy SEAL,' he said.

'How long were you with them?'

'Five years, sir.'

'You don't need to call me "sir", son,' said Yokely. He patted Martin on the shoulder. 'You did good work tonight, Dean. But you need to go now. And you need to forget this ever happened.'

Martin nodded. 'I understand.'

'No matter what you read in the papers or see on the TV in the coming weeks or months, you say nothing. To anyone.'

Martin nodded again. 'Absolutely.' He stood up and looked around as if looking for an excuse to stay.

'I'll fix you up with a ride so that you can collect your vehicle,' said Yokely.

'I'd appreciate that,' said Martin.

Yokely went back into the warehouse. One of the men on the ground was struggling but he wasn't going anywhere and a gag muffled anything he was trying to say.

Leclerc came in through the door. 'Richard, I found something.'

He held up a key attached to a plastic oval disc. 'Motel key. Park Motel, Long Island.'

Yokely frowned. The terrorists had either used the motel room to prepare for the attack or were planning to hide out there. Either way the room needed checking, and straight away. But he was short on manpower.

'Shall I head out there?' asked Leclerc, as if reading his mind.

'They could have backup, and they clearly have no problem getting weapons,' said Yokely. He looked at his watch, then back at Leclerc. 'I know this is unorthodox, but take Dean with you.'

Leclerc couldn't conceal his surprise. 'A civilian?'

'A civilian who's former Navy SEAL,' said Yokely. 'And he's clearly not rusty.' He nodded over at the guns on the floor. 'Give him the Glock.'

'You're sure about this?' asked Leclerc. The man wasn't being insubordinate, just checking that Yokely had thought it through. On Grey Fox operations every team member's views and opinions were listened to.

'We can't call in SWAT and we're short-handed until Gerry gets here,' said Yokely. 'We need to move now. If there's someone waiting for these three then they'll get spooked when they don't turn up. And if it was a planning base and they've cleared out already then we need to check it out before the room is cleaned.'

Leclerc nodded. 'I'm on my way.' He went over to the weapons on the floor and picked up the Glock.

'Best I talk to Dean,' said Yokely and went outside. Martin was smoking a cigarette and he looked over guiltily as Yokely walked out.

Yokely grinned. 'I've no problem with you smoking,' he said.

Garcia was standing by the black SUV, peering at the screen of his smartphone.

'I'm down to ten a day,' said Martin. He looked at his cigarette. 'I should give up, but . . .' He shrugged and smiled. 'I just like smoking.'

'Are you interested in helping us out?'

'Hell, yeah,' said Martin.

Leclerc came out, holding the Glock.

'I need you to help Peter here to check out a motel room in Long Island. If there is anyone there connected to tonight's terrorist incident, we need to know.'

Leclerc handed the gun to Martin. Martin checked it professionally, ejecting the clip, working the slide and looking down the barrel before slotting the clip back in.

Yokely reached into his pocket and took out his car keys. 'Best if you drop Tommy off on the way,' he said to Leclerc. 'You can use my car. No mention of what's going on, obviously.'

Leclerc smiled thinly and took the keys. He nodded at the gun in Martin's hand. 'You might want to put that away,' he said.

Martin tucked the gun into his belt. 'Good to go,' he said.

Leclerc and Martin went over to Garcia and after a quick conversation the three men climbed into Yokely's car and drove off. Yokely watched them turn on to the main road and head east. As the car disappeared into the night, a high-powered motorcycle left the road and drove towards the warehouse.

The biker parked next to the black SUV. As Yokely walked over, the biker took off his full-face helmet. It was Gerry McNee, wearing full motorcycle leathers, padded at the knees, hips, elbows and shoulders. He grinned when he saw Yokely and raised a gloved hand. 'Sorry I'm late,' he said. McNee was just over six feet tall, broad-shouldered, and like Leclerc had close-cropped hair. He had a square jaw and a white scar on his upper lip. He shook hands with Yokely.

'You've just missed Peter Leclerc,' said Yokely. 'And David Dalton is flying in from Seattle.'

'It's that plane, I'm guessing.'

'You're guessing right.' Yokely gestured at the door. 'We've got three inside, two of them still alive, and Peter's on the way to check out a motel they were using.'

'So hard interrogations?'

'Hard and fast and then disposal,' said Yokely.

McNee flashed him a tight smile. 'That's how it should be,' he said.

Chapter 15

Harper lit a cigarette as he waited for Charlotte Button to appear. He found an empty bench and stretched out his legs. He had sat down ten minutes before the arranged time and he looked around to see if anyone stood out. They didn't, but then professionals rarely did. After five minutes he stood up and walked a hundred yards or so before sitting down on another bench.

He saw Button walking by the Serpentine. She had cut her hair since he had last seen her and he didn't recognise the raincoat she was wearing, but other than that she looked pretty much the same as the first time he had met her, almost ten years earlier. She had a trim figure and legs that he was fairly sure were kept in shape by frequent running. She had a Michael Kors bag on her right shoulder and was carrying a copy of the *Evening Standard*. Her counter-surveillance techniques were as perfect as always; she changed her walking speed several times, dropped her paper once and looked behind her as she stooped to pick it up and sat for several minutes on a bench pretending to read the paper but really having a good look around her.

Eventually she came over and sat down on the opposite end of his bench, crossing her legs away from him and concentrating on her paper. 'How was the flight?' she asked.

'Uneventful,' said Harper. He blew smoke towards the Serpentine.

'The speed you got here, I'm assuming a direct flight.'

'My passport is kosher,' said Harper.

'I want as few people as possible knowing you're here, Alex.'

'Mum's the word.'

'The job I have for you isn't the normal sort of Pool job, Alex. I have to be up front with you on that. And after I've explained the situation to you, I'll understand if you turn me down.'

Harper nodded but didn't say anything.

'You heard about the stadium bombing, of course?'

'Sure,' said Harper. 'Bastards. Twenty-four dead, right?'

'Twenty-nine so far but there are another dozen casualties in intensive care who aren't doing well at all.'

'They should string them up,' said Harper.

'It was a suicide bomber, Alex. There's nothing to string up. Anyway, there will be a list of terminations connected to that bombing. I have one name so far but we obviously expect that to grow. I'd like you to do the jobs yourself, or bring in contractors, but those contractors must not be those used by the Pool.'

'You want to distance yourself?' asked Harper.

'Exactly,' said Button. 'On the financial side, the money will be coming from an account in the Cayman Islands, and the fee will be fifty per cent more than your usual rate, Plus any reasonable expenses will be covered – and, to be honest, even your unreasonable costs will be paid.'

'This is for the government?'

She stayed silent for several seconds, then turned the page of her paper. 'Does it matter?'

'It helps to know.'

'Then let's say it's semi-official. But there'll be no get-out-of-jail-free cards on this one.'

'Understood,' he said.

'I know you're a big fan of throwaway phones but for this operation I'm going to suggest we use iPod Touches and the Signal app.'

Harper nodded. 'Okay, I can do that.' Signal was one of the most secure ways of communicating, but the fact that an iPod was used meant that it had to be connected to Wi-Fi. The iPod wouldn't connect to any cellular network, which made it very difficult to spy on. Mobile phones left a trail as they moved and locked on to the strongest cell tower. Transmissions – calls and texts – could be intercepted and the location of the phone could be determined. Signal – produced by Open Whisper Systems – used encrypted instant messaging and voice calls and was one of the most secure apps on the market. It used ephemeral keys where a new cryptographic key was generated for each message as opposed to systems that used one decryption key for all messages. The combination of ephemeral keys and no cell-phone connection meant it was virtually impossible to intercept messages and calls.

'What sort of terminations do you want?' asked Harper.

'Quick ones,' said Button. 'I'll leave it up to you. We're looking to terminate anyone involved with the suicide bomber, Ali Naveed. He was granted asylum, claiming to be a teenage orphan, but we are fairly sure he was much older. Now, we already have one contact. On the morning of the bombing he made a call to a phone in Birmingham owned by another young Syrian refugee, Israr Farooqi. Farooqi is a cleanskin but his profile is very similar to Naveed's so I think we can assume he is on the same path. It might be helpful if you see if he has any intel on other jihadists. And in particular, whoever is running them.'

'So interrogation and termination? All good.'

'Over the next few days I should have more names for you. The police are searching Naveed's house and his foster parents are being questioned by the police as we speak. They are British-British and not at all religious, so it's likely they are innocent parties in this. Naveed has an uncle, Imran Masood, living in Bolton. He was granted asylum five years ago and is now a British citizen. Once he got his British passport he started to travel frequently back to Syria where he has been in contact with several members of ISIS. Again there is no concrete evidence that he was involved in the bombing.'

'So we're talking guilt by association? I don't have a problem with that, Charlie. In fact I'd like to see it as government policy. If these bastards knew that there were consequences for their actions they might think twice before blowing themselves up.'

'The tree-hugging Lefties would have a field day if that were to become official policy.'

'Fuck them,' said Harper. 'We're at war with these bastards, and they don't fight fair so why the hell should we? Just give me the list and I'll take it from there.'

'But to be clear, Alex, this job is not government sanctioned.'

'They never are, Charlie,' laughed Harper. 'That's why they use you. And that's why you use the Pool.'

Button flashed him a tight smile. 'They use me when they want to keep an operation at arm's length. Plausible deniability, as they say. But this is different. This is personal.'

'Personal?'

'I'm not going to say more than that, Alex, so please don't press me. And to be absolutely clear, I'm not using the Pool on this. I'm using you.'

Harper nodded and blew smoke down at the grass. 'If you know about this Farooqi, so do the authorities. Won't they have snapped him up?'

'We're ahead of the curve. The phone information is with MI5 and they will keep it to themselves until tomorrow. The phone was destroyed in the blast, obviously, so we won't be getting any information from the device, but the phone company has downloaded the call and text record and we'll have its location details later today.'

'But I'm going to have to move quickly, right? Once the cops have him I won't be able to get to him.'

'That's why I said it was a rush job, Alex.'

'And what about Masood?'

'Again, MI5 has that information but the police don't. He's in Five's database but the police have never looked at him. If the police do become aware of the uncle, I'll tell you immediately, obviously. But at the moment, you have a clear run. But Farooqi needs to be your priority.'

Harper flicked ash on to the grass. 'And there's no problem with the terminations looking like assassinations? Isn't it going to look like what it is – someone taking revenge?'

'It's a thin line,' said Button. 'We need the jihadists to understand that the rules have changed, but we don't want the Press on our case. I need you to throw out a few red herrings. There's a particularly nasty racist group on the rise – they've been attacking Muslims and nailing pig heads to mosque doors – so it wouldn't do any harm to point the blame their way. Once you have Signal up and running, contact me and I'll send you a list of their officials.'

'So you want me to frame innocent people for the killings?'

For the first time she looked over at him. 'Is that a problem?'

Harper smiled. 'Of course not, Charlotte. I just wanted to be sure, that's all.'

She slid her newspaper across the bench to him. 'There's some cash here to get you started. I'll have more for you soon.'

He picked up the paper and nodded when he saw the bulky manila envelope inside. 'I probably won't have much in the way of receipts,' he said.

'I won't be sweating the small stuff,' she said. 'And I trust you.'

Chapter 16

Present Day, London

Shepherd had fixed a map of the stadium to the wall and circled the location of the CCTV cameras with a red pen. On both sides of the map he had pinned photographs of Ali Naveed, head-and-shoulders shots taken from his asylum applications. There were two dozen Super-Recognisers in the room, eight regulars and sixteen new faces who had been brought in from their stations. They were a mixed bag – young, middle-aged, male, female, one Asian, two mixed-race, fat, thin, short and tall. The ability to be a Super-Recogniser didn't appear to be linked to any other genetic traits; you either had the talent or you didn't.

'Right, for those of you who don't know me, I'm Dan Shepherd. I'm on attachment from the Security Service and our immediate task is to find out how this man – Ali Naveed – managed to get a suicide vest into the stadium. Clearly he had help, and we need to identify whoever it was who helped him. We are going to assume that the person or persons who helped him worked at the stadium. There are thirty-two cameras inside the stadium and ten cameras covering the outside, with another four at the entrances. In the first instance we concentrate on finding out how he got into the stadium. Once we know which entrance he used we can focus on the cameras covering that area. I'm going to suggest that fourteen of you start now by checking those fourteen feeds. The rest of you can familiarise yourself with the staff database. Once you're happy that you have all the faces memorised, switch places with someone watching the entrance footage. Any questions?'

An officer held up his hand. He was in his early thirties with close-cropped red hair and piercing green eyes. 'Sorry,' he said. 'Eric Fitzpatrick, I'm from Kilburn nick. I absolutely appreciate the seriousness of this but I'm on earlies this week and I'm supposed to collect my daughter from school this afternoon.' He smiled apologetically. 'Sorry to bring it up but, you know—'

'Not a problem,' said Shepherd. 'We've all got families. Here's the situation. This room will now operate twenty-four-seven. My bosses have agreed to pick up all overtime payments for the foreseeable future at time and a half. But no one is forcing anyone to work. I understand how stressful recognition can be and I don't want anyone looking at faces and thinking about something else. So yes, if you need to go, go.' He pointed at a bald uniformed sergeant who was standing by the door. 'Sergeant George Hurry will be drawing up the rotas.' Hurry raised his hand in salute. 'The canteen should be open twenty-four-seven but George is also your go-to guy for food, coffees, anything you need brought in from the outside. I'll be here most of the time, but if not then Inspector Nick Hughes will be running the show.' The inspector was sitting at his terminal and raised his hand. He was a big man with wide shoulders who had been running the Super-Recogniser Unit for more than a year and everyone in the room knew who he was. 'There were forty thousand people at that match, so let's get started,' said Shepherd.

Chapter 17

Peter Leclerc drove in silence. Martin sat with his arms folded, staring ahead. He figured silence was the best option. He didn't want to appear overeager, and he didn't want to risk saying anything that would make him look stupid. The man with the tasselled shoes hadn't introduced himself but the name on his business card said 'Richard Yokely'. There had been no job title on the card, and no company name, just a couple of phone numbers and a PO Box number. But Martin was sure he worked for one of the government agencies, maybe the DIA or CIA, certainly something known by its initials. Garcia had been high up in Homeland Security but he was clearly deferring to Yokely, so Yokely carried weight. A lot of weight. They had dropped Garcia at his car in the mall parking lot, then headed for the Park Motel.

Leclerc had tapped the motel's location into the SatNav and it showed they were just five minutes away. Ahead of them was a pizza place, and above it a large sign showing a slice of pizza dripping melting cheese.

'We should get a pizza,' said Martin.

'We can eat later,' said Leclerc.

'If there's anyone in the room, they won't open for strangers,' said Martin.

Leclerc grinned. 'But they might for a guy with a pizza, even if it's the wrong room?' He nodded. 'Nice idea.' Leclerc turned off the road to pull in front of the pizza place. Martin hurried inside and bought a large pepperoni. He got back into the car and kept the box on his lap.

'Damn, that smells good,' said Leclerc.

Martin grinned. It did, too.

'Pepperoni?'

'With extra cheese.'

'You know this guy is almost certainly a Muslim so he won't be eating pepperoni?'

Martin shrugged. 'I wasn't planning on offering him a slice.'

The Park Motel was a two-storey H-shaped building with the reception in the central part and the rooms in wings either side. There was a car park in front and a sign indicating another car park at the rear. Leclerc switched off the SUV's lights and drove slowly around to the rear and parked.

'That's it,' said Leclerc, pointing at a room on the ground floor. 'One-two-six.' He pulled a Glock from his shoulder holster, checked it and then screwed in a bulbous silencer. 'Okay, so you play the delivery guy. He'll probably not open the door but if he does, you step aside and I'll force entry.' He handed Martin the key. 'If he doesn't open then you can use the key. Assuming the security chain is on, you need to unlock the door, open it and stand to the side. Again, I'll force entry. Try not to fire your weapon, we don't want the cops called.'

Martin nodded. 'Roger that.'

Leclerc smiled. 'Let's do it.'

They climbed out of the SUV. Martin walked straight towards the door across the parking lot. Leclerc hurried to the building and stood with his back to it, the gun at his side. The curtains were drawn in all the rooms and most were in darkness. There were televisions on in two rooms but they were both some distance away.

Martin reached the door, held the pizza box on his left arm and knocked on the door. 'Pizza!' he said. When there was no reply, he knocked again. 'Pizza!'

He heard a bump inside the room and he turned and nodded at Leclerc.

Leclerc was pressed against the wall, his gun still low.

Martin knocked on the door again. 'Pizza's getting cold.'

'I didn't order pizza,' said a voice from inside.

'Room one-two-six, it's already paid for.'

There was a security viewer in the door and Martin stood back, held up the pizza box and smiled amiably. The door stayed shut. He leaned forward and knocked again, a cheery, non-threatening knock.

The door opened. The security chain was on. Martin caught a glimpse of a dark-skinned face and a brown eye, and black hair. 'I didn't order no pizza.' A British accent, or Australian. Martin could never tell the difference. The TV was on, but the sound was turned down.

'It's paid for.'

'Just fuck off.'

The door began to close. The plan had been for Martin to stand to the side and for Leclerc to handle the entry but Martin could see there wasn't going to be time. He kicked out with his right foot, planting it under the handle and putting all his weight behind the kick. The door flew open, the chain ripped out of the door frame and the man inside staggered back. Martin turned and hit the door with his right shoulder. It slammed into the man and he staggered back again. Martin stepped into the room, taking in everything with one glance. An unmade bed, a stack of fast food cartons and wrappers, bottles of water, clothes strewn over a chair, two cell phones on a dressing table, three holdalls on the floor, an open bathroom door. The TV, showing CNN.

The man had a gun in his right hand. He snarled as he brought it up but he was slow and Martin's right hand was already reaching for the man's wrist. He grabbed and twisted and at the same time stamped down on the man's left foot. The man yelped and the gun fell to the floor. Martin let go of the wrist and chopped the man's throat with the side of his hand, being careful not to make it a killing blow. They wanted the man alive.

The man grunted and both hands went up to his injured throat, panic in his eyes as he fought to breathe.

Martin pulled back his hand, made it into a fist and chopped at the guy's solar plexus. The blow instantly paralysed his diaphragm and he went down, his chest heaving.

Leclerc had followed Martin inside and closed the door. He smiled as he looked down at the almost-unconscious Asian, now rolled up into a foetal ball. 'You know what was most impressive about the way you handled that?' asked Leclerc.

'The fact I didn't drop the pizza?' said Martin. He opened the box and offered it to Leclerc.

'Exactly,' said Leclerc, helping himself to a slice.

Chapter 18

Present Day, London

Harper walked back to Queensway and bought an iPod Touch for cash from a small electronics shop. He went to Costa Coffee, paid for an Americano and a croissant and sat at a table to activate the iPod. He used the shop's Wi-Fi to download the Signal app. Once he had the app up and running he sent a message to Button. He was halfway through his croissant when she replied: *That was quick . . .*

I don't hang around, he typed.

He finished his coffee and went back to his hotel room. He used a second throwaway mobile to make a call to a car dealer he'd used many times before. The only driving licence Harper had on him was his own and he didn't want to use that to rent a car the traditional way. Kev Wheeler was Harper's go-to guy for untraceable transport. Wheeler operated a small garage under a railway arch in Clapham. He made a nice living repairing cars and issuing MOTs but he had a sideline business that Harper had made use of on several occasions – renting out vehicles with ringer number plates. The vehicles were stolen but Wheeler would replace the number plates with the registration details of an identical vehicle in another part of the country. At any one time he had half a dozen vehicles stored in lock-ups around the city and he was the car rental company of choice for several London criminal gangs. Wheeler demanded a large payment upfront with the promise to rebuy so long as the vehicle hadn't been compromised.

Wheeler was happy to hear from Harper and agreed to pick

him up in Bayswater within the hour. Harper was outside the hotel when Wheeler pulled up in a white people-carrier. Harper climbed in and the two men shook hands. Wheeler was in his early thirties, tall and stick-thin and wearing stained overalls.

'Bit short notice, Lex,' said Wheeler, pulling away from the kerb. He had a rough Glasgow accent, not softened in the least by the ten years he'd spent in London.

'Yeah, it's been a bit of a rush,' he said.

'What do you need?'

'Something reliable and nondescript. Speed isn't an issue but I'll be up and down the motorway so a decent size. And a roomy boot.'

'I've got a Toyota Prius?'

Harper scowled at him. 'Don't piss about, Kev.'

Wheeler laughed. 'They're economical and you don't get more nondescript. But okay, I hear what you're saying. How about a three-year-old Avensis. Nice size boot.'

'Sounds better,' said Harper. 'What are the owner's details?'

'Dentist in Leicester. He's about your age. I've got all the info you need. Plus a copy of the insurance.'

Harper nodded. The fact that the car was a ringer meant that he would need to identify himself as the true owner of the vehicle in the unlikely – but possible – event that he was pulled over by the police. He could get away without providing the driving licence but at the very least he would be expected to know the name, address and date of birth of the owner. 'Sounds good,' he said.

Less than hour later he was driving north in a blue Toyota and Wheeler had eight thousand pounds in cash. Wheeler hadn't provided a receipt for the transaction but Harper knew that he'd have no problems getting the money back from Charlotte Button.

Chapter 19

Present Day, London

They found Ali Naveed after just two hours. He was wearing a black puffa coat, blue jeans and blue Nikes with a gleaming white swoosh on the side. It was a young PC who found him and she had whooped out loud. 'Got him!' she shouted.

Shepherd hurried over to her screen. There was no doubt, it was him. He patted her on the shoulder. 'Right everybody,' he shouted. 'We have Ali Naveed arriving at the stadium an hour and a half before the match started at the west entrance.' His fingers played across the keyboard and the image flashed up on one of the large wall-mounted screens. Shepherd went over to it. 'The jacket is fairly distinctive, but I'm really liking the shoes,' he said. 'I doubt there were too many Asians there wearing blue Nikes.' He walked over to the map of the stadium and tapped the entrance where Naveed had been spotted. 'Right, this is where he came in.' He looked over at Inspector Hughes. 'Inspector, could you draw up a schedule for the CCTV cameras adjacent to the entrance. We need to know where he went and more importantly, who he met.'

'I'm on it,' said Hughes.

'Also, we need to work backwards now from the entrance to see how he got to the stadium and if he arrived with anyone.'

As the inspector began tapping on his keyboard, Shepherd went over to Sergeant Hurry. The sergeant had taken off his tunic and rolled up his shirtsleeves and was on his third cup of coffee. Shepherd pulled up a chair and sat down next to him. 'Right, George, it's time to widen the net,' said Shepherd. 'Now that we know where Naveed came in, we don't need the full team on the stadium CCTV. We've got feeds from most of the council cameras around his house in Ealing. We need to start looking at who he met during the weeks running up to the attack. I don't yet know if he had a regular mosque so until we get that intel let's look at the four closest to his home. And the usual suspects for jihadist activity. Finsbury Park. Southall. Al Manaar.'

'That's a tall order,' said Hurry.

'We've no choice unfortunately,' said Shepherd. 'This guy was below the radar. No one saw him coming.'

'And what exactly are we looking for?'

'Basically anyone he meets. I need everyone to be up to date on the jihadist watch lists of MI5 and the Met, but it could well be that his contacts here are also under the radar. So let's start collating a list of everyone he is seen with. We're going to be getting feeds from Tube stations close to his house.'

The sergeant grimaced. 'North Ealing, Ealing Broadway and South Ealing. You're not asking much, Dan.'

'I know what I'm asking, believe me. But at the moment it's our only hope of running down his support network. MI5 have absolutely nothing on him and neither did SO15. But clearly a guy doesn't arrive here from Syria and put together a sophisticated terrorist operation like this without help. And if whoever planned this is still around, we could be facing more attacks.'

Hurry nodded. 'I hear you.'

Chapter 20

Ten Years Ago, New York

McNee took the gag from Rashid Makhdoom's mouth.

'I'm a British citizen, you can't do this to me,' said Makhdoom. 'You have to call the British embassy now.'

They had tied him to a chair in the middle of the warehouse, after stripping him of all his clothing. In Yokely's experience, the less clothing a person had on the more cooperative they were.

'I don't have to do a darn thing, sonny,' said Yokely. 'And so far as I know, you're a Pakistani who happens to have a British passport, so you watch your tone with me. I have some very good friends in ISI and I'm sure they would love to get their hands on you.'

The Inter-Services Intelligence was Pakistan's main intelligence agency and they were especially skilled at interrogation techniques that were banned in most civilised parts of the world. Yokely had sat in on several ISI interrogations in the wake of 9/11 and even he had been shocked by what he had seen.

'I'm fucking British.'

'You were born in Pakistan.'

'My parents left when I was two.'

'You've no idea how little that means to me right now,' said Yokely.

'I demand to speak to my embassy!' the man shouted.

Yokely smiled. 'What you're going to do is to shut the fuck up or I'll get my associate there to do it for you.'

'You can't treat us like this!' the man shouted.

Yokely nodded at McNee. McNee walked over to Makhdoom

and backhanded him so hard that blood spurted from his nose. The man screamed in pain but then clamped his lips together and stared sullenly at Yokely.

Yokely went back to his briefcase and took out a portable biometric scanner that he connected to his iPhone. He took it over to the bound man and waited while McNee untied his right hand. He grabbed the man's index finger and pressed it against the reader, then tied the right hand and repeated the process with the left. Yokely then used the camera to snap a photo of the man's irises, left and right.

The app on the iPhone used the Mobile Offender Recognition and Information System, which was mainly data on American citizens, but non-citizens who had committed offences were also put into the system. Yokely waited for the results to come through as McNee went over to Ibrahimi and began stripping off his clothes. He used plastic ties to bind the man's wrists behind his back, gagged him, then placed him on a chair facing Makhdoom. The two men looked at each other fearfully.

'Do not be afraid, brother,' said Makhdoom. 'Allah will protect us.'

'We'll see about that,' said McNee.

Yokely's phone buzzed. There was no record of Rashid Makhdoom on MORIS.

Yokely went back to the briefcase, put the phone away and took out a Glock semi-automatic, and walked over to stand in front of Makhdoom.

'Who gave you the Stinger?' he asked.

'You can't shoot me, this is America, you—'

Yokely shot Makhdoom in the heart. One shot. One loud bang. Blood blossomed on his shirt and his eyes widened, as much from surprise as pain. His mouth worked soundlessly but Yokely was already walking back to the briefcase. He put the gun back in the case, then walked over to stand in front of Omar Ibrahimi. He took the gag from Ibrahimi's mouth.

'You killed him!' gasped Ibrahimi, staring at the body across from him. Makhdoom had slumped in his chair. His chest had stopped moving but the red stain was still spreading across his shirt.

'Yes, I did, didn't I?' said Yokely. 'I guess his British passport didn't offer as much protection as he thought it would.' He pulled Ibrahimi's passport from his pocket. 'I wonder how being French will help you? *Qui vous a aidé à abattre l'avion?*' Yokely looked over at McNee. 'See that, Gerry? Did you know I spoke French?'

'Very impressive,' said McNee.

Yokely grinned at Ibrahimi. 'So, I'll ask you the same question that I asked your friend there. Who gave you the Stinger missile?'

'I don't know,' said Ibrahimi, his voice shaking.

'I don't believe you,' said Yokely.

'Hamid told us what to do,' said Ibrahimi. His face was bathed in sweat and he kept looking over at the body in the chair.

'Hamid bin Faisal?' He gestured over at the body on the floor. 'The dead guy? That's convenient.'

'He told us what to do.'

'And how did you meet Hamid?'

Ibrahimi frowned as if he didn't understand the question.

'Craigslist? Jihadists-R-Us? How did you meet him? You flew in separately. Did you meet him outside the United States?'

Ibrahimi shook his head. 'No. I met him here.'

'So you just flew into the US of A on the off chance you'd be able to commit a terrorist atrocity?' Yokely shook his head. 'You flew in to shoot down that plane, Omar. That's a fact. So someone must have trained you. Told you what to do. Where to go.'

Ibrahimi nodded quickly. 'Yes. Yes. That was Hamid.'

'So you knew Hamid outside of the United States?'

'No.'

Yokely sighed in exasperation. 'Then someone else must have briefed you before you came. Who was that, Omar? Who wound you up and set you off?'

Ibrahimi looked down at the floor. Yokely looked over at McNee. 'What do you think, Gerry? Is he deliberately being evasive or is he just stupid?'

'A bit of both, probably,' said McNee.

'Does Omar look Algerian to you?' Yokely asked him.

'I'm French,' said Ibrahimi.

'You have a French passport, that's true. But the passport says you were born in Algeria. And to be honest, Omar, I don't think that you were. You look like an Iraqi to me.'

'That's what I'd have said,' said McNee. 'Iraqi.'

'I am French!'

'You're not going to tell me I have to phone the French embassy are you?' said Yokely.

'Where are the police?' asked Ibrahimi. 'Who are you?'

'Well, the answer to the first question is that they are probably in a donut shop somewhere stocking up. As far as the second question goes, well, I'm the man with a gun who is asking you questions and really that's all you need to know.' He held his hands open and looked down at them. 'Ah yes, the gun.' He walked slowly over to the briefcase, his tasselled loafers crunching softly on the concrete floor. He picked up the silenced Glock and pointed it lazily at Ibrahimi's chest.

'Don't, please . . .' begged the man.

Yokely nodded at McNee. 'Run his prints through MORIS, will you?'

'Sure,' said McNee. He used the phone and reader to scan the index fingers of the man and then let the app do the work.

'So, Omar, assuming that is your real name, who taught you to fire the Stinger?'

The man frowned, feigning ignorance, but his duplicity was transparent. 'What? Me?' He shook his head. 'No, sir, it wasn't me.'

'You fired the Stinger. You shot the plane down.'

Ibrahimi shuddered. His face was bathed in sweat. 'It was Hamid.'

'It was you.'

'No, it was Hamid. It was Hamid. I swear on the words of Mohammed and all that is holy.'

'It was you, Omar. I've seen the video. You're wearing a scarf across your face but it's you.' He smiled tightly. 'And now you lied using the prophet's name, which means no heaven and no virgins for you. You need to tell me the truth, Omar, and you need to tell me the truth now. Who trained you? Who taught you to fire the Stinger? The Stinger is a complex piece of kit; you have to know what you are doing. Who trained you?'

Ibrahimi's lower lip was trembling.

Yokely pointed his gun at the man's chest and his finger tightened on the trigger. Yokely's phone rang. He smiled and lowered the gun. 'Saved by the bell,' he said. He pulled out his phone and looked at the screen. Karl Traynor. 'Yes, Karl.'

'Lots of shorting of American aviation stocks,' said Traynor. 'It started four days ago and ended six hours before the plane went down.'

'More than normal?'

'A thousand times more than normal. And most of it seems to have gone through Dubai at some point.'

'Do you have any names?'

'Not yet,' said Traynor. 'I'm working on it but they've gone to a lot of trouble to cover their tracks. Purchases were made through dozens of companies and those companies are themselves owned by other companies, many of them sells. But I've been following the money and there are two banks in Dubai that funnelled a lot of it.'

Yokely went over to the briefcase, put down his gun and took out the three passports. He gave the names and passport details to Traynor. 'Any financial transactions involving these three, especially over the past few weeks, would be much appreciated, Karl.'

'I'm on it,' said Traynor.

The call ended and Yokely put the passports and his phone back in the briefcase. He picked up the gun and smiled over at Ibrahimi. 'Now, where were we?' he mused.

'You can't shoot me,' said Ibrahimi. He swallowed nervously. 'Just hand me over to the FBI or the police. I will plead guilty. I am not ashamed of what I did.'

Yokely frowned. 'You murdered men, women and children in one of the most inhumane ways possible,' he said. 'How can you not feel shame?'

Ibrahimi jutted his chin up. 'We are at war,' he said.

'With who?' asked Yokely. 'With businessmen, holidaymakers, children with their mothers?'

'With America!'

'Then attack America,' said Yokely. 'Put on a uniform and pick up a gun and fight the good fight. But shooting down an airliner isn't war, it's terrorism.' He stood in front of Ibrahimi. 'Is the man who planned this from Dubai? Is he there now?'

'I have never been to Dubai.'

'That's not the question I asked you.'

'I don't know anyone from Dubai.'

'That's a lie,' said Yokely. 'Hamid bin Faisal lives there. He has a Saudi passport but lives in the United Arab Emirates.'

'Okay, so I know Faisal.'

'How long have you known him for?'

'Since I came to America. I told you. Yes, okay, he is from Dubai but I have never been to Dubai.'

Yokely smiled. 'So who introduced you to him?'

Ibrahimi frowned and said nothing.

Yokely pointed the Glock at Ibrahimi's chest. 'You're not helping me, Omar, and if you're not helping me then you're wasting my time. Who was running you, Omar? Who gave you the Stinger? Who organised this?'

'I don't know!' shouted the man.

Yokely sighed, then shot Ibrahimi in the chest. Twice.

The iPhone beeped and McNee looked at the screen. 'He's not on MORIS.'

Yokely unscrewed the silencer from the barrel of the Glock. 'No, they were all trained overseas, probably separately, then brought together for this operation. I don't think they even knew each other before they came to the States. Someone put them together, someone arranged the whole thing.'

'Any thoughts?'

Yokely shrugged. 'The key is the launcher. Whoever put this cell together supplied the Stinger. If we follow the Stinger, we'll find him.'

There was a quick knock on the door and Yokely went over

and opened it. Leclerc and Martin were there, a bound and gagged Asian in between them. Yokely waved McNee over.

'Gentlemen, meet Shabir Rauf.' Leclerc held up a holdall. 'He was waiting for them at the motel. Some interesting stuff you might want to take a look at.'

Yokely took the holdall. 'Gerry, make Mr Rauf comfortable, will you?'

McNee took Rauf inside the warehouse while Yokely went outside with Leclerc and Martin. 'How did it go?' he asked.

'Smooth,' said Leclerc. 'Dean here was a great help.'

'Good to know,' said Yokely. He patted Martin on the shoulder. 'Thank you.'

'I can do more,' said Martin earnestly. 'I was born for this.'

'I'm sure you were, but this operation is . . . Well, let's just say it's sensitive.'

'I've shown I can be trusted.'

'Yes, you have. But this isn't about trust. We're geared up for moving quickly, you're not. You've been a great help, but your work is done. For the moment anyway.'

Martin opened his mouth to argue but he could see from the look on Yokely's face that there would be no point. 'Okay,' he said.

'Peter here will drop you back at the mall. And remember—'

'It never happened?' Martin finished for him. 'Sure. I was never here. Neither were you.'

'Good man,' said Yokely, patting him on the shoulder again.

Leclerc and Martin walked over to the SUV as Yokely went back into the warehouse. McNee had stripped Rauf and tied him to a chair. They ran his fingerprints through the MORIS system, then Yokely unzipped the holdall that Leclerc had given him. There was a British passport in the name of Shabir Rauf, along with a dozen tickets flying out of Miami and Boston in the names of Rauf, Makhdoom and Ibrahimi, all on different airlines and to different cities in Europe. There were half a dozen throwaway mobile phones and two Glocks. Yokely put down the weapons and went over to Rauf. Rauf was eyeing the dead jihadists fearfully.

'They're all dead, Shabir. All three of your co-conspirators. I shot two of them; one of them was killed at the scene. So you are the last man standing.' He smiled. 'For the moment.'

Rauf started to speak but the gag muffled everything.

McNee went over and untied it.

'I was just holding the tickets, I didn't know what they were going to do, I swear,' he said.

'You swear on the words of Mohammed, the prophet?'

Rauf nodded frantically. 'Yes, I do.'

Yokely looked over at McNee and shook his head sadly. 'I can't get over the fact that they can lie so easily,' he said. 'Could you lie on the Bible?'

'Definitely not.'

'Me neither.' Yokely looked at Rauf. 'That's the difference between our religions, isn't it? When a Christian swears on the Bible, it means something. That's why we use Bibles in courts of law. But you . . .' Yokely shrugged. 'The Koran means nothing to you. You just use it for your own ends.'

'I am a good Muslim!' shouted Rauf.

'But that's not true, otherwise you wouldn't have sworn a lie on the name of the Prophet. Now who gave you the Stinger?'

'I don't know.'

'Who trained you?'

'I was in Afghanistan. Two years ago.'

'To be trained by al-Qaeda?'

Rauf nodded.

'Is that where you met Rashid and Omar?'

'No, we met for the first time in America.'

'Who put you together? Who arranged everything?'

Rauf took a deep breath. 'If I tell you, will you let me go?'

'If you don't tell me, I will kill you the way I killed your friends, that much I can tell you.'

'Who are you? FBI? CIA? Why aren't you in uniforms?'

'I'm a man with a gun who has questions that you need to answer, that's all you need to know.'

Rauf nodded at the bodies in the chairs. 'You killed them?'

'What do you think?'

Rauf nodded. 'I think you killed them.'

'Then tell me what you know. Tell me who was running you. Who was pulling your strings?'

'I need you to swear that if I tell you, you will not kill me the way you killed my friends.'

'I swear,' said Yokely.

'On the Bible,' said Rauf. 'I want you to swear on the Bible that you will not kill me.'

Yokely took a deep breath. 'Fine,' he said eventually. 'I swear, on the Bible, that I will not kill you if you give me the information I want. Now, who told you what to do? Who organised this?'

Rauf swallowed nervously, then nodded. 'His name was Hakeem. We met him for the first time in the motel.'

'The Park Motel?'

Rauf nodded.

'When?'

'Two nights ago. We checked in and he came around with a truck to give us the missile.'

'What's his full name?'

'He just said Hakeem.'

'Describe him.'

'Fifty, maybe fifty-five. A bit fat. A long beard going grey.'

'What was he wearing?'

'Regular clothes. Blue jeans. Trainers. A long grey coat. He was always playing with prayer beads.'

'Nationality?'

'I don't know. He wasn't the chatty type.'

'And this was the first time you met him?'

Rauf nodded. 'We were told to go to the motel and wait and that we would receive the missile and our instructions.'

'This Hakeem, did he know any of you? Had he met any of you before?'

'No.'

'Not Ibrahimi?'

'I don't think so.'

'You don't think so?'

'When Hakeem arrived he knew who we were but I don't think anyone knew him.'

'And was Hakeem alone?'

'There was someone with him. Driving the truck.'

'What did he look like?'

'I don't know. He stayed in the truck.'

Yokely held up the man's passport. 'You are from Leeds?'

'Born and bred.'

'How does a young guy from Leeds end up blowing a jet out of the sky over New York?'

'I didn't. I was in the motel.'

'But you knew what you were doing. You must have done when you saw the Stinger.'

Rauf stared at Yokely, his eyes burning with hatred. 'You're not a Muslim; you wouldn't understand.'

'Try me.'

'You're killing Muslims all over the world, mate. In Iraq, in Afghanistan, in Somalia. It's a Crusade. How could we not fight back?'

'Killing civilians is fighting back? Killing women and children?'

'Muslim women and children are killed every day. The Jews murder women and children in Palestine and you Americans encourage them.'

Yokely held up his hand. 'Okay, enough,' he said. 'I'm sorry I asked.'

'Look, I've told you everything you wanted to know. We're done here, right?'

Yokely picked up the Glock and screwed the silencer into the barrel.

'You swore on the Bible that you would not kill me!' Rauf protested, his voice trembling.

'Yes, I did,' said Yokely. Yokely handed the gun to McNee, who walked up to Rauf and shot him in the heart, point blank. Rauf stared at McNee with hate-filled eyes as he died. McNee stared back, a slight smile on his face, until Rauf's head slumped on to his chest.

McNee handed the gun back to Yokely, who put it back in his briefcase. He picked up his phone and called Sam Hepburn at the NSA. 'I've a name and some phones for you to check, Sam.'

'You've been a busy boy. As have I.'

'You've got something for me?'

'Damn right, I do. That Stinger was one of a dozen that went through an arms dealer in Sarajevo. The paperwork is all legit, nothing underhand that I can see. The dealer's name is Alex Kleintank and he's been in the business for more than a decade. He was one of the first into Afghanistan supplying the contractors out there. He's been busy in Iraq recently.'

'Do you have an address, picture, anything?'

'All of the above,' said Hepburn. 'He had to register with the government before he could be awarded any contracts and he did. He has all the necessary accreditations so we have all his details. I'll send you an email.'

'Do we have any idea how it got from Sarajevo into the States?'

'No way of telling but it wouldn't be difficult.'

Yokely gave Hepburn the numbers of the phones they had found in the motel, and ended the call. He took McNee outside and they opened the back door of the van. Inside were half a dozen large plastic barrels and a pallet of orange bottles of drain cleaner. Drain cleaner was primarily sulphuric acid, which would make short work of a body. After just a day or two submerged in the chemical, identification would be next to impossible, and after a week there would be almost nothing left.

'I'll get the delivery door open and you can drive in,' said Yokely. He went back into the warehouse as McNee climbed into the cab.

Once Yokely had opened the load bay door, McNee drove the van inside and switched off the engine.

Yokely went over to the Stinger launcher. McNee joined him. 'A Stinger FIM-92? Nice bit of kit,' said McNee

'Can you store this some place safe?' asked Yokely. 'There's a camcorder, too. Somewhere they'll be safe but I can dig them out if needs be.'

'I've got a place.'

Yokely nodded. 'Okay, let's get started.'

McNee climbed into the back of the van and handed out blue plastic suits, black gloves and overshoes, facemasks and goggles. The drain-cleaning fluid was very caustic and the fumes were dangerous.

They put on the gear and McNee lowered down four barrels, one at a time.

They heaved the four dead jihadists into the barrels. All of the men were fairly short and lean so there was no problem fitting them in. Then they unscrewed the caps off bottles of drain-cleaner and poured them in. There was no fizzing or spluttering but the sulphuric acid fumes built up fairly quickly, so they moved away for a few minutes to let the fumes disperse before going back and adding more. Taking it in short bursts meant that it took the best part of half an hour to fill the barrels. McNee fitted plastic lids and used metal straps to lock them shut. As he was sealing the last barrel, Leclerc returned.

Yokely stripped off his protective gear and dropped it into a garbage bag. 'How's our boy?' he asked Leclerc.

'He's not happy about being sent on his way. But he's a team player.'

'He's a former SEAL, that's a pre-requisite. How did he perform?'

'Like a pro. I'd work with him again, no problem.'

'Okay, that might happen. Once this job is over.' He nodded at the barrels. 'So, this gets rid of the four jihadists. I need you in Sarajevo right away. The Stinger was supplied by a Dutch arms dealer who's based out there. Alex Kleintank. He had a dozen and one of them was used to shoot down the plane at JFK. Find out where he is, who he's meeting, his personal situation, but keep your distance.'

'I'm on it,' said Leclerc. He went outside and less than a minute later Yokely heard the car start and drive off.

'Sarajevo?' said McNee, frowning. 'Strange place to be based, no?'

'Arms is a multi-national business; he's probably just a middleman,' said Yokely. He nodded at the launcher. 'But that went through his inventory, which means he's partly responsible for what happened.'

'So, we head out there?'

'And Dubai. And the UK. Rashid Makhdoom lived in London. The French connection I'm not sure about. Omar looked more Iraqi than Algerian. Let's see what the databases turn up.'

'Either way we've a lot of flying to do.'

Yokely nodded. 'And we'll have to use scheduled flights and false names,' he said. 'We can't be leaving any trails on this. How are you fixed for passports?'

'I'm good,' said McNee. 'I've a couple of genuine Canadian passports left over from my last operation.'

'Everyone loves the Canadians,' said Yokely. 'Canadian and Irish passports will get you in everywhere, just about.' He picked up his phone and called David Dalton. Dalton answered almost immediately. 'Where are you, David?' asked Yokely.

'On the way to the airport,' said Dalton. 'All revved up and raring to go.'

'Slight change of plan,' said Yokely. 'I need you in the UK, ASAP. How good are your anti-terrorism sources there?'

'I've a good contact in Europol, Italian but he lives in London. And there's a guy in MI5 who owes me a few favours.'

'I'd avoid Europol if possible,' said Yokely. 'In my experience they leak like a sieve. I need you to check out two jihadists, now deceased. Rashid Makhdoom from London and Shabir Rauf, from Leeds.' Yokely spelled out their names, then gave Dalton their dates of birth and passport numbers. 'I need to know what they have in the way of relatives, especially those on any watch lists. I need to know where they were radicalised and who by.'

'I'm on it,' said Dalton.

'We'll be with you in a few days. Set us up a safe house in London, and we'll need equipment.'

'You'll need me to handle disposal?'

'Definitely,' said Yokely.

Chapter 21

The sky was darkening when Harper pulled into the service station to the west of Manchester. Jony Hasan's silver BMW was already parked and Harper pulled up next to him. Hasan wound down his window and grinned at the Toyota. 'What the fuck is that?' he asked. He was in his early thirties, a dark-skinned Asian wearing an Armani leather bomber jacket, with a thick gold chain around his neck.

'It's called low-key,' said Harper.

'It's called a piece of shit, that's what it's called,' laughed Hasan. 'You wouldn't catch me dead in one of those.'

'It's reliable with good mileage,' said Harper. 'So fuck the fuck off.'

Hasan chuckled. 'Come into my office and we'll talk,' he said.

Harper got out of his car and climbed into Hasan's BMW. The men bumped fists. 'Thanks for the short notice,' said Harper.

'Nothing's too much trouble for my best customers,' said Hasan. 'What do you need?'

'Something small that packs a punch. And totally non-traceable.'

'What did you buy last time? It was a Smith & Wesson SD9 VE, wasn't it?'

Harper nodded. 'Yeah. Sixteen rounds in the clip. Maybe something a bit smaller?'

'Revolver or automatic?'

'I'm going to need a silencer, so automatic.'

Hasan wrinkled his nose. 'How do you feel about six in the clip?'

'Six is fine. I'm not planning on any spray and pray.'

'I've got a brand new Beretta Pico. Just over five inches long, .380ACP, weighs under twelve ounces.'

'Sounds perfect.'

'Yeah, but the one downside is that I don't have a silencer for it. A silencer will triple the length, which sort of spoils the fact that it was designed as a pocket pistol.'

Harper wrinkled his nose. 'Noise might be a factor.'

'I could probably get you one within forty-eight hours. Worst possible scenario I can get one made for you.'

Harper shook his head. 'I need it tonight.'

'Then no can do,' said Hasan. 'But you could fix yourself up something, right? Cobble something together.'

'I suppose so.'

'Worst possible scenario, shoot through a pillow or wrap a blanket around your hand. That calibre will shoot through no problem.'

Harper nodded thoughtfully. 'How much?'

'They're hard to get,' said Hasan.

'For fuck's sake, Jony, cut the sales pitch. Just give me the number.'

'Eight hundred quid, ammo included,' said Hasan. 'If you return it unfired I'll give you four hundred for it.'

Harper took out his cigarettes. 'Nah, I'll be firing it, no question.'

He pulled out his cigarette lighter but Hasan waved a warning finger at him. 'This motor is new – don't you go stinking it up.'

'Sorry, mate,' said Harper, putting the cigarettes and lighter away. 'How about we say six hundred for cash?'

'It's always cash, Lex. This is a fucking cash business. But if it'll speed things up, seven hundred. And I'll throw in a couple of extra clips.'

'With ammo?'

'Of course. An empty clip's no use to anyone, is it?'

'Deal,' said Harper.

Hasan held out his hand. Harper fished out a wad of notes

and peeled off seven hundred pounds. He handed it to Hasan, who put it in his pocket before climbing out of the car. He went around to the boot, opened it and rummaged around for a few minutes before returning to the driver's seat with a large Tupperware container. He handed the container to Harper and closed the door.

Harper ripped the top off the container and took out the gun, which had been wrapped in an oily cloth. It did appear to be brand new. Harper sniffed it, then checked the mechanism. He nodded. 'Nice,' he said.

'You sound surprised,' said Hasan. 'Have I ever let you down?'

Harper slipped the gun into his jacket pocket and gave the cloth and container back to Hasan. 'You know what would happen if you did, mate,' said Harper. He grinned, but he was only half joking. 'There's a couple of other things I need,' he said.

'I've got a boot full of kit,' said Hasan, reaching for the door handle. 'Let me show you my wares.'

Harper shook his head. 'I need a lock-up in Birmingham. Somewhere quiet. Size isn't too important. But I'll be up to mischief there so it mustn't be traceable.'

'What sort of mischief, Lex?'

Harper grinned. 'Do you really want to know? Let's just say that you probably won't be able to use it again and you wouldn't want it traced back to you.'

Hasan nodded thoughtfully. 'Yeah, I've got a place. I haven't used it for a while and I was planning on getting rid.'

'Where is it?'

'South of the city. Quiet area, no one will disturb you. It used to be a chop shop but the guy who ran it was sent down on drugs charges and won't be out for three or four years. Place is pretty much abandoned.'

'Pretty much?'

'I used to use it to store vehicles but I'm not doing much in Birmingham these days.'

'Sounds perfect. How much?'

Hasan wrinkled his nose. 'Ten grand.'

Harper could hear the uncertainty in the man's voice and he resisted the urge to smile. 'Let's say five.'

'Split the difference.'

Harper nodded. 'Seven five it is.' He nodded at his car. 'Let me get the cash.' He got out and went over to the Toyota. The envelope that Button had given him was in the glove compartment. He counted out seven thousand five hundred pounds in fifty-pound notes, then went back to give them to Hasan.

Hasan grinned and pocketed the cash. 'Always a pleasure doing business with you, Lex. I'll text you the details.'

'The key?'

'There's one close by. There's a drainpipe spout to the left of the door. The key's in there.'

'There better had be, mate.'

'Cross my heart,' said Hasan.

'I trust you,' said Harper. 'One last thing. I need personnel. Someone reliable, someone who can do what needs to be done without fucking it up, and someone who knows me or my reputation and what will happen if they let me down.'

'I thought you had your own team?'

'I need someone at a distance for this,' said Harper.

'Belfast Mick is around.'

'Really? What's he up to?' Mick O'Hara was a former IRA hard man who had left political violence behind him once the Good Friday Agreement had wiped away the eighteen murders he had committed in Northern Ireland, but had transferred his skills to the private sector with considerable success. The bulk of his work involved chasing up debts but he was able to offer permanent solutions to problems, provided the price was right.

Hasan held up his hand. 'Client confidentiality, Lex,' he said. 'But I can tell you that a job he was expecting to do fell through last night so he's at a bit of a loose end.'

'Have you got a number for him?' Hasan looked uncomfortable and Harper waved his hand dismissively. 'I know, I know, client confidentiality. Look, I'll give you my number and you get him to call me, okay?'

'Sounds like a plan,' said Hasan.

Harper gave him the number of one of his throwaway mobiles, fist-bumped him, then climbed out and got back into his Toyota. He filled the tank with petrol and headed south. He was ten minutes outside Birmingham when O'Hara called him. Harper took the call on hands-free. 'Mick, you Irish bastard, how the hell are you?'

'Mad as fucking hell,' growled the Irishman. 'But what can you do?'

'Where are you?'

'Manchester.'

'Can you get to Birmingham tonight? I'll make it worth your while.'

'You got a job for me, Lex?'

'If you're interested.'

'Fuck, yeah.'

'I'm checked into the Ibis at Birmingham Airport. Call when you get there.'

Harper ended the call. O'Hara was a good operator and would come in handy for what he needed to do next. Five minutes later his phone beeped. It was a text from Hasan with details of the Birmingham lock-up.

Chapter 22

It was just after midnight when one of the Super-Recognisers spotted Ali Naveed arriving at the stadium. He had climbed out of a van about a quarter of a mile away. A council CCTV camera set up to monitor traffic had caught the van turning off the main road and stopping. Naveed climbed out of the front passenger seat, waved at the driver and walked off. The puffa coat and the distinctive Nikes made him easy to follow as he joined the crowds streaming towards the stadium.

The CCTV picture was clear enough for them to read the registration number and to see the sign on the side. The van belonged to a Lebanese restaurant in Edgware Road. They couldn't see the driver but two cameras further down the road had a better view through the windscreen and they could clearly see a young Asian man with a neatly trimmed beard behind the wheel.

'Well done,' Shepherd said to the PC who had spotted Naveed getting out of the van. 'Follow the van back, see if we can find out when Naveed was picked up. And let's see where the van started from.'

The PC grinned. 'The name on the side is probably a clue,' he said.

'Sure, but we don't take anything for granted,' said Shepherd. He went over to Hurry, who was munching on a slice of pizza. 'Do you mind?' asked Shepherd, pointing at the pizza.

'Help yourself,' said Hurry. 'You paid for it.'

Shepherd took a slice and sat down next to the sergeant. 'How are we getting on inside the stadium?'

'Slowly but surely,' said Hurry. He had a diagram of the stadium on his desk and he had plotted the jihadist's progress using small red crosses. Numbers by the crosses referenced the CCTV camera that had picked up the image. 'He turned left, and walked around for a bit, to-ing and fro-ing. He kept checking his watch as if he was waiting for something. Or someone.'

'Did he talk to anybody?'

Hurry shook his head. 'No. But ten minutes after entering the stadium he went to the Gents.'

'Could he have picked up the vest there?'

'I don't think so. He was in and out within ninety seconds. I don't think that would be enough time to get his coat off, fit a vest and put his coat back on.'

Shepherd nodded. 'Okay. Could he have met a contact in there?'

'It's possible. We're looking to see if any members of staff went in prior to Naveed.'

'What did he do after visiting the toilets?'

'He walked around. So far we haven't seen him talk to anybody. But he used his mobile twice.'

'Does it look as if he was waiting for anyone?' asked Shepherd.

'It's difficult to say,' said Hurry. 'He's was looking around and you can sense that he's nervous, but given what he intended to do, that's understandable.'

Shepherd patted him on the shoulder and walked back to his own terminal. He needed to tell Patsy Ellis about the van that Naveed had arrived in but he didn't want to do that with more than a dozen officers in earshot. He looked at his watch. It was half past twelve. Ellis had said to call her at any time so he'd put that to the test.

The canteen was open twenty-four hours a day, though at night there were only sandwiches and muffins on offer. Shepherd bought a chicken salad sandwich and a coffee and took it to a table by the windows. There were only two other officers there and they were deep in conversation on the other side of the room. He took out his phone and rang Ellis. She answered almost immediately so he figured she wasn't in bed yet, and he quickly filled her in on the details of the van that had delivered Naveed to the stadium.

'What about the vest?' she asked. 'Do we know how he got it?'

'We're working both ends as we speak,' said Shepherd. 'We see him come into the stadium and we know where he was when he detonated, so it's just a matter of time. I'd say we'll have reviewed all the relevant footage by midday.'

'Excellent, Dan, thank you. And please, keep me informed. As I said, night or day, don't worry about the hour.'

'Understood,' said Shepherd. He ended the call and went back downstairs. Hurry was sitting back in his chair, rubbing his eyes. 'You need a break,' said Shepherd. 'We all do.'

'What about you?' asked Hurry. 'You've been here longer than me.'

'I'm going to pop home to shower and change, maybe grab a nap,' said Shepherd. He knew from experience that working too long could be counterproductive when it came to facial recognition; it was easy to overlook something when the brain was tired. The unit recommended that its operators didn't stare at the screens for more than thirty minutes without a break, and ideally they should get up and walk around for at least five minutes.

'I'll probably do same in about an hour,' said Hurry. 'I've got two more operators coming in. I'll brief them and then head off. I'll have them follow the van. We have the stadium footage in hand.'

'If anyone does spot Naveed getting the vest, call me right away,' said Shepherd.

'Definitely,' said Hurry. He sipped his coffee, blinked his eyes several times and stared at his screen again. Shepherd headed for the lift.

Chapter 23

Harper showered and changed and switched on the TV to watch Sky News. The stadium death toll had now passed thirty. Five were children. He had bought a couple of sandwiches and a coffee at a service station on the drive back and he was just about to take a bite out of the second one when his mobile rang. It was O'Hara. Harper said he would meet him in the hotel bar and ten minutes later he found the Irishman on a stool nursing a pint of Guinness. O'Hara grinned when Harper walked in. He slid off his bar stool and embraced him in a crushing bear hug.

'Fuck me, you're a sight for sore eyes,' said O'Hara. 'How long's it been?'

'Three years? Berlin?'

O'Hara grinned. 'Yeah. Berlin.' He was a big man, a few inches over six feet tall and almost as wide, with a square jaw and slicked-back greying hair. He was wearing a caramel brown leather jacket that was stretched across his broad shoulders as if the seams would burst at any moment. He waved at the stool next to his and the two men sat down. Harper ordered a beer and they waited until the barman had served him before continuing their conversation.

'So Jony says you're at a loose end,' said Harper.

O'Hara's eyes narrowed. 'Yeah? What else did he say?'

Harper held up his hands. 'Mate, he's all about client confidentiality. He just said a job fell through, that's all.'

'Yeah, he's fucking right,' said the Irishman. 'Bloody nightmare. A couple of business types fell out big time and one was selling off assets on the cheap to his friends. Stripping the company. The other partner hires me to do the job, and pays a third up front. I do all the planning, get the kit, I'm all revved up and ready to go and the target keels over and dies. Heart attack. Getting out of his car and he just dies.'

'How close were you to carrying out the contract?'

'I was going to do him in the morning when he left his house. I mean, how fucking unlucky was I, huh? All my ducks in a row and the guy goes and dies of natural causes.'

'So the client wouldn't pay the balance?'

O'Hara shrugged. 'Wasn't much I could do, was there? Okay, I could have got heavy with him but then word would get around. I'd be the guy who charges for work he doesn't do, and you know as well as I do that your reputation is all you have in this business.'

'I hear you,' said Harper. 'But long story short, you're available?'

'I'm here, aren't I? What's the job?'

'Two jobs. Syrians who may or may not have been up to no good.'

O'Hara frowned. 'So it's a government job? You know I'm not sanctioned for Pool work?'

'It's complicated,' said Harper. 'But I'll pay you your normal rate and both jobs should be easy enough. Are you up for it?'

'Fuck, yeah,' said O'Hara. 'You know I'd love to be part of the Pool and have the old get-out-of-jail-free card.'

'It's not as simple as that,' said Harper. 'Anyway, the two hits are a young Syrian refugee here in Birmingham. Israr Farooqi. I have an address and the plan is to do him tonight. The other target is another Syrian, Imran Masood. He lives in Bolton. I was planning on doing him first thing in the morning.'

'Sounds like a plan,' said O'Hara.

'I'm figuring straightforward hits, but we need to do something creative, point the finger at a racist group. Maybe plant the gun down the line.'

O'Hara nodded. 'How much?'

'Five grand each. Really I just need another pair of eyes. I'm happy to pull the trigger.'

'Ten for the two works,' said O'Hara. He rubbed his hands together. 'When do you want to get started?"

Harper raised his glass. 'As soon as we're done with these.' His iPod Touch vibrated in his pocket. He took it out and looked at the screen. It was a message from Charlotte Button. A name and address. Khuram Zaghba. A house in Acton, West London. And a picture of an Asian male with a neatly trimmed beard. And a note: *Target Three. Treat as priority.*

Harper put the iPod away and picked up his glass. He raised it in salute to O'Hara. 'Looks like we're going to be busy,' he said. 'We need to get to London, pronto.'

Chapter 24

Present Day, London

Shepherd let himself into the riverside apartment that he had been renting for the past six months. 'Dan?' called Katra from the kitchen.

'No, it's a heavily armed burglar come to strip you of your valuables,' said Shepherd, taking off his coat and hanging it on the back of the door.

Katra came out of the kitchen, grinning. 'Why would you say that?' she laughed, before giving him a hug that turned quickly into a kiss.

He returned the kiss and pressed himself against her. He wasn't happy at the role he'd been given at work, but the one upside was that he was able to spend more time with Katra. She had moved down from their house in Hereford and up until the stadium bombing he had been home every evening by seven o'clock at the latest, and they'd been able to spend pretty much every weekend together. It was a much more stable lifestyle than his undercover days and Katra clearly relished the time she spent with him. While Shepherd was equally happy to have more time to spend with her, he hadn't switched from the Serious Organised Crime Agency to MI5 to spend all day sitting in front of a terminal watching CCTV footage and he wanted to get back to what he did best – undercover work.

'I thought I said you should go to bed?' said Shepherd.

'I wanted to wait for you. Are you hungry?'

'I'm tired more than hungry,' he said. 'But yes, I guess I should eat.'

'There's bograc in the oven.'

Bograc was one of Katra's Slovenian culinary specialities, a sort of beef goulash, and one of Shepherd's favourites. 'Sounds good,' he said. 'Let me shower first.'

He headed to the bathroom while Katra went back into the kitchen. It was only when he stood in the shower that he realised just how tired he was. The adrenaline had been full on while he had been working but as the hot water played over his body he felt a sudden urge to burrow beneath the covers and sleep.

He dried himself and changed into fresh clothes before going through to the kitchen, where Katra had a plate of steaming bograc in a bowl on a plate with a stick of freshly baked crusty bread. She had opened a bottle of red wine and she poured some into a glass as he sat down. 'I can't drink, baby,' he said. 'I've got to go back to the office.'

Her jaw dropped. 'It's night-time, Dan.'

'We're on a big case,' he said. He picked up a fork. 'That suicide bomber at the football stadium. We have to check all the CCTV.'

'But anyone can do that, surely.'

'Thank you very much,' he said.

'You know what I mean,' she said, sitting down opposite him. 'It's just checking cameras, isn't it?'

'There's a bit more to it than that,' he said, but actually he knew that Katra was right. When it came to the ability to recognise faces, he was no better or worse than any other member of the unit. He picked up his glass and toasted her. 'But one glass isn't going to hurt.'

She forced a smile, picked up her glass and clinked it against his. They both drank, then Shepherd tucked into his meal. He was on his third mouthful when his mobile rang. It was George Hurry. 'We've got him getting the vest,' said Hurry.

'I'm on my way,' said Shepherd. He ended the call and looked over at Katra. It was clear from her crestfallen expression that she knew what was happening. 'I'm sorry,' he said.

Katra shrugged. 'It's okay,' she said. 'It's bograc. It'll keep.' She gathered up the plates and put them in the oven. Shepherd could see that she was unhappy but right then there was nothing he could say or do that would make it better, so he just grabbed his coat and headed for the door.

Chapter 25

Ten Years Ago, Sarajevo

Richard Yokely and Gerry McNee flew into Sarajevo on the same Austrian Airlines flight, but sitting in different parts of the plane. McNee flew economy and Yokely was at the front of the plane. Yokely could have pulled rank but a team was a team so they had played rock, paper, scissors and he'd got the better seat anyway. Leclerc had sent a man to pick them up. He was in his fifties wearing a scuffed leather jacket and a flat cap and holding a piece of cardboard with the words MR WOLF on it. Leclerc's attempt at humour. Yokely nodded at the man. 'I'm Mr Wolf,' he said. McNee suppressed a smile and shook his head.

The man took a mobile phone from his pocket and gave it to Yokely, then headed out of the terminal. Yokely checked the phone as they walked over to a battered Mercedes. There was a single number in the contacts book and he called it as the man took their bags and put them in the trunk.

'Welcome to Sarajevo,' said Leclerc. 'The driver is Zoran. He looks shabby but I've used him before and he's a hundred per cent reliable. I've got Kleintank under surveillance as we speak so best you meet me here. Zoran knows where to drop you. Call me again when you're on the street.'

Yokely and McNee climbed into the Mercedes – Yokely in the front and McNee behind the driver – and they headed west away from the terminal. Yokely had been to Sarajevo several times over the years, and it wasn't one of his favourite cities, even before the conflict had ripped the former Yugoslavia apart. The conflict had officially ended in 1999 but much of the bullet and shell damage had yet to be repaired. Sarajevo had been under siege by the Bosnian Serb Army from April 1992 until the end of February 1996, during which time almost fourteen thousand men, women and children were killed. Now the city was bustling with shoppers and students and new tower blocks were appearing everywhere.

They drove through the city centre, some of the roads still pockmarked with damage from mortars, then down a narrow road lined with apartments before Zoran pulled up. 'Here,' he said gruffly. 'I drop you here.'

The two men climbed out and retrieved their bags from the trunk. As Zoran drove away, Yokely took out the throwaway phone and called Leclerc.

'I see you,' he said as soon as he answered. 'About a hundred feet ahead of you, on the left. Blue Toyota.'

Yokely and McNee carried their bags to the Toyota. McNee popped the trunk and tossed the bags in as Yokely got into the front passenger seat. Leclerc had swapped his safari outfit for a heavy jacket, coarse trousers and work boots. He handed Yokely a photograph of a man in his mid-thirties getting out of a Mercedes.

'As the name suggests, he's Dutch. Used to be in the French Foreign Legion and they are tough motherfuckers so don't be misled by the thousand-dollar suit and handmade shoes.'

He pointed at a metal-sided warehouse in the distance. 'He's in there with six men. Three are his bodyguards, all big and all armed. Three other guys went in about fifteen minutes ago. They didn't seem to be carrying so I'm guessing customers.'

'How are we fixed for kit?'

McNee got into the back seat. 'In that bag next to Gerry,' said Leclerc.

McNee unzipped the nylon holdall on the seat next to him. Inside were two Glocks, two silencers, a dozen clips of ammunition and a large black stun gun. He handed one of the Glocks and silencers to Yokely.

'There are a couple of holsters in there,' said Leclerc. He lifted his own jacket so that Yokely could see the butt of the Glock he was carrying.

The two men took off their jackets and adjusted the holsters.

'You guys hungry?' asked Leclerc.

'You brought food?' asked McNee.

'No, but there's a café down the road that does sandwiches,' said Leclerc.

'When did Kleintank go in?' asked Yokely.

Leclerc looked at his watch. 'About three hours ago. Then, like I said, his visitors arrived fifteen minutes ago.' The door in the side of the warehouse opened and three men stepped out. 'That's them,' said Leclerc.

The three men walked down the road as a big man in a leather jacket pulled the door shut behind them. The man on the left was in his late thirties, with receding hair and a broad chest. The man on the right looked like his younger brother. They were laughing at something the man in the middle had said. Yokely's eyes narrowed as he recognised the man in the middle. He was dark-haired, of average build and height, but Yokely knew that there was nothing average about Dan 'Spider' Shepherd. Shepherd had served in the SAS, probably the world's best special-forces unit, and had switched to working as an undercover cop. These days he worked for the Serious Organised Crimes Agency, Britain's equivalent of the FBI. Yokely had met the man in London two years earlier and had been impressed with his professionalism. But what the hell was he doing with an arms dealer in Sarajevo?

The three men climbed into a car and drove off.

'What do you think?' asked Leclerc.

'I think we need to strike while the iron's hot,' said Yokely. 'We don't know when we'll get another chance. So Kleintank has just got the three heavies?'

Leclerc nodded. 'I followed them here and they unlocked the door to get in so I'm assuming the place was empty then. There's no CCTV and no alarm that I can see.'

'There's as good odds as we'll get,' said Yokely. 'Are we all good to go?'

McNee and Leclerc nodded.

They climbed out of the SUV, keeping their weapons hidden as they jogged over to the main entrance. Yokely tried the door. It was locked or bolted, which was hardly surprising.

McNee and Leclerc moved to opposite sides of the door. Yokely held his Glock down by his side and knocked on the door, three sharp, confident knocks. He took a deep breath and let it out slowly. They didn't hear any footsteps but the door opened a fraction. There was a figure there, but whoever it was they didn't speak.

'Room service,' said Yokely.

A man said something in a language Yokely didn't recognise.

'Room service,' repeated Yokely. He flashed a beaming smile. 'I'm here to turn down your room.'

The door opened another couple of inches. The man was big, a good three inches taller than Yokely, and broad. But that wasn't a problem as Yokely wasn't planning on getting into a fist fight with him. He brought up the Glock and fired twice in quick succession, once to the top of the chest, just below the throat, and a couple of inches to the right and lower where he hoped the man's heart would be. As soon as he had put the two shots in the man he forced the door open. The man was staggering back, two red roses blossoming on his shirt.

There were three other men in the warehouse. Kleintank was on his feet, the other two were sitting at a table. Kleintank was about five feet eight inches tall, wearing a black cashmere overcoat and gleaming patent leather shoes. His mouth was open in surprise.

The man Yokely had shot fell to the ground, his breath rasping in his throat as he died. Yokely walked towards Kleintank, his gun pointing at his chest.

Yokely heard Leclerc and McNee enter the building behind him and the door shut. Without looking he knew that Leclerc would move left and McNee would head right.

The two men at the table pushed away their chairs and stood up. The chairs hit the ground as they pulled out automatic weapons but Leclerc and McNee were too quick for them. Half a dozen shots rang out in less than a second and both men slumped to the ground. The Dutchman slowly raised his hands above his head. 'I'm not armed!' he shouted.

Yokely smiled. 'You can see the irony in that,' he said. 'You being an arms dealer and all.'

'There's no money here but you can take anything you want,' said Kleintank.

'We're not here to rob you,' said Yokely.

Kleintank frowned. 'So what do you want?'

'Information. Specifically about a dozen Stinger missiles that passed through your hands recently.'

Kleintank shook his head. 'I don't have any Stingers.'

'Maybe not now. But you had a dozen. Consecutive serial numbers.'

Kleintank shrugged. 'I handle a lot of inventory.'

Yokely nodded at Leclerc and Leclerc punched Kleintank in the face. Kleintank staggered back, blood streaming from his nose.

'Don't fuck me around, Kleintank,' said Yokely. 'You had twelve. Who did you sell them to? And if I even think I'm going to hear the words "client confidentiality" I will put a bullet in your ball sack.'

'Iraq,' said Kleintank. He pulled a handkerchief from his pocket and dabbed at his nose. 'They went to Iraq.'

'You were selling to al-Qaeda?'

'I sold to a couple of guys with beards. They were in town buying from me and a couple of other dealers. They were buying anything they could get their hands on and paying in cash. They didn't tell me who they were or where the weapons were going but the shipper they used is an old friend. They were going to Iraq. I don't know who was using them in Iraq, and I didn't care. Cash is fucking cash, right?'

'You were selling ground-to-air missiles to terrorists and you don't care what they do with them, right?'

Kleintank sneered at Yokely. 'And who do you think makes them? You're American, right? It's your fucking country that manufactures them. Do your arms companies give a fuck who the end user is? Of course they don't. Don't pass judgement on me. I'm just a middleman. It's your country that starts these fucking wars and then sells the weapons to fight them. You need to—'

Leclerc punched Kleintank in the face again, this time so hard that the Dutchman went down like a sack of potatoes.

Yokely shook his head and sighed. 'Peter, the man is entitled to his opinion.'

'Couldn't think of any other way to shut him up,' said Leclerc. 'You think the Stinger used to shoot down the plane came from Iraq?'

'No, I don't. Strip off his clothes – being naked usually focuses the mind.'

Leclerc bent down and began pulling off the Dutchman's expensive shoes.

Yokely heard footsteps off to his left and he pulled out his gun. He frowned when he recognised the man. It was Dan Shepherd. Why the hell had he come back to the warehouse?

Yokely looked over at Leclerc and McNee. 'It's okay, I know him,' he said. The two men relaxed and went back to stripping the clothing off Kleintank.

Yokely walked towards Shepherd, an amused smile on his face. 'You do turn up at the most inconvenient times, don't you?' he asked.

'What the hell are you doing here, Richard?'

'Tidying up some loose ends. How did you get in?'

'Side door,' said Shepherd. 'I have unfinished business with Mr Kleintank. I'm a bit surprised to see you, but you do have a habit of turning up when I least expect it.'

'I'm going to have to ask you to go now, Spider.'

'I can't do that,' said Shepherd.

'Yes you can. You turn around and you walk away and you don't look back.'

'Is he dead?' asked Shepherd, gesturing at Kleintank.

'Not yet,' said Yokely.

'You're going to kill him, right?

'Not your business, old friend.'

'We're not friends, Richard. We're just guys whose paths cross from time to time.'

'You owe me.' Yokely's finger was still on the trigger of his Glock but the barrel was now pointing at the floor.

'I owe you a favour,' said Shepherd. 'I don't owe you a man's life.'

'Not just any man,' said Yokely. 'But that's not the point. You owe me. You owe me big time. So turn around and walk away. You're right, we don't have to be friends but I'm going to do what I have to do no matter what.'

'You did a big favour for me, I'm not denying that. But there's a hell of a gap between a debt of honour and being an accomplice to a cold-blooded murder.'

'I don't need your complicity,' said Yokely. 'I just need you to go.'

'Why?'

'Because I don't want you here.'

'I mean why do you want to kill him. What's he done?'

The gun moved. Now it was pointing at Shepherd's knee but Yokely didn't for one moment think of pulling the trigger. Spider Shepherd was an ally in a world full of enemies. 'You're making this very difficult for me, Spider.'

'You think murder is easy?'

Yokely snorted. 'If it was anyone else but you—'

'What, Richard? What would you do? Would you shoot me, is that what you're saying?'

The gun didn't move but the finger tightened on the trigger. Yokely shook his head slowly. 'I've got a job to do. And you're in my way.'

'This is Sarajevo, this is way out of your jurisdiction.'

Yokely grinned. 'I represent the United States of America, which means the whole God-damned world is my jurisdiction. And it's like George W said, you're either with us or you're against us.' He gestured at Kleintank with the gun. 'Him, he's against us. What about you, Spider? Which side are you on?'

'There's no sides in this,' said Shepherd. 'There's just you and me and the guy you're threatening to kill.'

Yokely took a deep breath and then exhaled slowly. He stared at Shepherd, his lips a tight line. The barrel of the gun moved slowly until it was aimed at Shepherd's stomach. 'You heard about the plane that crashed leaving JFK?'

Shepherd nodded. 'Engine failure, they're saying. It crashed into the sea.'

'Yeah, well they're saying what they've been told to say,' said Yokely. 'The real situation is being kept under wraps. Islamic fundamentalists shot it out of the sky. And they shot it out of the sky with a missile supplied by that piece of shit. So he made his choice and now it's time for him to pay the piper.'

Yokely had no idea what Shepherd was doing in Sarajevo, but from the flurry of questions that followed it was clear he was also investigating Kleintank's missile sales.

'Can we go somewhere and talk?' said Shepherd eventually. 'I'm getting nervous hanging around here.'

Yokely looked over at Leclerc, who was pulling off Kleintank's underwear. 'Keep him on ice,' said Yokely.

Leclerc nodded. 'Like he was in a freezer,' he said.

Yokely flashed Shepherd an apologetic smile. 'He watches a lot of Tarantino movies,' he said.

'Don't we all,' said Shepherd.

Chapter 26

A waiter with a well-tended goatee placed cups of coffee on the table in front of Shepherd and Yokely, smiled and left. Yokely stirred in two spoonfuls of brown sugar but Shepherd left his untouched. They chatted a while before Shepherd got to the point. 'I've infiltrated a group of armed robbers who need a missile for the robbery they've got planned,' he said. 'The guy who put the job together gave us Kleintank's name for the ordnance.'

'And the plan is to point a missile at the tellers and demand they hand over their takings? Sounds a bit like overkill.'

'There's a wall involved,' said Shepherd. 'We were in the market for a few RPGs but all Kleintank had was a training Grail. I told Kleintank that we weren't interested so we're going to have a rethink about where we're going to get the RPGs from. But while I was chatting with Kleintank he let slip about the Brits who bought a Grail and who wanted a Stinger and I came back for a chat.'

'A chat?' said Yokely. He grinned malevolently. 'We're not too different, you and I, are we?'

'Chalk and cheese,' said Shepherd. 'I was just going to talk to him.'

'About what?'

'About the Brits he sold the Grail to. They've now got a Grail and a Stinger and that can only mean one thing.'

'You think they're home-grown fundamentalists who want to bring down a plane? Nasty.'

'I was going to pass any info on to our anti-terrorism people,' said Shepherd. 'But that's a non-starter after what you've done to Kleintank.'

'Don't expect me to apologise for doing my job,' said Yokely. 'First I knew you were involved was when you came barging in with a bad attitude.' He sipped his coffee and then told Shepherd that he would interrogate Kleintank and share any intel with him. He figured he owed the man that much.

'You could blow my case, Richard. If Kleintank talks to my guys, alarm bells could start ringing.'

'Give me some credit, Spider. We'll keep him on ice, as my Tarantino-loving colleague said. We'll take him well away from here.'

'Rendition?'

Yokely grinned. 'Haven't you heard, we don't do that any more. We'll find a place here, somewhere secluded. You let me know when you're in the clear. Deal?' He smiled. He was lying, of course. There was going to be no rendition for Kleintank, just a bullet or two in the chest.

They finished their coffees soon after and Shepherd left. Yokely went back to the warehouse. He knocked twice on the door and Leclerc let him in.

Kleintank was hanging upside down, naked, from a metal beam in the ceiling. Blood had trickled from between his lips on to the floor. His eyes were closed but his chest was heaving. His wrists had been tied behind his back. Yokely walked over to the holdall and took out the stun gun. It was over a foot long, black and baton-shaped with two steel prongs at one end and a button for a trigger. He pressed the button and sparks arced across the gap.

'Give him some water,' said Yokely.

Leclerc picked up a plastic bottle of water and McNee helped lift the Dutchman so that Leclerc could put the bottle to his mouth. Kleintank coughed and spluttered but managed to swallow some of the water.

He blinked up at Yokely. 'Who are you?' he asked. What do you want?'

'We need to talk, Alex,' said Yokely, brandishing the stun gun.

'About what?'

'Your customers.'

Kleintank coughed. 'What do you want to know?'

Blue sparks crackled across the top of the stun gun. 'Everything.'

'You don't have to do this,' said Kleintank. 'I'll talk.'

'Then talk. Did all the Stingers go to Iraq? And don't lie to me.'

'No,' said Kleintank. 'Not all.'

'The rest. Who did you sell them to?'

'A dealer in Dubai.'

'His name?'

'Jamahl Benikhlef.'

'Spell it.'

Kleintank slowly spelled out the name. 'I think along the line it was Bin Khalif but Benikhlef is on his passport.'

'Where in Dubai do I find him?'

'I don't know. We don't socialise. But he mentioned the marina, the new one. Said I should buy there. Maybe he lives there.'

'What did this Benikhlef want with Stingers?'

'He didn't say. I didn't ask. We're middlemen, we buy and sell.' He coughed and spluttered, then spat to clear his mouth. 'You don't have to do this to me, I'll tell you everything you need to know.'

'I prefer it this way,' said Yokely. 'Did he buy anything else from you?'

'He only wanted Stingers. He wanted more but the ten were already on their way to Iraq. Look, let me down, I can't think, all the blood is going to my head.'

'You're doing just fine, Alex,' said Yokely. He tossed the stun gun back in the holdall. 'The three men who were here before. What are they buying?

'They want RPGs. I don't have any. I offered them a training Grail but they didn't want it.'

'And you sold another Grail recently?'

Kleintank nodded. 'Two Brits bought it.'

'Names?'

'I only got the name of the white guy. Paul Bradshaw. Former soldier. He fought in Iraq. Knew his stuff.'

'And he was with an Asian?'

'A Pakistani Brit. I didn't get his name. Then another Asian came in with the money.'

'This Bradshaw, what did he want?'

'A Grail missile with a guidance system. The practice model wasn't good enough. So I put him in touch with a French guy, down in Nice. Marcel Calvert. He was in the Legion. He was going to sell him a Stinger.'

'How did Bradshaw know to contact you? It's not as if you guys advertise on Craigslist, is it?'

'Friend of a friend. Word of mouth. I think it was a guy who he'd served with who now works for Blackwater.'

Yokely nodded. 'Thank you, Alex, you've been very helpful. Now, do you have a contact number for this Bradshaw?'

'My phone. In my coat.'

Yokely went over to Kleintank's cashmere overcoat and fished an iPhone out of one of the pockets. 'Password?'

Kleintank gave him the digits and Yokely tapped them into the phone. 'Thank you,' he said.

'Now will you let me go?' asked Kleintank.

'Have you told me everything?'

'Yes,' said Kleintank.

'You are sure?'

'Yes!' screamed the Dutchman.

Yokely took the gun from its holster and shot Kleintank twice in the chest. Kleintank's body went into spasm as blood dripped on to the floor, then he went still. Yokely turned to look at Leclerc. 'Peter, are you okay going point in Dubai? It's a while since I was there.'

'Sure.'

'Who do you suggest we use?'

'Michael Bardot in Abu Dhabi is always reliable for kit. Puts a bit of distance in there. He can drive into Dubai with any equipment we need.'

Yokely nodded. 'Good call.' Yokely had worked with Bardot before. Another Navy SEAL who had moved into the commercial sector. 'Fix up some potassium chloride. I don't want to be making too many waves in Dubai.' He looked at his watch. 'Okay, Peter, see if you can get to Dubai tonight. Gerry and I will fly over tomorrow.'

Leclerc dropped Yokely and McNee at the Marriott Hotel and headed for the airport. The two men checked in and went to their rooms. Yokely took a couple of miniature whiskies from the minibar, poured them into a tumbler and took a sip before calling Karl Traynor on his throwaway mobile. The FCEN analyst answered almost immediately. Yokely gave him Benikhlef's details. 'Can you check if he was involved in any of the airline stock shorting?' asked Yokely. 'And try an alternate spelling of the family name.' He spelled out Bin Khalid. 'Also, we've got a Saudi name who lives in Dubai. Hamid bin Faisal. Have a look at him, too.'

'I'm on it,' said Traynor.

Yokely showered and changed into a clean shirt and chinos before phoning Spider Shepherd. Yokely got to the point immediately and told Shepherd what Kleintank had said and gave him Paul Bradshaw's details and phone number.

'You can spread the word, but you can't ever identify your source,' said Yokely. 'You have a good day now.' Yokely ended the call.

He used the hotel phone to call McNee. 'Fancy dinner?' asked Yokely.

'Hell, yeah. Drinks first? I know a place.'

Yokely chuckled. There wasn't a city in the world where Gerry McNee didn't know a place.

Chapter 27

'How do you want to handle it?' asked O'Hara. Harper had been deep in thought for the best part of twenty minutes, staring at the Acton house where Khuram Zaghba lived. It was just after midnight and the house was in darkness. Harper and O'Hara were sitting in the Toyota with the engine running to keep the interior warm. Generally the richer the target, the easier it was to get to. Harper was considering his options. High-profile targets often had security systems and even bodyguards, but more often than not they lived in detached houses. Targets at the lower end of the income scale tended to share flats and houses and there were always other people around.

'I don't think we've got time to fuck around,' said Harper. 'I've got a couple of fluorescent jackets in the boot; we'll say we're with British Gas and that there's been a leak. As soon as he opens the door, we slot him.'

'That works,' said O'Hara.

'Are you okay to do the dirty if necessary?' asked Harper. O'Hara had a Glock with a silencer and it made more sense to use a silenced weapon, though Harper hoped not to have to use a gun.

'Happy to do the honours,' said O'Hara. Harper held out the iPod Touch so that O'Hara could see what Zaghba looked like. O'Hara nodded. 'What about collateral damage?' he asked.

'He's a bad 'un so we can assume anyone unlucky enough to be with him is also a bad 'un and I don't want to be leaving any witnesses behind.'

O'Hara nodded. 'Let's do it then.'

Harper pressed the button to open the boot and the two men climbed out of the car. There was a box of disposable latex gloves in the boot and they both put them on, then Harper handed O'Hara a fluorescent jacket and a hard hat. O'Hara grinned and put them on.

Harper followed suit and then slammed the boot shut. 'Good to go?' he asked.

O'Hara nodded. 'Locked and loaded, as the Yanks say.'

The two men walked across the road, scanning for any potential witnesses, but the road and pavements were deserted. It was a cloudy night and the street lights were few and far between. They walked up the path to the front door. The house had been divided into flats and there were six bells to the left of the door. Zaghba lived in Flat 5. Harper pressed the bell and waited. There was no response and he had to press it another two times before the intercom crackled into life.

'Yeah?' said a voice, thick with sleep.

'Mr Zaghba, this is Peter Wilkinson from British Gas. We've had reports of a gas leak in the building – could you buzz me in so that we can check the gas levels in your flat.'

There was a few seconds' silence and then the door lock buzzed. Harper pushed the door open. The hallway was in darkness but there was a light switch on the wall and when he pressed it a single bulb came on. There were two doors on the ground floor so Harper assumed that Zaghba's flat was on the floor above. He headed up the stairs, his shoes squeaking on the bare boards.

Zaghba had opened his front door and was peering down. He was wearing boxer shorts and a Manchester United replica shirt. 'I can't smell anything,' he said.

'Our sensors are a thousand times more sensitive than the human nose,' said Harper. 'Do you mind if we come in? We just need to check your kitchen.'

'It's a bedsit,' said Zaghba, 'and like I said there's no smell of gas.'

'It'll only take a minute,' said Harper, reaching the top of the stairs. He flashed Zaghba a reassuring smile.

'Sure, whatever,' said Zaghba.

He opened the door and Harper walked past him into what appeared to be the only room – there was a double bed, a wardrobe and a small kitchen area. A doorway led into a small bathroom that smelt of bleach.

Zaghba followed Harper. 'See. Nothing.'

O'Hara stepped into the room and kicked the door shut behind him. As Zaghba turned, O'Hara pulled out his Glock.

'What the fuck, bruv?' said Zaghba. 'Waste of time trying to rob me.'

There was a small table by the side of the bed with an alarm clock on it. In one smooth movement Harper picked up the table, tossed the clock on to the bed and brought the edge of the table crashing down on to the back of Zaghba's head. Blood splattered across the floor and he went down without making a sound. Harper raised the table again and smashed it against the man's head. The skull cracked and blood pooled across the carpet.

'Fuck me, Lex, you don't mess around, do you?' whispered O'Hara.

Harper put the table on the ground and pulled a Ziploc plastic bag from his pocket. Inside were half a dozen pieces of streaky bacon and he placed them across the dead man's back and legs. Then he pulled a can of black spray paint from the pocket of his jacket and wrote 'FUCK ISLAM' and 'DEATH TO MUSLIM PIGS' across the wall.

O'Hara chuckled as he watched Harper work.

'Make yourself useful and see if there's a laptop around,' said Harper. 'And grab his phone.'

O'Hara did as he was told as Harper continued to spray racial epitaphs on the walls. When he'd finished he put the can in his pocket.

'No computer, by the look of it,' said O'Hara. He picked up Zaghba's phone and pocketed it.

Harper gestured for O'Hara to open the door. They slipped

out, pulling the door closed behind them, and went down the stairs, listening carefully to check that there was no one moving around. The house was still and they opened the front door and headed for the car.

'So the bacon and the graffiti are to make it look racial?' said O'Hara, as they took off their fluorescent jackets and got back into the Toyota.

'That's the plan,' said Harper.

'Nice,' said O'Hara. He unscrewed the silencer from his Glock and slipped it into his pocket. 'I tell you, Lex, I'd like to do more jobs for the Pool.'

'Strictly speaking, this isn't a Pool job.'

'I know, but you know what I mean.' He put the gun in its underarm holster. 'The jobs are, you know, cleaner. Simpler. A lot of the contracts I get these days are disputes, one side against the other, so they can get messy. And there's always the possibility of someone taking offence at what you've done and going for revenge.' He handed Harper Zaghba's phone.

Harper slid the phone into his pocket and nodded. 'I'll keep in touch after this is over,' he said. 'You never know.'

Chapter 28

Shepherd took off his coat as he rushed over to George Hurry. He dropped down on to a chair next to the sergeant. 'What have you got, George?'

Hurry tapped on his keyboard. 'Naveed went into a storage room half an hour before he detonated. We didn't see it earlier because there's only one camera covering that area and even then it's only a partial view.'

A frozen CCTV filled one of the big screens on the wall. There were more than a dozen United fans in view. 'There, on the right, you can see the door?' said Hurry.

Shepherd nodded,

'It's used for storing cleaning supplies and accessed with a keycard.' Hurry pressed a key and the figures on the screen started to move. 'Naveed appears from the right,' said Hurry. Ten seconds into the footage, Shepherd saw the distinctive puffa jacket and Nikes of the target. Naveed walked straight to the door, reaching into his pocket. He took out a keycard, swiped it through the reader and pushed open the door. He disappeared inside and the door closed behind him. 'He was inside for just shy of ten minutes,' said Hurry. He pressed a key to fast-forward the footage and after nine minutes had passed he returned to real time. The door opened and Naveed reappeared. He walked out and the door closed behind him. Hurry froze the picture. 'You wouldn't notice it unless you were looking for it, but the jacket is just a bit larger now. As if he had put on something underneath it.' His fingers played across the keyboard and the image split into two – on the left a shot of Naveed using the keycard and on the right, him emerging from the storage room. Shepherd studied the two images and nodded. Hurry was right. The coat was slightly bulkier. Naveed had gone into the room and put the vest on.

Shepherd sighed and sat back. 'Okay, so now we know where Naveed got the vest. Two things. We need to know whose card he used to access the room.' He looked at his watch. It was one-thirty in the morning and he figured the stadium staff wouldn't be in until eight at the earliest. 'I'll make the call on that first thing. And we need to find out who put the vest in the storage room. Can you assign someone to monitor that feed in reverse, see who else went in?'

Hurry grinned. 'Already on it,' he said. He gestured over to Eric Fitzpatrick, who was sipping a coffee as he stared at his screen. Figures were moving backwards at several times normal speed.

'I thought you had to take care of your girl?' Shepherd asked him.

'I did the school run but the wife's on duty now,' he said, his eyes not leaving the screen. 'I'm here for the duration.'

Chapter 29

O'Hara clicked the seat backwards and stretched out his legs. 'This is the best car you could get? It's a piece of shit.'

Harper grinned over at him. They were on the M40 heading towards Birmingham, in the middle lane and driving at just below the speed limit. 'It's perfect for flying below the radar,' he said.

'I'm a Range Rover man,' said O'Hara. 'Now that's a vehicle.'

'Yeah, I bet. Black with tinted windows. Mate, you stick out like a sore thumb. A car like this, no one remembers.'

O'Hara folded his arms and sighed. A sign flashed by. They were ten miles from Birmingham. 'What's the plan?' he asked.

'We've got one target in Brum, then another in Bolton. Both ragheads.'

'Jihadists?'

'Don't know, don't care. They're jobs, that's all that interests me. We'll do the Birmingham one first. Israr Farooqi. Young guy who snuck in as a refugee. We need to off him but we're looking for intel, too. I've got a lock-up we can use to interrogate him.'

O'Hara nodded. 'What sort of intel?'

'The guy that bombed the stadium phoned Farooqi before the attack. Be nice to know why, and also what this Farooqi is planning. But we're under time pressure. The bomber has an uncle in Bolton, which is about two hours from Birmingham. Be handy to do both tonight.'

O'Hara looked at his watch. 'Bloody hell.'

'I know, it'll be tight.'

'I need to eat, too.'

'To be fair, Mick, you could do with losing a few pounds. Just saying.'

'Fuck you very much.'

'If you're really hungry I've a couple of sandwiches in the bag on the back seat.'

'Why the fuck didn't you say?' O'Hara twisted around in his seat. He opened the bag and took out two plastic-wrapped sandwiches. He read the labels out loud. 'Ham and cheese, prawn salad. Which do you want?'

'Have them both, mate, I'm good.'

O'Hara grinned and wolfed down both sandwiches.

Farooqi lived in a terraced house in the south of the city. Harper parked close by and used his smartphone to locate the lock-up that Hasan had given him. It was about three miles away. He plotted a route from the house to the lock-up, then put the car in gear.

'Now what?' asked O'Hara.

'Just want to make sure there are no surprises,' said Harper. He drove to the lock-up. It was at the end of a quiet street close to a railway line. 'Mick, do me a favour and get the key, it's in the drainpipe next to the door. Have a quick look around, yeah?'

O'Hara nodded. He climbed out of the car, looking left and right as he headed to the lock-up. He bent down by the drainpipe and groped inside. He took so long that Harper began to worry that the key wasn't there but eventually O'Hara straightened up and flashed him a thumbs-up. He looked around, then walked over to the door and unlocked it. He disappeared inside.

Harper scanned the street and pavements but there was no one else around. After three minutes O'Hara reappeared, locked the door and jogged over to the car. He climbed in. 'Hasn't been used for a while,' he said. 'Seems secure enough.'

Harper drove back to the house where Farooqi lived and parked again. He switched off the engine and studied the building. If they had time to spare they could just wait outside and catch Farooqi as he entered or left, but the clock was ticking. According to the message Button had sent, Farooqi lived in Flat 3 but that wasn't much help as he had no way of knowing how many flats there were on each floor.

'Are we going to pull the gas trick again?' asked O'Hara.

'I think we just say we're immigration officers,' said Harper. 'It's not unusual for them to run checks at all hours. I just worry about getting him into the car without being seen.'

'We walk him out,' said O'Hara. 'People tend to cooperate if you stick a gun in their ribs.'

Harper looked up and down the street. There didn't seem to be any obvious CCTV cameras. But two men escorting an Asian man to a car was the sort of thing a passer-by might notice and remember. It would cut down the walking time if he parked closer to the house. 'Okay, we ring the bell and identify ourselves as Border Force. Assuming he buzzes us in we gain access to his flat and do a quick search. Then we march him out. You get into the back of the car and as soon as he's in you put him to sleep. Nothing too drastic, we need to talk to him.'

'No need to teach this grandmother to suck eggs,' said O'Hara.

Harper started the car again and drove over to the house. There was a garage to the right and a parking space in front of it. Using the parking space increased the chance of the car being noticed but even if it was, it couldn't be traced to him so he decided it was a risk worth taking. He switched off the lights and killed the engine.

The two men got out of the Toyota and walked to the front door. There were six buttons on the intercom unit, numbered one to six. Harper pressed number three, long and hard. After a few seconds they heard a hesitant 'Who is it?'

'Is that Mr Israr Farooqi?' asked Harper, putting as much authority into his voice as he could.

'Yes.'

'We are from the Home Office, Mr Farooqi. It's nothing to be concerned about but we need to check your residential status pursuant to your asylum application.'

'What? I don't understand.'

'We need to check your living arrangements.'

'It's late.'

'Yes, I realise that, but the Home Office has the authority to check your residential status at any time of the day or night. Failure to confirm your status could jeopardise your asylum application.'

Harper waited. After a few seconds the lock buzzed and O'Hara pushed open the door. They went inside. The light clicked on immediately, presumably a motion detector switch. Harper nodded up the stairs. O'Hara went first. Farooqi's flat was at the rear of the building. There was a brass number '3' in the middle of the door, and no security viewer. Harper knocked and the door opened almost immediately. It was on a security chain. Farooqi peered through the gap. 'Can I see your identification?' he asked.

'Of course you can, sir,' said Harper, stepping away from the door and reaching inside his jacket. He caught a glimpse of Farooqi's sweatshirt and jeans.

O'Hara shouldered the door hard and the screws holding the chain in place ripped out with the sound of tearing wood. O'Hara kept the momentum going and the door hit Farooqi and knocked him back. O'Hara pushed the door wide and grabbed Farooqi around the throat. The man's eyes bulged as O'Hara forced him back against the wall.

Harper slipped inside and closed the door. 'Easy, Mick,' hissed Harper, but Farooqi's eyes had already glazed over. O'Hara loosened his grip on the man's throat but it was too late – Farooqi was out for the count and he slid down the wall like a puppet whose strings had been cut. 'For fuck's Mick, don't tell me you've killed him.'

'He's okay,' said O'Hara. 'Just a bit too much pressure on the carotid. He'll be awake in a minute or so.'

'He better had be or I'm cutting your fee in half,' snapped Harper. 'Nothing too drastic, I said. They were my exact words.'

'Okay, okay, what do you want me to do, open a fucking vein?'

'Forget it,' said Harper. 'Just make sure he's on his feet in the next couple of minutes, I don't want to hang about.' He looked around. The flat was tiny. The room they were in had a plastic sofa and a low coffee table, and by the window a small wooden table with two matching chairs. There was a Sony laptop on the coffee table. It was open but the computer was off.

There was a copy of the Koran on the table by the window. It was an Arabic version and there were two Arabic books next to it. Harper picked up the Koran and flicked through it. Hundreds of passages had been highlighted in yellow but there were no scribbled notes.

Harper went through to a small bedroom with a single bed and a cheap teak-effect wardrobe. There was an Islamic prayer mat on the floor by the window. On the bedside table was a Samsung phone. He picked it up. It was password-protected. He slipped it into his pocket. The cramped shower room was dirty and the ceiling dotted with black mould; water was dripping from the plastic shower head.

Harper went back into the main room, where O'Hara was slapping the unconscious man's face.

There was a laptop case on the floor next to the coffee table. Harper picked it up and slid the laptop into it. O'Hara looked over his shoulder. 'Sorry about this, Lex. Bastard won't wake up.'

'You can carry him,' said Harper. 'But gag him and tie him in case he comes around in the boot.'

O'Hara nodded. He stood up and went over to the kitchen area. He ripped the cord out of an electric kettle and used it to tie Farooqi's hands behind his back, then he stuffed a pan cleaner into the man's mouth and held it in place with a roughly tied dishcloth.

'Okay, out we go,' said Harper. 'Stay behind me and don't move until I say we're clear.' He took out his car keys and eased open the door. The hallway was in darkness but the light came on as soon as he stepped out. He held up his hand to tell O'Hara to stay where he was and he listened intently. There was a television on somewhere in the house and muffled voices from the floor above. But they were alone in the hallway. He padded down the stairs. O'Hara followed with Farooqi slung over his shoulder.

Harper reached the front door and slowly opened it. A car drove by and disappeared down the road. He looked left and right. On the other side of the road an old woman in a heavy coat was walking a black and white spaniel. The dog crouched and the woman pulled a plastic bag from her pocket. When the dog had finished its business, the woman picked it up with the bag and walked off. Another car drove by. Then a motorcycle. Harper gritted his teeth and waited.

After the sound of the motorcycle had faded into the distance, he stepped out of the house. He looked around, then when he was satisfied the pavements were empty he waved for O'Hara to follow him out. He held the door open for O'Hara, quietly closed it behind him and then hurried over to the Toyota and opened the boot. O'Hara dropped the still-unconscious man into the boot and closed it.

'See now, that worked out quite well, didn't it?' said O'Hara.

'Yes, Mick,' said Harper, his voice loaded with sarcasm. They got into the car. Harper started the engine and drove on to the road. He waited until he was several hundred yards from the house before switching on the car's lights. He looked over at O'Hara and grinned. 'Mind you, the look on his face when you had him by the throat, it was priceless.'

'I think he shat himself,' said O'Hara. He chuckled. 'He's going to be doing a lot worse than that by the time we're done with him, right?'

'Damn straight,' said Harper.

Chapter 30

Present Day, London

'Got him!' said Eric Fitzpatrick. He sat back and punched the air triumphantly. Shepherd rushed over to his workstation but was narrowly beaten by Sergeant Hurry. Fitzpatrick had frozen the CCTV footage showing a young Asian man at the door to the storage room, holding a black nylon kitbag.

As Shepherd and Hurry joined him he pressed the key to restart the footage. The man on the screen used a keycard to open the door and slipped inside. The door remained closed for almost a minute, then it opened again and the man reappeared, this time without the bag in his hand. Fitzpatrick froze the picture. 'Usman Yussuf,' he said. 'He works in the accounts department. He's been employed there for almost a year. He keeps his face away from the camera most of the time but you can see enough of it when he comes out to make an ID.'

'I'm going to need an address.'

'Yeah, bit of a cock-up there,' said Hurry. 'We've got names and dates of birth to go with all the human resources photographs but we don't have addresses.'

'You're joking. How did that happen?'

'I guess whoever compiled the database thought that identification was what mattered. And we've identified him. But for an address we'll need to get access to the human resources database and they don't start work until nine o'clock.'

Shepherd looked at his watch. Nine o'clock was only a few hours away. Plus there was a chance that Yussuf would turn up for work himself, which would make their job a whole lot easier. 'Eric, follow him on the cameras and see where he goes.'

'Will do,' said Fitzpatrick.

Shepherd went back to his desk. It took him just a few minutes on his terminal to ascertain that neither the DVLA nor the PNC had any information on Usman Yussuf. He didn't have a driver's licence and he wasn't on the police database. Shepherd logged into MI5's database and drew a blank there, too. He was a genuine cleanskin, totally unknown to the police and security services. He phoned Patsy Ellis. This time it took longer for her to answer and she had clearly been asleep, but she thanked him for calling and told him not to worry about the lateness of the hour. He briefed her on what little they knew about Yussuf.

'Good work, Dan,' she said. 'I'll contact Border Force and get a watch put out for him at all airports and ports in case he decides to run. Let me know what else you turn up.' She ended the call.

He looked at his watch and wondered if he should phone Katra but then decided against it. If she was asleep she wouldn't thank him for waking her up, and if she was awake she would want to know when he'd be coming home and that was a question he couldn't answer just then.

Chapter 31

Ten Years Ago, Dubai

All the flights from Sarajevo were full and the only tickets Yokely could get at short notice meant leaving at nine o'clock in the morning with a twelve-and-a-half-hour stopover in Istanbul, with the second leg of the flight getting in at just before six o'clock the following morning. Leclerc was waiting for them at Dubai Airport and took them to an SUV in the parking lot. Michael Bardot was in the driving seat. He was a big man and had put on a few pounds since leaving the SEALs, but even in his polo shirt and chinos his military background was still in evidence, with his razor-sharp haircut and impenetrable Oakley sunglasses. He fist-bumped Yokely and did the same to McNee.

'Okay, so, good news, bad news,' said Leclerc. 'Benikhlef lives in a penthouse in one of the luxury blocks in Dubai Marina. 'Full-on security, CCTV everywhere, so even if we could get in we'd be caught on camera. The vehicles are fully secure in the underground car park, and there's no way we could mount a surveillance operation outside the tower. There are some very rich and powerful people in that building so it's as secure as Fort Knox.' He smiled at the look of disappointment on Yokely's face. 'The good news is that he keeps a mistress on a boat in the marina and he's there most evenings.'

Yokely nodded his approval. 'That is good news,' he said.

'It'll make disposal easier, too,' said McNee. 'We can make the boat go boom, we don't even need C4. I can set it to blow with just fuel and a timer.'

'The one drawback is that the mistress will be there,' said Leclerc. He looked over at Yokely.

Yokely shrugged. 'If she's his mistress she'll know who he is and what he does. Same with the bodyguards. Collateral damage. It's all good.'

'Then we can do it tonight,' said Leclerc.

'How are we fixed for kit?' asked Yokely.

'Michael has done us proud,' said Leclerc. 'A nice selection of semi-automatics and silencers and a couple of Ingram MAC-10s.'

'All part of the service,' said Bardot.

'And the potassium chloride?'

'I have a litre,' said Bardot. 'Overkill but it's easier to buy in bulk.'

'And what about Hamid bin Faisal?'

'He's a Saudi but he has a residence here.'

'Any family?'

'An uncle. Runs a marketing company, mainly running promotions for luxury clothing companies.'

'Name?'

'Mohammed Al-Hashim.'

'Any suggestions that the uncle is involved in terrorism?'

'He's not on any watch lists,' said Bardot.

'Do you have an address for Hamid bin Faisal?'

Bardot nodded. 'And the uncle.'

'Let's check out his home first before we decide what to do about the uncle.' He looked at his watch. 'How about we do that now? Strike while the iron's hot?'

'Sounds like a plan,' said Bardot.

The drive to bin Faisal's house took just over half an hour. It was a gated development but there was no security and Bardot followed a white SUV through as the gates opened. 'I checked it out this morning, there was no one at home and he seems to live alone.'

'What does he do for a living?' asked Yokely.

'He works for his uncle. I phoned the company yesterday and was told he's on vacation until the end of the month.' He nodded at a two-storey yellow villa, flat-roofed with a large satellite dish on the top. There was a Wrangler Jeep parked outside.

'Does he own or rent?' asked Yokely.

'His uncle owns it. The uncle owns a fair bit of property around Dubai.'

Bardot parked in front of the villa. He took them around to the back where there was a wooden decking area. There was a door that led to the kitchen. There was no burglar alarm and it took Bardot less than a minute to pick the lock and get them inside.

Leclerc went upstairs while McNee checked out the kitchen.

Yokely looked around the sitting room. There was hardly any furniture, just a sofa and a coffee table and a bookcase. Yokely looked at the bookcase. One shelf was filled with Islamic books, mainly in Arabic but there were a few in English. There were several copies of the Koran. The largest was a hardback and it was peppered with Post-It notes. Sections had been highlighted in yellow. Yokely read through some of them. It wasn't pleasant reading.

'As to those who reject faith, I will punish them with terrible agony in this world and in the Hereafter, nor will they have anyone to help.'

'Soon shall We cast terror into the hearts of the Unbelievers, for that they joined companions with Allah, for which He had sent no authority.'

'The punishment of those who wage war against Allah and His messenger and strive to make mischief in the land is only this, that they should be murdered or crucified or their hands and their feet should be cut off on opposite sides or they should be imprisoned; this shall be as a disgrace for them in this world, and in the hereafter they shall have a grievous chastisement.'

'I will cast terror into the hearts of those who disbelieve. Therefore strike off their heads and strike off every fingertip of them.'

'Surely Allah loves those who fight in His cause.'

It was as if bin Faisal was looking for justification for what he was planning to do in the United States. Yokely closed the book and put it back on the shelf with the others. There were a handful of New York guidebooks, and a folded map of the city. Yokely unfolded the map but there were no marks on it. There were several military books, mainly detailing the equipment used by armed forces around the world. There was a folded sheet of paper in one of the books. Yokely opened it at the marked page – it was a chapter on ground-to-air missiles.

There was an empty box on the floor that had contained a video recorder, almost certainly the camera that had been used to film the downing of the jet.

Leclerc came down the stairs with an Apple laptop. 'Password protected,' he said, handing it to Yokely.

Yokely looked at his watch. It was just before nine in the morning. 'How about Gerry and I check into our hotel and we can give the computer a going over?' he said to Leclerc. 'You and Michael can drop us off and then go check out the uncle's whereabouts.'

'The uncle's on your list?' asked Leclerc.

'He was taking care of a jihadist who blew a passenger jet out of the sky, Peter. So yes, the uncle's on my list.'

Yokely and McNee checked into the Jumeirah Dar Al-Masyaf at Madinat Jumeirah. The hotel was as luxurious as any Yokely had ever seen, set among lush gardens, waterways and massive swimming pools, with traditional abra boats and golf carts ferrying guests between their villas and the resort's many restaurants.

The hotel wasn't far from the Palm, and Yokely could see it in the distance from one of the rooms in his palatial villa. After he'd tipped the bellboy who had spent five minutes showing him all the facilities on offer in the villa, Yokely placed the computer he'd taken from bin Faisal's house on a desk. He used his cell phone to call Sam Hepburn at the NSA. Hepburn sounded sleepy when he answered but he was as enthusiastic as ever. Hepburn was one of the smartest men Yokely had ever met, holding two degrees from MIT and a Masters from Harvard, but he was far from being a nerd. He played tennis at a level that would have allowed him to join the professional circuit if he'd wanted to and ran at least five miles a day, most of that on a running machine in his office. He'd once told Yokely that he slept for only four hours a night and Yokely had no reason to think he was lying.

'It's a MacBook, one of the latest models by the look of it,' said Yokely. 'It's password-protected.'

'Not a problem,' said Hepburn. 'Can you switch it on and connect a phone to it?'

Yokely took another cell phone and connected it to one of the laptop's USB slots. He gave the number of the cell phone to Hepburn and a minute later the phone buzzed. The screen stayed the same, prompting for a password, for several minutes, then the prompt went and the desktop flashed up with more than twenty files on a background of what appeared to be a mosque in a Middle Eastern country.

'There you go,' said Hepburn. 'You're in.'

'Can you do me another favour?' asked Yokely. 'I'm pretty sure the owner was using a draft file to communicate with his handler. Can you have a quick look? I'm assuming he's not been stupid enough to store his passwords.' It was a standard way of keeping communications off the grid. The National Security Agency and the British equivalent – the Government Communications Headquarters – could indeed read any email ever sent. But if two people shared an email account and only ever left messages in the draft folder, there was no transmission so no way that the email could be intercepted.

'Give me a couple of minutes,' said Hepburn. 'I'll call you when I'm done.'

Yokely went over to the minibar and opened it. Despite the Muslim ban on all things alcoholic, it was packed with wine and spirits, including two very good bottles of champagne. Yokely took a bottle of Evian water and went out on to the terrace. He sat on a wooden bench and lit one of his small cigars. He was halfway through it when Hepburn called him on his cell phone. 'It's a Google account,' said Hepburn. 'At least, it was a Google account. It was closed three days ago. Have you got a pen? I'll give you the email address and password.'

Yokely wrote down the details. 'Can you recover any messages that were on the account?'

'It'll take time and I'll need you to leave the laptop online while I do it. It's either that or do it through Google and they tend not to be too cooperative these days.'

'I'll leave it on and connected,' said Yokely. 'What about when he set up the account? He must have put in some details when he started off.'

'I'll check.'

'You're a star, Sam.'

'No need to blow smoke up my ass, Richard. I'm on the case.'

Yokely spent the afternoon and early evening in his room. Hepburn called him back just before five o'clock. 'All done,' he said. 'If you check the laptop now you'll see all the messages are back, including the ones that were in the draft folder.'

'You're a wizard, Sam,' said Yokely. He thanked Hepburn and sat down in front of Hamid bin Faisal's laptop. He went through to the email account that bin Faisal had used to communicate with whoever was running him.

There were more than a dozen messages in the folder, half from bin Faisal and half from someone using the name Saladin, and Yokely cursed under his breath when he saw that they were all in Arabic. He reached for his cell phone and called Michael Bardot. 'I need your Arabic skills, now,' said Yokely. Bardot said he'd be right up.

Yokely helped himself to a beer from the minibar. He was halfway through it when Bardot knocked on the door.

Yokely showed him the laptop and Bardot sat down and leaned forward to peer at the messages. 'Okay, this guy Saladin is checking that he has the right visa to visit the States. That's one of the earliest. The later emails are telling him what to do when he gets to the States and explaining that there will be someone at the airport to meet him. They'll be holding a card with his name in Arabic.'

'Anything about what he is supposed to be doing there? Details of what they have planned?'

Bardot shook his head. 'There's a lot of Islamic rhetoric. Bringing the fight to the infidels, the joy of jihadism, a lot of quotes from the Koran, all the usual shit.'

'What about details of the people he'd meet in the States?' asked Yokely.

'Again, just general stuff. Loyal warriors, their names will live for ever, true jihadists, almost as if he's worried that he might be changing his mind.'

'It's a lot to organise, and if any one link falls apart the whole operation fails,' said Yokely. He walked over to the window and looked out over the Persian Gulf. On the horizon, oil tankers were heading west towards the Arabian Sea loaded with oil for the infidel. If it wasn't for the oil, the Emirates would be nothing but desert and the mega-rich Saudis would still be riding their camels from oasis to oasis. And much of the money that paid for the oil was used to fund terrorism around the world. The West was effectively funding the attacks on itself and no one seemed capable of breaking the circle.

'So who is this Saladin?' asked Bardot.

'It's the guy who was running the jihadists in New York,' said Yokely. 'I'm assuming Saladin is just an alias. He's obviously not going to use his real name.'

'That makes sense,' said Bardot. 'Saladin was one of the greatest Muslim warriors. Full name An-Nasir Salah ad-Din Yusuf ibn Ayyub. He led the Muslim fight against the European powers during the Third Crusade.' Bardot sat back. 'He's going to be hard to find, this guy, isn't he? He goes to a lot of trouble to cover his tracks.'

'Everyone makes mistakes,' said Yokely. 'Or they run into bad luck. Either way, we'll get him eventually.'

Bardot looked at his watch. 'I'm going to have to get moving,' he said. 'I'll be back to pick you and the guys up at eight.'

'Everything's lined up?'

Bardot nodded. 'All good to go,' he said.

'And Jamahl Benikhlef?'

'I've got his place being watched now by a couple of guys I use in Dubai. They're reliable and they don't know what we're up to, no need to worry on that score.'

Yokely grinned. 'I'm not worried, Michael,' he said. 'You're a pro. I wouldn't be using you if you weren't.'

Chapter 32

Harper bent down and undid the makeshift gag from around Israr Farooqi's mouth. Farooqi spluttered and spat out the pan cleaner. His chest heaved as he sucked air into his lungs. He was lying on his side, his hands still tied behind his back with the electrical cord.

They were in the garage and the Toyota was parked on the forecourt outside. There were no windows in the building and the door was closed and bolted. There were two fluorescent lights overhead but Harper had only switched on one. There was space for half a dozen cars with an inspection pit at one end and workbenches pushed up against one wall. Behind the benches were racks of tools. Steel girders ran across the ceiling and the floor was bare concrete stained with oil.

Farooqi rolled on to his back and looked around, blinking tears from his eyes. 'Who are you?' he gasped.

Harper ignored the question. 'Israr, you're going to tell me what I want to know eventually, so you might as well tell me now and save yourself a lot of pain.'

'Who are you?' he repeated. 'Why are you doing this?

'Why does that matter?'

'You're not cops because cops aren't allowed to do this to people, not in this country.'

O'Hara drew back a foot and kicked Farooqi in the side. Farooqi screamed and tried to roll away from his attacker but O'Hara kicked him again.

'We're not cops, Israr,' said Harper. 'And we're not spooks

either. We're nobodies. We don't exist. Which is why we can do whatever we want to you and there will be absolutely zero consequences.'

Farooqi frowned. His English wasn't great, Harper realised. He stood over the man and glared down at him. 'We can do what the fuck we want to you. Do you understand?'

Farooqi nodded fearfully.

'So, answer my questions and we won't hurt you. But if you don't answer . . .' He nodded at O'Hara, who went over to the tool rack and selected a pair of bolt cutters. He went back to Farooqi and squatted down next to him and grabbed his right ankle. He was barefoot, his feet stained with dirt from the lock-up's floor. Farooqi tried to pull his leg away but he had little strength left and he began to sob. 'You get the picture, right?' said Harper. 'My friend will happily cut off all your toes. And your fingers. And probably make you eat them.'

'What do you want?' asked Farooqi.

Harper took out the man's phone. 'The password for this, for a start.'

Farooqi nodded and gave Harper the digits to open the phone. Harper tapped them in and nodded. 'Well done,' he said. He put the phone back in his pocket and went over to one of the workbenches where he'd put the laptop case. He unzipped it and took out the computer. He placed it on the bench and opened it. He pressed the button to boot it up. It was also password-protected. 'And I want the password for this,' he said.

'Jihad,' said Farooqi. 'The password is Jihad.'

'Are you serious?' He tapped in JIHAD and it was accepted. Harper shook his head. 'How stupid are you?' he asked. He walked over to Farooqi and looked down at him. 'You know the man who blew up the football stadium?'

Farooqi shook his head. 'No. No, I do not. I swear on the Koran, I swear on the life of my parents.'

Harper frowned. 'I thought you were an orphan,' he said. 'Isn't that the story you told? A poor little orphan boy who needed asylum? But anyway I know you are lying – Naveed called you not long before he blew himself up.' He nodded at O'Hara, who deftly inserted Farooqi's middle toe between the blades of the bolt cutter and snapped the handles together. The steel blades snipped the toe off as easily as if they were cutting a piece of cheese. Blood spurted over the blades and Farooqi screamed and then went ashen. His whole body was shaking.

O'Hara straightened up and nodded approvingly at the bolt cutters. 'Nice bit of kit,' he said.

'Tell me the truth, Israr,' said Harper. 'You've got another nine toes and ten fingers. And a dick, of course. Though we'll save the dick until last.'

Farooqi swallowed nervously. 'Yes, I knew him.'

'From where?'

'We were fighters in Syria. We were both told to come to the UK and to seek asylum here.'

'Why?'

'Because we are to bring the fight to the UK.'

'You were to become a terrorist?'

'Not a terrorist. A jihadist. It is the West who are the terrorists.'

Harper sneered at the man. 'I'm tempted to get my friend here to cut off another toe just to stop you talking shit,' he said. 'But I'm in a hurry. Who sent you to England?'

'Our commander.'

'What was his name?'

'Mohammed al-Hafiz.'

'And what did he tell you to do in England?'

'Please, my foot, it hurts,' said Farooqi.

'It'll hurt a lot more if we cut off another toe,' said Harper. 'What were you told to do?'

'The commander said we were to make our way to England. If we couldn't get to England we were to go to France. We were to claim asylum. And we were to wait.'

'Wait? For what?'

'He said someone would contact us. A man. A man called Saladin.'

'Saladin?'

Farooqi nodded. 'We were told Saladin would contact us and tell us what to do. That was why Ali called me. To tell me that Saladin had contacted him and that he was ready to die for Allah.'

'Ali?'

'The jihadist who attacked the stadium. His name is Ali.'

'You say Saladin contacted Ali. How?'

'By email. And they met in London, two weeks ago. At a mosque.'

'Which mosque?'

'He didn't say.'

'Have you met him? This Saladin?'

'No.'

'Has he contacted you?'

'Not yet.'

Harper frowned. 'So what, he just sends you an email when he wants you?'

Farooqi shook his head. 'Before we left Syria we were given an email address to check. We check it every day.'

'A draft folder?'

Farooqi nodded again. 'When Saladin is ready, that is how he will contact me.'

'What's the email address?'

Farooqi told him.

'And the password?'

Farooqi gave him the password.

'What will this Saladin want you to do?'

'I don't know. We are just told to wait.'

Harper rubbed the back of his neck. He was dog-tired, but they still had a lot to do. 'Okay, we're done,' said Harper. He nodded at O'Hara. 'Do the honours, will you?' O'Hara pulled out his Glock and was about to screw in the silencer when Harper held up his hand. 'Let's keep the gunshots to a minimum, shall we?'

O'Hara shrugged and put the gun away. 'Saves me money,' he said. 'Jony'll buy it back if it hasn't been used.' He walked over to the tool racks and stood with his hands on his hips for a while before selecting a bodywork hammer. He took it off the rack, hefted it in his right hand and then walked over to Farooqi.

Farooqi knew what was coming and tried to push himself along the floor but there was nothing he could do. He began to babble incoherently as O'Hara raised the hammer and brought it crashing down in the middle of his forehead. The skull splintered and the hammer went in a good inch. O'Hara grunted as he wrenched it out and brought it crashing down a second time. Farooqi went still and blood pooled around his head. O'Hara straightened up and tossed the bloody hammer on to the floor.

Harper put the laptop back in its case. Blood was still oozing from the shattered skull and spreading across the floor. There were several cans of spray paint on the bench and he picked up one at random. It was red and he sprayed 'DEATH TO MUSLIM PIGS' on the wall, then sprayed a rough cross on Farooqi's chest. He put the spray can in the laptop case and nodded at O'Hara. 'Let's go,' he said.

'Bolton?'

Harper nodded.

'You are a fucking machine, Lex,' said the Irishman.

Harper laughed and headed for the door. On the way he picked up the hammer, wrapped it in a piece of cloth and put it into the laptop bag.

Chapter 33

Shepherd walked into the office with a tray of coffees from the canteen and as soon as he saw the look of triumph on the face of George Hurry and Eric Fitzpatrick he knew that something was up. The sergeant waved Shepherd over. He was standing behind Fitzpatrick and they were looking at CCTV footage on the big screen on the wall. It was from the camera overlooking one of the toilets. 'Not long after Yussuf put the bag in the storage room, he visited the same toilet that Naveed went to.'

'So he hid the keycard there? That's why Naveed went in?'

Hurry nodded enthusiastically 'That's what it looks like. It's possible that Yussuf had never met Naveed, he was just told to drop the vest in the storage room and leave the keycard in a hiding place in the toilet.'

Shepherd stared at the screen and watched as Yussuf walked into the toilet. He was inside for three minutes, then he came out and walked purposefully away.

'Good job, Eric,' said Shepherd. He put a coffee down on Fitzpatrick's desk and gave one to Hurry. 'So, have we accounted for Naveed's every movement within the stadium?' he asked.

'Pretty much,' said Hurry. 'There are a few gaps but never more than a minute or so. I doubt that the missing periods will add anything to our understanding of what happened.'

Shepherd nodded. 'I agree. Okay, let's start looking more closely at that van and see if we can nail down when it picked up Naveed.'

'We have the van leaving the restaurant at five p.m. with just Zaghba on board. And we have it dropping Naveed off a short walk from the stadium. But filling in the gaps is going to take time. There are several possible routes and there's a good chance he'll have taken a detour to pick up Naveed.'

'I know it's not going to be easy. Also, once the day shift reports in, we need to get people looking at Naveed's life before the bombing, who he met, where he went. We need to see if he was meeting up with any known jihadists.'

Shepherd dropped down on to his chair. 'Someone clearly put this together,' he said. 'Someone must have briefed Naveed, and Yussuf, and Zaghba, and whoever made the vest.' He rubbed his chin as he stared at the screen. It had frozen, with Yussuf almost out of view. 'He must have had some way of contacting them, and he'd know that phones can be tracked and that most of London is covered by CCTV.'

'You're thinking email?' said Hurry.

'Emails can be read by GCHQ. The bad guys tend to communicate through draft folders. They've been doing it for years and the system is pretty much uncrackable.'

'The anti-terrorist boys will have been around to Naveed's house already,' said Hurry. 'If he had a computer they'll have it and their technical boys will be on it.'

Shepherd nodded. 'Sure. But Naveed was in foster care. I'm not sure how many foster parents give their charges laptops. Maybe they did, and I'll check first thing, but in the meantime why don't you get someone to identify all the Internet cafés within a mile of where Naveed lived. I doubt there'll be too many. Then see if we can get CCTV outside those premises and get sight of Naveed going in.'

Hurry nodded. 'I'm on it.'

'Naveed must have been in contact with his handler either on the day he blew up the stadium or at least the previous day. He'd need confirmation that he was to go ahead. So time-frame wise let's stick with forty-eight hours.'

'I'll switch Eric on to it,' he said. 'Eric, you okay with that?'

'I'm on it, said Fitzpatrick, his fingers playing across his keyboard.

Chapter 34

Harper and O'Hara reached Bolton at five o'clock in the morning. Dawn was just a couple of hours away. Imran Masood lived in a terraced house in a run-down area of the town. The doors and window frames were rotting, there were missing tiles on the roofs and the cars parked in the roads were old and uncared for. Discarded fast-food wrappers lined the gutters and even the feral cats that slinked by seemed reluctant to linger in the area.

'Salubrious,' said O'Hara. 'Reminds me of parts of Belfast. The nasty bits.' He nodded over at the house. 'So what's the story?'

'This guy is the uncle of the guy who bombed the stadium. We just take him out.'

'Collateral damage?'

Harper shrugged. 'He's bad and anyone who lives with him has to be bad, too.'

'And we make it look racial again?'

'Nah, this one we can just slot, no need for anything fancy.'

'You want me to do it?'

'I want to use my gun but I don't have a silencer,' said Harper. He looked up and down the road. 'I'm not happy about firing an unsuppressed weapon in an area like this.'

'Most people don't give a fuck,' said O'Hara. 'If they don't know what it is they'll assume it's a car backfiring. If they recognise it for what it is they usually don't want to get involved.'

Harper nodded. The house hadn't been converted into flats,

which meant Masood almost certainly wasn't living there alone.
He used his smartphone to check the electoral register. There
were five registered voters at the house, including Masood. They
all had the same surname so Harper figured the man lived with
his wife and grown-up children.

'I'm happy to use the Glock,' said O'Hara.

'Might be best,' said Harper. 'But I'll need it afterwards.
Someone else is going to take the fall for it.'

'You do like to overcomplicate things, don't you?'

'It's a complicated business,' said Harper. He sighed. He wasn't
happy about the way they were rushing, but there was nothing
he could about that – Button had made it clear that he was up
against a tight deadline. There were no lights on in Masood's
house or in the houses either side. But the street was far from
empty, despite the late hour. At the end of the road, three young
Muslim men were standing next to a small hatchback passing
what looked like a marijuana cigarette between them. An Asian
man in a long robe and a knitted skullcap was walking purposefully along the pavement followed by two heavyset women in full
burkhas. Four houses down from Masood's home, two elderly
men with straggly beards were deep in conversation.

Harper had parked in a side road and switched off the lights
and didn't appear to have attracted any attention. But the area
was clearly populated, in the main by immigrant families, and
two white men knocking on a door at that hour was obviously
going to be noticed.

He started the engine and drove away from the house. He took
a left. There was an alleyway running behind the houses, dotted
with wheelie bins. 'We'll go in the back way,' he said.

'Makes sense,' said O'Hara.

Harper found a parking space at the side of the road, reversed
in and switched off the engine. The entrance to the alley was
about fifty feet away. The good news was that there were no
CCTV cameras in the vicinity and it didn't look as if it was the
sort of area where the police patrolled, certainly not on foot.
'Okay,' he said, 'Let's do it.'

They got out of the car and walked towards the alley. A Toyota Prius drove by, probably an Uber taxi, and they turned their faces away. The alley was in darkness but there was enough moonlight to make out the potholes in the ground and the rubbish left behind last time the bins were emptied. Wooden doors led to the backyards of the houses left and right. Harper counted off the doors until he reached what he was sure was Masood's house. The door wasn't locked and Harper pushed it open. Behind was a small paved yard. They slipped inside and Harper closed the door behind them.

They stood in silence for almost a minute, then tiptoed over to the kitchen door. The top half was composed of six glass panels. Harper tried the handle but wasn't surprised to find it locked. To the right of the door was the kitchen window. Harper peered through. The door to the hallway was closed.

He used his elbow to break the glass panel closest to the handle, one blow that made a cracking sound followed by the tinkle of glass hitting the ground. Harper winced and waited to see if there was any reaction from inside the house. The lights stayed off and they didn't hear anything from inside. Harper gingerly removed the rest of the broken glass from the panel and placed it on the ground, then reached through and felt around. The key was in the lock and he turned it until it clicked. He turned the handle and pushed open the door.

They stepped inside and Harper gently closed the door. He led the way across the kitchen. A tap was dripping and the fridge motor was humming but other than that the house was silent.

O'Hara followed him through the kitchen and into the hallway, where they stopped again and listened for a minute or so before tiptoeing up the stairs.

They reached the top of the landing. There was a door to the left and as they listened they heard a soft snoring. Harper eased the door open. The sound of snoring got louder. There was enough light coming in through the window to make out two figures on the bed – a middle-aged man and a woman who was almost twice his size. It was the woman who was snoring, lying on her back with her mouth open. Her husband was curled up on his side with his back to her.

Harper closed the door and turned to face O'Hara. 'Let's see who else is here,' he whispered.

O'Hara nodded and gently opened the next door. It was a smaller bedroom with a single bed. A bearded Asian man in his late twenties was fast asleep. O'Hara pulled the door closed. There was another man, this one in his early twenties, asleep in a third bedroom. There were two single beds in the room and one was empty. The only other door led to a bathroom. Either the electoral roll was wrong or one of the occupants was missing.

Harper ran through his options. He really wanted to use the Beretta but even if he shot through a pillow or wrapped a towel around the gun, the noise would wake up everyone in the house. That meant they would all have to die. He wasn't against the idea in principle – if Masood was a hardline Islamic fundamentalist then his family would almost certainly be the same way. After what Masood's nephew had done, Harper didn't really care whether his family lived or died. He was more concerned about the logistics of the operation, and it would be a lot messier if there were four victims.

'Give me the Glock,' whispered Harper. O'Hara handed it over. Harper held out his hand for the silencer. O'Hara gave it to him and Harper screwed it into the barrel of the gun. Then he pulled out his Berretta and passed it to O'Hara. 'I'll slot Masood, and his wife if she wakes up,' whispered Harper. 'If either of those two are disturbed then do what you have to do.' He nodded at the Berretta. 'But if you fire it, we'll have to leg it PDQ.'

O'Hara nodded. 'Last resort,' he said.

Harper flashed him a tight smile and opened the door to Masood's bedroom. The woman was still snoring. He walked around the bed and stood close to Masood. He aimed the gun at the man's temple. One shot to the head would be enough. His finger tightened on the trigger. Purists never referred to silencers on guns; they were always suppressors. The reason was that no gun could ever be truly silenced. All a silencer did was reduce the amount of noise produced by a shot – usually by about thirty decibels or so. It could take the sound down from a loud crack to a fairly loud pop, but there would still be noise. The question was, would it be enough to wake the woman? If it was, he would have no choice other than to put a bullet in her head.

'Be lucky,' he whispered to her. He pulled the trigger and Masood's head exploded over the pillow.

The woman stopped snoring but her eyes stayed shut and her mouth was wide open. There was a soft gurgling sound at the back of her throat and then she began to snore again. Harper smiled and headed for the door. His iPod Touch vibrated in his pocket. It was a message from Button: *New intel on Masood's sons. All have ISIS connections. Treat as hostile.*

Harper sighed. She would probably moan about him only getting two of the sons, but then she should be grateful that he got the message in time. He pointed the Glock at the woman's head and pulled the trigger. She died mid-snore. He didn't know if the wife had ISIS connections but if her husband and her sons were jihadists then she had forfeited the right to a long and happy life.

He went back into the hallway. O'Hara was peering into the nearest bedroom. He turned and frowned at Harper. 'Two shots?' he mouthed.

'Change of plan,' whispered Harper. 'Watch the other one.' He pushed the door open, walked over to the bed and shot the sleeping man in the head, point blank. The man twitched once and then lay still as the pillow soaked up his blood. Harper turned and walked quickly back into the hallway.

O'Hara had the door to the last bedroom open and he pushed it open for Harper, who went over to the bed, casually aimed the Glock at the sleeping man's head and pulled the trigger. The skull imploded and the pillow glistened with blood.

'What the fuck's going on?' asked O'Hara as Harper rejoined him in the hall.

'They're all dirty,' said Harper. 'I'll keep the Glock. Okay?'

'Sure,' said O'Hara. 'I wasn't planning on taking it back with me anyway. You'll pay me, right?'

Harper grinned. 'Of course I'll pay you, you soft bastard.' He stopped as he heard a key slotting into the lock of the front door. The same thought hit them both instantaneously – the third son. O'Hara flattened himself against the wall. Harper did the same. They were both breathing shallowly. Harper smiled to himself. It looked as if Button was going to get what she wanted.

He listened as the man downstairs closed the door behind him. If he came upstairs, all well and good. It became more problematical if he decided to go to the kitchen because then he'd see the broken window. Harper's finger slid over the trigger and he moved his head slightly, giving his ears the best chance of picking up the slightest sound. The man coughed, then started walking to the kitchen. Harper moved quickly to the top of the stairs. He headed down on tiptoe, keeping close to the wall to minimise any squeaking of the boards. He reached the bottom of the stairs and turned left, raising the gun. The man disappeared into the kitchen and a second later the lights flicked on. Harper moved along the hallway, holding his breath. A loose floorboard creaked underfoot but it was muffled by the carpet. He took another step, and another. The man turned to look at the kitchen door and Harper knew he had seen the broken window. A frown flashed across the man's bearded face and then he stiffened. He turned to look at Harper but by then Harper was just four feet away from him and he shot him in the middle of the face. The nose disappeared and blood spurted down the man's beard as he slumped to his knees, then he pitched to the side. His head scraped against the fridge, leaving a smear of treacly blood as he fell to the floor.

O'Hara came up behind Harper. 'You're on fire tonight,' he said.

Harper shrugged. 'It's not as if they're shooting back, is it?' he said. He stepped over the body, taking care not to tread in the spreading pool of blood. He switched off the light and waited for O'Hara to join him at the door before opening it. They put their guns away and stepped into the yard. The alley was clear and they got back to the Toyota without being seen.

'Please tell me we're done for the night,' said O'Hara.

'Mate, we've done everything we've been asked to,' said Harper. 'I'll be pushing for a bonus after this.'

'So what's the plan now? Crash in a hotel?'

'To be honest, I'd be happier back in London,' said Harper. 'You can sleep while I drive.'

'But we'll stop for food on the way?'

Harper grinned. 'Breakfast is on me,' he said.

Chapter 35

Ten Years Ago, Dubai

Yokely, McNee and Leclerc climbed out of the SUV. All three had semi-automatics in underarm holsters and silencers in their pockets for when they needed them. McNee had a small nylon backpack containing the equipment he needed to blow up the boat.

Bardot wished them luck, then drove off. The sun had just gone down below the horizon and there was only a smear of red in the darkening sky.

'Right guys, game faces on,' said Yokely.

They were casually and expensively dressed, in brand name clothes they had bought from shops in the marina's upmarket mall. Yokely had a blazer, dark trousers and a Ralph Lauren shirt. Leclerc had chosen a black Hugo Boss suit with a grey shirt and McNee had shopped at Prada. The backpack alone had cost over a thousand dollars.

As they wandered through the marina they looked like three wealthy middle-aged men, out for a stroll and possibly a meal in one of the many world-class restaurants and cafés in the area. Dubai Marina was a two-mile stretch of the Persian Gulf shoreline, flanked by tower blocks containing some of the most expensive apartments in the city. The first phase had only just been completed and there were still dozens of buildings being constructed. There were several marinas where multi-million dollar yachts and cruisers were moored, linked by a canal that gave access to the Arabian Gulf. Many of the boats never left their moorings, though. They were for show, and for entertaining, rather than sailing.

They walked along the jetty. Yokely spotted the bodyguards immediately. Big men in dark suits wearing earpieces. They both looked over at the three men. One was about six feet from the rear of the boat. The other was further along, abreast of another boat.

They reached the first bodyguard. He was over six feet tall, his head shaved and his hands the size of small shovels.

'Wow, you're a big one,' said Leclerc. 'Isn't he a big one?' he asked McNee.

'Fucking huge,' said McNee. 'What do you think he is? Two hundred and fifty pounds?'

'Three hundred,' said Leclerc.

Yokely continued to walk. 'Come on, we'll be late!' he shouted.

'We just want to know how big this guy is,' said Leclerc.

'Leave him alone.'

The bodyguard stood with his feet planted shoulder width apart, his hands clasped together in front of his groin. 'I suggest you do as your friend says,' he growled. His eyes widened when he saw the silenced Glock pointing at his groin. 'I need you to walk quietly and calmly to the boat,' said Yokely. 'You do anything other than that and I will shoot you in the groin. Then in the head. Okay?'

The man raised his hands slowly.

'You can keep your hands down,' said Yokely. 'Just start walking.' He gestured with his gun and the man did as he was told. Yokely kept two paces from the bodyguard and his finger firmly on the trigger. The threat he had made had not been an empty one – any sign that the bodyguard wasn't following his instructions and Yokely would shoot.

They reached the stern. McNee had climbed on board and was aiming his gun at the first bodyguard. The bodyguard glowered at Yokely as he stepped on to the deck. Leclerc followed him. The stern of the boat had been fitted out for entertaining, with a U-shaped seating area and a table large enough to seat six. Beyond it was a ship's wheel and a hatch that led below decks.

Yokely kept his gun aimed at the second bodyguard's back as he climbed on to the boat. The two bodyguards looked at each other, unsure what they should do. Yokely didn't give them the chance to come to any conclusion. He shot them both in the heart. The smaller one dropped immediately but the bigger man stayed where he was as blood trickled down the front of his shirt. Yokely put a second bullet in the man's sternum. This time he fell with a dull thud.

Yokely looked around. The jetty was still deserted. He headed for the hatch as Leclerc and McNee dragged the two bodies to the table and rolled them underneath where they would be out of sight.

Yokely went down a set of wooden steps into a large entertainment area with modern low-backed sofas, a large-screen TV on one wall and a galley. Through the windows to his left he could see the marina's tower blocks. A door led to the bow, which was where the main cabins were. He waited for Leclerc to join him before easing open the door. It led to a wood-panelled corridor. There was a door to the side but it was ajar and the cabin was empty. They moved down the corridor on the balls of their feet. There was a second door. It was open. The cabin was large with a double bed and an overstuffed sofa.

The final door was closed. Yokely turned and nodded at Leclerc, then slowly turned the handle and eased the door open.

Benikhlef was naked, lying on his back while a blonde girl sat astride him. His hands were up on her breasts and as she moved the tattoo of a tiger writhed on her back as if it were alive. He was grunting in time with her movements and his feet twitched as if he was being electrocuted.

Yokely stepped into the cabin and tapped her on the back of her head with the silencer. She flinched and then twisted around. Benikhlef gasped and his erection swung from side to side as she jumped off the bed and flattened herself against the wall.

'Don't scream,' said Yokely. 'Whatever you do, don't scream!'

Her eyes were wide and panicking and she looked frantically at Yokely and then at Leclerc and then she opened her mouth to scream. Yokely pointed at her. 'If you make a sound, you die,' he said.

She closed her mouth and nodded fearfully.

Benikhlef sat up and pushed himself back against the headboard. 'If you want money, I have money in the safe,' he said. 'Just let me get it.' He held up his left arm and showed Yokely the diamond-studded gold watch on his wrist. 'This is a Patek Philippe,' he said. 'Take it.' He pulled off the watch with trembling hands and threw it at the end of the bed. 'It's yours.'

'We're not here for you or your watch,' said Yokely.

Benikhlef's erection had subsided and he groped for a black silk robe. He wrapped it around his shoulders. 'What do you want?'

'I just want to talk,' said Yokely. 'About a couple of Stinger missiles that passed through your hands.'

Benikhlef frowned. 'You are American? Who do you work for? The CIA? The FBI?' He smiled ingratiatingly but Yokely could see the fear in the man's eyes. 'I have friends in the CIA. They often ask me for information and I am always happy to help them.' He pointed at the door behind Yokely. 'Let us at least take this out of the bedroom. We can have a drink, like civilised men.' He smiled and nodded. 'I will tell you whatever you want to know,' he said. 'There is no need for violence.'

'I'm happy here,' said Yokely. 'Too much glass out there. And don't worry about your bodyguards, they've been taken care of. You see, here's what I don't understand; you say there's no need for violence, but you've made a fortune from it, haven't you?'

'I am just a middleman,' said Benikhlef. 'I buy and I sell and I make a profit.'

'The two Stingers you bought from Alex Kleintank. Who did you pass them on to?'

Benikhlef swallowed nervously. 'You have spoken to Alex?'

'We had a conversation, yes.'

Benikhlef swallowed again. 'And he told you he sold me two

Stingers?' He shrugged, trying to appear casual, but he was clearly worried. 'Of course I will not deny it. He sold, I bought. It was a transaction. I buy and sell to Alex many times a year.'

'Because you are both middlemen, making an honest buck?'

Benikhlef could hear the sarcasm in Yokely's voice so he didn't answer.

'You sold that Stinger to terrorists and they shot down a plane with more than three hundred men, women and children on board,' said Yokely.

Benikhlef's jaw dropped. He shook his head. 'No,' he said. 'That is not possible.'

'Who was the buyer?'

'His name was Hakeem. He said he was going to take them to Iraq, I swear.'

'What was his full name?'

'I don't know. He was introduced to me as Hakeem. He is a Palestinian.'

'Describe him.'

Benikhlef ran a hand over his face, wiping away the sweat. 'He was fifty, maybe a bit younger. Had a long beard, straggly. It was streaked with grey. He had a string of amber beads that he was always playing with.'

'Misbaha?'

Benikhlef nodded. 'Yes, Misbaha.'

The Misbaha were Muslim prayer beads, usually thirty-three or ninety-nine on a string used by devout Muslims to keep track of their prayers.

'And where did he take delivery?'

Benikhlef tried to swallow but his mouth had gone so dry that he almost gagged. 'Serbia,' he said.

'So you bought them from Kleintank in Sarajevo and sold them to Hakeem in Serbia?'

Benikhlef nodded. 'Yes.'

'And what about shipping? To Iraq?'

'Hakeem said he would take care of shipping. I just sold him the missiles.'

Yokely's smile tightened. 'You're lying, Jamahl. Please don't insult my intelligence again.'

'I am telling you the truth.'

Yokely pointed his gun at the woman and shot her twice in the chest. She slumped against the wall of the cabin, shuddered and slid down the wall like a marionette whose strings had been cut.

Benikhlef gasped and covered his mouth with his hands. 'Why did you—?'

'You don't seem to think I am serious, Jamahl. I thought killing your bodyguards would do the trick but clearly not. You either tell me everything you know or I will kill you and then I will go upstairs to your lovely penthouse home and kill every member of your family. I will do that with a smile on my face, Jamahl, because it will go some way to redressing the balance of all the lives your missile took.'

Benikhlef was trembling now, staring at the body of the woman in horror.

'Who shipped the missiles?'

'I did. Hakeem came here, to Dubai. He explained what he wanted and I gave him the price.'

'He paid cash?'

Benikhlef nodded again.

'What is this Hakeem's full name?'

'I don't know. I just know him as Hakeem.'

'And how did he know to deal with you?'

'A friend introduced us.' Benikhlef was still staring at the body, his voice a dull monotone. All the fight had gone out of him, as if he knew what was coming and had accepted it.

'Did you meet a man called Hamid bin Faisal?'

Benikhlef shook his head.

Yokely took out a photograph of bin Faisal and showed it to Benikhlef. Benikhlef looked at it and shook his head again.

Yokely put the picture away. 'This mutual friend. Who is he?'

'Abdul Aziz Al Amin.'

'Where is he from?'

'He is a Saudi. But he lives here, in Dubai.'

'He introduced you to this Hakeem?'

Benikhlef nodded. 'Yes. Abdul is a long-standing friend to al-Qaeda, he has been for many years. He helps them with funding.'

'Where does Abdul live?'

'He has a villa on the Palm Jumeirah.'

'Nice,' said Yokely. The Palm Jumeirah was an artificial archipelago that had been built by dredging sand from the floor of the Persian Gulf and spraying it to form land in the shape of a palm tree, producing enough new land to house sixty-five thousand people in some of Dubai's most luxurious homes. There were dozens of top hotels and restaurants on the Palm and it had become one of Dubai's main tourist attractions.

'It is Abdul that you want,' said Benikhlef. 'He is al-Qaeda's man, he hates America and everything it stands for. I like America. Last year I took my grandchildren to Disneyworld. You know Disneyworld? In Florida.'

'Yes, I know Disneyworld,' said Yokely. He fired once, shooting Benikhlef in the dead centre of the chest. Benikhlef's eyes went blank almost immediately and his head slumped.

Yokely unscrewed the silencer and slid the Glock back into his holster. He went back up on deck, where McNee was already pulling equipment from his backpack. Wiring. A timer. A can of lighter fluid.

'Do you need help with the fire?' Yokely asked.

'No, I'm good,' he said.

'Peter and I will get started on dinner,' he said.

Leclerc drove Yokely to an Italian restaurant overlooking the marina. Yokely asked for a table by the window and the greeter – a beautiful Indian girl with waist-length glossy black hair and a beaming smile – said that wouldn't be a problem. They followed her gently swaying hips across the room to a table that was perfect. Yokely thanked her and slipped her a twenty-dollar bill. It wasn't the local currency but in Yokely's experience dollar tips were appreciated the world over. He took out his throwaway mobile and called Karl Traynor.

'Still nothing on Benikhlef,' said Traynor.

'I have another couple of names for you,' said Yokely. 'The first one is a Saudi but he spends a lot of time here in Dubai. Abdul Aziz Al Amin. The other is also a Saudi but he seems to live in Dubai. Mohammed Al-Hashim. He has a nephew, Hamid bin Faisal, but he's dead.'

'I'll get back to you as soon I have anything.'

Yokely waved over a waiter and ordered a bottle of Nuits-Saint-Georges. They were halfway through the bottle when McNee arrived. He sat down as Yokely poured wine into his glass.

'All good?' asked Yokely.

'Oh yes,' said McNee.

They all clinked glasses.

'So what's the plan?' asked McNee. 'Are we taking care of this Abdul Aziz Al Amin?'

'At the moment he's top of my list,' said Yokely. 'And the uncle is a close second. We'll get Al Amin sorted tomorrow morning. Then Michael can drive us to Abu Dhabi and we'll fly out of there.' He clinked his glass against theirs. 'We have a plan, gentlemen.'

As they ordered their food from a waiter, there was a dull thud down in the marina, followed by a yellowish ball of flame that enveloped Benikhlef's yacht. Within seconds the whole boat was aflame and the fire spread quickly to the boats on either side

There were people on the boat to the starboard side of Benikhlef's and they frantically jumped off and ran along the jetty. People were getting off boats all around the marina and staring at the fire, many of them videoing it on their smartphones.

The boat to the port side of Benikhlef's yacht was ablaze now but there didn't seem to be anyone aboard. The jetty had now caught fire and flames were spreading quickly.

'I think you might have overdone it, Gerry,' said Yokely.

McNee shrugged. 'Guys, it's not an exact science.'

'Clearly not,' said Yokely. 'Let's just hope they're all insured.'

Chapter 36

Charlotte Button woke up to the sound of her mobile phone ringing. She groped for it and sat up, blinking her eyes until she could focus on the screen. It was just after six in the morning and Patsy Ellis was calling.

'Yes, Patsy.'

'Sorry about the early call, but I have some information for you,' said Ellis.

Button ran a hand through her hair. 'No problem, I was planning on an early start anyway.'

'I just wanted to fill you in on a development,' said Ellis. 'CCTV has thrown up a member of the stadium staff who appears to have supplied Naveed with his suicide vest. His name is Usman Yussuf. He works in the accounts department, apparently.'

'Send me the details and I'll pass them on to my people,' said Button.

'Unfortunately there's a problem. Yussuf is a complete cleanskin and we don't have his address on any of the databases. The only people who do have an address for him are the stadium's human resources department and they're not in the office yet.'

'Are the police aware of him?'

'Unfortunately yes, so I don't see there's any way you'll be able to get to him first. Really I'm just calling to keep you in the loop. There is a chance he's already gone into hiding or left the country, but if he hasn't I expect him to be picked up early this morning. As soon as I have the details, I'll send them to you. I'll also be looking at Yussuf's family and friends to see how that pans out. How are things progressing?'

'Quickly, and efficiently,' said Button. 'Acton was interrogated and dealt with last night. Bolton and Birmingham were taken care of in the early hours. I passed on the information about Masood's sons and they were all in the house, so they were done in one fell swoop. We need to talk about muddying the waters because it's going to be a huge media story.'

'How about lunch?'

'Lunch?'

'That meal between breakfast and dinner. I'm sure you've heard of it.'

'I assumed you'd be in the office all day. The threat level is still at critical, isn't it?'

'Yes, it's still critical, but we all have to eat,' said Ellis.

'Then lunch it is,' said Button.

Chapter 37

Present Day, London

Shepherd walked into the café and looked around. It was just after seven-thirty and the clientele was a mixture of night workers grabbing a meal on the way home and early starters tucking into breakfast. Don Margrave was at a corner table with a full fry-up in front of him – eggs, bacon, sausage, mushrooms and beans. There were two slices of toast on the side and he was already halfway through a mug of tea. He didn't get up but put down his knife and shook hands with Shepherd. 'Wasn't sure if you were going to be eating,' he said by way of apology.

'No problem. I can't stay long – we're all flat out at the moment, obviously.'

He sat down and a waitress came over. He ordered tea and a bacon roll. 'I tell you what, throw a sausage and an egg on it,' he said.

'Breakfast roll it is,' she said and went over to the hatch to relay the order to the cook.

'So you're still with the Super-Recognisers?' asked Margrave.

Shepherd nodded. 'Exiled to Siberia, but to be fair we're leading the fight on the stadium thing. We ID'd the van driver who took him to the stadium and the employee who got the vest in for the bomber.'

'Nice one.'

'Yeah, there's no doubt the system works. It's just . . .' He shrugged.

'It's as boring as fuck?'

Shepherd laughed. 'Yeah, it's fighting crime through a

computer terminal and while it gets results, it's not what I signed up for.'

'Kicking down doors and handcuffing bad guys loses its appeal after a while,' said Margrave. He took a bite out of a slice of toast and washed it down with a gulp of tea. Margrave was a high-flyer with the Met's Counter Terrorism Command, also known as SO15. Margrave was in his late twenties but had already been assigned a senior role with the National Counter Terrorism Policing Network, under which all the police forces in the UK shared intel in the fight against terrorism. The NCTPN worked with the Home Office and MI5 and liaised with intelligence and criminal justice agencies around the world. Shepherd had met Margrave shortly after he had been assigned to NCTPN and had kept in close touch with him. He was a good no-nonsense copper who seemed to be more concerned about getting the job done than climbing the slippery promotion pole.

'I hear you. But I wasn't built for sitting at a desk.'

'I did notice you'd put on some weight since the last time I saw you.'

Shepherd laughed. 'Yeah. Katra has moved down to London to take care of me while I'm based here, and she is one hell of a cook. That plus the fact I'm sitting at a terminal all day means I'm a few pounds heavier.' He patted his stomach. 'You're right. I'm going to start exercising more.' The waitress brought over his roll and a cup of tea. Shepherd grinned. 'I'll start tomorrow.' He poured a splash of ketchup on his egg, bacon and sausage and took a bite.

'So what do you need?' asked Margrave, attacking his meal again. 'I'm assuming this isn't social.'

Shepherd took a swig of his tea. 'I just want to pick your brains about the way the stadium investigation is progressing,' he said. 'All the intel from my group is flowing one way and there's not much getting out to the media. But I wanted to give you the nod about something we turned up last night. We know how Naveed got his explosive vest. One of the stadium employees, a Usman Yussuf, took it in and hid it in a storage room. Then he left his keycard in a toilet. Naveed collected the keycard, got the vest, and bang!'

Margrave frowned. 'That's news to me.'

'We only got the intel a few hours ago. The problem is we have his name and we know what he does at the stadium, but someone screwed up and we don't have an address. He's not on the electoral roll or the PNC and he doesn't have a driver's licence. Until we can access the human resources database at the stadium we don't have an address.'

'Our guys know this?'

'Sure, the Met gets all the intel we produce, and I liaise with my bosses. But even MI5 databases don't show him.'

'A complete cleanskin?'

Shepherd nodded. 'Probably by design. My boss has informed Border Force but you know how useless they are so there's a good chance he's already out of the country. But if he has stayed put obviously your guys need to go in first thing.'

'I'll make sure that happens,' said Margrave, reaching for another slice of toast.

Shepherd took a bite of his roll and a gulp of tea before continuing. 'So what's happening about the driver of the van that took Naveed to the stadium. Khuram Zaghba. Lives in Acton?'

'Our guys went around but there's no answer, so they assume he's not there.'

'They didn't kick the door down?'

'They need a warrant for that.'

'Seriously?'

'He's just a van driver, he's not wanted, not believed to be armed. A couple of detectives went around and knocked on his door.'

'If it was me I'd have sent an armed response unit in.'

'In a predominantly Muslim area? Recipe for disaster, that would be.'

'Don, we have him on video delivering a suicide bomber to his target. If that doesn't merit an armed response then I don't know what does.'

'Decisions like that are taken above my pay grade,' said Margrave. 'But I'm told that a warrant will be obtained later today and they'll have a locksmith with them this time.'

'Better late than never,' said Shepherd. 'Though if he was in there when the detectives were knocking he's probably done a runner by now.' He took another bite of his roll. 'How's the investigation going with regard to Naveed?'

'Total cleanskin, as you probably know, but really that's because he slipped through the cracks like so many of these so-called refugees we allowed in. You wonder about the sanity of those in charge, don't you? A guy turns up on our doorstep and claims to be a sixteen-year-old unaccompanied minor. We just welcome him in and put him with a foster family without running any of the most basic checks. I mean, does no one think about giving these guys a medical? Any dentist worth his salt would be able to give you the true age within a year or two. We've had so-called sixteen-year-olds being put into schools where they are a foot taller than their classmates and we've had rapes and assaults by the score, most of them hushed up. It's as if there was a bloody conspiracy, run from the top. We estimate there are hundreds of guys like Naveed scattered around the country. Add that to all the home-grown jihadists we've got coming back and it's a bloody nightmare. We've done away with almost all border checks on people leaving the country, and British passport holders can now swipe themselves through an automatic gate to get back in without even talking to Border Force. I mean, how stupid is that? If a Brit comes back from six months in Syria or Iraq or Pakistan then you'd think that someone would take them to one side and ask them what the fuck they've been doing. And if they don't have a reasonable explanation then at the very least put an electronic tag on them for a year or two.'

Shepherd chuckled. 'I'm sure the human rights brigade would have something to say about that.'

'Fuck them, you and I both know what it's like in the real world, Spider,' said Margrave. 'Most of the time we're playing catch-up with these guys. Naveed's story will come out eventually and will show that he was an ISIS fighter who lied about his age to get into the UK solely for the purpose of committing a terrorist act. But will those who let him into the country be held responsible? Of course they won't. And the liberal media will bleat about it not being an Islamic problem, that the percentage of jihadists is tiny compared with the overall Muslim population, but that's not the bloody point, is it? The point is that one nutter like Naveed can kill more than thirty innocents and injure more than a hundred at a bloody football match and for what? They want Britain to become an Islamic state? Well that's never going to happen, is it? And I will personally kill anyone who tries to stop me eating bacon.'

He continued to tuck into his breakfast. His emotional outburst was clearly having no effect on his appetite.

'Anything on his phone records?' asked Shepherd. 'Someone must have been running him.'

'I haven't seen them. Can't you access the records through Five?'

'Yeah, but like I said I'm out of the loop.'

'I'll have a look and let you know.'

'Did he have a computer at home?'

Margrave shook his head. 'No. But he had a smartphone. It looks as if he had it on him when he detonated.'

'I'm looking at all the Internet cafés within walking distance, checking CCTV footage to see if Naveed was using them. You might want to get the computers checked at school. He must have been getting his instructions from somewhere. Any thoughts on the vest? It's unlikely that Yussuf would have put it together.'

'That's down to the forensics boys and whatever they can find at the scene. Could take weeks.' He popped the final piece of toast into his mouth and swallowed. His plate was clean and he sat back and burped. He grinned. 'Better out than in.'

'The key to this investigation is to track down Naveed's handler,' said Shepherd.

'He might not even be in the country,' said Margrave. 'If they communicate by email or text, he could be anywhere.'

'What mosque did Naveed go to, do we know?'

'Argyle Road was his regular one, but according to his foster parents he visited several in the area. In the early days they dropped him off and picked him up but over the last few months he insisted on going alone. Said he didn't want to be driven to his place of worship by non-believers.'

'Nice. Where are the foster parents?'

'Helping us with our inquiries, as they say. We moved them out of the house while the forensics boys do their thing, but they're happy to cooperate. They're livid, actually. They say that the boy should never have been sent to them, that they told social services several times that he wasn't what he claimed to be and the husband had actually been thinking of calling the anti-terrorist hotline. The school had also complained about him as he had been bothering some of the girls, but that problem was solved when he just stopped going.'

Shepherd shook his head in annoyance. There had clearly been a plethora of red flags about Naveed and if anyone had taken it upon themselves to have acted, the terrorist incident at the stadium could have been nipped in the bud.

Margrave looked at his watch. 'Okay, I've got to dash. Good to see you again, Spider. I hope you get back on active duty sooner rather than later.'

'You and me both,' said Shepherd. He still had half his breakfast roll to finish. 'I'll get the bill.'

'You're a prince among men,' said Margrave. He stood up and picked up his raincoat from the back of his chair. 'If anything comes up, I'll call you.'

'Don't forget Yussuf.'

Margrave tapped the side of his head with his finger. 'I might not have your eidetic memory but I can remember one simple name,' he said. 'I'm on it.'

Shepherd picked up the remains of his roll as the detective left the café. He hated being on the outside of an investigation and not being able to see the big picture. If it wasn't for picking Don Margrave's brains he wouldn't have a clue how the operation was progressing. He just hoped that Patsy Ellis would follow through on her promise to move him back to a more active role within MI5, because if she didn't he would probably have no choice other than to leave and find employment elsewhere. That wasn't a prospect he was looking forward to. If he left MI5 under a cloud his options would be restricted and that would mean having to work in the private sector. He shuddered. That wasn't something that appealed at all. He enjoyed working for the forces of good, even though more often than not he felt rules and regulations were constantly holding him back. At least he knew he had right on his side and that the targets he went up against deserved to be put behind bars. Things in the private sector were considerably less cut and dried and morality often took second place to whoever was picking up the bill. He put down the remains of his breakfast roll. He'd lost his appetite.

Chapter 38

Ten Years Ago, Dubai

The ringing of Yokely's cell phone woke him from a dreamless sleep. He groped for the phone. The number was withheld but that was true of most of the calls he received, so he pressed the green button to take the call. It was Karl Traynor from the Financial Crimes Enforcement Network. 'What time is it there?' asked Traynor.

'Early,' said Yokely, sitting up and squinting at the digital clock on the bedside table. 'Just after six.'

'Ah well, the early worm catches the bird, as they say.'

'That makes no sense at all,' said Yokely. 'Okay, so what do you have for me?'

'I struck gold with one of the names you gave me. Abdul Aziz Al Amin. He's covered his tracks well and I probably couldn't prove to a court what he did, but I've no doubt he's dirty. None of the option buys came through his bank accounts or companies of his, but there are just too many links for it to be coincidental. For instance, there was a flurry of purchases through a broker based out in the Cayman Islands. The brokerage is really nothing more than a plaque on a wall but Al Amin has half a dozen of his companies in the same building. There were more purchases from a bank in Jersey and Al Amin has accounts at the same branch. And there's money moving out of his accounts that matches the value almost to the dollar of the price of several of the sell options. He's been very clever at covering tracks, but I think I'm on to him.'

'That's great, Karl. Thanks. What about the other two? Bin Faisal and Al-Hashim?'

'No shorting that I can see, and they're not on any financial watch lists. They're clean.'

Yokely snorted. 'They might not have shorted the shares, but trust me, neither of them are clean,' he said. 'Okay, as always I owe you, Karl. And we never spoke, obviously.'

'Obviously,' said Traynor.

He ended the call and Yokely shaved, showered and changed into clean chinos and a polo shirt, then he phoned Peter Leclerc.

'Where do we stand, Peter?' he asked.

'The kids have left for school. He's still in the house with his wife.'

'Bodyguards?'

'No. It's all low-key.'

'Do we have any idea what time he leaves?'

'No, but his car is here so I'm assuming he drives himself in. My suggestion would be that Michael and I go in now and secure the house. But that means the wife will be there.'

'I'd be happier if the wife wasn't there, obviously.'

'She doesn't have a job. But she's the wife of a wealthy man, so she probably shops a lot and lunches with friends.'

'Okay, send Michael to pick me up when you're ready.'

Yokely sat in the lobby reading a copy of *Gulf News* until Bardot arrived outside the hotel in a white BMW SUV. Bardot was wearing his Oakley sunglasses and Yokely could see his own reflection in the dark lenses.

'How did it go?' Yokely asked as Bardot drove away from the hotel.

'Smooth as silk,' said Bardot. 'The wife left about an hour ago. They have two cars, a Mercedes and a Porsche. She took the Porsche. She was all dolled up so we figure she's off to see friends. Or a lover. Either way she'll be a while.'

The drive to the Palm Jumeirah took less than ten minutes. The artificial archipelago might well have looked like a spreading palm tree from space – or even a high-flying plane – but at ground level all Yokely could see was sweeping roads and villas that seemed to have been pushed together to maximise the use of land. The entire area was a building site and most of the construction workers labouring under the fierce Middle Eastern sun seemed to be Indian or Bangladeshi. The layout of the area meant that every home had water access, but there were only a few yachts or boats to be seen and most of the villas that had been finished didn't appear to be occupied.

An eight-lane motorway formed the trunk of the Palm, with mile-long roads left and right forming the fronds. Almost all the traffic on the roads was construction-related. There were only a few palm trees in evidence but as they drove by one Yokely realised it was fake, a well-disguised cell-phone tower.

'When will this be finished?' Yokely asked.

'A year or two,' said Bardot. 'There's a building boom across the Emirates at the moment. They say that a quarter of the world's cranes are currently in Dubai. It's a work in progress. But once the building work is done they'll start on the landscaping. It's becoming very popular. They were selling villas off-plan for a million bucks and now they're changing hands for four million and more.'

'And no terrorism?'

Bardot chuckled. 'Yeah, funny that. The place is full of Westerners, you've got five-star hotels selling booze by the bucketful, and you've got bars full of hookers. You'd have thought al-Qaeda might have taken offence.'

'Pay-offs?'

'On a massive scale, I'd say, but no one will admit to it, obviously. Plus they allow the al-Qaeda people to operate here without any hassle and their money is allowed to go through the banks with no restrictions. I can't see how long it'll continue, though. They hate Western values and Western habits and the Emirates are home to them in spades.' He nodded at a gleaming white house ahead of them. 'This is Al Amin's.'

It was two storeys with a flat roof and a turret that looked like a clock tower, with a double garage on the left. The garden was bare and the villas on either side were still being constructed, though there were no building workers in evidence. There was a black SUV parked in front of the garage and Bardot pulled up next to it. They climbed out of the BMW and the heat hit Yokely immediately. He shaded his eyes against the sun with his hand as they walked to the front door. Bardot knocked and Leclerc opened it.

They stepped into a hallway. The air con was full on and it was blisteringly cold. They walked across a white marble floor under a massive circular chandelier to another room, this one with a black slate floor. Two low-slung sofas had been pushed against the wall and Al Amin had been tied to a chair in the middle of the room. McNee was standing behind him, a Glock in an underarm holster.

Al Amin was wearing a thawb with blue and yellow vertical stripes. He was fat, almost obese, and sweating profusely despite the air conditioning. He was bald and had a fleshy neck and puffy bags under his eyes. Duct tape had been used to tie the man to the chair, binding his wrists and his ankles.

'You are in charge?' he asked Yokely.

Yokely nodded. 'I am.'

'If this is a kidnapping, just tell me how much you want and I will get the money brought to you from the bank.'

'That's very generous of you, but this isn't about money.'

'What then?'

'Information.'

'And for that you needed to tie me to a chair? Why did you not just ask me, like a man?'

'Because the information I want is the sort you will not want to give me. This way you know that I am serious, and that there will be repercussions if you do not tell me what I want to know.'

Al Amin stared at Yokely for several seconds. Then he nodded. 'You are American?'

'Yes.'

'CIA? NSA? FBI? DEA?'

'You don't need to know who sent us,' said Yokely. 'That's not important. What is important is that you answer my questions and that you answer them quickly, because if your wife or children return while we are here . . .' He shrugged. 'Let's just say it would be better if they didn't.'

'You are threatening my wife and children?'

'I am threatening you, Abdul Aziz. Your family would be collateral damage.' He looked around, and walked over to one of the sofas. He sat down. 'Do you mind if I smoke?'

'What?'

Yokely took his pack of cigars out. 'Can I smoke?'

Al Amin frowned. 'Yes. Of course. How could I stop you?'

'It's only polite to ask,' said Yokely. He took out a small cigar, slipped it between his lips and lit it with his Zippo. He inhaled and blew smoke before speaking. 'Al Amin means truthful, doesn't it?' he said. 'So try to live up to your name.'

'Or what? You will kill me?'

'You know an arms dealer by the name of Jamahl Benikhlef?'

'Yes, I know him,' said Al Amin grimly. 'And I know that you killed him. Yesterday you killed Jamahl. You blew up his boat, didn't you?' He snarled at Yokely. 'I knew a boat would not go up in flames like that.'

'Benikhlef bought some Stinger missiles that were used to shoot down a passenger jet in New York. He bought them from a dealer in Amsterdam to sell on to a British jihadist.'

Al Amin shook his head. 'No, no, that is not true,' he said. He continued to deny everything while Yokely smoked his cigar. Eventually Al Amin fell silent.

Yokely looked at him and smiled coldly. 'If you lie to me again, Abdul, I will kill your wife and I will kill your children and I will kill your brothers and I will kill their children.'

'What sort of man are you?' spat Al Amin.

'An angry man,' said Yokely. 'A vengeful man. The missile you helped source was used to shoot down a plane with more than three hundred innocent civilians on board.'

'There are no innocents. Not in the war against the Crusaders who kill our people around the world.'

'I understand that view,' said Yokely. 'But you realise that I can apply the same logic to your wife and your children and your brothers and their children. There are no innocents, they share your blame.'

'You would kill children?'

'I have done in the past, Abdul, and I have no doubt I will do so again. The man you introduced to Jamahl. Who was he?'

Al Amin glared malevolently at Yokely, then the fight went out of him. 'Hakeem Khaled,' he said.

'From?'

'He is a Palestinian but he has a British passport.' Al Amin smiled. 'He hates the British as much as he hates the Americans, but they gave him asylum and a passport.'

'Describe him.'

'Fifty years old, maybe. He has a long beard that is going grey. He's a big man, a strong man.'

'And how do you know him?'

'I have known him for many years.'

'That's not an answer.'

Al Amin closed his eyes and shook his head. 'I have funded him in the past. When he needed it, I would arrange it.'

'You funded his terrorist activities?'

'You say terrorist, I say freedom fighter. He fought back against the Israeli oppressors, how could a good Muslim not assist him?'

'What sort of terrorist activities?'

'He sent suicide bombers into Tel Aviv. Many, many times. Until the Israelis discovered who he was. They tried to kill him so he fled to France, and then to London.'

'And you knew he was planning to shoot down a plane?'

'He didn't tell me what he wanted the missiles for.'

Yokely sighed. 'I don't believe you.'

'It's true. He didn't tell me and I didn't ask.'

'The missiles were shipped to the United States, that must have been a clue.'

Al Amin shook his head. 'I didn't know where they were going or what he planned to do with them.'

Yokely nodded slowly. 'So you're just another middleman, are you. A facilitator. Nothing that happened is your fault?'

'Hakeem wanted to purchase the missiles. I helped him. I knew I was helping the cause, and that is my duty as a good Muslim. But you cannot blame me for what happened.'

'And again, you didn't know what he was planning to do?'

'I swear by the Koran and all that is Holy.'

Yokely stared at Al Amin for several seconds. 'You see, I know you're lying. Not only did you know that he was planning to shoot down a plane, you set out to profit from it. You sold airline stocks short so that when the shares fell you would make millions.'

Al Amin's mouth opened in shock and he began to stammer but Yokely cut him short with a wave of the gun. 'You lied to me,' said Yokely. 'You know what that means.'

'I'm sorry, I'm sorry,' said the man. 'Please, I implore you in the name of Allah, spare my family. It is not right that they should suffer because of my actions.'

'You lied to me,' said Yokely.

'I'm sorry!' he wailed. 'Shoot me, kill me, take my life, but please do not harm my family. I beg you.'

'What about the families who died on that plane? All those women and children? Did you care about them?'

Al Amin bowed his head and closed his eyes as he sobbed.

'Look at me, Abdul.' When the man didn't react, Yokely repeated his command, louder this time.

Al Amin raised his head and opened his tear-filled eyes. 'Please, I beg you . . .' he whimpered.

'Hush,' said Yokely. 'Be a man. Understand? It is time for you to be a man and not cry like a little girl.'

Al Amin nodded.

'If you lie to me again we will wait here until your children return from school and I will kill them in front of you. And I will do the same with your wife.'

'Please, no . . .'

'Do you understand? Do you understand what will happen if you lie to me again?'

Al Amin nodded again.

'Do you have a phone number for Khaled?'

'He won't use phones. He says the authorities listen in.'

'So how do you contact him?'

'By email. But we never send the emails; he says that the NSA and GCHQ read all emails.'

'So you share an account and leave messages in the draft folder?'

Al Amin nodded.

'I need you to tell me the email address and the password.'

Al Amin told him the Gmail account name and the password to get access to it.

'Does Khaled come to Dubai often?'

'Not often.'

'When he travels, he uses his British passport?'

'Yes.'

'And what about the UK. Where does he live?'

'London. But I don't have an address.'

'Where could I find him?'

'He is often at Finsbury Park Mosque. The famous one.'

Yokely nodded. The US intelligence services often described the London mosque as an al-Qaeda guesthouse in London, a hotbed of Islamic radicalism. It was where Abu Hamza – the hook-handed preacher of hate – had spewed his anti-West hatred before the Brits had put him in a high-security prison for inciting violence and racial hatred.

'Is he an imam?'

'No, but he does teach there.'

'Jihadism?'

'He helps those young men who want to embrace jihad, yes. It is his calling.'

'That and killing innocent civilians. That's his calling.' Yokely felt his heart race and he took a deep breath to calm himself.

Al Amin saw the tension on Yokely's face. 'You will spare my family?' he asked.

Yokely considered the question for several seconds and he felt the anger within him slowly subside. 'Yes.'

'You swear?'

Yokely nodded slowly. 'I swear. Unless I discover that you have lied to me, in which case I will come back and kill them all.'

'I have not lied to you,' said Al Amin.

'Then we're good,' said Yokely. He nodded at Leclerc. 'Let's do it,' he said.

Al Amin began to struggle but the bonds held tight. Leclerc took a ball gag from his pocket, popped the ball into Al Amin's mouth and fastened the strap behind his neck. Al Amin tried to talk but the ball made it impossible. Leclerc went over to his backpack and took out a plastic case. He popped it open and took out a large hypodermic filled with a clear liquid. Al Amin's struggling intensified, and his head thrashed from side to side as Leclerc walked over to him.

Leclerc knelt down. Al Amin's ankles were taped to the chair so it was relatively easy to push the needle into a vein between Al Amin's big toe and the toe next to it. He pressed the plunger slowly and injected all 50cc of potassium chloride solution into the man's foot. Al Amin's eyes were wide and fearful and the veins in his temples were throbbing.

Leclerc stood up and put the hypodermic back in the case. Yokely walked over and stood next to Leclerc. States in the USA that killed their murderers with lethal injection invariably used a combination of substances but it was usually a high dose of potassium chloride that did the job. Too much potassium in the blood causes hyperkalemia, which leads to heart arrhythmia and then a full-on heart attack or cardiac arrest. It was possible to detect higher than normal potassium levels in the body of the deceased shortly after death but you had to go looking for it. Al Amin was overweight and out of condition and a prime candidate for heart failure so Yokely doubted anyone would see anything sinister about the death.

Al Amin stopped struggling. His chest was heaving and there was panic in his eyes. His eyes began to flutter and his legs strained at the tape holding them to the chair, and then his eyes went blank and he went still.

Yokely patted Leclerc on the shoulder. 'Good job, Peter,' he said.

Leclerc removed the gag and used a knife to slice through the duct tape. 'What you said about the kids. Was that the truth?'

Yokely smiled thinly. 'What do you think?'

'I'm not sure. I don't think I could.'

'I think you could, Peter, under the right circumstances.'

'Maybe so.' He sighed. 'So you're not going to answer my question?'

'Do you want me to?'

Leclerc tilted his head on one side. 'I guess not.'

Yokely slid his gun into its holster. 'I'll do whatever I have to do to protect my country,' he said. 'Let's leave it at that.'

He took out his cell phone and called David Dalton but the call went straight through to voicemail. Yokely realised it was the early hours in the UK and Dalton was probably asleep. He left a message. 'I need you to check out a name with your Brit contacts,' he said. 'Hakeem Khaled. Palestinian with a British passport. Lives in London, attends the Finsbury Park Mosque.' He ended the call, put the phone away and went over to help Leclerc.

Once they had arranged Al Amin's body so that it looked as if he had died from natural causes, they headed back to the hotel. Yokely ordered a coffee and a steak sandwich and while he was waiting for it to arrive he sat down at his desk and opened the laptop he'd taken from Hamid bin Faisal's house. He logged on to the email account that Al Amin had given him. There was one email in the draft folder, Saladin talking to Al Amin. It was in English. There was a long quote from the Koran:

And slay them wherever ye catch them, and turn them out from where they have turned you out; for tumult and oppression are worse than slaughter; but fight them not at the Sacred Mosque, unless they first fight you there; but if they fight you, slay them. Such is the reward of those who suppress faith.

Yokely knew that the next verse – which Saladin had omitted – portrayed Islam in a more peaceful light: *But if they cease, Allah is Oft-forgiving, Most Merciful.*

The message afterwards was short and to the point. 'The goods have arrived, *Allahu Akbar*. You will get your reward in heaven, my friend.'

Yokely was sure there would have been more correspondence between Khaled and Al Amin but the most secure method was to delete them after they had been read. He phoned Sam Hepburn, gave him the email details and asked him to see what he could come up with.

As he was finishing the call, Yokely's sandwich and coffee arrived. He ate the sandwich as he watched CNN. There were still no details on what had happened to the plane. Various experts spoke about engine failure and pilot error and freak weather and bird strikes. A security expert raised the possibility of a bomb having been on board the plane and explained how luggage – in the hold and in the cabin – was checked. A former FBI agent spoke at length about the shoe bomber, a Brit called Richard Reid who had attempted to detonate explosives packed into his shoes on a flight from Paris to Miami a few days before Christmas 2001. Reid had failed and was serving three life sentences plus a hundred and ten years at ADX Florence, a supermax security prison in Colorado. Security checks had been tightened since then but the expert warned that Islamic terrorists were constantly looking at new ways of downing passenger jets. No one mentioned the possibility of a missile strike, but Yokely knew that it would only be a matter of time before the truth came out.

Al-Qaeda had yet to claim responsibility for the attack. There was probably confusion within the terrorist organisation. Khaled had seen his colleagues being confronted by the security guard so he must have assumed that they were captured. The fact that there had been no announcement of any arrests would have made no sense to the terrorists, though they might assume that the captured jihadists were cooperating with the authorities. Yokely figured that Khaled and anyone else involved in the planning of the attack would be lying low or would have fled the country already. Khaled had bolted without the video camera, which meant al-Qaeda had no proof to back up any claims it made, but Yokely doubted they would wait much longer before taking the credit.

It took the NSA analyst less than an hour to restore the emails. When Yokely went back into the account the email in the draft folder was much longer, with more than twenty messages spread over a three-month period. Many of the messages contained quotes from the Koran, and again Saladin chose his words carefully. Jamahl Benikhlef was never referred to by name, only as 'our friend', but it was clear who they were talking about. Al Amin had made the introduction and Khaled had flown to Dubai twice for meetings with him.

The fact that Saladin wanted to purchase missiles also wasn't mentioned, though several times he referred to 'arrows'. It was the 'arrows' that Saladin was thanking Al Amin for in the last message.

Yokely sat back and sighed. Al Amin had introduced Khaled to Jamahl Benikhlef. Benikhlef had bought the missile from Alex Kleintank in Sarajevo and arranged to have it shipped to the US. And they had done it without once coming to the attention of the CIA or MI5 or Mossad or any of the West's intelligence services. Khaled was clearly a cunning bastard and was now top of Yokely's hit list. The problem was, he was no closer to locating the al-Qaeda mastermind than when he had first been given his mission.

Chapter 39

George Hurry had gone home for some much-needed sleep but Inspector Nick Hughes was at his station, his jacket hanging on the back of his chair and his sleeves rolled up. He was sitting back in his chair, his hand on a mouse that allowed him to control the speed of the CCTV footage he was reviewing. Although he was in charge of the Super-Recogniser Unit, Hughes was a talented observer and always led from the front. He made sure that no one worked longer then he did and took fewer breaks than anyone in the unit.

'Nick, who's checking the mosque footage for Ali Naveed?' asked Shepherd.

'Matt Goddard,' said the inspector, gesturing at a fresh-faced dark-haired man in a grey suit. 'He's new to the team but he's got a good eye.'

Shepherd thanked him and went over to Goddard to introduce himself. 'Dan Shepherd, I'm here to liaise with MI5,' he said. Goddard shook his hand. On the terminal was footage from a CCTV camera that covered the approach to what was clearly a mosque, a brick building with a green dome and a tall minaret flashed in white. Outside were a group of several dozen Asian men, all bearded and most wearing robes. The scene could easily have been anywhere in the Middle East but Shepherd knew that it was the Acton Mosque, only a few miles away from where the unit was based.

'I've just been told that Naveed is a fan of the Argyle Street Mosque,' said Shepherd. 'Can you see what footage is available there?'

'No problem,' said Goddard. 'Any idea of the time frame?'

'He was a regular there so I'd be surprised if he hadn't visited over the days prior to his death. But we're more interested in who he talked to, who he went and left with. We're looking for his contacts. His foster parents used to drive him but then they stopped. I'm hoping that he started attending with someone else and obviously we'd like to know who that someone is.'

Goddard nodded. 'Anyone in particular I should be looking for?'

'Unfortunately not. Best bet is for you to save any footage of him that you find and run it by me. I'm up to speed on all the jihadists on MI5's watch list. There's an imam at Argyle Road who is a definite problem. His name is Shakeel Al-Heweny. I'll send you over a picture. He's a clever one – you'll see him on TV all the time as the friendly face of Islam, "we must all work together to bring peace", that sort of thing. But Five has tapes of him talking in private and he's a nasty piece of work. We're pretty sure he's sending young men out to join ISIS in Syria and he runs courses in jihad, but again only in private. The thing is, if Al-Heweny is one of Naveed's handlers he's not likely to be embracing him in the street. Contact would have been behind closed doors, for sure.'

'I'll get the feeds and let you know as soon as I get anything,' promised Goddard.

Chapter 40

Harper stretched out his legs and blew smoke up at the darkening sky. It had been threatening to rain all day but if anything the clouds were starting to thin out. There was a chill in the air and he'd turned up the collar of his jacket against the wind that was blowing against his back. A red setter ran over, sniffed his shoes and the holdall at his feet and then ran back to its owner, a young woman in a sheepskin jacket and Ugg boots. 'Sorry!' she called.

'No problem,' said Harper, waving his cigarette. In the distance he saw Charlotte Button She had her mobile phone to her ear but he couldn't tell if she was on a call or faking it. The mobile phone was a Godsend for surveillance and anti-surveillance. Watchers could use their mobile phones to talk to each other while following a target, and being on a mobile meant that your eyes were free to look at whatever you wanted. Button was on a path parallel to where he was sitting. She was wearing a long coat that looked like cashmere and had a large Louis Vuitton bag over her left shoulder. Her chestnut hair was loose and shifting in the wind as she walked. Harper took a long pull on his cigarette. Two teenagers rollerbladed by Button. A woman with a pram walked by her, her eyes fixed to a smartphone. Two women in full burkhas with a dozen Harrods carrier bags led a gaggle of noisy children towards Bayswater. In the distance, a group of young children were riding ponies in single file. It was just a normal day in Hyde Park and so far as Harper could see no one was paying Button any attention.

She seemed to have reached the same conclusion and headed his way, still deep in conversation on her phone. She put it away as she got closer, then sat down on the far end of the bench and crossed her legs away from him. 'You've been a very busy boy, Alex,' she said, arranging her coat over her knees.

'When you're paid by results there's no point in hanging around,' he said. 'And speaking of payment . . .'

Button smiled. She took a copy of the *Evening Standard* from her bag and placed it on the bench between them, looked around and then pushed it towards him. 'There's twenty thousand in cash,' she said. 'On account.'

'Cash will do nicely,' said Harper. He picked up the newspaper. It was folded around a bulky envelope. He knew that he didn't need to count it, at least not in front of her.

'I'm guessing you weren't working alone,' said Button.

'I had help. There was a lot to do and not a lot of time.'

'Specifically?'

'Just one guy. Mick O'Hara.'

'The Irishman? Alex, he's a bit of a loose cannon.'

'It was a rush job, Charlotte. Beggars can't be choosers. Yes, he's got a temper and you wouldn't want him thinking for himself, but if you keep him on a short leash he's an asset.'

'I'll take your word for that.'

'He didn't put a foot wrong, I swear.'

'Where is he now?'

'He's booked into a cheap hotel not far from here in case I need him again. And he'd like to do more work for the Pool.'

Button flashed him an icy stare. 'Alex, just so we are crystal clear on this, Mick O'Hara will never, ever, work for the Pool.'

Harper held up his hands in surrender. 'Message received and understood.'

'Put your hands down, Alex. You look ridiculous.'

Harper grinned and did as he was told. There were times when Charlotte Button treated him as if he was an unruly pupil in her class, but truth be told he quite liked her telling him off. And he could see from the glint in her eye that she was only half serious.

He used his left foot to push the holdall towards her. 'There's a few things in there you might like,' he said. 'Farooqi's laptop and phone. And Zaghba's mobile. I've got the passwords for Farooqi's stuff but not for Zaghba's.'

'No problem, I'll get it done.'

'Farooqi said that Naveed told him that he had met Saladin. In London.'

'When?'

'A couple of weeks ago. He said Naveed and this Saladin met at a London mosque.'

'And do we know who this Saladin is? His real name?'

'They only know him as Saladin. That's what Farooqi said and under the circumstances, I don't think he was lying.'

'Had Farooqi met Saladin?'

'No. Farooqi was waiting for instructions. They use the old draft folder technique.'

'You have the email account?'

Harper winked at her. 'Of course.'

'I have another name for you, but he's on the run and I don't yet have a location for him. His name's Usman Yussuf and he works for the accounts department at the stadium. He brought the vest in. The police checked his address this morning but there's no sign of him.'

Harper nodded. 'So what happens next?'

'Stay close,' she said. 'I'll probably have more names for you soon.'

'And what about the guys you want framing?'

'What do you have?'

'I have the gun. Untraceable. And I have the spray paint cans. And I have the hammer that was used to off Farooqi.'

'Can you plant the gun? Ideally on some drugs gang up in the Bolton area?'

'Does the Pope shit in the woods?'

Button nodded thoughtfully. 'Actually, no, I'll get someone else to do it. If you got caught with it then the whole house of cards would come tumbling down.'

'I appreciate your vote of confidence.'

'You know what I mean. The best-laid plans and all that. Best we get the planting done one step removed. Can you be back here in two hours? I'll have the gear collected.'

Harper nodded. 'No problem.'

Button picked up the holdall. 'Always a pleasure, Alex,' she said.

'Right back at you,' said Harper. He lit a cigarette. 'I'll watch you go, make sure you're not being followed.'

'Bless you,' she said. 'Seriously, Alex. Thank you. In an uncertain world, you are one of the few men I can totally rely on.'

'Careful, Charlotte, you'll make me cry.'

'Oh, I doubt that any woman could bring tears to your eyes.' She smiled and he could see the warmth in it. 'You take care, Alex. I'd hate it if anything ever happened to you.'

'I'll be fine,' he said.

Button nodded. She turned away and walked south, in the direction of Harrods. Harper watched her go, not because he thought for one moment that she was being tailed; he just liked the way her backside moved under her coat and the way her chestnut hair swung from side to side with every step. He blew smoke at her and smiled through it. 'One day, Charlotte,' he whispered to himself. 'One fine day.'

Chapter 41

Present Day, London

Shepherd's mobile rang on his desk. It was Don Margrave. He took the call and went out into the corridor.

'I've got news on the driver, Zaghba. Our boys just forced their way into his flat.'

'And?'

'He's dead, mate.'

'Dead?'

'Not living. Deceased. He has ceased to be. He's expired and gone to meet his Maker. He's a stiff. Bereft of life, he rests in peace.'

'Very funny,' said Shepherd. 'What happened?'

'Someone smashed a table over his head and sprayed racist slogans on his walls.'

Shepherd's jaw dropped. 'No bloody way.'

'Yeah, his phone is missing and racists don't generally steal phones. And there are no signs of forced entry. But all sorts of stuff about Muslims and pigs on the wall, apparently. There's a forensics team in there as we speak.'

'So what happened? He lets in a racist and lets him hit him with a table?'

'Had to be someone he knew, right? Or someone with a decent story to get him to open the door and turn his back on him.'

'Any idea of time of death?'

'After midnight. Before four a.m.'

'What do you think, Don?'

The detective sighed. 'If it was a one-off, I might buy the racist attack. Someone could have followed him in and cold-cocked him after he opened his door. But the uncle was also killed last night.'

Shepherd frowned. 'Whose uncle?'

'Naveed's. Imran Masood. Syrian refugee. He was granted asylum almost ten years ago and is now a British citizen. I say "is". I mean "was". He and his family were shot in their beds last night.'

Shepherd froze. 'What?'

'Execution style. A bullet in the head for the old man, his wife and their three sons. It happened last night. In Bolton. The north of England.'

'I know where Bolton is,' said Shepherd laconically. 'Five killings? There's been nothing on the TV.'

'Media blackout at the moment until they decide how to play it,' said Margrave.

'Sounds like a professional hit, doesn't it?'

'No one heard a thing so they must have used some sort of silencer.'

'Suppressor,' said Shepherd. 'They're called suppressors. But you're right. Someone would have heard five shots if they hadn't been suppressed.'

'Hang on, in the movies and on TV they always call them silencers.'

'Well they're wrong. There's no such thing as a silencer. All you can do is suppress the sound of a shot, not silence it.'

'Well you learn something new every day,' said the policeman. 'I'm not sure how professional a job it was because the killer gained access by breaking a window downstairs. And one of the victims was shot in the kitchen.'

'Sounds rushed,' said Shepherd. 'The suppressor suggests professionals but if it had been better planned they wouldn't have broken a window.' He scratched his chin. 'Could the uncle have been involved in the planning of the stadium bombing?'

'It's possible,' said Margrave. 'But there are no recent calls between Naveed and Masood. They could have used call boxes, of course. It's being looked at.'

Shepherd's forehead creased into a frown as he processed what the detective had told him. Could it be a coincidence? Who the hell would kill a family of five? Families did die together but it was usually in car crashes or house fires; it was incredibly rare for someone to break into a house to shoot and kill an entire family. 'It wasn't racist, was it?'

'A preliminary check hasn't turned up any reports of racism against the family but we'll dig deeper today. It might be a complete coincidence. Some sort of honour killing maybe. There were three sons and one of them might have been fucking someone he shouldn't have been fucking. Their community can react pretty violently to situations like that.'

'Yeah, but they usually throw acid or use knives. This takes honour killing to a whole new level.'

'It can't be a coincidence, can it?' said the detective. 'The hairs are standing up on the back of my neck. How's your Spider sense?'

'I'm with you, it can't be a coincidence'

'Do you think it's ISIS tidying up loose ends?'

'Killing anyone involved? They've never done that before. And it would screw up recruitment wouldn't it?'

'Only if it became public,' said Margrave.

'And there's no evidence that the Masood family were involved in the planning or execution of the stadium bombing?'

'No, but the uncle has ISIS connections and the three sons were all out in Syria at some point, presumably fighting alongside ISIS. It's a weird one, that's for sure.'

'You said the Masood killings were clinical, a single shot to the head in every case?' said Shepherd.

'That's right. And nothing was taken from the scene, according to the Bolton cops. Not that they'd know that for sure, obviously. And there were no racist slogans in Bolton. So if you were looking just at the scenes, sure you wouldn't think they were connected. Except Imran Masood was Naveed's uncle and Khuram Zaghba drove Naveed to the stadium.'

'What about Usman Yussuf?'

'No sign of him at the house. We got his address first thing but he'd already cleared out. Most of his clothes and personal effects had gone so he's on his toes, obviously. They got the bag in the storage room and it's being tested for explosives as we speak. If Yussuf turns up I'll keep you in the loop. There's something else you might be interested in.'

'I'm all ears,' said Shepherd.

'Naveed made a number of calls the day he blew himself to Kingdom Come,' he said. 'One was to another Syrian refugee, Israr Farooqi. Like Naveed, Farooqi claimed to be a child refugee but even social services in Birmingham had their doubts. He was put with a foster family but moved into a place on his own.'

'Council funded?'

'Apparently not, so he's getting money from somewhere. Doesn't seem to have been employed. According to his neighbours he kept to himself and rarely went out.'

'He's been questioned?'

'We sent a couple of our guys up to knock on his door first thing this morning but he wasn't there. They spoke to a neighbour who said they heard a ruckus late at night so they got a warrant and had the lock picked but the flat was empty. There was damage to the security chain, though, as if the door had been forced. But that could have happened at any time. He might just have done a runner. Just a thought, but maybe you could bring your area of expertise into play. Birmingham doesn't have as much CCTV as London, but you might be able to see when he left and if he was with anyone.'

'I'll give it a go,' said Shepherd. 'Text me the address.'

'Will do,' Margrave promised.

Chapter 42

'That's his car,' said Bardot. A gleaming black Bentley with tinted windows had pulled up in front of the tower block where Mohammed Al-Hashim's offices were based. Bardot and Yokely were in a white SUV with Dubai plates. Bardot hadn't said where he'd got the car from but they were both wearing surgical gloves so that they wouldn't leave prints. Their windows were also heavily tinted so no one could see inside.

It was a ten-mile drive to the secure compound where Al-Hashim lived, most of it along a six-lane highway. Bardot and Yokely had done the drive three times that afternoon, each time with Gerry McNee following on a high-powered Kawasaki motorcycle. The bike had been stolen to order and false plates had been fitted. Leclerc hadn't taken part in the rehearsals, he'd been stationed outside the office block to check that the target didn't surprise them by leaving early.

Now he was riding pillion, a Glock in an underarm holster. There was no need for a suppressor, not on a bike that would be travelling at close to sixty miles an hour when he took his shot.

Leclerc and McNee were both wearing full motorcycle leathers and full-face helmets with tinted visors. They were parked by the pavement around the corner from the entrance to the building, engine running.

'Here they come,' said Leclerc.

Al-Hashim was wearing the full Saudi gear – a long white thawb that Yokely always thought of as a man dress and a red and white checked keffiyeh headdress. He was carrying a Louis

Vuitton briefcase. His bodyguard followed him, a sure sign that the man had not been trained in close protection – a professional bodyguard would have exited the building ahead of his principal. The bodyguard hurried around Al-Hashim and opened the rear door of the Bentley. He was wearing a too-tight suit and it was clear he wasn't armed.

Al-Hashim got into the rear seat. The bodyguard closed the door and went to the front of the vehicle to sit by the driver.

'And off we go,' said Bardot. He put the SUV into gear and edged into the traffic. Yokely checked in the wing mirror. The Bentley was a dozen cars behind them.

Bardot drove smoothly, following the route to the highway. By the time they turned on to the major road, the Bentley was seven cars behind them. They couldn't see the bike but that was to be expected: there was no reason for them to be anywhere near the target until the last minute.

The traffic picked up speed on the highway. Bardot kept one eye on his rear-view mirror. The driver of the Bentley didn't appear to be interested in switching lanes, which made Bardot's job easier. All he had to do was to keep in the same lane as the target. It didn't matter how many cars were between them, not until they reached the section of the road where they had planned to carry out the hit.

Yokely flinched as a siren kicked into life but he relaxed almost immediately when he saw that it was an ambulance. The ambulance sped past them, lights flashing and siren wailing.

They had decided the best place for the hit was half a mile before the turn-off that the Bentley was going to use. That was just two miles ahead of them.

Bardot clicked his tongue. 'He's moving.'

Yokely checked the wing mirror. The Bentley was indicating it wanted to move into the lane on its left. The traffic was heavy and no one was giving any ground so the indicators were on but the Bentley stayed in its lane. Bardot's fingers were poised on his own turn indicator. They needed to stay in the same lane as the target.

Eventually a Mercedes slowed, giving the Bentley space to move across. As the Bentley moved, Bardot flicked his turn indicator and edged over. The Porsche to his left initially refused to give way but when he realised Bardot was moving come what may he braked and banged on his horn.

Yokely kept his eyes on the wing mirror. There were now just three cars between them and the Bentley, including the Porsche. The Porsche driver accelerated and pulled around their SUV. His windows were almost black but Yokely had no doubt that the driver was yelling at them and probably giving them the finger, too. The Porsche continued to accelerate, but then had to brake to avoid a truck ahead of him. The driver was clearly in full-on testosterone mode and he zigzagged impatiently and then broke right, missing the truck by inches.

'Prick,' said Yokely.

'Yeah, but probably an Emirati prick, which means we have to be careful. Only the Emirati citizens are allowed that degree of tinting and if we have a bust-up with him on the road the cops will automatically side with him.'

'Because we're foreigners?'

'Because we're the worst sort of foreigners,' said Bardot, flashing him a thin smile. 'White foreigners. There's nothing they like more than putting one of us behind bars. Any excuse.'

Yokely checked the wing mirror again. There was a white Toyota just behind their SUV, then a minivan, then the Bentley. A dozen or so cars behind them was the motorbike, gaining on them.

Yokely looked at the road ahead. They were about half a mile from the killing zone. 'All good, Michael?' he said.

'All good,' said Bardot.

Overhead signs gave information on the upcoming turn-off. Yokely checked the wing mirror again. There were still two cars between them and the target.

The Kawasaki was just four cars behind the Bentley. It was coming up on the driver's side because the traffic was lighter there. But Yokely knew that at the last moment the bike would cross over to the other side so that they would be closer to Al-Hashim. Leclerc was left-handed, which would be an advantage.

Bardot was breathing slowly and evenly, his eyes flicking between the road ahead and his rear-view mirror. They were almost there. 'Ready when you are,' he said.

Yokely checked the wing mirror again. The bike was now tucked in behind the Bentley. matching its speed. As he watched, the bike eased over to the right side of the Bentley. Leclerc's hand was moving to unzip his jacket.

'Go for it,' said Yokely.

Bardot took his foot off the accelerator and let the speed bleed off. The gap between them and the car in front widened quickly. He looked in his rear-view mirror. The white Toyota didn't realise that the SUV had slowed until he was almost up against its rear bumper and the driver braked suddenly. The driver of the minivan behind the Toyota was sitting up high so he'd seen the SUV slowing and was already braking. The Bentley slowed just as Leclerc pulled out his Glock and fired at the offside rear window. The glass shattered into a thousand cubes. Leclerc fired twice more and then McNee accelerated and streaked away. Yokely caught a flash of red and black and then they were gone.

Bardot accelerated. Behind them several cars had collided in panic and there was a blaring of horns and the sound of tyres screeching. Thirty seconds later they were turning off the highway. Job done.

Chapter 43

Present Day, London

The man was good, no doubt about that. Harper had been keeping a watchful eye out for Button's bagman and had come up with three possibilities before the middle-aged man in a pinstripe suit and a Burberry raincoat sat down on the bench next to him. For a moment Harper wondered if the guy was gay and wanted to pick him up, but the man just nodded curtly.

'Charlotte sent me,' he said. There was just a trace of a Newcastle accent.

'Do you always dress like that, or is it a disguise?' asked Harper.

The man's face remained impassive and he didn't answer.

'You look very smart,' said Harper. He pushed the black nylon kitbag along the bench towards the man. Inside were the two cans of spray paint that he'd used, along with the bloodstained hammer and the Glock. He had taken the magazine out of the weapon, even though the Glock's trigger safety mechanism was pretty much faultless.

'Have a nice day,' said the man. He picked up the bag and walked away.

Harper didn't bother to watch, just lit a cigarette and headed back to his hotel.

Chapter 44

Present Day, London

Shepherd sipped his coffee as he stared at his screen. The address that Don Margrave had given him for Farooqi was a residential street in the south of Birmingham. Shepherd had gone to Google Earth to take a look at the house and the surrounding area. The house had been divided into flats or bedsits and there was a line of doorbells at the side of the front door. Farooqi had lived in Flat 3. Shepherd sat back and linked his fingers behind his head as he stared at the screen, wondering what he should do next. He called Sergeant Hurry over and showed him what he was looking at.

'Naveed telephoned another Syrian refugee, a guy called Israr Farooqi,' explained Shepherd. He tapped the location of the house. 'This is where he lives. Can you see what CCTV feeds are available in the area of the house and patch them through to me?'

'Sure.' Hurry peered at the screen. 'Birmingham? Yeah, they've got fairly good CCTV coverage and West Midlands Police are usually cooperative. I'll see what I can do.'

They were interrupted by Eric Fitzpatrick as he stood up at his workstation. 'Dan, I've got Ali Naveed walking into an Internet café near Ealing Broadway station the morning of the bombing,' he said excitedly.

'Excellent!' said Shepherd and hurried over.

Fitzpatrick sat down and tapped on his computer, transferring the image on his computer to the big screen on the wall. Shepherd smiled when he saw that Naveed was wearing his distinctive

Nikes and the same puffa jacket he had had on over the suicide vest. The image was clear enough to make out his features and Eric paused the image just as he stepped across the threshold. 'He arrived at just before ten in the morning and was there for less than five minutes.' He played the video on fast-forward and they watched as Naveed left the shop.

'Well done,' said Shepherd, patting him on the shoulder. 'Can you give me a printout of him entering, one where his face is clear?'

Eric nodded. 'Sure.'

Shepherd went over to Sergeant Hurry. 'George, I'm going to pop out to talk to the owner of an Internet café that Naveed visited.'

'Are you sure? I should be passing the intel on to SO15.'

'I know, but we're going to need to lock down the computer he used, so the sooner the better. I'll get an MI5 computer forensics guy to meet me there. It'll just save time.'

The sergeant nodded. 'Go for it,' he said. 'I should have the Birmingham feeds ready for you by the time you get back.'

Shepherd headed out and caught a black cab to Ealing. On the way he called Amar Singh, one of MI5's top technical experts, and explained what he was doing. Singh agreed to meet him at the Internet café.

It took the cab almost fifty minutes to cross London to Ealing Broadway station. Singh was already on the pavement waiting, as always overdressed in a dark blue Armani suit and well-polished Bally shoes. He had a Cartier watch on his wrist and was carrying a Ted Baker travel bag. Shepherd paid off the driver and shook hands with Singh before taking him along to the Internet café. It was a single room with two dozen computer terminals in four ranks of six. To the left was a counter with a coffee machine, a display case of snacks and sandwiches and a cash register manned by a burly Indian with a sweeping moustache.

Shepherd smiled. 'Are you the owner?'

'I'm the owner's son but it's a family business so, you know . . .' He shrugged. He waved his arm at the computer terminals, most of which weren't being used. 'One day all this will be mine.' He smiled ruefully as if it was the last thing he wanted.

'And your name, sir?' asked Shepherd.

'Khan,' the man replied. 'Akbar Khan. And who's asking?'

Shepherd took out his Metropolitan Police warrant card and showed it to Mr Khan. He'd been issued with the card after joining the Lambeth unit and it was easier to flash it than to explain that he was with MI5. 'Do you remember this man coming in, on the morning of the fifteenth? At twenty past ten.' He held out Ali Naveed's picture.

Mr Khan squinted at the printout and shrugged. 'What is he, an asylum seeker?'

'Why would you say that?'

'Because he's an Arab and he's young. We get a lot in here, checking up on their asylum applications and talking to their relatives in whatever shithole they're from. They usually try to haggle about the cost and they never spend on coffee or food. And a lot of them look at porn sites, and watch them with the volume up until we tell them to use headphones.'

'But do you recognise him?'

Mr Khan laughed harshly. 'They all look the same to me,' he said.

'Is there any chance that you would remember which computer he used?'

Mr Khan shook his head. 'Like I said, they're in and out all day and if they don't give me a problem I don't pay them any attention.'

Shepherd pointed up at a CCTV camera in the corner of the room. 'Please tell me that works?'

Mr Khan turned to look at it and nodded. 'Sure it does. And we keep the video for a full year. We had a visit from your child pornography unit last year. That was a bloody asylum seeker, too. He'd been watching child porn and we were almost put out of business. Now we video everything, just in case.'

'Excellent,' said Shepherd. 'So let's have a look at the footage for the fifteenth, twenty past ten.'

Mr Khan nodded and turned to a laptop behind him. He tapped on the keys and looked over his shoulder. 'The fifteenth?'

'Yeah. Twenty past ten.'

Mr Khan tapped on the keyboard again.

'Do you mind if I have a look?' asked Shepherd.

Mr Khan stepped to the side. 'Sure.'

Shepherd bent down and looked at the screen. It showed Naveed walking in, handing some money to a man at the counter and then going to sit at a terminal, the one that was furthest from the door.

'Who is that?' asked Shepherd, pointing at the man who had taken Naveed's money.

'That's my brother. Akhtar.'

Shepherd turned to look at the terminal. 'We're going to have to take that computer away with us, I'm afraid,' he said.

'For how long?'

'For as long as it takes, unfortunately.'

Singh was already walking towards the computer, unzipping his bag.

'Don't you need a warrant or something?' asked Mr Khan.

'I'll give you a receipt,' said Shepherd. 'And if there is any damage you'll be reimbursed.'

Mr Khan wrinkled his nose. 'It's all shit anyway,' he said. 'The computers are four years old and the keyboards get hammered. We're trying to get the old man to turn it into a sandwich shop, that's the way to make real money these days.'

Singh unplugged the monitor and speakers and put the tower and the keyboard into his bag. Shepherd filled out a receipt for Mr Khan and he and Singh went outside.

'How long do you think it'll take to find out who Naveed was talking to?' asked Shepherd.

'Assuming he was using a draft folder, not long at all,' said Singh. 'We know when he was on the computer. It won't be difficult.'

'Keep me in the loop, yeah?'

'Sure. Anything in particular?'

'I'm just being nosy,' said Shepherd. 'How are you getting back?'

Singh grinned and nodded at a brand new Audi A4 parked down the road. 'My new pride and joy,' he said.

'They pay you too much,' said Shepherd.

Singh laughed. 'Not for what I do,' he said. 'And I'd make twice as much in the private sector.' He walked towards the Audi as Shepherd flagged down a black cab.

Chapter 45

Charlotte Button had long been a fan of the J Sheekey seafood restaurant in Covent Garden and appreciated the fact that Patsy Ellis had chosen it for their meeting. The fact that it was more than a mile from MI5's headquarters in Millbank was a bonus. Ellis and Button were old friends but after Button had burned her bridges, eyebrows would be raised if they were seen socialising.

Ellis had arrived first and had taken a small table tucked away in the corner of one of the more private rooms. There was a bottle of Pinot Grigio in front of her and she was halfway through her first glass. She smiled when she saw Button and stood up. There were dark patches under her eyes and her make-up couldn't disguise the unhealthy pallor of her skin.

'Charlie, darling.'

They air-kissed.

Button sat down and put her Louis Vuitton bag on the floor next to her chair. The maître d' had taken her coat at the door. She was wearing a blue suit, a close match to the one that Ellis was wearing. They had always had a similar taste in clothes, though it was less a coincidence and more that Ellis had been Button's mentor at MI5 and she had copied many of the traits that had made her boss such a success in the service.

A waitress appeared and poured wine into Button's glass.

Ellis lifted her glass and toasted Button. 'Thank you,' she said. 'Thank you for coming and thank you for . . .' She smiled. 'You know what for.'

They clinked glasses and both drank. Button took a sip of the chilled white wine, but Ellis took two large swallows. When she put the glass down, the waitress reappeared and refilled it. Ellis caught Button's look and she smiled defensively. 'One glass, darling. And we are celebrating.'

'You're entitled,' Button said.

Ellis nodded. 'The funeral is on Tuesday.'

'I'll be there.'

Ellis took a deep breath to steady herself. 'Thank you.'

'Does anyone at Five know that you were Eleanor's godmother?'

Ellis shook her head. 'No, and there's no reason for them to, either. Her parents are civilians, there's no blood connection and they were never mentioned during my positive vetting.'

'And how's Tony?'

'He's a rock. But you know Tony. He's a great one for locking away his emotions. He'd have made a great spy.'

'I've always thought that.'

'He was approached at Cambridge. He turned them down without a second thought. Funny old world. If things had gone differently he could have been running Five and I'd be . . . What would I be, Charlie?'

'Not a housewife, that's for sure,' said Button. 'Five is lucky to have you, Patsy. This country is lucky to have you.'

Ellis blinked away tears. 'I can't thank you enough, Charlie.' She reached across the table and held Button's hand.

'Hush,' said Button. 'I'm happy to do whatever you want.' She lowered her voice and leaned towards her. 'But I have to ask. Does it make you any happier?'

Ellis sniffed. 'What about you? When you killed the men who murdered your husband? How did you feel?'

Button sighed. 'I wasn't happy. It didn't bring him back. But at night, when I was trying to get to sleep, the fact that I had done something to avenge him, yes, it was a comfort. If they had still been walking around, breathing air and living life, that would have eaten me up. But they were dead and fuck them, they deserved to die.'

Ellis forced a smile. 'Exactly,' she said.

'But why not have them questioned, Patsy? The people I'm using are well able to do basic interrogations. They might have useful intel.'

'And what would I do with said intel? How could I explain it?' She sat back and picked up her glass. 'Fuck them,' she said.

Button nodded in agreement. 'Yes. Fuck them.'

Ellis let go of Button's hand. The two women clinked glasses and this time they both drank enthusiastically. Ellis beat the waitress to the bottle and refilled both glasses. They ordered. Button asked for the fish pie, which she had pretty much every time she visited Sheekey's. Ellis ordered the lemon sole.

They waited for the waitress to leave before continuing. 'I have Farooqi's laptop for you,' said Button. 'And his phone.'

'Where is he? The police went around to his flat but he wasn't there and the security chain was broken.'

'I don't know exactly but he won't be found until we want him to be found. What do the police think?'

Ellis smiled ruefully. 'They tend not to be great thinkers, in my experience,' she said. 'All I have is a report that an armed response unit went in and the cupboard was bare. They are assuming he did a runner but that doesn't explain the busted door, obviously. Because there were no signs of a struggle inside the apartment they are assuming that the damage was done earlier.'

'Farooqi was questioned and he said that he was awaiting activation,' said Button. 'His handler used the codename Saladin.'

Ellis frowned. 'Saladin? That sounds familiar.'

'The first sultan of Egypt and Syria and led the Muslim military campaign against the Crusaders. At one point he ruled over Egypt, Syria, the Yemen and a big chunk of North Africa. But as he died in 1193, we can assume it's not him.'

'I thought your degree was in English.'

'Google,' said Button. She sipped her wine. 'Now according to Farooqi, Naveed called him to say that Saladin had given him his task.'

'So they shared the same handler?'

Button nodded. 'I can't find anything on him but you might have more luck. According to Farooqi, Naveed met this Saladin at a London mosque. We don't know which one unfortunately.'

'I'll reach out to the Americans. And the Europeans. Though since the Brexit referendum, European cooperation has fallen to new lows.' She ran her finger around the rim of her wine glass. 'The problem is, they'll want to know where the intel came from.'

'It's on the laptop.'

'And how did I get the laptop?' She forced a smile. 'It's getting complicated, Charlie.'

'I did warn you. But you need to get your technical boys to look at it. Who knows what intel is on it?'

Ellis nodded. 'The problem there is that I can hardly turn up at Thames House with his laptop, can I?'

'How about we send a tip so that Farooqi's body is discovered. We could put a left luggage ticket on the body, which leads to the computer. The phone can be on the body. Once we've set the scene we can give the police an anonymous tip.'

Ellis nodded. 'That sounds very workable.'

'Farooqi and Zaghba weren't shot. The proverbial blunt instruments did the trick. And there was racist graffiti left at both scenes. We can use the spray cans to point at a racist group. And I have the murder weapon that was used to kill Farooqi.'

'Can you do that?'

'Just say the word.'

Ellis nodded slowly. 'Okay,' she said. 'Yes. Please.' She sipped her wine but the sip quickly turned into a gulp. Her hand trembled slightly and she took extra care when putting the glass back on the table. She forced a smile. 'So this Saladin is running the jihadists who have come over from Syria? There could be others?'

'I would say that's a definite possibility,' said Button. 'Obviously he needs looking at. He could be someone from the higher echelons of ISIS, he could be an up-and-coming unknown, for all we know he could be a bloody Brit.'

'The degree of sophistication suggests that he's been around for a while,' said Ellis.

'But until we get some hard intel, it's all guesswork. I'll get the laptop set up, put the hammer and cans in place, then I'll make a call.'

'Today?'

'I don't see why not,' said Button. 'As soon as I have my ducks in a row, I'll let you know.' She took a sip of wine. 'Patsy, I'm on the outside these days of course, but I did have a thought.'

'I'm listening.'

'This Saladin has to be the ultimate target, obviously. It looks as if he planned the bombing and put it all together.'

'That being the case he has probably already left the country.'

'Yes, true. But Farooqi has a line of communication in place. Through the email draft folder. I presume that it's a two-way street. So a message could be sent to Saladin and if GCHQ was on the ball . . .'

'They could track his location.' Ellis nodded. 'Good idea, Charlie.'

'But that means keeping Farooqi's death under wraps. You'd need a D Notice on it immediately. Complete news blackout. As soon as it becomes known that Farooqi is dead . . .' She shrugged but didn't finish the sentence.

'I'll make sure that happens,' said Ellis. She smiled. There was a haunted look in her eyes and Button figured it would be there for some time to come. 'The Masood family is a bit more prob-lematical,' Ellis went on. 'The Greater Manchester Police have kept a lid on it but I think it'll be in the papers tomorrow or at least the day after. Not that I'm shedding any tears over them. They were all potential jihadists, just waiting for the call.'

'Who is handling the investigation in Bolton?'

'GMP, but bearing in mind the family's jihadists connections the Met has offered to send some of their anti-terrorist police up to assist. Five Asians shot dead in their beds. We obviously need to muddy the waters but it's not the normal sort of racist attack, is it?'

'I did have a thought about that. We could make it look drug-related.'

Ellis raised her eyebrows. 'That might work.'

'Lots of drug- related activity in that neck of the woods. We plant the gun on a local dealer, make it look as if the Masood family were dealing or importing. It wouldn't be hard. It'd put the cops on the wrong track and provided they had a name in the frame they probably wouldn't bother looking elsewhere.'

'Can you fix it?'

'Of course. Just say the word.'

Ellis thought about it for several seconds, and then nodded slowly. 'Yes. Do it. Please.'

'And do you have other names in the pipeline?'

'The cops have pulled in half a dozen of Naveed's contacts and are interrogating them as we speak,' she said. 'As you know, usually they are released within a day or two, no charges and no bail.'

'What about the employee who took the vest in for Naveed?'

'Usman Yussuf? No sign of him but we're looking. Border Force are on the lookout but I won't be holding my breath.'

Button knew what Ellis meant. There were few if any checks on people leaving the country, mainly as the result of government cutbacks. But even if Border Force had the manpower, usually people leaving the country weren't a priority, the theory being that if they left they would be someone else's problem. Button nodded. 'How is the investigation going, generally?'

'It's not really an investigation, more fact gathering. We know who took Naveed to the stadium. We know who took in the vest. Forensics are trying to piece together what's left of it to see if there's any sort of signature but that could take for ever. Shepherd is doing his thing with the CCTV and we'll follow up on all Naveed's contacts. But the way things stand, we'll probably never know all the details. As you said, Saladin is the key, but at the moment all we have is a name.'

Their food arrived. As always the fish pie smelled delicious and Button tucked in with relish. Ellis picked at her fish but clearly didn't have much in the way of an appetite. Considering what she had been through, Button was surprised she could eat at all. She didn't seem to have any problem with the wine, though, and even before Button had got halfway through her pie, Ellis had ordered a second bottle.

Chapter 46

Ten Years Ago, London

Yokely and Leclerc flew into London on separate flights. McNee had booked them rooms in the Sheraton Skyline Hotel at the airport and he and Yokely had breakfast in the restaurant while they waited for Leclerc to arrive. Over coffee and eggs and bacon, Yokely briefed McNee on Rashid Makhdoom's family.

'Rashid lived with his parents in a house in Stoke Newington, North London,' said Yokely. 'It's a big immigrant area, lots of Turks and Iraqis there. It's not far from Finsbury Park Mosque. According to David's MI5 contact, Rashid is a cleanskin, not on any watch lists. His brother is a different matter. Latif Makhdoom is three years younger and was born in London. He went to Pakistan a year ago, ostensibly to attend a wedding there, but MI5 believe he crossed the border into Afghanistan and spent several months training with al-Qaeda. Their father made the trip with Latif and the wedding does seem to have taken place but the father returned on his own.'

McNee nodded. 'So the father must have known what the boy was up to.'

'I'm sure of it,' said Yokely. 'Plus both the boys lived at home; the parents must have seen their sons being radicalised. The fact that the father went to Pakistan with the son while the mother stayed at home is a red flag to me. Now, Latif was on MI5's radar but Rashid wasn't. There's no evidence that Rashid was training in Afghanistan but the Brits are pretty lax with their borders, as we know. People are checked coming in but there are no checks on people leaving most of the time. Right, we're going to take care of the whole family. I'm thinking a fire?'

'It happens,' said McNee.

Yokely handed McNee a piece of paper with the address of the house. 'Go ahead and put a plan together.'

McNee buttered a triangle of toast. 'What about the other UK guy? Shabir Rauf? What's his situation?'

'David's up north checking him out. Rauf has an uncle on the no-fly list, but Rauf himself is another cleanskin. We'll take out the uncle for sure. Let's see what else David comes up with. The imam at the mosque Rauf attended is a firebrand and is known to be sending potential jihadists over to Afghanistan for al-Qaeda training.'

'So the imam too?'

Yokely nodded. 'Definitely.'

David Dalton arrived in London late afternoon and went straight to their hotel. He met Yokely, McNee and Leclerc down in the bar. They grabbed a corner table away from prying eyes and over beers he gave them details of Shabir Rauf's imam, an Egypt-born cleric who had been granted British citizenship shortly before the 9/11 attacks. His name was Mohammed El Saadawi and MI5 had been watching him for some time after it had become clear that young men from the mosque were travelling to Pakistan and staying for months at a time, presumably crossing into Afghanistan for al-Qaeda training. The imam taught special classes in the evenings, ostensibly studying the Koran, but in reality he was grooming his favoured students to be jihadists and once he was satisfied they were ready, he arranged for them to be sent to Afghanistan for specialist training.

'The mosque is in a place called Dewsbury, south of Leeds,' said Dalton. 'It's one of the biggest mosques in the UK and can hold up to four thousand men.'

'Four hundred, you mean,' said Leclerc.

'Four thousand,' said Dalton. 'It's huge. There are more than three hundred thousand Muslims in Yorkshire. The mosque is in a place called Savile Town and of the four thousand people living there fewer than a hundred are white British. You have to see it to believe it.' Dalton had a briefcase with him and he opened it and took out half a dozen surveillance photographs. He spread them out over the table. The imam was tall and stick-thin with a long beard and a hooked nose. In several of the photographs he was wearing a long thawb robe and riding a woman's bicycle.

'He rides to and from the mosque on this bike,' said Dalton. 'He's single, and according to MI5 has a thing about pre-pubescent boys, which at some point they hope to blackmail him with.'

'Is he under surveillance?' asked Yokely.

'Not at the moment. Not on a regular basis, anyway. My contact says they're working on putting an undercover agent into the mosque so they're leaving him pretty much alone until that comes off. Do you need to talk to him, or just off him?'

'A chat would be good,' said Yokely. 'What do you have in mind?'

'He rides to the mosque every morning at about half four in time for morning prayers. It would be easy enough to pick him up. And there's a self-storage place that's open twenty-four hours a day on the main road to Leeds. I could fix us up with a unit. No one would disturb us and the roads are quiet at that time of the day.'

'Morning it is. We can do the family in Stoke Newington tonight and head straight up to Dewsbury to grab the imam first thing.'

'So no sleep then?' asked McNee.

'Plenty of time for sleep when you're dead,' said Leclerc.

McNee scowled at the Canadian. 'I can keep going longer than you, Peter, any day of the week.'

'Challenge accepted,' said Leclerc.

'I don't think it's doable,' said Dalton. 'Even at night it's a four-hour drive minimum to Dewsbury from Stoke Newington. We'd need to be in place by four.'

Yokely grimaced. Dalton was right. 'Okay, so we come back to the hotel here and check out first thing. Get to Dewsbury early afternoon. We can do a recce of his house and mosque and get the lie of the land. And we can check out the storage unit facility.' He sipped his beer. 'What about disposal?' he asked Dalton.

'I can pay for the unit for a year in advance. Providing there's no smell, it won't be disturbed. Wrap it in plastic and we're good to go. We can either leave it there to decompose or move it later.'

'Do that,' said Yokely.

'What about the uncle?' asked McNee. 'Didn't you say he was on a no-fly list?'

'The Americans won't let him fly but he's got a pretty common name – Mohammed Ahmad – so there could just be some confusion,' said Dalton.

'The Brits aren't looking at him?'

Dalton shook his head. 'No, he and his nephew aren't on any British watch lists.'

Yokely nodded slowly. 'Okay, then maybe the uncle has a pass. Let's see what the imam says. And what about the ringleader, this Hakeem Khaled?'

'Nothing so far,' said Dalton. 'MI5 haven't heard of him and neither have the anti-terrorist cops. If he was a Palestinian who was given asylum there'll be a Home Office file on him but my contacts there are non-existent.'

'Mine aren't much better,' said Yokely. 'Homeland Security don't know of him, either, and there's no record of him flying into the country under that name. Looks like Khaled is managing to keep below the radar. But I'm on his case. Okay, can you get everything ready for Dewsbury? And we'll need night-vision goggles for tonight.' He looked over at Leclerc. 'And we'll need your lock-picking skills, Peter.'

Chapter 47

There were two men in the van that had been painted in the livery of a Birmingham plumbing company. The men wore matching blue overalls and heavy workboots and soft black leather gloves. They had parked in front of the lock-up and had spent ten minutes just sitting there, getting the lie of the land. The lock-up was secure and pedestrians were few and far between.

The man behind the wheel was the older of the two but only by a few years. Both were bald, though the older man's bald skull was a choice rather than genetic. He nodded at his companion. 'In you go,' he said. 'Any problems I'll beep the horn twice. Three times means get the hell out and expect the worst.'

Neither man was armed. They had documentation that showed they had been hired to carry out an inspection on the property so, even in the unlikely event that the cops turned up, there was a good chance they would be able to talk their way out of the situation.

The passenger climbed out of the van and slammed the door shut. He walked over to the door and bent down at the drainpipe there. He found the key immediately and used it to open the door and slipped inside.

He heard the buzzing of flies immediately and seconds later the smell of dead flesh assailed his nostrils. He put a hand over his mouth as he switched on a small Maglite torch. The beam found the body in seconds, the head covered in flies. He walked around to approach the corpse from the feet and knelt down.

He took a mobile phone from his pocket and slipped it into the back pocket of the man's jeans.

The man's wallet was in the left side pocket of the jeans and he fished it out. He took a folded piece of paper from the breast pocket of his overalls and placed it in the wallet. It was a receipt for a left luggage locker in the Bullring Shopping Centre, just a few miles away. Inside the locker was Farooqi's laptop computer. The man put the wallet back into the dead man's jeans pocket and then retraced his steps to the door.

Chapter 48

Present Day, London

Shepherd spent all of Saturday afternoon and most of the evening staring at the CCTV footage from the camera closest to where Farooqi lived. He took a five-minute break every half an hour to rest his eyes, but at six o'clock he took a complete break and went up to the canteen, where he ordered fish and chips and coffee.

Nick Hughes was sitting at a table tackling a chicken curry and Shepherd went over to join him.

'How's it going?' asked the inspector. 'George says you're looking at footage from Birmingham.'

'I'm checking on a Syrian refugee that Naveed phoned. Trying to see if he left with somebody, but it's not easy. A needle in a haystack doesn't come close.' He poured a large dollop of ketchup on his plate but as he picked up his knife and fork his mobile rang. It was Katra.

'Dan, where are you?' she asked.

It was clear from her tone that she wasn't happy and he could understand why. Since the bombing he had been working pretty much non-stop and only went home to shower and grab a few hours' sleep.

'You said we'd go shopping at Portobello Market,' she said.

'I know, and I'm sorry,' he said. 'I'm just working flat out.'

'What are you doing at the moment?'

'Right now, I'm eating. Then I have to get back to work.'

'You could have come home to eat. I could have cooked for you.'

'It would have taken too long, I'm sorry,' he said.

'I hardly see you at the moment. I thought the reason I moved down to London was so that I could spend more time with you.'

'I know, and once this case is over we'll spend lots of time together. But a lot of people died, Katra, and a lot more are still in hospital. They deserve justice for what happened to them.'

She didn't say anything but he could sense that she wasn't mollified.

'I'll make it up to you, I promise,' he said.

Inspector Hughes tried to suppress a smile but didn't do a very good job of it. Shepherd grimaced, stood up and went over to an empty part of the canteen. 'I'm really sorry but sometimes the job is like this,' he said. 'You didn't really see it when you were in Hereford and I was here or wherever, but believe me, there are many times when my job isn't nine to five and there's nothing I can do about it. I can't stand up and say I want to pack up work and go to see my lovely girlfriend, no matter how much I want to.'

'Lovely?' she repeated.

Shepherd laughed. 'Yes, lovely. Listen, of course I'd rather be at home drinking wine with you and watching a movie than sitting in a room with a bunch of sweaty policemen, but this is important. We're catching terrorists, Katra.'

'I'm being stupid, aren't I?' she said in a soft voice that sounded close to tears.

'No, it shows how much you love me,' he said. 'I'd be really worried if you didn't care what time I got home.'

'I do care,' she said.

'I know you do. And I will be home at some point, I just don't know when. But I will make it up to you.'

'Okay,' she said. 'I'm sorry.'

'You've nothing to apologise for. And I'll try to get home before midnight.'

She said goodbye and that she loved him but Shepherd could tell that she was close to tears. He put his phone in his pocket and went back to his fish and chips.

'Plays havoc with the family life, doesn't it?' said Hughes.

'When the shit hits the fan, sure. But it doesn't happen that often, to be fair. My speciality was working undercover and that can be twenty-four-seven for days on end. And before that I was in the army and that really plays havoc with family life.' He attacked his meal and suddenly realised how hungry he was.

'You've been around,' said Hughes. 'I joined the police as a graduate and haven't worked for anyone else.'

'I was with a police undercover unit after the army, and that was good fun. I'm not sure I could do what you do for ever.'

'It's valuable work,' said Hughes. 'And I did my fair share of RTAs and break-ins when I was on the beat.'

'I didn't mean to denigrate what you guys do,' said Shepherd. 'I can see how you get results. It's just not for me. I need . . .' He shrugged as he tried to find the right word.

'The adrenaline rush?'

'Yes. Maybe. The knowledge that you could get hurt if things go awry. What's the worst thing that could happen in the Super-Recogniser Unit? A bad back from sitting too long?' He saw the inspector's face fall and he quickly apologised. 'That came out wrong. It's a valuable job, I get it, and your arrest rate is way higher than mine ever was as an undercover agent. But it's not how I want to spend my career. I want to put guys away, and I want to be there when it happens, not just see it on an internal email a few days after I've put in my report. Does that make sense?'

'It makes perfect sense,' said Hughes. 'And I don't take offence. Me, I prefer fighting crime at a computer terminal. I like the fact that no one is going to spit in my face or make a spurious racism complaint about me or accuse me of being part of a system designed to suppress the common man. I come in, I sit down and I catch criminals because I'm good at recognising. That's good enough for me.' He shrugged. 'Mind you, it's a pain not getting paid overtime.'

'That's right, ranks above sergeant don't, do they? Same as my job. No overtime either.'

'You can't have everything,' said Hughes. 'But it's a bugger, isn't it? One of the PCs was saying he's hoping to get a new kitchen out of his overtime from this case.'

'Every cloud . . .' said Shepherd. He finished up his meal and headed downstairs with Hughes, taking a fresh coffee with him. He sat down, sighed and clicked the mouse to restart his CCTV footage.

Chapter 49

Jon Barnes lived in a semi-detached house about four miles from the lock-up where Israr Farooqi had been tortured and killed. It was late evening and the house seemed to be empty. The two men sat in their van and watched it for half an hour and saw no movement outside. A red and white flag of St George had been hung from one of the bedroom windows, the bottom weighed down so that it didn't blow around.

According to the information they'd been given, Barnes drove a four-year-old Jaguar XF and there was no sign of it outside the house or parked in the road.

The passenger climbed out of the van and opened the side door. He took out a metal toolbox with the insignia of the plumbing firm on the side. In the top pocket of his overalls he had a job note with the name and address of a house around the corner. In the unlikely event that he was asked to explain why he was at the house, producing the job note would make it look as if it was a simple mistake. He'd blame the GPS and all would be well.

He closed the side door and walked across the road, swinging the toolbox casually. He walked up the side of the house to where two wheelie bins were backed against the wall. One green and one black. He put the toolbox down and opened it. Inside was a carrier bag containing a blood-spattered hammer and a can of red spray paint. He opened the lid of the black wheelie bin and moved the rubbish around to make a space at the side. He dropped the carrier bag in and pulled rubbish over it, then closed the lid and picked up the toolbox again. He looked around, satisfied that nobody had seen what he'd done, and walked jauntily back to the van.

Chapter 50

Present Day, London

Shepherd woke to the sound of his mobile phone ringing.

'What time is it?' asked Katra sleepily.

He grabbed the phone and squinted at the screen. 'Eight o'clock,' he said. It was Don Margrave.

'You've only been in bed four hours,' she said.

Shepherd sat up.

'And it's Sunday.' Katra glared at him, then turned over and wrapped the quilt around herself.

He slid off the bed and padded naked into the hallway to take the call. 'Don, hey, how's it going?'

'The whole Israr Farooqi thing has kicked off and I thought you'd want a heads-up.'

'What happened?'

'Crimestoppers got an email tip-off about a body in a lock-up garage south of Birmingham. Turns out to be Farooqi. Someone had chopped off a toe and smashed in his skull. That someone then sprayed anti-Islamic graffiti on the walls.'

'Are you serious?'

'It gets better. The Birmingham cops then get a phone tip-off from a call box saying that a guy called Jon Barnes was connected to a racist killing. Barnes is a nasty piece of work and the Brummie cops were chomping on the bit so they used the tip-off as an excuse to go through his house with a fine-tooth-comb. They found a hammer with blood on it and a can of spray paint in his rubbish.'

'Oh, come on.'

'I'm just telling you what the cops have told us. The blood on the hammer is Farooqi's. They haven't matched the paint yet but the paint in the lock-up is red and so is the spray can they found with the hammer.'

'And what does this Jon Barnes say?'

'He's screaming fit-up. But then he always does. He runs the Anti-Muslim Brigade and they have a habit of burning out Asian families. There was one three months ago when a mother and a baby died. Barnes always has an alibi but his Facebook posts hint that his group deserves the credit.'

'Okay, but this isn't setting fire to a house, is it? Someone abducted Farooqi. How far is the lock-up from where he lived?'

'Four miles. Five maybe.'

'So someone takes him across town and what, chops off a toe before killing him? Why not kill him in his house? And why chop off a toe?'

'Torture maybe?'

'So why just one toe?'

'What are you thinking?'

'I'm thinking maybe someone was trying to get information out of Farooqi. And the fact that they only took off one toe suggests that he started talking pretty quickly. Why would the leader of a racist group be doing that?'

'I'm just telling you what the Brummie cops told me,' said the detective. 'How was I to know you'd be looking the gift horse right down the throat.'

'But you hear what I'm saying, Don? This is a guy who burns out Asians and boasts about it on social media. Why does he suddenly move into abduction, torture and bludgeoning to death? And who tipped off the cops in the first place?'

Margrave laughed. 'You understand how the anonymous tip process works, right?'

'You know what I mean. Who could have known there was a body in the garage? The killer, obviously. And why would anyone leave a murder weapon out with his rubbish?'

'I'm starting to regret phoning you now,' said Margrave. 'I guess you don't want to hear the really good news.'

'Go on, I'll bite.'

'His phone was there. And there was a left luggage receipt in his wallet. The cops checked the locker and you'll never guess what they found inside.'

'A suicide vest?'

The detective chuckled. 'Chance'd be a fine thing,' he said. 'No, it was Farooqi's laptop.'

'He kept his laptop in a left luggage locker?'

'Seems like clever tradecraft to me. Anyway, the phone and the laptop are being rushed to your technical boys as we speak.'

'So they realise it's terrorism and not racist?'

'I'm not sure that the Brummie cops had a change of heart. My understanding is that MI5 stepped in and asked for the laptop and the phone. They've also slapped a D Notice on the story so you won't be seeing anything in the media. Hopefully you'll be able to get the intel from the horse's mouth.'

'I'll give it a go,' said Shepherd. 'Any news on Yussuf?'

'Still missing, believed to be on the run,' said the detective. 'Though after what's happened to Farooqi I'm wondering if someone got to him, too.'

'Seriously?'

'I really don't know, Spider. Nothing about this case surprises me any more. Though there's nothing to suggest that Yussuf was abducted. Like I said before, he'd taken clothes with him, and his toothbrush. People who are abducted don't usually pack a bag first.'

'Fingers crossed,' said Shepherd. 'Do me a favour and text me the address where the body was found.'

He ended the call and went back into the bedroom. Katra was sleeping. Shepherd considered getting back into bed but he wasn't tired; the adrenaline had kicked in again and all he really wanted to do was to get back to the office.

Chapter 51

'What do you think?' asked the woman. She was in her early thirties, blonde with too much make-up and wearing a pink tracksuit with JUICY written across the bottoms.

Sitting in the driving seat was a man who hadn't shaved for several days. Like his companion he was wearing a tracksuit but his was blue and Adidas. He was also in his thirties and while he slouched in his seat, a closer look would have determined that he was in good physical condition. The woman was fitter than she looked, too, and was more than capable of holding her own against most men. She had a black belt in Shotokan karate, was expert at Krav Maga, the military self-defence system devised for the Israeli security forces, and was an expert shot with small arms and rifles.

The car was an old Ford Escort with a couple of fluorescent orange dice hanging from the mirror and a back seat littered with fast-food wrappers and pizza boxes. They were in a run-down part of Salford and the car and the outfits helped them to blend in. They were looking across the road at a brand new BMW Five Series, black with tinted windows and gold wheels.

'Personally, I'd rather put it in the boot, hide it in the spare tyre,' said the man.

'Yeah, and I'd like a date with Brad Pitt but I don't see that happening in the foreseeable future. Look, he didn't get back until four in the morning.' She looked at her watch, a pink Casio. 'It's now ten-thirty. He could be sleeping all day for all we know. Then who knows where he'll be tonight.'

'What about getting inside the house?'

The woman shook her head. 'Way too risky while he's in there.' She folded her arms. 'I say we put it in the car now, under the passenger seat. It makes sense to keep a gun there. Nobody would question it.'

'You'll be seen.'

'Not if I'm lucky.'

'That's your plan? To depend on luck?'

'If I time it right it'll be fine. Walk alongside the car. Open the door. Gun under the seat. Close the door. Four seconds. Five at the most.' She nodded at the upstairs bedroom window. The blinds were down. And the curtains were closed in the downstairs window. 'He's not going to see anything.'

'No, but people in the street will.' Further down the road a woman was pushing a stroller with a toddler in it. An old woman was walking slowly with two carrier bags and behind her was a shaven-headed bruiser of a man with a large brown pit bull on a lead.

'The passenger door is on the road side. I'll be covered. You can drive up and that'll cover me from the other side. Four seconds, Pete. Tops.'

Pete sighed. 'I don't like it.'

'What are our options? We sit here on our arses all day doing nothing until we get a phone call and we're asked what the fuck is the delay? Or we say that we're sorry but the job is just too difficult. Either way our careers come to an abrupt end. We can't even do a simple drop.'

'Yeah, but it's not simple, is it, Katy? And if we get caught, then what? You want to explain how you've got a murder weapon in your hand? Because I sure as fuck don't.'

'I'm just saying, we can't sit here all day.'

Katy had a key fob in her right hand. The previous night they had been following the BMW and had got close enough to clone the car's keyless entry code. The driver had been going into a nightclub and Katy had asked him for a cigarette. The device – the size of a packet of cigarettes – had been in her pocket and it picked up the fob's wireless code and recorded it. That code was now stored on the key fob Katy was holding, allowing her access to the BMW whenever they needed it.

'I'll use the stroller as cover. It'll work.'

'What do you want me to say, Katy? I don't think it's a good idea.'

'Well what is? We sit here until he wakes up. Then he goes out and what? You saw what happened at the club – he gets waved to VIP parking and there's security everywhere. I don't see we have any choice here. Urgent, Charlie said. Remember?'

Pete nodded. He remembered. He tapped his fingers on the steering wheel, then nodded. 'Okay.'

'Don't worry,' she said. She looked around. 'I'll walk to the corner shop back there. I'll have the stroller as cover and I'll wait until the pavements are as clear as they get. You park up at the end of the road. When I start walking, time your drive so that we reach the BMW together. I'll cross the road, you pull up next to me. I'll make the drop, you drive off, I get on to the pavement and walk away. You drive around the block and pick me up.'

He sighed. 'You make it sound so easy.'

'Four seconds, max. It'll be fine.'

'I hope so.' He grinned. 'And don't call me Max.'

She punched him lightly on the shoulder and got out of the car. He popped the boot and she went around to the rear and took out the stroller. She pulled the hood down so that no one could see that it was empty. The Glock was wrapped in a cloth. Next to it was a box of flesh-coloured latex gloves and she pulled on a pair before picking up the gun and slipping it into the stroller. She slammed the boot shut and lifted the stroller on to the pavement. She lit a cigarette and blew smoke up at the overcast sky as Pete drove away, then she pushed the stroller towards the corner shop. Her heart was racing and the cigarette wasn't helping. It wasn't that she was scared; the chances of the police coming along or the target suddenly appearing were infinitesimal – the worst that could happen is that someone might see what she was doing but even if that did happen it wasn't the sort of area where people called the police. It was more that she didn't want to fail. They had been given a task to carry out and she wanted everything to go smoothly. She blew smoke down at the pavement and flicked ash. Four seconds, max. She smiled. It was going to be fine.

Pete appeared at the far end of the road. There was no traffic and only a handful of pedestrians. She took another drag on the cigarette and began pushing the stroller.

An old man with waist-length dreadlocks and a Bob Marley hat stepped out on to the pavement and turned to pull his front door shut behind him. Katy steered around him.

She heard a rapid footfall behind her and turned to see half a dozen schoolkids running down the pavement. They whizzed past her as if trying to see how close they could get without actually hitting her. She took another pull on the cigarette. Pete was driving down the road towards her, at just above walking speed. She blew smoke, then looked over her shoulder and pushed the stroller into the road, walking diagonally so that she would reach the BMW.

A moped drove down the road, heading towards Pete. It was an UberEats delivery driver, clearly looking for an address. Katy said a silent prayer that he wasn't going to the target's address. She paused in the road and took a drag on her cigarette, then relaxed as the moped continued on its way. She flicked away the butt and pushed the stroller towards the BMW. She reached into the pocket of her tracksuit and pressed the key fob. The BMW's lights flicked on and off.

Pete was about fifty feet from her and she slowed as she walked parallel to the BMW. She took a quick look over her shoulder. There were a few pedestrians but most of them were looking at their smartphones as they walked.

Pete timed his arrival perfectly, drawing level with the BMW just as she reached for the passenger door handle. She pulled open the door. Bent down and pulled the Glock from the stroller, and slipped it under the passenger seat. She closed the door and straightened up as Pete drove away.

She manoeuvered the stroller around the rear of the BMW and lifted it on to the pavement. As she walked away she clicked the key fob again, relocking the car. She smiled to herself. Job done.

Chapter 52

Ten Years Ago, Leeds

Yokely looked at his watch. It was four o'clock in the morning. He was sitting in the back of a van with the name of an Indian restaurant on the side. Dalton was in the driving seat. Yokely was dressed in black and holding a ski mask in his hands. His phone buzzed to let him know he'd received a text message. It was from McNee: *On way.* The imam had left for the mosque. McNee was parked up on a motorbike a short distance away from the imam's house. His brief was to follow the imam at a safe distance.

'Target is on the way,' said Yokely. He yawned. It had been a long night. They had taken care of Latif Makhdoom and his parents, making it look as if they had been killed in a fire at their Stoke Newington home, then driven up to Leeds. Yokely had managed to snatch a few hours' sleep in the back of the van, but he was still bone tired.

Leclerc was also in the back of the van and he nodded. Like Yokely, he was dressed in black and carrying a ski mask. On the floor of the van they had duct tape, a stun gun and a hood to throw over the imam's head.

The van was in a supermarket car park, its front pointed towards the road. The engine was off. Yokely watched the second hand on his Rolex Submariner crawl around. After four minutes he patted the back of Dalton's seat and Dalton started the engine. The three men in the back pulled on their ski masks and Yokely picked up his stun gun. He pressed the button on the side and bright blue sparks cracked between the two prongs. Forty-six million volts and totally illegal in the United Kingdom.

'Here he comes,' said Dalton. 'Two hundred yards.'

There were no windows in the rear of the van so Dalton was going to have to be their eyes. 'A hundred and fifty,' said Dalton. 'The road's clear, we're good to go.' He revved the engine.

Leclerc put his hand on the door handle, ready to pull the door to the side. They would be facing the imam on his bike.

'A hundred yards,' said Dalton. 'Ready to move.'

Yokely took a deep breath and exhaled. 'Here we go,' he said.

'Fifty yards,' said Dalton. He eased on the accelerator and the van edged forward.

'Twenty yards.' He stamped on the accelerator and the van leapt into the road and then almost immediately he braked.

Leclerc pulled on the handle and slid the door open. The imam was almost on top of them, his eyes wide with fright. He was wearing a white skullcap and a grey thawb and had a carrier bag hanging from his handlebars and the brakes were squealing as he tried to stop.

Leclerc jumped out. The imam tried to steer in front of the van but he was moving too quickly and didn't make it. The bike slammed into the van and the front wheel crumpled. The imam fell to the side but Leclerc was already moving, grabbing him by the scruff of the neck and heaving him into the van.

Yokely helped drag the imam inside and shouted 'Clear' as he pressed the stun gun against the man's neck and pressed the trigger. The imam went into convulsions, his feet thrashing against the van floor.

Leclerc grabbed the bike, threw it into the van and climbed in after it, then pulled the door shut.

Dalton stamped on the accelerator and they sped off down the road.

Leclerc tied a gag around the imam's mouth and pulled the hood over his head.

Yokely used the duct tape to bind the man's feet and wrists together, then pulled off his ski mask. He grinned at Leclerc. 'Well done.'

Dalton drove to the storage unit. It was on the ground floor with a roll-up metal door. The entrance to the facility was covered by CCTV and there were cameras on all the floors, but the unit Dalton had taken was in the middle of a row of twenty with no direct CCTV coverage. The van could be driven alongside the unit and no one would see what was being taken inside through the side door of the vehicle.

Yokely climbed out, unlocked the sliding door, then raised it and Leclerc handed him the bike. As Yokely put the bike in the corner of the unit, Leclerc dragged out the unconscious imam and dropped him on the floor. He pulled the van door shut and banged on the side. As Yokely pulled down the storage-unit door, Dalton drove the van away.

There was a wooden chair in the middle of the unit and Yokely used duct tape to bind the imam's arms and feet to it. Leclerc picked up a bottle of water, pulled the hood off the unconscious imam and then poured water over him. After a few seconds, the imam began to cough and splutter. Yokely untied the gag.

El Saadawi continued to cough and blink his eyes. Eventually he focused on Yokely. 'Who are you?' he asked.

Yokely ignored him and went over to a black holdall. He opened it and took out a hammer.

'What do you want?' asked El Saadawi. He looked over at Leclerc. 'What is this? Who are you?'

'Look at me, Mr El Saadawi,' said Yokely. 'I'll be the one asking you questions.'

'Questions? What questions?' He looked around, trying to work out where he was being held. 'What is this place?'

The imam had been wearing sandals but they had come off in the van. Yokely squatted down, hefting the hammer.

'What do you want?' asked the imam, his voice trembling.

Yokely smiled up at him. 'I want you to answer a few questions, Mr El Saadawi. But in my experience, people don't tell me anything until they're in pain. So bear with me while I break a few of your toes and then we'll get to the questions.' He raised the hammer.

'No!' shouted the imam. 'What questions, what do you want to know?'

'There's no point in telling you because you'll say you don't know what I'm talking about, you know nothing, it's all a big mistake etcetera etcetera. So then I'll have to hurt you and only then will you tell me the truth. I'm in a bit of a rush, Mr El Saadawi, so to save time I'll go straight to the toe-smashing, if you don't mind.' He lifted the hammer again and took aim at the imam's left big toe.

'For the love of Allah and his prophet, please!' shouted El Saadawi. 'Just ask what you want and inshallah I will be able to answer.'

'Inshallah? If god is willing? I'm not sure if this is about God, Mr El Saadawi. Religion, maybe. Jihad, certainly. But I don't think God's hand is in this.'

'What do you want to know?' gasped the imam. 'Please, ask your questions.'

Yokely sat back on his heels. 'Okay, let's try it your way. Shabir Rauf. You sent him to Afghanistan for training, didn't you?'

El Saadawi opened his mouth to argue but Yokely raised the hammer. 'Yes, yes, I sent him to Afghanistan,' stammered the imam. 'But to further his studies, that is all.'

'Studies in Stinger missiles and bomb-making, no doubt,' said Yokely. 'Where is he now?'

'I don't know.' Yokely lifted the hammer again. 'I swear on the prophet, I don't know!'

'Shabir's uncle, do you know him?'

'He has many uncles.'

'Mohammed Ahmad.'

'He is at the mosque sometimes. A few times a week.'

'Did you send Shabir to America?'

The imam frowned. 'America? No.'

'Well someone did.'

'Not me, I swear. After he was in Afghanistan he stopped coming to the mosque.'

'You didn't know what he was doing there? In America?'

'No.'

'Well someone must have sent him. If not you, then who? Have you heard of Hakeem Khaled?'

The imam's lips tightened and his eyes hardened. 'I'm not familiar with the name,' he said.

Yokely smiled at the obvious lie. 'Really? I'm told he frequents the Finsbury Park Mosque.'

'I rarely travel to London,' said the imam. 'It is not a pleasant city. I am happier here.'

'How do you contact this Hakeem Khaled?'

'I told you, I do not know this man.'

'I don't believe you,' said Yokely. 'I assume it involves an email draft file. I need you to give me the email address and password.'

The imam shook his head. 'You are wrong.'

'Let's see how a few broken toes changes that,' he said. He nodded at McNee, who moved to stand behind the imam. The imam glared at Yokely as he picked up the hammer again. Yokely raised the hammer but the imam said nothing. Yokely shook his head sadly, then brought the hammer smashing down on the big toe. It split and blood splattered across the concrete floor. The imam screamed but Leclerc had already clamped his hand over the man's mouth, muffling the cry.

Yokely sat back and Leclerc released his grip on the man's mouth. 'So I'll ask you again. Do you know Hakeem Khaled?'

The imam nodded tearfully. 'I know him.'

'And you put him in touch with Shabir?'

'Yes.'

'Did Hakeem say what he wanted Shabir to do?'

'No. He told me to send him for training, which I did. On his return, I did not see Shabir again.'

'When did Shabir come back from Afghanistan?'

'A month ago. Six weeks, maybe.'

'And how did you talk to Hakeem?'

'Through an email account.'

'I need you to give me the name of the account and the password.' Yokely raised the hammer threateningly.

'Yes, yes,' said the imam. He gabbled the Yahoo account name and password and Leclerc wrote it down.

'Well done, Mr El Saadawi. You've saved yourself a great deal of pain.' He stood up and put the hammer back in the holdall.

'What happens now?' asked El Saadawi. 'You will let me go?'

'No,' said Yokely. 'That's not going to happen, I'm afraid.'

The imam opened his mouth to scream but Leclerc had the plastic bag ready and he whipped it over the man's head. The screams quickly changed into grunts as the bag pulsed in and out. The imam strained at his bonds, his eyes glaring at Yokely through the transparent plastic, but then he went quiet and his eyes slowly closed.

Leclerc was already unwrapping a roll of plastic sheeting.

'What about breakfast?' asked McNee.

Yokely looked at his watch. It was coming up to seven o'clock in the morning. 'I don't see why not,' he said. 'Then we'll head back to London.'

'Excellent,' said McNee. He grinned. 'I know a place.'

Chapter 53

Present Day, London

As soon as he got to the Super-Recogniser Unit in Lambeth, Shepherd went over to talk to Sergeant Hurry. 'George, can you do me a favour?' he asked. He took the sergeant over to his desk and tapped in the address of the lock-up where Farooqi had been found. Then he tapped in the address of Farooqi's flat. 'That Syrian refugee I told you about, the one in Birmingham. He's just turned up dead.' He tapped the location of the house. 'This is where Farooqi lived.' He moved his finger and tapped the lock-up. 'This was where his body was found. Looks like he was abducted and killed not long after the stadium bombing.'

Hurry nodded. 'Okay.'

'Can you see what CCTV feeds are available on the direct route, but also look at alternative routes as well? Then can you get the feeds patched through to me?'

'Sure.' Hurry went back to his desk while Shepherd used Google Maps and Street View to check the area as best he could.

It took Hurry less than an hour to patch in feeds from several dozen CCTV cameras on the routes between Farooqi's flat and the lock-up where he died. He had also prepared a map of the area showing the location of the camera sites. Most were council run and used for monitoring traffic and potential trouble spots in the city. Hurry compiled an on-screen map using Google Maps and had also produced a large printout that Shepherd placed at the side of his keyboard. He was setting himself a huge task, he knew that, and he wasn't thrilled about the amount of work involved. Farooqi clearly hadn't walked from his flat to the lock-up, which meant that he had travelled in a vehicle of some kind, almost certainly under duress. Shepherd had to make an educated guess on the time frame, but the torture had been minor, which meant Farooqi had given up intel to his captors fairly quickly. He was probably only held for a few hours, so the total time from being picked up to being killed would probably be around three hours. Shepherd decided to double the time frame to be on the safe side. The vehicle must have driven to the flat, picked up Farooqi and then driven to the lock-up. There were half a dozen routes between the two locations and all had CCTV coverage at some point. The problem was that there were no CCTV cameras in the street where Farooqi lived or close to the lock-up. He was going to have to watch all the footage on all the possible routes and spot any common vehicles that were near the flat and then later near the lock-up. It was going to be a mammoth under-taking, and while his photographic memory was near faultless, he'd never used it like this before.

Shepherd remembered everything he had ever seen or done – he could recall every conversation he'd had and every face he'd seen. Once he had something in his long-term memory, it was there for ever. His short-term memory was also close to perfect. He'd always been able to memorise facts and as a party trick as a kid he'd memorise the order of a deck of playing cards in less than a minute. But what he was asking his memory to do on this occasion was something completely different – he was going to be looking at hundreds upon hundreds of vehicles and looking for a match, and that wasn't something he'd done before.

He counted the CCTV camera locations. There were thirty-seven. Watching all thirty-seven feeds for six hours would take more than two hundred hours. He couldn't delegate the task to anyone else because the Super-Recognisers were all about recog-nising faces and bodies – so far as he was aware none of them had the same eidetic memory as his. This was going to have to be a solo job. He sighed and clicked on the feed nearest to

Farooqi's flat, then settled back in his chair. It was going to be a long week.

Shepherd sat back in his chair and sipped his coffee, then stood up and stretched his legs. It was now almost midday and he'd spent two solid hours watching the CCTV footage on the main road from Farooqi's flat to the lock-up. It was mind-numbingly boring; all he was looking at was vehicles coming up to a set of traffic lights and either going through or stopping depending on the colour of the lights. At this stage he was just remembering the colour and type of the vehicles and he was able to play the footage at three times the normal speed. Once he had watched the full six hours of the feed he would switch to another camera. His hope was that he would see the same vehicle in both feeds, and if he did he could then try to get a decent view of the registration plate.

Shepherd's mobile phone rang. It was Amar Singh. He took the call. 'Hey, Amar. You working weekends as well?'

'Everyone's in,' said Singh. 'Just wanted to fill you in on what was on the hard drive I took from the Internet café.'

'I'm listening,' said Shepherd.

'He went to a Yahoo email account and opened a draft file. He had deleted the conversation but we were able to recover it from the servers, so all good. He spoke to someone called Saladin. There's a lot of stuff from the Koran but basically Saladin was telling Naveen that he was going to heaven and that his name would be revered as a hero for all time, the normal sort of stuff you tell someone when you want them to blow themselves to smithereens.'

'Any idea who this Saladin is?'

'Unfortunately not. But I've been able to go back over the last few months and see what was in the draft file. This Saladin has been grooming Naveed for a long time. And they had a meeting. A couple of weeks ago.'

'Where?'

'The Argyle Street Mosque in Ealing.'

'That's his regular mosque. What day?'

'The second. At first prayers.'

'You're a star, Amar, thanks. What happens next?'

'I'll be passing my report on to Patsy Ellis. It's up to her what happens next. I'm not sure how much is going to happen on a Sunday but we'll see. And mum's the word, yeah?'

'Amar, I've got the best security clearance there is.'

'Yes, but you're on attachment to the Met and Ellis has made it clear that all intel has to go through her office prior to getting clearance for release to the Met.'

'Even SO15?'

'The Met in its entirety, Spider, so technically that would include you. So like I said, mum's the word.'

'Message received and understood,' said Shepherd, and ended the call. He sat down, clicked his mouse to restart the CCTV footage and settled back in his chair.

Chapter 54

Present Day, Salford

Carlton Chapman patted his girlfriend's expanding belly. 'Babe, you sure you've not got twins in there?'

She laughed and pressed herself against him. 'It's just the one boy, but he's going to be a big one,' she said. Her hand moved down between his legs. 'Come back to bed, you know how horny I am right now.'

Chapman laughed. 'Babe, it was you getting horny got you pregnant in the first place.' He cupped her full breast in his hand and squeezed gently. 'I love the way your tits are filling out,' he said. 'You look so damn hot right now.' He looked at his watch, a gold Rolex Sea-Dweller. 'I'm late as it is.' He had to drive over to Liverpool to see about a consignment of coke that was coming in from Ireland and the Liverpool boys were sticklers for punctuality. But Jay-lee was only wearing one of his T-shirts and it barely reached the top of her long, caramel legs. It was her amazingly long legs that had first attracted him to her, but it was her skills in bed that had kept him with her for the last six months, almost exclusively. Chapman had seven children by four different women scattered across Birmingham, plus another two in Manchester. Those were the ones that he knew about and supported; he wasn't a big fan of condoms but he did enjoy one-night stands.

'What time will you be back?' she asked, rubbing his crotch gently.

'I don't know. It's business babe and you know you can't set your clock to it.' He kissed her on the cheek but she reached up to grab the back of his neck and pulled him down to her, kissing him hard on the lips before he broke away, laughing.

He was still laughing as he walked over to his BMW and pressed the key fob to unlock it, but his smile froze as six armed police officers charged towards him shouting for him to get down on the ground. He stopped, stunned, staring at the Kevlar helmets, bulletproof vests and high-powered carbines. He blinked, wondered what the hell was happening, then his legs were swept from underneath him and he hit the pavement, hard. 'What the fuck,' he gasped.

His legs were kicked apart and something pressed down in the middle of his back. Someone was still yelling at him to lie down. His arms were grabbed and twisted around and he felt flexicuffs being fastened around his wrists.

His left cheek was pressed against the pavement but through his right eye he could see the cops pulling open the doors of his car. One of them was groping under the front passenger seat. Chapman grinned savagely. They were wasting their fucking time. He never kept anything in his car – no guns, no drugs, no cash. There was none in the house either. He paid people to carry what he needed.

'Gun!' shouted one of the armed cops.

'What the fuck do you mean, gun?' sneered Chapman.

The armed officer held up a Glock pistol. 'Gun!' he shouted. 'Am making safe.'

'Oh fuck the fuck off,' said Chapman. 'I wouldn't be seen dead with a fucking Glock.'

The officer ejected the magazine and checked there wasn't a round in the breech before putting the pistol back where he had found it.

Chapman was hauled to his feet and marched over to a waiting van. He didn't bother protesting his innocence. He knew there was no point. He would leave that to his solicitor down the line. When arrested by the police there was only one rule – don't say one word to the bastards.

Chapter 55

Shepherd was in the canteen buying a round of sandwiches and coffees for the unit when his mobile rang. It was Don Margrave.

'I hadn't realised how much work would be involved in keeping you up to speed,' said the detective.

'Sorry, mate. But I'll make it up to you one day.'

'How exactly?'

Shepherd laughed. 'In my experience, most favours get repaid eventually. So what have you got for me?'

'GMP have just pulled in the killer of Masood and his family. Drug dealer in Salford by the name of Carlton Chapman. They found the murder weapon in his car.'

'Nice police work,' said Shepherd.

'Well, to hear GMP talk you'd think that. But I'm told they got a tip-off saying the gun was in his car. They sent in a couple of ARVs and lo and behold, the Glock was under the front passenger seat.'

'And what does Chapman say?'

'Chapman has gone all three wise monkeys, but his lawyer says the gun was a plant. And to be fair, Chapman's prints aren't on the gun or the cartridges and there's no gunshot residue on his hands. But, you know, gloves . . .'

'Any D Notice on this?'

'Hell no, GMP even had a tame TV crew along to film it. It'll be all over the evening news.'

'What about Masood's background and the fact that his sons had been fighting for ISIS?'

'It's been touted as a drug-dealers-falling-out story,' said Margrave.

'How do you feel about that?'

'It's possible,' said Margrave. 'There's a lot of drugs in Bolton so there could have been an argument over territory. And the youngest son has been in prison for drugs.'

'Dealing?'

'Possession.'

'You don't kill customers, you kill rival dealers,' said Shepherd.

'The Manchester police are looking into it.'

'What, they had a drug-dealing family on their patch that they didn't know about? That doesn't make their drugs squad look good, does it?'

'You know GMP aren't known for their smarts,' said Margrave. 'Let's see what they come up with. But for the moment, the deaths of Masood and his family are being put down to a gang-land execution. I just wanted you to know.'

'I appreciate it. Thanks.'

'And how are you spending this lovely Sunday morning?'

'I'm watching CCTV footage, trying to see who abducted and killed Israr Farooqi.'

'Good luck with that.'

'Cheers, Don.' Shepherd ended the call and stared at his phone thoughtfully. He had a bad feeling about the way things were going. A very bad feeling. It was all just too convenient. An anonymous call leads the police to Farooqi's body and another call gives up his racist killer. Another anonymous call gives them the killer of Imran Masood and his family. Either the police were getting very lucky or someone behind the scenes was trying to draw attention away from what was really happening. He was going to have to talk to Patsy Ellis again. And soon.

Chapter 56

Ten Years Ago, Washington DC

Christopher Mullins let himself into his house and put his briefcase down by the hall table. The answering-machine light was flashing and there were twenty-two messages. He sighed. He went through to his study and poured himself a large measure of Macallan twenty-year-old single malt. His wife had bought it for him for their twentieth wedding anniversary and he had always kept it for special occasions. He figured that today was as special an occasion as they got, so he sipped it and went back into the hallway. He took out his mobile phone. There were six missed calls from his PA, Jenna. He knew what she was calling about and didn't want to talk to her. There were three missed calls from the White House. He took another sip of the single malt. It was beautifully smooth and gave him a nice warm feeling across his chest.

He pressed the button to listen to the messages on the answering machine. The first was from Jenna, wanting to know why he wasn't answering his cell phone. The second was from the White House, telling him the President wanted to talk to him. The third was Jenna again, sounding more anxious this time. The fourth was from one of the political correspondents at the *Washington Post*, just requesting a call back. Mullins had known the journalist for more than a decade and she was one of the few he trusted. The fifth call was from CNN, again requesting a call back.

The sixth call was Jenna again. 'Where the hell are you?' She never spoke to him like that. Never. The seventh call was the *Washington Post* reporter again. She said that CNN were preparing to run a story that his wife and son had been on the plane that went down at JFK. She wanted him to call back. There was a hardness to her voice as if she was upset that CNN had the story and she didn't.

Call number eight was from the *New York Times*, asking for a call back. Then a call from the Head of News at CNN confirming that they were about to go public with a story that his family had been on board the doomed jet. 'We need to talk to you, obviously, but we will be airing the piece come what may,' said the Head of News.

Call number nine was from the White House, insisting that he called the President immediately. Mullins didn't listen to any more. He walked away and into his study. He closed the door and took a long pull on his whisky. It really was a good whisky, possibly the best he'd ever tasted.

On a cabinet was a framed photograph – a family picture taken the previous Christmas. His wife had insisted that they all wear red shirts and Santa hats. Mullins had laughed at the idea but the photograph was pretty much his favourite. They all looked so happy, so at ease with each other. His wife had one hand on his shoulder and the other on their son's arm. She was looking up at him and the photographer had caught the love in her eyes. Their son was laughing at something the photographer had said, and his eyes were sparkling, full of life. Nine years old. Tears pricked Mullins' eyes and he blinked them away.

He took the photograph over to his desk and sat down. He placed the picture in the middle of the desk and refilled his glass with whisky. He opened the top right-hand drawer of his desk and took out a semi-automatic. It was a Colt 45. His father's gun. His father had died five years earlier and the gun had been specifically mentioned in the man's will. It seemed to Mullins that the gun had mattered more to his father than the millions of dollars and the property he had left to his only son. The gun mattered because it had saved his life several times in Vietnam, where he served as a captain.

Mullins had never actually fired the weapon. But it was loaded.

He took a long drink of whisky and swallowed. He ejected the magazine, then slotted it back into place. He pulled back the slide mechanism and released it, slotting a round into the chamber. He stared at the picture again and blinked away tears.

He had spent an hour or so on the Internet googling the best way to commit suicide with a handgun. He got close to two million hits and there was a lot of advice. Most people seemed in agreement that a shotgun was the weapon of choice, but he didn't have a shotgun.

When it came to using a handgun, the most popular site was the right temple, for right-handers. The mouth was second and the forehead was third. Shots under the chin were not recommended as people tended to flinch when they pulled the trigger, resulting in a non-fatal shot. One recommendation was to shoot through the mouth with a high-energy cartridge, aiming down so that the bullet went through the top of the spinal cord. It sounded too technical and he had rejected the idea. Shots to the front of the head risked only damaging the cerebral cortex and that might not be fatal.

It was on the fourth or fifth site that he visited that he read about the technique of filling your mouth full of water before inserting the gun in the mouth. The water intensified the explosion and the head virtually disintegrated when the trigger was pulled. Death was certain and instantaneous. It sounded to Mullins like the perfect way to go. He planned to add an extra refinement though, substituting the water with a twenty-year-old malt whisky.

He looked at the photograph and smiled at his wife and son through the tears. 'I'll be with you soon,' he said. He really believed that. He was a committed Christian, had been his whole life, and he knew that suicide was a sin, but he was sure that once he passed over he would be with his family again. He sipped his whisky, then took a longer gulp. He swallowed slowly and let the warmth spread across his chest. He smiled. The whisky was a good idea. There were much worse ways to go. He tilted his head back and poured in as much whisky as he could, then pressed his lips together and put the glass on the desk. He picked up the gun and sat back, keeping his eyes on the photograph as he slipped the barrel of the Colt between his lips. Whisky started to leak around the metal so he pulled the trigger immediately. As the Internet had promised, death was certain and instantaneous.

Chapter 57

Present Day, London

First thing Monday morning, Shepherd was at Thames House, the Grade 2 listed building on the north bank of the river close to Lambeth Bridge that had been MI5's headquarters since December 1994. Patsy Ellis kept Shepherd waiting for almost half an hour in her outer office before her secretary ushered him in. She didn't appear as pleased to see him as the last time he'd been there.

'I'm not sure why you thought we needed a face to face,' she said. She smiled but there was little or no warmth in it.

'There's something I need to run by you and I didn't think a phone call was appropriate.'

She waved him to sit. She looked tired. There were dark patches under her eyes and deep wrinkles across her forehead.

Shepherd sat down and folded his arms, then realised that made him look defensive so he put his hands on his knees and tried to relax. It was tough to do because he knew that Ellis wasn't going to be happy with what he was about to say. He took a deep breath and forced a smile. 'So, here's the thing,' he said. 'You've heard about Carlton Chapman, the drug dealer up in Salford who's just been arrested for the murder of Imran Masood and his family?'

Ellis frowned. 'I hadn't heard that. But then if it's a drugs case, it probably wouldn't cross my desk.'

'But Imran Masood is Ali Naveed's uncle. Or was. But the tense isn't important. What is important is that Masood and his family were all shot.'

'And the killer has been arrested, you say?'

'Alleged killer. The gun was in his car. It's being tested for fingerprints and DNA.'

'So why is this of such interest to you? It was a drug dispute, was it?'

Shepherd shrugged. 'There's no evidence that the Masood family were involved in the drugs trade.'

'The fact that another drug dealer killed them is a sign that there is some drug connection, don't you think?'

'Imran Masood travelled to Syria regularly and was an ISIS sympathiser. His three sons are all believed to have had terrorist training in Syria and are thought to have fought with ISIS.'

'They wouldn't have been the first terrorists to have been involved in the drugs trade.'

Shepherd resisted the urge to snap at her. She seemed to be deliberately being obtuse but she was his boss and losing his temper wouldn't get him anywhere. He took a deep breath. 'Okay, but then look at what happened to Khuram Zaghba. We identify him as the driver of the van that delivered Ali Naveed to the stadium and within a day he's been murdered.'

'In a racial attack.'

'In a supposed racial attack,' said Shepherd. 'A few strips of bacon and some graffiti means nothing. Could have been the killer muddying the water.'

'Muddying the water?' repeated Ellis. 'Can you hear yourself, Dan? You're saying there's a killer who killed a suspect in a terrorist case who then goes to the trouble of making it look as if the attack was racist?'

'So you think it's a coincidence?'

'I think that coincidences happen, yes. I hear what you're saying, and it's duly noted. But I think you're reading too much into the situation.'

'Two people closely connected to a suicide bomber are killed within hours of each other.'

'One was an assassination by a drugs dealer who is now in police custody, the other was battered to death in an apparent racist attack.'

Shepherd shook his head. 'There's more,' he said. 'Israr Farooqi. Naveed made a call to him. He's also a refugee from Syria.'

'I'm aware of that.'

'And he's just turned up tortured and killed in a lock-up a few miles from where he lived. Someone had hacked off one of his toes.'

'And there was racist graffiti at the scene, I'm told.' Her eyes narrowed. 'But how do you know about that? There's a D Notice in force.'

'A pal in SO15 tipped me off.'

'Really? And who might that pal be, pray tell?'

Shepherd ignored the question. 'So you know what's happened? The Birmingham cops got a tip-off that a guy called Jon Barnes was involved and the cops found the murder weapon at his house, along with a can of spray paint.'

'So there's no mystery there then. It was a racially motivated killing.'

'In a lock-up six miles from where the victim lived? And what about the fact that Farooqi was tortured? Barnes runs the Anti-Muslim Brigade, which makes a habit of burning out Asian families. It's a big jump from arson to abduction, torture and murder.'

'Who said anything about abduction?'

'What, you think that he went there on his own?'

'He might have done. We don't know. Maybe Farooqi was lured there, maybe he went to meet someone. I don't think you can start making assumptions about abduction.'

'Fine. But you have to ask why this Jon Barnes suddenly moved from arson to torture and why he was stupid enough to keep the murder weapon and the paint.'

'In my experience, generally racists aren't that bright. It's really a prerequisite of being a racist, don't you think?'

'But you can see a pattern here, can't you? Masood, Zaghba and Farooqi, all connected to Naveed one way or another, and all dead.'

Ellis held up her hands and shrugged. 'I don't know what you want me to say.'

'You think it's a coincidence?'

'In the absence of any concrete evidence linking the deaths, yes, that would be my conclusion.'

Shepherd took a slow, deep breath before continuing. 'I'm told that MI5 now has Farooqi's laptop and phone.'

Her eyes hardened. 'And who told you that? Your friend in SO15? I'm starting to wonder if your friend is in the right job.'

'He was just keeping me in the loop,' said Shepherd. 'I have the requisite security clearance.'

'But that's not your brief, Dan. Your brief is to organise the review of any CCTV footage that is pertinent to the investigation, and to keep me informed of any developments. Not to go gossiping with the police.'

'It helps me to have sight of the bigger picture,' said Shepherd. 'And by keeping abreast of developments I know what CCTV footage to be looking at.'

She said nothing for several seconds as she stared at him with unblinking eyes. He met her gaze, unwilling to look away. He didn't want to be confrontational but he wasn't going to let her browbeat him.

'So to be absolutely clear, what exactly are you suggesting?' she said eventually. 'That someone killed Masood and his family and framed a drug dealer for the murders, and that same someone killed Khuram Zaghba and also tortured and killed Israr Farooqi?'

'I'm suggesting that we look for a connection, yes.'

'See now, Dan, that sounds like a conspiracy theory you've read on one of the crazier parts of the Internet. On a par with the Americans never went to the moon and that planes never hit the twin towers.'

'Maybe there's some sort of cover-up going on. Maybe Masood, Zaghba and Farooqi were party to some information that someone wants to keep secret. Maybe they were killed to keep that secret.'

'What secret? What could they possibly know? They're hardly masterminds, are they? They are foot soldiers in this war. And who is killing them? ISIS? Racists?'

'I don't know,' said Shepherd. 'Maybe it was their own people.

Maybe they did know something and someone in ISIS decided it would be safer to take them out. And it would make sense for them to make it look as if it was the work of racists to throw us off the scent.'

'Wouldn't they want the killings to stand as a warning?'

'It's never good publicity to kill your own,' said Shepherd. 'Look, what I'm saying is that there's something not right going on. And that perhaps we should look at it.' Shepherd stood up. 'I just thought I should express my concerns.'

'Duly noted.'

He headed for the door.

'One thing, Dan, before you go,' said Ellis. 'I will pass on your concerns. And I will get the three killings looked at again. But no more off-the-books chats with investigators. Your role is not, and I repeat not, to cut across ongoing lines of inquiry. Clear?'

Shepherd nodded. 'Clear.'

'Just concentrate on the task you've been given.'

'I understand.'

She dismissed him with a curt wave of her hand.

Shepherd left the office and went down in the lift deep in thought. Working undercover was often a matter of life and death and a key part of surviving was to be able to read people, to tell when they were being truthful and when they were lying. Shepherd knew without a shadow of a doubt that Ellis was hiding something. It was clear from her reaction that she knew that Farooqi's laptop and phone had been sent to MI5 for analysis. Shepherd hadn't pressed her because he could see that she was already on the defensive but there was clearly something not right. According to Margrave, MI5 had been quick off the mark to request the laptop and the phone. The question was, how had they known to ask for it? Farooqi lived in Birmingham and it had been the Birmingham cops who had received the tip-off about the body. They wouldn't have known that Ali Naveed had phoned Farooqi, or that Farooqi was in any way connected to a terrorism investigation. Margrave had said that it had been officers from SO15 who had gone to Farooqi's flat. So far as the

Birmingham cops were concerned, Farooqi's torture and murder were racially motivated. That being the case, there would be no reason to pass the details on to the Met and if the Met hadn't been told then they couldn't have passed the information on to MI5. The fact that MI5 had requested the laptop and phone so quickly and had been ready with a D Notice right from the off suggested they had prior knowledge of the discovery of the body – and that opened up a whole new can of worms.

Chapter 58

McNee's breakfast place was a small restaurant frequented by truck drivers on one of the main roads out of Leeds. They talked as they tucked into plates of egg, bacon, sausage and baked beans.

'We really need to find this Hakeem Khaled,' said Yokely. 'He's the one who put it all together. The Brits don't seem to know about him. Or at least he's not on any of their watch lists. But they gave him a passport so he must be in the system.'

'What about the States?' asked McNee. 'There must be a record of him flying in or out?'

Yokely shook his head. 'He must have used another passport under another name because there's no record of a Hakeem Khaled flying in before or after the downing of the jet. I need to access the email account that El Saadawi used.'

'There's an Internet café down the road,' said McNee. He looked at his watch. 'Should be open in half an hour.'

'Perfect timing,' said Yokely.

They finished their breakfasts and ordered more coffees. At nine o'clock, Yokely walked down the road to the café and paid for an hour's Internet access. He left McNee and Leclerc drinking coffee, figuring that three Americans sitting around a single computer might look suspicious. He sat down in front of a terminal that had been used so often, the lettering on many of the keys had worn away.

Yokely tapped in the password that El Saadawi had given him to access the Yahoo account. He opened the draft folder. There were two emails. Yokely opened the first one. He smiled when he saw that it was from Saladin, the name that Khaled had used when talking to Hamid bin Faisal. And his smile widened when he saw that the email was in English.

The two men had taken it in turns to write on the draft email, and they had added to the message rather than deleting what had already been written. There was a lot of Islamic rhetoric and both men were careful with their language. There were no references to weapons or missiles or terrorist acts. Shabir was referred to by name, which was careless tradecraft, but all they talked about was how Shabir would be getting to the US and how he would be met. El Saadawi also talked about other worshippers at his mosque who he planned to send to Afghanistan for what he called 'further study'.

Yokely stared at the email for several minutes, deep in thought. Khaled wouldn't know that El Saadawi was dead. There was a chance – albeit a slim one – that Khaled would respond to any messages left in the draft file. There was only one other person using the café and he had headphones on and was Skyping his girlfriend, so Yokely took out his cell phone and called Sam Hepburn at the National Security Agency. It was only when Hepburn answered that Yokely remembered the time difference – it was the early hours in Maryland.

'Sam, sorry, were you sleeping?'

'No problem, Richard, I had to get up to answer the phone,' said Hepburn, his voice loaded with sarcasm.

'I'm really sorry, Sam. But I'm in the middle of something important. Are you at home?'

'That tends to be where I sleep, yes.' Yokely heard Hepburn whisper to someone, probably his wife, telling her that it was a work call. 'Go ahead, Richard, what do you need?'

Yokely explained that he was about to leave a message in a draft folder and he wanted Hepburn to monitor the account and locate whoever responded.

'I can do that, no problem,' said Hepburn. 'I can set it up from here. It'll take me about five minutes. Give me the account name and password.'

Yokely gave him the information, thanked him and ended the call. He waited five minutes and then added a message to the email in the draft folder.

Think not of those who are slain in Allah's way as dead. Nay, they live, finding their sustenance in the presence of their Lord. I will be in the UK next week. Can we meet?

He closed the file and opened the second message in the draft folder. The original message had been created two months earlier and again the updates had been added with no deletions. There was an MP4 video file attached to the email. The name of the file was BRADSHAW. Yokely clicked on it. It was a white man, mid-thirties, holding a Grail missile. Behind him was an al-Qaeda flag. The video was about three minutes long. Bradshaw had a black and white checked keffiyeh scarf around his neck. He spoke earnestly, staring at the camera with deep-set eyes. The West was intent on destroying Muslims around the world, they hated the religion as much as they feared it, and it was the duty of every Muslim to fight the aggressor. He was going to teach the West a lesson they would never forget, he said. He finished his rambling speech with an impassioned '*Allahu Akbar*', the effect of which was somewhat spoiled by the fact that he then had to crawl forward to stop the videoing.

Yokely sat back in his chair. Bradshaw was the man Alex Kleintank had talked about, the British Muslim convert who wanted to buy a Grail missile. From the sound of it, he had managed to acquire one. In a perfect world Yokely could just pass the intel on to Dan Shepherd or his boss, Charlotte Button, but Yokely and his team were supposed to be below the radar. And if Bradshaw was apprehended then that might well lead the British to Kleintank and El Saadawi and who knew what else. Yokely was going to have to take care of it, and quickly.

He went back to the email. There was a discussion back and forth about renting an office by the Thames. A high floor with a view across the river and no CCTV coverage in the corridors.

The office had been rented in the name of a shelf company and the keys sent to a mailbox in Mayfair. The video was to be released to various news outlets once Bradshaw had carried out his mission. Again there were many quotes from the Koran, including, 'But do not think of those that have been slain in God's cause as dead. Nay, they are alive! With their Sustainer have they their sustenance.' It sounded as if Bradshaw was intent on a suicide mission.

He cleared his browsing history, switched off the computer and walked out of the café. He lit one of his small cigars and walked slowly back to the restaurant, where McNee and Leclerc were still nursing their coffees. They looked at him expectantly.

'Slight change of plan,' he said. 'We have a new target. A British jihadist who is planning to create havoc in London. I've got the address of an office he's going to be using. And it looks like we're going to have to move quickly.'

Chapter 59

Present Day, London

There were more than two dozen officers sitting at workstations when Shepherd got back to the unit. Sergeant Hurry was still at his desk and Inspector Hughes had drafted in another two Super-Recognisers to watch footage from the Argyle Street Mosque, going back three months. Anyone who was seen with Ali Naveed was identified and run through the various anti-terrorism databases. So far they had found three matches, young men who had returned from Syria after fighting with ISIS. All three were on MI5's watch list, though none was under active surveillance. Shepherd figured the fact that they were now linked to a suicide bomber who had killed three dozen people meant that would almost certainly change.

While Shepherd had been out of the office, Eric Fitzpatrick had turned his attention to another Internet café, this one on Ealing Road. He had seen Naveed entering two weeks earlier, three times in one day. Shepherd phoned Amar Singh and gave him the details and Singh promised to go over straight away to collect any computers that Naveed had used.

Shepherd settled down in front of his screen and picked up the map showing the routes between Israr Farooqi's flat and the garage. He'd watched the footage from three of the feeds in their entirety and had discovered more than a dozen vehicles that had been both close to the flat and also in the area of the lock-up. Eight were Uber cabs, seven of which were variations of the Toyota Prius and one of which was a Skoda. Six of the eight were driven by young men with Muslim names but none was on either the police or MI5's database.

Three of the vehicles were pizza delivery vans. Shepherd couldn't get details of the drivers but the companies that owned the vans seemed genuine. He had marked them all down for further investigation as a pizza van would be the perfect cover for moving a body, dead or alive.

One of the vehicles belonged to an emergency plumbing firm and there were so many sightings in the area that Shepherd figured it was out on calls, but again he made a note to have the van checked out.

One of the cars was a red Hyundai hatchback driven by a young Muslim guy by the name of Muzhar Jhangir who was as busy as the pizza delivery vans, appearing on all three of the feeds at various times. Jhangir wasn't known to the security services but he was of interest to the Birmingham Police Drugs Squad, who were reasonably sure that he was a heroin and crack cocaine dealer. He had only one conviction, for marijuana possession as a teenager, but there was plenty of intel that suggested he was connected to a major British-Pakistani drugs gang. Shepherd sent off a memo to the Drugs Squad telling them of Jhangir's night-time activities and suggesting that they pull in his car at some point.

Shepherd made himself comfortable and clicked his mouse to restart the feed he had been watching. It was mind-crushingly boring. All he was doing was watching cars drive down a road. The time code said it was just after one a.m. and the camera was covering a junction with traffic lights. Shepherd was already about halfway through the feed and the traffic had died down after the first couple of hours and most of his time was spent watching the lights change. A Mercedes sports car pulled up at a red light. A Porsche pulled up next to it. There was no sound but Shepherd knew that engines were being revved and as soon as the lights changed the two cars raced off. Shepherd smiled to himself. Boys and their toys.

The lights changed. Vehicles came and went. All Shepherd had to do was to keep his eyes open. Concentrating didn't help; his memory functioned on automatic. When he did see a car he recognised, it was as if there was a tickle somewhere in his head, followed by the memory of where he had seen it before. He didn't have to strain or try; it just happened.

Half an hour passed. He recognised one of the Uber cars again. The guy was clearly having a busy night. Then a silver grey Toyota Avensis pulled up at the lights. Shepherd tensed and leaned forward to get a better look at the number plate. He had seen the car in an earlier feed, close to Farooqi's flat. With no effort at all he could recall the time when the Avensis had appeared in the other feed. Ten minutes to midnight. The time on the feed he was looking at was one thirty-five. The timing was right if the Avensis had driven to the flat, picked up Farooqi and was now driving him to the lock-up.

He tapped into the DVLA database and within seconds had ascertained that the car was taxed and insured and belonged to Nicholas Brett, a dentist in Leicester. Brett had been caught in speed traps in the Leicester area twice over the past year and had six penalty points on his licence. Shepherd checked him out on the Police National Computer but there was nothing. Other than a few speeding tickets, Mr Brett was a model citizen. Shepherd frowned, wondering why a Leicester dentist was driving around Birmingham at night. He pulled up the man's driving licence and studied the photograph. Middle-aged, a full head of hair, almost smiling for the camera.

He entered the number into the National Automatic Number Plate Recognition Data Centre database. The National ANPR centre was based in Hendon, North London, and its computers read and analysed more than 100 million number plates every day, storing the information for two years. The ANPR was run separately from the Police National Computer and officers would often cross-check the two databases. The police, and the security services, could use the ANPR database to track vehicles across the country, and often identify the drivers, depending on the quality of the pictures and video. They had real-time access to all the country's ANPR camera data, though records less than ninety days old needed an inspector's authority to be viewed, and over ninety days the inquiry had to be counter-terrorism-related and a superintendent had to sign off on it.

Shepherd was only looking for sightings for the past three days, and all inquiries from the unit were automatically approved by Inspector Hughes.

He sat back and looked at the results of his search. The Avensis had been seen and videoed in London, Manchester, Birmingham and Leicester, more than a hundred times in all. The sightings were in chronological order and his heart began to race when he realised what route the car had taken. The car had started in London and then driven up to Manchester. After Manchester the car had travelled down to Birmingham and then on to London. In London the car was photographed twice in Acton, not far from where Khuram Zaghba had been killed. One of the cameras had caught the car at just before midnight but there was a sighting just thirty minutes earlier in Leicester, which didn't make any sense.

The fact that the car was in Acton was suspicious enough, but it was then seen driving back to Birmingham. It was in the Birmingham area for more than two hours before being driven to Bolton in the early hours of the morning. That couldn't possibly have been a coincidence. The car had been in the area of all three murder scenes.

But it was the Leicester sightings that made no sense and on some occasions the car seemed to be in two places at the same time.

He went back into the ANPR database and requested all sightings of the Avensis between four days ago and eight days ago. He got his answer within seconds. There were several dozen matches – all of them in the Leicester area. Shepherd sat back and stretched out his legs. There was only one conclusion to be drawn – the car that was in London, Manchester and Birmingham was a ringer, using the same plate as Mr Brett's vehicle. That suggested a professional was at work, which meant that Shepherd was definitely on the right track.

He went back to the list of sightings and began checking the ones in London. Most of them were traffic cameras and enforcement cameras and, while they gave a decent view of the car and the registration plate, they were no help in identifying the driver.

There were several decent shots of the front windscreen in some of the footage from cameras in Birmingham and Manchester. In the Manchester shots it looked as if the driver was alone but in some of the Birmingham footage Shepherd was fairly sure there was someone in the front passenger seat.

In one of the Highways Agency camera feeds he saw the Avensis turn off a major road and head for a service station. He froze the image several times but he couldn't ever get a clear look at the driver. He called over to Sergeant Hurry, who was watching a CCTV feed on fast-forward. 'George, can you do me a favour?'

The sergeant froze his feed and looked over. 'Sure.'

'I've got a Highways camera covering a service station to the west of Manchester. If I ping over the time and date and the location can you see what feeds we can pull in from the station itself? Ideally covering the pumps.'

'No problem,' said Hurry.

Shepherd copied the details and sent them in an email. 'I'll do a canteen run,' he said. 'What do you want?'

'I'd love a bacon roll and a coffee,' said Hurry.

'Ketchup or HP sauce?'

Hurry laughed. 'The eternal question. Surprise me. But no sugar in the coffee. No surprises there.'

More than a dozen officers immediately chimed in with orders for bacon rolls and coffee and it was half an hour later when Shepherd returned with a laden tray. He handed out the food and drinks, then sat down at his desk.

George Hurry came over and patted him on the shoulder. 'You're good to go. I sent you links to three downloads, there are two cameras covering the forecourt and another at the cash register.'

'You're a star,' said Shepherd. 'Brilliant.'

He sipped his coffee and checked his emails. There were three links as Hurry had promised. He clicked on the first one and opened the video file. It was from a camera covering the approach to the pumps. He fast-forwarded it until he saw the Avensis arrive, then watched it at regular speed. It was the right car but there was too much glare on the windscreen, so it was all he could do to make out the outline of the driver. There didn't seem to be a front seat passenger.

He clicked on the second link. This was footage from a camera covering the exit from the pump area. He fast-forwarded to the same time and saw the nose of the Avensis but it stopped just short of giving him a full view of the car. The driver got out but at no point was his face visible as he put petrol in the tank.

Shepherd clicked through to the final link. It was from a camera high up in a corner, looking down at the cash register and showing a section of the floor between the door and the counter. Shepherd played the footage at regular speed, keeping a close eye on the time code. His heart began to pound as he reached the time when the driver of the Avensis was putting fuel in. Then the door opened and a man walked in. Five feet ten, maybe five feet eleven, wearing a black jacket and dark jeans. Shepherd couldn't see all of the face but it was already clear it wasn't Nicholas Brett, the Leicester dentist. The man had his head down as he walked towards the counter, his hand pulling a wallet from the jeans. He kept his head down as he took two twenty-pound notes from the wallet.

'Look up, look up, damn you,' whispered Shepherd, leaning towards the screen. Almost as if he had heard, the man lifted his head and smiled at the man by the cash register. Shepherd's mouth fell open as the cashier took the cash. He pressed the mouse to freeze the image and he stared at the image in amazement. 'Lex fucking Harper,' he whispered. 'What the hell are you up to?'

Chapter 60

Present Day, Surrey

There were almost a hundred mourners at the funeral. Eleanor and Sarah Coles were laid to rest in a pretty churchyard in Surrey. The Coles family were regulars at the church and counted the vicar as a friend. The sky was cloudless, it was a warm day and those who had turned up in dark coats had them unbuttoned.

After the service the mourners walked out into the graveyard and watched as the two coffins were lowered into the ground. Eleanor's was glistening pine, but Sarah's smaller coffin had been painted in United's colours. They were placed next to each other in a single grave.

Lucy and Clive Coles stood silent in grief, and from the glazed look in the mother's eyes it appeared she had taken some form of medication to help her get through the day. Her husband stood on her left, his arm protectively around her, but he seemed more in need of support than she did. Patsy Ellis stood on Lucy's right, her arm linked through her friend's, her face stone hard.

The vicar finished speaking over the grave and the mourners drifted away. Lucy Coles burst into tears and her husband clasped her to his chest.

Ellis left the grieving parents and walked over to join Button.

'It was a lovely service,' said Button, though she knew the words were empty. What could be lovely about consigning two girls to the ground? Parents should never have to bury their children; it was against the natural order of things.

'Yes, it was,' said Ellis. 'And it's a lovely church.' She nodded at the grave. 'Lucy and Clive have the plot next to where Eleanor and Sarah are buried. Lucy said it comforted her to think that one day they would all be together. How fucking sad is that?'

Button felt her eyes prick with tears. 'I'm so sorry,' she said and stepped forward and hugged Ellis.

'It's okay, it's okay,' said Ellis. She sniffed and blinked back her own tears. 'So, we have a location for Saladin,' she said.

'Really? Where?'

'The Afghan–Pakistan border. There is a network of caves there that ISIS uses as a training camp. We placed a message in Farooqi's email draft folder, talking about the stadium bombing and saying that he wanted to be used in the service of jihad.' She smiled ruefully. 'Bloody nonsense, right? You wonder what goes through their heads.' She sighed. 'Anyway, Saladin got back the following day with a load of nonsense from the Koran, basically telling him to be patient. Amar Singh had rigged it so that it looked as if there was a technical problem – he froze the page and then made it look as if the message hadn't loaded so Saladin had to retype it. They ended up keeping him online for almost twenty minutes. He was using a sat phone just outside the cave complex. We have the sat phone number, which is a bonus.'

'It means he could be targeted with a drone, right?'

Ellis grimaced as if she had a bad taste in her mouth. 'The problem is we still don't know his real name or what he looks like. Yes, we could target the phone but there's no guarantee that the person using it at the time would be Saladin.'

'So how do we move forward?'

'At the moment we don't. I'm still waiting to hear back from the Americans, though the delay suggests to me that they have nothing on him. The French haven't come across the name and the Germans are being their usual unhelpful selves. All we can do now is wait to see if Saladin gets back in touch with Farooqi.'

'And what about Yussuf?'

'Still no sign of him. It's possible he left the country before we started looking for him.' She took Button's arm and gently squeezed it. 'Thank you,' she said. 'Thank you for coming and thank you for everything you've done.'

'You don't have to thank me,' said Button.

'Yes, I do,' said Ellis.

Chapter 61

Ten Years Ago, London

'That's him,' said Dalton. He pointed at a man pulling a wheeled suitcase from his Toyota Prius over to the elevator that led to the building above. They were in an underground car park and had been waiting the best part of an hour for Paul Bradshaw to arrive. Dalton was in the driver's seat of the black Range Rover, Yokely was sitting next to him and Leclerc was in the back. The man was wearing a leather jacket and chinos. He was wearing glasses and his hair seemed unnaturally black, as if it had been dyed. It was certainly darker than it had been in the al-Qaeda video that Yokely had seen.

They watched as Bradshaw disappeared into the elevator with his suitcase.

'Well, he doesn't have a Grail in there, the shape's not right,' said Yokely.

'This is his third trip today,' said Dalton.

'He had a case each time?' asked Yokely.

'He takes it in and about fifteen minutes later he brings it out,' said Dalton. He was holding an iPad and he showed it to Yokely. It was a view of the corridor in the building. 'Twelfth floor,' he said.

Dalton had put a small camera in the corridor, a Wi-Fi model with enough battery power to keep it going for a few hours. Yokely looked at the screen and watched as the man emerged from the elevator, pulled the suitcase down the corridor and then unlocked an office door. After a few seconds he disappeared inside.

'What would his target be?'

'The office is riverside so he has a clear view of the South Bank – the National Theatre, Royal Festival Hall and the London Eye.'

Yokely raised his eyebrows. 'The London Eye? That makes sense.'

The London Eye was the huge Ferris wheel that dominated the South Bank of the Thames. There were thirty-two pods on the wheel and each of the pods could carry a maximum of twenty-five passengers, which meant that when the Eye was full there were eight hundred men, women and children on board, the equivalent of two fully loaded jumbo jets. The giant wheel was sponsored by British Airways and access to it involved passing through full security screening including metal detectors. But a single Grail missile fired from the other side of the river would destroy it in seconds.

'How do we play this?' asked Leclerc.

'We're going to have to take him out ourselves, and handle the disposal. If the authorities are involved it'll fuck up our operation.'

Leclerc nodded. 'I can handle the lock.'

The door to the office opened and Bradshaw walked out, pulling the suitcase. 'Where does he go?'

'A house in Kilburn. Gerry follows him on his bike. Full-on security. CCTV, reinforced doors. Always at least two occupants.'

They watched the floor indicator above the door click up to number twelve and then stop. Five minutes later, the elevator went down three floors, stopped and returned to the parking garage. The doors opened and two young men in suits carrying briefcases went over to a black BMW.

Over the next fifteen minutes, a dozen people came down in the elevator and drove away. Then the elevator went up to the twelfth floor, stopped and came down to the parking garage. Bradshaw came out, pulling the suitcase. It was clear that the case was now empty. He swung it into the back of his Toyota and drove off.

Dalton called McNee on his mobile. 'Target heading out now.'

McNee was outside on his high-powered motorbike. He

confirmed that he had eyes on the target and that he was following him.

Yokely considered his options. He needed to know exactly what was happening in the office on the twelfth floor, and sooner rather than later. Bradshaw was obviously taking something into the office, but was the missile already there? If it was, he could fire it at any point. But if they broke into the office and Bradshaw realised he'd been discovered, he could bolt.

Dalton could see that Yokely was deep in thought so he sat quietly.

'Okay,' said Yokely eventually. 'We wait. For a while longer at least.'

It took Bradshaw half an hour to drive to the house in Kilburn. Once he'd gone inside, McNee phoned Dalton. He called again twenty minutes later to say that Bradshaw was leaving the house, this time with a metal trunk.

'Large enough for a Grail missile launcher?' asked Yokely.

'Affirmative,' said McNee.

Yokely ended the call and twisted around in his seat. 'Right, Peter, time to demonstrate your lock-picking skills.'

'You're going in?' asked Dalton.

Yokely nodded. 'You keep a watch here. As soon as he arrives, call me.'

Yokely and Leclerc got out of the Range Rover and went over to the elevator. Leclerc had a keycard that he tapped against a reader before pressing the button to summon the elevator. They rode up to the twelfth floor.

The door to the office that Bradshaw was using was also accessed with a keycard. Leclerc had a piece of specialist kit designed to open keycard locks. He slotted in a card that was connected to a small handheld computer unit. The card was able to read the opening code in the lock's memory and the computer played it back. It took less than five seconds to open the door and they slipped inside.

The views over the Thames were spectacular. Yokely went over to the window and phoned Dalton. 'We're in,' he said.

'You need to see this,' said Leclerc.

Yokely turned to look at Leclerc. He was at the far end of the office. Against the wall were boxes of Calor gas cylinders and stacks of jerry cans. Leclerc opened one of the cans and sniffed. 'Petrol,' he said. 'This is what he's been bringing in inside the suitcases.'

Yokely nodded. The backblast from the Grail missile would ignite the petrol and the heat would explode the gas cylinders, blowing out a big chunk of the front of the building. It probably wouldn't be enough to bring the building down, but that wasn't his intention. Bradshaw just wanted to make sure that his mission was a suicide one. He intended to die in a blaze of glory.

At the far end of the main office was a door that led to a windowless storeroom. Yokely nodded at the bare shelves. 'We can wait here,' he said. They both had Glocks in underarm holsters and were carrying silencers.

They stayed by the window until Dalton phoned them to let them know that Bradshaw had arrived downstairs. Yokely and Leclerc slipped into the storeroom and pulled the door closed.

Dalton called again. 'He's in the elevator now.' Yokely ended the call and made sure that his phone was on silent. They took out their guns and screwed in the silencers.

Yokely and Leclerc stood where they were, their guns at the ready. They heard the door open, then the sound of something heavy being placed on the floor and the door being closed.

There was the sound of something being opened, and then a grunt. Then Bradshaw began mumbling something, something that sounded like an Islamic prayer.

Yokely nodded at Leclerc, who reached for the door handle. Yokely had the gun in his right hand and he counted off 3-2-1 with his left. Leclerc pulled the door open in one smooth motion and Yokely stepped into the main office.

Bradshaw was kneeling in the middle of the office, the Grail launcher on his shoulder. There was a metal trunk at his side, the lid open. The missile was pointing at the window. In the distance, on the other side of the river, the London Eye, turning so slowly that there was no perceptible movement.

'*Allahu Akbar*,' Bradshaw muttered.

Yokely could see Bradshaw's finger slipping over the trigger mechanism so he fired three times in quick succession, all the shots aimed at the man's head. The head exploded in a mass of blood and brain matter that splattered across the carpet. The Grail launcher hit the ground with a dull thud and for a second Yokely's heart was in his mouth even though he knew a blow wouldn't be enough to launch the missile.

Leclerc stood next to him and looked down at the body. 'Nice grouping,' he said.

'The third shot went a bit wide.'

'Still hit the target,' said Leclerc.

Yokely unscrewed the silencer and slid his Glock into its underarm holster. He took out his cell phone to call Dalton to tell him that they were ready for him to arrange disposal, but then he saw that he had an incoming call. The caller was withholding their number.

'Richard Yokely?' It was a woman's voice.

'Yes.'

'Hold for the Defense Secretary, please.'

Yokely frowned, wondering why Chris Mullins was calling him, and why he was getting his assistant to place the call. But the man who came on to the line wasn't Mullins.

'Where the fuck are you?' snapped the man in a nasal Boston accent. It was Robert Follis, who as far as Yokely was aware was running the Defense Intelligence Agency and not the Defense Department.

Yokely looked down at the body on the floor and realised that it probably wouldn't be in his best interests to be precise about his location. 'London,' he said. 'What happened to Chris Mullins?'

'He killed himself yesterday.' From the man's tone it was as if he was blaming Yokely for the suicide.

Yokely felt as if he had been hit in the stomach and his jaw dropped.

'Are you still there?'

'Yes,' said Yokely. 'Did he leave a note?'

'No. But the Press was on his case. They discovered that his wife and boy were on the plane that went down at JFK. They were travelling under assumed names so it took time to come out. You understand what has happened here, Richard? What Mullins ordered, what you have been doing, none of it has the approval of the White House. You've been on a revenge mission from day one.'

Yokely's head was swimming as the realisation of what had happened hit home. 'Where does that leave me?' he asked.

'That's a very good question, Richard. The words Shit, Creek and Paddle come to mind. You need to stand down with immediate effect, obviously. And any teams you have in place also need to stand down. And you need to get yourself to Los Angeles, ASAP.'

'Not Washington?'

'The President doesn't want you anywhere near the White House, Richard. I'm sure you can understand why. We're fixing up a meeting on the West Coast and, believe me, you've got some explaining to do.'

The line went dead. Yokely stared at his cell phone, his mind in turmoil. What the hell had happened?

Chapter 62

Present Day, London

Shepherd spent most of Tuesday checking all the sightings of Lex Harper's car and drawing up a timeline on a map. By early afternoon it had become clear that Harper had driven up to Manchester, then down to Birmingham and then back down to London, to Acton. From Acton, presumably after he had battered Khuram Zaghba to death, he drove back up north to Birmingham to torture and kill Farooqi. Then on to Bolton to kill the Masood family. It had obviously been one hell of a night.

From Bolton the car had headed south and entered London on the M1 before vanishing, presumably into a garage or car park.

The first sightings were on the M1 driving north to Manchester. The timeline suggested that Harper had been collecting something, a weapon perhaps. Or an accomplice. Then the car was parked in a hotel car park at Birmingham Airport. Shepherd had asked Sergeant Hurry to see if they could get a feed from the hotel's CCTV system but that was proving difficult and Hurry had asked if they wanted the local cops to go around and collect the footage on a hard drive. Shepherd was reluctant to do that as it would have meant having to explain what he wanted to look at and he preferred to keep Lex Harper's involvement to himself, for a while at least.

Shepherd and Harper went back a long way. There had been a time, during his SAS days, when Shepherd had been a skilled sniper. For several months he had been assigned Harper, then a young paratrooper, to be his spotter and guardian, the man who watched over him and helped determine wind, distance and accuracy as Shepherd took his shots. Harper's tough no-nonsense attitude and harsh sense of humour went down well with all the SAS guys, and he and Shepherd formed a good team.

Harper had all the skills and mental toughness necessary to pass Selection and join the SAS if he'd wanted to, and he and Shepherd had many long conversations during which Shepherd had tried to persuade him to do just that. But Harper never really enjoyed being a soldier. He actually relished combat and was never bothered about taking lives – it was taking orders that he never found easy. They resigned from the army at about the same time. Shepherd quit to join an undercover police unit and Harper just left. Shepherd wasn't entirely sure where Harper went, or what he was doing, or which side of the law he was on while he was doing it, but eventually Harper reappeared as a member of the Pool, an ad-hoc team of men and women, many former military, who were used to do the jobs that the government didn't want to be associated with. In recent years Shepherd's former boss Charlotte Button had run the Pool. She would put together teams as and when needed to carry out all sorts of dirty operations, up to and including contract killings. Shepherd scratched his head. Was it at all possible that the Pool had been behind the deaths of Israr Farooqi, Khuram Zaghba and Imran Masood and his family? Why would the government want suspects in a terrorist case to be murdered rather than brought to trial? But if it wasn't a Pool operation, why was Lex Harper involved? Did he have a personal reason for wanting Zaghba, Masood and Farooqi dead? That would make sense if perhaps a relative or a friend of Harper's had been killed in the stadium bombing and Harper wanted revenge and was bent on killing anyone who might have helped Naveed. Harper was the type who would want to take matters into his own hands. Shepherd frowned as he tried to make sense of what he'd discovered. How had Harper known about Farooqi so quickly? Or Masood? Or Zaghba? There was no way that Harper could have known about the three men and their connections to Ali Naveed. MI5 had discovered that Ali Naveed had phoned Farooqi, and they knew that Masood was Naveed's uncle. That information wasn't generally known, so someone must have passed it on to Harper. But who? If it was Charlotte Button then it would have been a Pool operation and again that made no sense. There was no advantage to be gained by killing Israr Farooqi instead of arresting and questioning him. The same went for Imran Masood and his family. And what about Khuram Zaghba, the van driver? Zaghba had been murdered only hours after he had been identified as the driver of the van that had delivered Ali Naveed to the football stadium. How could Harper possibly have known that? Shepherd's mind whirled as he considered all the options.

It was late evening by the time Shepherd had decided what to do. It took him almost an hour to come up with the right bait: Andrew Millen. Shepherd took a deep breath and composed himself. He took no pleasure in what he was about to do, and he knew that he was putting Andrew Millen's life on the line in order to prove if his suspicions were correct. Not that Millen was an innocent. Far from it. Born in the UK to Roman Catholic parents, he got into trouble as a teenager experimenting with drugs, which he paid for by stealing cars, and he'd served time for assault. While he was in prison he converted to Islam and after his release he was known to have fought with ISIS in Syria before slipping back into the UK in the winter of 2016. MI5 had him under observation for almost six months but it was clear that he had been schooled in counter-surveillance techniques and the watchers were unable to pin anything on him. The decision had been taken to withdraw the surveillance in the hope that he would be lulled into a false sense of security. In Shepherd's view the decision had been a mistake, but then no one had asked his opinion.

He took another deep breath, exhaled slowly and then rang Patsy Ellis's number. She answered almost immediately and he apologised for calling at such a late hour.

'It's not a problem, Dan, what do you have for me?'

'I've got a lead on Yussuf,' said Shepherd. 'I'm pretty sure he's staying with a jihadist on our watch list. A guy called Andrew Millen. British born but converted to Islam while in prison a few years ago. He changed his name to Mohammed al-Britani by deed poll. He's on Five's watch list but is being treated as a low priority. I've got CCTV footage of Yussuf and Millen together close to Millen's house in Harlesden.'

'Are they there now?'

'There's no camera close to the house but there's footage of them heading in that direction three hours ago.'

'Has this been passed to SO15 yet?'

'It'll be done in the morning. As I said, we're not a hundred per cent sure that Yussuf is there. But it'll need checking out. It was more to let you know that he's still in the country.'

'Okay, well thanks for keeping me in the loop, Dan. How are things going there?'

'Noses to the grindstone, but we're making good progress,' said Shepherd.

'Are you still in the office?'

'Just heading home,' lied Shepherd. In fact he was going to drive towards Harlesden, where he figured he had a long night in front of him.

Chapter 63

Lex Harper was lying on his bed watching *Newsnight* when his iPod Touch buzzed and he looked at the screen. It was Charlotte Button calling.

'Where are you?' she asked as soon as he answered.

He could tell from her tone that she was under pressure so he gave her a straight answer. 'My hotel. London.'

'You need to get to Harlesden now. I'll send you the address and a picture of the target. His name is Andrew Millen but he also uses the name Mohammed al-Britani. He did time for assault when he was in his teens and became a Muslim while he was behind bars. He's been in Syria with ISIS but isn't currently under surveillance. The intel we have is that Usman Yussuf is staying with him.'

'What is wrong with Five these days?' asked Harper. 'How can someone like Millen not be under a bloody microscope? Or better still, locked up in Belmarsh.'

'Don't go looking gift horses in the mouth, Alex. The fact that they're not watching him will give you a clean run, at least until the morning.'

'What happens in the morning?'

'The cops will be picking him up, so you need to get a move on.'

Harper sat up. 'I'm on it.' He ended the call and phoned O'Hara. 'Are you ready to go?'

'Just got out of the shower.'

'Well get your clothes on sharpish,' said Harper. 'We've got a rush job.'

Chapter 64

Ten Years Ago, Palm Springs, California

The President wasn't happy. It wasn't the first time that Yokely had been in the man's presence – it was actually the fourth – but on all the previous occasions he had been part of a group and only there to supply information. This time there was just him, the head of Homeland Security and the new Defense Secretary, Follis, and Yokely was the focus of the President's unhappiness. It wasn't a pleasant position to be in.

The President shook his head as he stared at the floor, his mind in turmoil. 'How the hell does something like this happen?'

The question was rhetorical so neither Yokely nor the head of Homeland Security said anything. The Homeland Security chief was Piers Sutherland, his haggard face and almost white hair making him look older than his sixty years. He was wearing a dark blue suit, a dazzling white shirt and a red tie that he'd loosened to give himself more room to breathe. The President was wearing golfing gear, a pale blue short-sleeved shirt, brown and white checked trousers and white golfing shoes. They were sitting in a private room in the members' area of an exclusive golf club outside Palm Springs, a regular haunt of the President's whenever he was on the West Coast. Yokely had been ushered in through a rear entrance by two unsmiling Secret Service agents.

'Why did no one tell me what was going on?' The President glared at Sutherland.

Sutherland flushed. 'Mullins said you needed to be kept at a distance, that it had all been cleared with you but that all communication would be through him.'

'And you thought that I would condone the torture and murder of innocent civilians?'

'Hardly innocent, Mr President,' said Sutherland.

The President pointed a finger at Sutherland's face. 'Women have been murdered for no other reason than they were related to terrorists,' he said. 'And it's going to be laid at my door. At my desk.'

'Christopher didn't tell me that families would be targeted,' said Sutherland. 'He said that Yokely would be working his way up the food chain, and that he wouldn't be concerned about collateral damage.'

'He's been executing people all over the world, that's not collateral damage,' said the President. 'And you're complicit in this.'

'With respect, Mr President, I don't see that I'm complicit in anything. The Defense Secretary said he was speaking with your voice.'

The President looked at Yokely. 'What were your instructions?'

'To kill anyone involved in the downing of the jet and anyone connected or related to them.'

'Women?'

Yokely nodded.

'Children?'

'He said he wanted to wipe out their genes, Mr President.'

The President groaned and rubbed the back of his neck. 'Did you follow through on that? Did you kill children?'

'No, Mr President.'

'That's something, at least. So what is the death toll, exactly?'

'Four in Queens, the cell responsible for shooting down the plane. Four in Sarajevo. Six in Dubai. Four in London. One in Leeds.'

'How many women?'

'Two. One in Dubai, one in London.'

'Nineteen murders,' said the President. 'And they can all be laid at my door.' He rubbed the back of his neck again. 'This is a nightmare.' He shook his head at Yokely. 'You didn't think to question what you were being asked to do?'

'Things were moving very quickly. A plane had gone down and a lot of people had died. The scenario put before me was that we had three terrorists in custody, along with the weapon and a video of them shooting down the plane. There was no doubt that the men were guilty, and no doubt that they could lead us to the rest of the cell. They weren't in the system, which meant that we could be more creative in our approach.'

'That's what Chris said? He said that?'

'His words exactly, Mr President. And at the time, he said he was speaking with your voice. He said we had a limited time frame in which to act, and that we had your authority to do whatever was necessary.'

'And you didn't think it worth checking any of this with me?'

Yokely grimaced. He knew that he was going to have to tread carefully because shit tended to flow downhill and he was the lowest-ranking person in the room. 'Can I speak frankly, Mr President?'

'It's about time you did.'

Yokely grimaced again. 'You and the Defense Secretary had a very special relationship, Mr President.' He looked over at Follis. 'The former Defense Secretary, I mean, obviously.' He looked back at the President. 'You went to college with him, you played golf with him, your wives are best friends.' Yokely realised what he'd said and he quickly corrected himself. 'Were best friends,' he said. 'He was in your office twice a day, he had one-to-one time whenever he needed it.'

'And your point is?'

'My point, Mr President, is that the Defense Secretary, the former Defense Secretary, had a direct line to you that no one else comes close to matching.' He groaned again as he realised that he was still using the present tense. 'Came close to matching,' he said. 'I'm sorry, I can't get used to the fact that he's dead.'

'Tell me about it,' said the President.

'There was no way I could second-guess him. If I had called you and you had approved his actions, it would have looked as if I'd been going behind his back. And I don't think either of you would have forgiven me for that.'

The President looked over at Sutherland. 'What about you, Piers? Didn't you think to keep me in the loop?'

'May I speak as frankly as Richard has just done?' said Sutherland.

'Just spit it out, Piers,' snapped the President. 'I really don't have time to fuck around.'

'Mr President, I got to where I am by hard bloody work, by putting in so many hours at my desk that I broke two marriages and produced three kids who wouldn't care if I dropped dead tomorrow. I've got to where I am because of that, not because I'm your friend or because I let you beat me at golf. If it came to a confrontation between Christopher and me I know that my feet wouldn't touch the ground so when he said that he had spoken to you and that he was handling it, then I took what he said as Gospel. To be fair, that wasn't the first time that I had been in that position, so no, I didn't think to keep you in the loop because the Defense Secretary assured me that you were already in it.'

The President swallowed, and then stood up and started to pace around. 'I am so screwed,' he said. 'No one is going to believe that I didn't know what was happening. Hell, they're going to assume that it was all my idea and that Chris was acting on my behalf. And then he goes and kills himself without leaving a note. The fucker could at least have confessed to everything and left me in the clear. But now the conspiracy theorists are going to have a field day. Look at the Clintons and Vince Foster. Half the population thinks they are behind his death.'

'And they might be right,' said Yokely, sourly. He had never been a fan of Bill Clinton, and Hillary even less so, and he'd been asked to do some pretty unsavoury things during their tenure in the White House.

'That's not the point,' said the President. He stopped pacing. 'So exactly how many people know about what's happened? Other than the three of us?'

'I've had a team of five,' said Yokely. 'All Grey Fox and all totally trustworthy.'

'You'd trust them with your life?'

'I already have done,' said Yokely.

'Who else?'

'One of my people, Tommy Garcia,' said Sutherland. 'He was the first at the scene.'

'Any more of your people?'

Sutherland shook his head. 'Garcia called me at home and filled me in. I told him to get straight out there and not to mention it to anyone else.'

'Local police?'

'Thankfully, no,' said Sutherland. 'The terrorists were discovered by a security guard and he's the one who called Garcia. Garcia had interviewed him for a position a few weeks ago. The security guard is former Special Forces, Navy SEAL as it happens.'

'Do we at least have him under wraps?' asked the President.

'He's back at work. We've had him under surveillance and he doesn't seem to be a security risk.'

'What about financing? Who or what funded this killing spree?'

'I have access to various Grey Fox accounts,' said Yokely. 'Some of those accounts are buried so deep that you'd need a submarine to find them. It has to be that way because most of their operations require total deniability.'

'Deniability is all well and good, but this is still going to get out,' said the President. 'The Press are already on to the fact that Chris's family was on that plane. And eventually someone somewhere will notice the murders. It might take a month or a year but eventually it will get out and someone is going to put two and two together. And when that happens, the Press will be looking for someone to pin it on.'

'We can tell the truth,' said Follis. 'We can tell them that Christopher was grief-stricken and reacted instinctively—'

'—by sending a government-trained, government-financed killer on a murdering spree?' the President finished for him. 'That leads them straight to my office. Straight to my desk. Christopher told you and Yokely that he was acting with my authority and he's not in a position to retract that now, is he?'

'No, he's not,' admitted Follis. 'Mr President, isn't the best strategy simply to come clean, to tell it like it is? That the Defense Secretary was acting on his own initiative, motivated by grief brought on by the loss of his wife and son.'

'You think the media will let us get away with that?' the President replied. 'They'll say that we're using Chris as a fall guy, shovelling the blame on a man who can't defend himself.'

'But that's not the truth,' said Follis.

'Don't be so naive. The media doesn't care about the truth, they want a story, and it's a better story to blame the President. And even if they can't prove it, the mud will stick. And Grey Fox is my responsibility. There's no way I can prove that I didn't authorise Yokely's actions. It's impossible to prove a negative.'

'Richard can confirm that he was following instructions from the Defense Secretary.'

'He can never go public, on anything, ever. Grey Fox is a can of worms that has to stay well out of the public eye.' The President stopped pacing and rubbed the back of his neck. 'Damn that security guard. If he'd just phoned the police then none of this would have happened.'

The President sat down again. He waved at a drinks cabinet. 'Piers, pour me a brandy.'

Sutherland went over to the cabinet and picked up a bottle. 'Rocks?'

'Neat. Pour one for yourself.' He threw a tight smile at Yokely. 'Help yourself to a drink if you want one. It looks like you could do with one.' Follis wasn't offered a drink – he was a well-known teetotaller.

'I'm fine, Mr President. Can I make a suggestion?'

'If it can get me out of the shit-filled hole I'm in, fire away.'

Sutherland put a tumbler of brandy in front of the President and he took a sip without thanking him.

'The four jihadists in Queens are gone and will never be found,' said Yokely.

'You sound certain of that.'

'Dissolved in acid, so yes, I'm certain. Al-Qaeda have already claimed the credit for the attack. I'm assuming they haven't released their names until they find out what's happened to them. Now, there were two jihadists that escaped. I am fairly sure one was the guy who put it all together and the second was the driver. We don't know who he is. They were in a truck and one guy got out. He saw the security guard jump his colleagues, but he didn't hang around to see the outcome. So far as he knows his colleagues could have overpowered the security guard and gone to ground. We took one of the jihadists from a motel in Long Island. There was some damage to the door but we cleaned up after ourselves. So my suggestion is this. We carry out a drone attack on an al-Qaeda camp and obliterate it, then we announce that we are sure that the jihadists who carried out the attack were there and that they were killed. We show video of the Predator attack, the missile striking, the aftermath. But the names we release won't be the names of the men in Queens. Al-Qaeda are hardly likely to call us on the lie, are they? What are they going to do? Name the four men they sent to bring down the jet and say that they are missing in action? No, they'll probably just claim the names we give as martyrs.'

'And Chris's suicide?'

'As Piers said, he killed himself, distraught with grief. There's no reason a note couldn't be found, even at this late stage. An email perhaps, to a close friend. Perhaps it went into a junk file and has only just now been found.'

'And the rest of the deaths? The twenty people you killed?'

'We went to a lot of trouble to make them look like accidents,' said Yokely. 'There was a straightforward shooting in Dubai but that man had enemies. We disposed of the four in Sarajevo and they were an arms dealer and his bodyguards, so no one would be too surprised if they disappeared.'

'What about this jihadist who got away?'

'We can continue to hunt for him. He's hardly likely to go public on what happened, is he?'

The President nodded slowly. 'So we get justice for the dead. The public is happy. The wounds heal. But it depends on no one connecting the deaths to the jihadists. That's the key.'

'I can probably come up with some names that will fit the bill.'

'They'd have to be dead.'

Yokely smiled. 'They will be.'

The President nodded. 'That might just work.' He flashed Yokely a tight smile. 'Remind me to never get on your bad side,' he said.

'I just follow my orders, sir,' said Yokely.

The President sipped his brandy. 'There's one loose end we need to tidy up.'

Yokely frowned, not understanding. He was fairly sure that he had covered all the bases that needed covering.

'The security guard,' said the President. 'What was his name?'

'Dean Martin,' said Yokely.

The President laughed. 'Are you serious?'

'That's his name. He's a good guy, sir. As Piers said, Navy SEAL.'

'But can we rely on him?' The President looked at Sutherland. 'Why wasn't he hired?'

Sutherland looked uncomfortable. 'He wasn't suitable.'

'Because?'

'His psychological profile was . . . flawed.'

'Flawed? Stop beating around the bush, Piers. You're not being interviewed on CNN here.'

'He has PTSD, that's why he left Special Forces. Nightmares, flashbacks, anger-management issues. He just wasn't suitable for a role in Homeland Security.'

'Grey Fox could probably use him,' said Yokely quietly. He had a nasty feeling that he knew where the conversation was headed.

'Please don't tell me that Grey Fox hires people with mental health issues, because that's not what I want to hear right now,' said the President.

'He helped us, at the start,' said Yokely. 'If it hadn't been for him, we'd never have caught the jihadists in the first place. And he helped us bring in a fourth guy.'

'No one is saying he wasn't helpful,' said Sutherland. 'It's just that we don't know what's going to happen down the line. If he talks out of turn . . . he could bring down the presidency. No one is going to believe that the President didn't authorise the operation. We have to make sure that this stays buried, and that means we have to bury Martin.'

'Collateral damage?' said Yokely, unable to keep the bitterness out of his voice.

'A casualty of war,' said the President. 'Look, I can see you've got a personal connection to the guy, so you don't have to do it yourself. We can use someone else in Grey Fox.'

Yokely put up his hand. 'No,' he said. 'It's my mess. I'll clear it up.'

The President smiled. 'Good man,' he said. 'Always the pro.' He finished his drink and looked at his watch. 'And I've got time to finish my round, so the day's not a complete loss.'

As the President walked out with Sutherland following, Yokely's cell rang. It was Sam Hepburn.

'That draft file hasn't been accessed,' said Hepburn. 'Just thought you might want to know.'

'Thanks, Sam. You can drop the investigation now. I've been told to stand down. I appreciate all your help but we're done.'

'You okay? You sound a bit tense?'

Yokely chuckled drily. 'I've had better days, Sam. But I've had worse.'

Chapter 65

Present Day, London

It was just after three o'clock in the morning when Shepherd spotted Lex Harper at the wheel of the three-year-old Toyota. It was the same vehicle that Shepherd had tracked across the country. It was a good choice of car, nondescript and with no distinguishing features, unlikely to attract the attention of the police or be remembered by eyewitnesses. There was another man in the front passenger seat. He was bigger than Harper with black hair and a broad chin. Shepherd didn't recognise him.

The Toyota prowled quietly past the house where Millen lived in a small ground-floor flat. Shepherd sat back and waited. He was in his BMW X5 with the engine and lights off, tucked away in a side street with a clear view of the house.

It was another five minutes before the Toyota reappeared, this time from the other direction. Shepherd figured Harper was checking the area for escape routes and potential problems. The Toyota parked about fifty yards from the house, on the opposite side of the road.

Shepherd got out of his SUV, closed the door as quietly as he could and walked towards the Toyota, moving softly and approaching the car from the offside rear. He reached the rear door without being seen and he grabbed for the handle and pulled it open. The two men whirled around in surprise but before they could react he had slipped on to the back seat and closed the door behind him.

'What the fuck?' exploded the man in the passenger seat. He

pulled a gun from his holster and pointed it at Shepherd. 'Who the fuck are you?'

'It's okay,' said Harper. 'He's a friend.'

The man kept the gun pointed at Shepherd's face. 'I asked you a question.'

Shepherd stared back at him. The gun was a regular Glock, a staple of law enforcement around the world. Its double-trigger safety system meant that it didn't need a safety switch and was almost impossible to fire by accident. But the five-and-a-half-pound trigger pull and less than half an inch of trigger travel meant that firing it in anger was relatively easy. And the man staring back at him certainly looked angry.

Harper put his hand on the gun. 'Mick, it's okay. I know him.'

'What the fuck's he doing?'

'I don't know,' said Harper. 'Why don't we ask him?'

'This is fucked up,' said O'Hara, scowling.

'I hear you.'

'And you've told him my name.'

'Fuck yeah, an Irishman called Mick, you're well fucked now. Anyway, Spider here is with MI5 so if he wanted to track you down he has the resources.'

'A spook?'

'Yeah, but one of the good ones. Look, Mick, if we had a problem we'd be surrounded by armed cops and lying spread-eagled on the ground, so as we're not let's hear what he has to say.'

O'Hara reluctantly put his gun away.

'Thank you,' said Shepherd. He turned to look at Harper. 'Who are you working for, Lex?'

'You know I can't tell you that.'

'The Pool? Or is this off your own bat?'

'It's a job,' said Harper.

'Government-sanctioned?'

Harper grinned. 'I couldn't possibly comment.'

'This isn't fucking funny, Lex. Do you have any idea what you're involved in?'

Harper's face hardened. 'Fuck you, Spider. Of course I do. I'm dealing with the vermin behind the stadium bombing. And you shouldn't be shedding any tears for these scumbags.'

Shepherd nodded at the house. 'Except the guy in here had nothing to do with the stadium. He's a jihadist and he's planning something, that's for sure, but he wasn't involved in the stadium bombing. And the one thing I can assure you is that Usman Yussuf isn't in there.'

'How the fuck do you know about Yussuf?' Harper frowned. 'What the fuck's going on?'

'That's what I'm asking you. I can tell you this much – whatever you're doing isn't officially sanctioned and is going to blow up in your face. Now, is this a Pool operation?'

Harper shook his head. 'No,' he said quietly.

'Charlotte Button?'

Harper sighed. 'I'm sure you'd worked that out for yourself already. First rule of interrogation, never ask a question you don't already know the answer to.'

'This isn't an interrogation,' said Shepherd. 'This is just two old friends having a chat. When did Charlie give you this job?'

'A few hours ago.'

Shepherd cursed under his breath. He gave the fake intel to Ellis and she must have been on to Button immediately. But why? Why would the acting head of MI5 be taking matters into her own hands? And why would she act through Charlotte Button and not official channels?

'So what's the problem?' asked Harper.

'The problem is that the name you were given isn't a valid target. I came up with the name and gave it to someone I've started to suspect might not be on the level. The fact that Button gave you the name and that you and Mick are here tooled up proves that my suspicions are correct, which means that I have to put a stop to it.'

'You're saying you're gonna try and stop me carrying out the hit?' asked Harper. 'Because from where I'm sitting, you don't have a gun and Mick and I have two between us.'

'You're not going to shoot me, Lex. There'd be no money in it.'

'No, but Mick might.'

'You can fucking count on it,' growled the Irishman.

'How about this?' asked Shepherd. 'I'll send a text. Just one text. And I'm pretty sure the job will be cancelled.'

Harper stared at him for several seconds and then nodded slowly. 'Okay,' he said.

Shepherd reached inside his jacket and the Irishman immediately pointed his gun at Shepherd's face. Shepherd slowly took out his iPhone, showed it to both men and then tapped out a message to Patsy Ellis: *Intel on Andrew Millen and Yussef is incorrect. Mistaken identity. Am on the case.* He sent the message and smiled at Harper. 'Okay, let's see what happens next.'

'How long do we give it?' asked Harper. 'We don't want to be here when dawn breaks.'

'It won't be long,' said Shepherd.

'What the fuck is going on?' asked the Irishman. He gestured at the house. 'Are we offing this raghead or not?'

'We'll give Spider a few minutes to work his magic,' said Harper. 'We've nothing to lose.'

'Unless the cops go by and wonder why there are three white men sitting outside a raghead's house.'

'Cops hardly ever patrol these days,' said Harper. 'They're usually in the office staring at screens or sitting on the motorway catching speeding cars. We're cool.' He lit a cigarette and offered one to the Irishman.

Shepherd wound down the window as the two men puffed away. They sat in silence. Harper's phone rang less than five minutes after Shepherd had sent the text message to Ellis. Harper answered. 'Yeah? Outside. Just about to go in.' He listened for several seconds before speaking again. 'Well, that's all well and good but we're locked and loaded. You're going to have to pay the full whack.' He listened again and then shrugged. 'Okay, fine. And the expenses as well. We're right up to the wire on this.'

He ended the call, put the phone away and twisted around in his seat. 'So what just happened?'

'The job's off?' asked Shepherd, though he already knew the answer to his question.

'The lovely Charlotte says we are to walk away. No explanation, but she'll pay the fee and cover the costs.' He looked over at the Irishman. 'It's been called off, Mick, but we get paid so all's well.' The Irishman shrugged and put his gun away. Harper looked back at Shepherd. 'This is not good.'

'No, it's not,' agreed Shepherd.

'The shit is going to hit the fan, isn't it?'

'At some point, yes.'

'Fuck.' Harper slapped the steering wheel and swore again.

'So what's happening?' asked the Irishman, clearly confused.

'What's happening is that we've been used to do someone's dirty work, and that someone has been caught by the short and curlies,' said Harper. 'You, my friend, need to get back to Ireland as quickly as possible.' Harper looked over his shoulder. 'How fucked am I, Spider?'

Shepherd shrugged. 'It won't come from me, Lex. I was never here. I just wanted to check if my suspicions were right. I'm not a hundred per cent sure what's happening, but at some point it'll all come out. My end of it anyway. But it looks to me as if Charlotte Button is being used as a cut-out, so whether your name is in the frame will be down to her.'

'I trust Charlotte,' said Harper emphatically.

'I'm sure you do,' said Shepherd. 'And she couldn't do what she does without being totally reliable. You just need to be careful when the authorities get on the case, and by authorities we're talking the Security Services and the cops. I found you, Lex. And trust me, it wasn't difficult.'

'You set me up, you didn't find me.'

'I got you on CCTV.'

'Shit.'

'The cameras are everywhere, you know that. Now, I'm not saying that they'll be as efficient as I am, but you need to know they could be coming for you at some point. So if I were you, I'd head back to the Land of Smiles.'

'Is he fucking serious?' the Irishman asked Harper.

'Yeah, mate, I'm afraid he is.'

'We just run off with our tails between our legs like a couple of bitches?'

'Mick, Spider here is doing us a favour. We've been used and that's down to me not being more careful. Our only option now is to go into defensive mode and to get the hell out of Dodge.' He turned to look at Shepherd again. 'Thanks.'

'Not a problem, Lex. Do me one favour, don't mention this to Charlie.'

'What's going to happen to her?'

'I don't know. But whatever it is, I don't want her tipped off.'

Harper nodded and Shepherd climbed out of the car. The moment he slammed the door shut the car sped off down the road. Shepherd watched it go. Harper had asked the very question that was on his own mind. Just what the hell was going to happen to Charlie Button?

Chapter 66

Dean Martin took a bottle of Budweiser from his fridge and popped off the cap. He'd picked up a pizza on his way home from work and he was planning to watch a football game he had recorded on his Tivo and fall asleep on his sofa. That was more often than not how he ended his day, though he'd vary the pizza with Chinese, Thai and the occasional bucket of KFC. He took a swig of beer and flipped open the pizza box. Double pepperoni. His favourite.

He picked up the remote but before he could press anything his doorbell rang. He frowned. He never had visitors. He padded barefoot over to the door of his apartment and peered through the security viewer. He frowned again when he saw who the visitor was. Richard Yokely. He was dressed almost the same as when they'd met at the warehouse but his blazer was now black and the blue tie was lighter and spotted with black dots. He opened the door. The shoes seemed to be the same – gleaming black leather with tassels.

'Sorry about the surprise visit, Dean,' said Yokely amiably.

'No problem, sir,' said Martin, holding the door open. 'I was just going to eat pizza. Can I get you a beer?'

'A beer would be good,' said Yokely. Martin closed the door as Yokely walked over to the single armchair and sat down. 'And please, drop the "sir". Richard is fine.'

'Budweiser okay?' asked Martin, opening the fridge.

'The King of Beers,' said Yokely.

Martin popped the cap off a bottle and handed it to Yokely.

Yokely raised the bottle in salute and then took a long swig. 'You're welcome to share my pizza,' said Martin.

Yokely patted his stomach. 'I've already eaten.' He looked around the room. 'You keep yourself tidy,' he said.

By 'tidy' Martin knew that Yokely was referring to the fact that the flat was virtually empty. Other than the sofa, the armchair, a small wooden table with two wooden chairs and an empty pine bookcase, there was nothing in the room. No pictures, no ornaments, no personal items, just the furniture that had come with the rental apartment.

There wasn't much more in the bedroom. A bed, a bare dressing table and a side table. If Yokely had opened the wardrobe he would have seen four uniforms, five sweatshirts and two pairs of jeans, and a drawer full of neatly folded underwear and socks. The military had taught Martin to keep his living space ordered and that had followed him into civilian life.

'I'm not here much,' said Martin, dropping down on to the sofa. 'I'm either at work or the gym. This is just a place to sleep.' He closed the lid of the pizza box and waited for Yokely to get to the point.

Yokely nodded as he looked around and Martin recognised the look of a predator getting the feel of his surroundings. He kept his hands together in his lap.

Yokely looked back at Martin and smiled, but his eyes were hard. His hand moved smoothly inside his jacket and reappeared with a Glock. His finger was on the trigger and he held the gun on the arm of the chair, the barrel pointed at the centre of Martin's chest. It was a Glock 19, pretty much the perfect weapon for concealed carry. Fifteen 9mm rounds in the magazine and another one in the chamber. It was a second generation, which meant it was missing the accessory rail and the finger grooves, but they weren't needed on a gun that was tucked away in a shoulder holster and used at close range.

Martin said nothing. He knew there was nothing he could say that would change the outcome. Yokely was a professional and any decisions had already been taken.

'Dean, they sent me to kill you,' said Yokely quietly. 'They want all the witnesses out of the picture.'

Martin said nothing. He just stared coldly at Yokely, his right hand clenched tightly on his bottle of beer.

'You understand what I've just said,' said Yokely eventually.

Martin's knuckles whitened as he tightened his grip on the bottle. 'What about your team? The men who were with you? What about Peter?'

'They're family,' said Yokely. 'And in their eyes, you're not.'

'Didn't I prove my worth?'

'Yes, you did. I told you at the time, you did well. And I meant it. But the powers-that-be, they're worried that at some point you might talk.'

Martin shook his head. 'I won't.'

'They looked at your medical reports, the psych evaluations, and they think you're unstable.'

Martin shrugged. 'They're probably right.'

'So they're worried that at some point down the line you might tell somebody.'

'Who? Who would I tell?'

'A journalist. Or maybe you get drunk in a bar one night and let your guard down.'

'I don't get drunk,' said Martin. 'And I don't do drugs. And what I definitely don't do is shoot off at the mouth. Stuff I saw and did in the Sandbox . . .' He tapped the side of his head with his left hand. 'Locked away in here and I never talk about it. To anyone.'

Yokely looked at him, long and hard. 'It's a shitty world, some-times.'

'Most of the time,' said Martin. He returned Yokely's stare. 'I could probably get to you and snap your neck before you could kill me, unless you were lucky and got me in the heart or the head.'

'That wouldn't be luck, Dean. I do this for a living.'

Martin shrugged. 'I could too. You could put me on your team.' He wasn't going to beg for his life, but it was important for Yokely to know that there were options.

'I suggested that.'

'And?'

'Your psych evaluations. No one disputes your skill sets, but there's a mental side to the job and that's where you come up short.'

Martin swallowed. 'So that's it. A bullet in the head, then disposal?'

'That's the plan.'

'That's one hell of a shitty plan.' He leaned forward slowly and placed his bottle on the coffee table, his eyes fixed on Yokely.

Yokely smiled thinly. 'No argument here,' he said.

'Fuck,' said Martin as he sat back. 'Fuck, fuck, fuck. I was only trying to help. Just wanted to do what was right for my country. And for that, I get killed?'

'Life isn't fair,' said Yokely.

'Ain't that the fucking truth.' Martin forced a smile. 'At least it'll be a pro doing the job.' Martin closed his eyes and took a deep breath. He pictured Yokely aiming the gun at his heart and getting ready to pull the trigger. Martin frowned as he remembered that there hadn't been a suppressor on the gun. There were more than twenty apartments in his block and neighbours all around him. Neighbours who would hear the shot and recognise it for what it was. Why was Yokely, a true professional, not using a suppressor? He opened his eyes. Yokely was still looking at him. The gun was still pointing at Martin's chest. But Yokely's finger was no longer on the trigger.

Chapter 67

Present Day, Surrey

Charlotte Button rarely slept well, and hadn't since the day that a jihadist assassin had murdered her husband and almost killed her. She still lived in the same house she'd shared with her husband; moving out would have meant leaving far too many memories, and if the memories faded then the killer would have won and she wasn't prepared to allow that to happen. Sleep always came in short snatches, never more than a couple of hours at a time, so when her front doorbell rang she was awake instantly. She sat up. It was six o'clock in the morning, which meant it wasn't a delivery or a meter reading, and the postman rarely appeared before nine. She picked up her TV remote and clicked several times to get a view of the front door from one of the many security cameras that had been installed in and around the house. Her eyes widened when she saw who was standing on her doorstep, grinning up at the camera and waving. Richard Yokely.

She grabbed a robe and put it on as she padded down the stairs. His grin widened when she opened the door.

'Sorry about the pre-dawn raid,' he said. 'The early bird and all that. How the hell are you, Charlotte?'

Button frowned. 'What's going on, Richard?'

He ran a hand through his short, grey hair and as his smile widened she couldn't help but glance at his gleaming teeth, so white they were either veneers or chemically treated. 'We need to talk and we need to do it away from prying eyes. What sort of coffee maker do you have?'

'A Nespresso.'

'Well, if it's good enough for George Clooney, it's good enough for me,' he said. 'Do you think I could persuade you to make me a cup, the coffee on the flight over was undrinkable.'

She stared at him for several seconds, then opened the door wider. He stepped inside and she pointed at the kitchen door. 'Kitchen's down there. You make the coffee while I get dressed.'

'I hear and obey,' said Yokely. As he went by her she caught the scent of sandalwood. He was wearing a beige trench coat and he took it off as he headed for the kitchen. Under the coat he had a dark blue blazer and black slacks and his trademark black loafers with tassels. Button hurried upstairs and pulled on a pair of jeans and a floppy pink sweater. She stood looking at her reflection in the mirror, wondering if she should put on some make-up, but decided against it. It wasn't a social visit.

When she got to the kitchen Yokely had two coffees ready and waiting.

'I did a cappuccino and an Americano. You can choose.'

'Americano for the American makes sense,' said Button, taking the cappuccino and sitting on one of the stools at the breakfast bar. 'Richard, much as I enjoy the company, what the hell do you want?'

He sat on the stool next to her and sipped his coffee before answering. 'I'm here about Saladin,' he said, watching her carefully to see her reaction.

She kept her face impassive. 'That's interesting.'

'I thought you might think so.'

'But as you know I'm in the private sector these days. Any information on Saladin really needs to go to MI5.'

'Well, that's where the request for intel on Saladin came from, of course. Courtesy of the lovely Patsy Ellis.'

'So I suppose it's Patsy you really should be talking to about this.'

'She was a mentor of yours, wasn't she?'

'Mentor is a bit strong, Richard. She's always been ahead of me on the career curve and we've always got along well.'

Yokely raised one eyebrow. 'Birds of a feather, I always thought.'

'I'll take that as a compliment,' said Button.

'It was meant as one,' said the American. 'I've always had the greatest respect for Ms Ellis. Though of course we never had the same connection that I've always felt you and I enjoyed.'

'Will you be getting to the point anytime soon, Richard?' asked Button.

'Absolutely,' said Yokely. He took a packet of small cigars from his jacket pocket and gestured at the door. 'Would you mind if we took this outside?'

'Of course not,' said Button, standing up. 'I could do with some fresh air.' She nodded at his cigars. 'Which means you staying downwind of me, of course. I was never a fan of cigars.'

'Not a problem,' said Yokely.

They went outside into the back garden. The sun was coming up, reddening the horizon. Yokely lit a cigar and blew smoke up at the sky contentedly.

'Did Patsy really think she could do what she did without anyone finding out?' he asked, not looking at her.

'Richard, knowing how good you are at playing your cards close to your chest, I'm reluctant to say too much until I know exactly what's in your hand.'

Yokely smiled. 'You think I'd bluff you?'

'I think you'll try to bluff anyone, Richard. It's in your nature.'

He chuckled drily. 'Well let me tell you what I know,' he said. He moved his head closer to hers and lowered his voice, even though there was no one within earshot. 'I know that a number of people have died, all of them connected to that nasty shit who blew himself up at the football stadium last week. His uncle. And the uncle's family – though that did strike me as overkill, literally. Then another Syrian refugee was killed in Birmingham. Tortured before he died, I believe. And then another Asian was killed in London. Battered to death. It looks like a racist incident but the fact that all of the deaths are connected to the stadium bomber leads me to an inescapable conclusion.'

'Which is?'

He turned to look at her. 'Why, that someone is out for revenge,

Charlotte. It's as plain as the pretty nose on your face.' He took another drag on his cigar and blew smoke. 'It isn't generally known that Patsy's goddaughter was one of the victims of the stadium bombing, is it?'

'I think she wanted to keep it low-profile.'

'Understandably,' said Yokely. 'The media these days – vultures. Whatever happened to journalism as an honourable profession?'

'I don't think it ever was, really.'

'Well, it's a thousand times worse these days. Opinion masquerading as fact, putting people's grief out for everyone to wallow in. I can see why she would want it kept out of the papers.'

'And she is acting head of MI5,' said Button. 'Announcing that her goddaughter was killed in a terrorist attack would be handing the terrorists a major propaganda coup.'

'Exactly,' said Yokely. He took a long drag on his cigar and blew smoke up at the clouds before continuing. 'So, we're looking at seven killings all connected to the bomber. Seven that I know about. Yet there appears to be no official sanction for a government operation to that effect.'

'As you know, Richard, I am no longer a civil servant.'

'Of course,' said the American. 'Very much at arm's length these days. How is the Pool?'

Button smiled thinly and ignored the question.

'Need to know?' said Yokely, and he chuckled again. 'So, we have seven or more dead Muslims, none of them any great loss it has to be said. And what evidence there is suggests that right-wing racist groups or drug dealers are responsible. According to the papers, anyway.'

'And you can't believe them these days, can you? Not with all that fake news around,' she said.

'Fake news? Exactly what I was thinking. Some very clever misdirection is what it looks like to me. But then nobody seems interested in my opinions so I keep them to myself these days.'

'But you are happy to share your opinions with me, of course.'

He smiled, clearly enjoying the banter. 'Of course. We go back a long way, you and I, Charlotte. We have a rapport. An understanding.' He sighed. 'Listen. If someone I loved was murdered by a terrorist – or anyone for that matter – I'd be taking matters into my own hands. No question. There's nothing wrong with revenge, Charlotte. Never has been and never will be. And I know you understand that more than anyone, after what happened to your husband and all. It was revenge that got you to where you are now.'

'I think we're done, Richard,' said Button, turning to go.

'I'm not here to criticise or interfere, I'm here to help,' he said quietly. 'Walk away if you want, but you'll be turning down a golden opportunity.'

'An opportunity?'

'You're looking for the man who facilitated the explosion at the football match,' said Yokely. 'The bastard that groomed the bomber and set him up with the explosives and logistics. Hakeem Khaled. AKA Saladin. Present whereabouts, unknown.'

'You have his name?' Button's heart was pounding but she forced herself to stay calm. Yokely clearly knew everything. But if he had wanted to make life difficult for her then there would be no need for the early morning wake-up call. He had something else in mind and she had no choice other than to hear him out. She folded her arms.

'Charlotte, we're on the same side here,' said Yokely. 'Trust me, I'm here to help. If MI5 is on the ball – and it usually is – I'm assuming they are trying to locate Khaled, though they only know him as Saladin. What is holding you back is that you don't know what he looks like. But I have an asset who has seen him, face to face. An asset who can identify him for you.'

Button frowned. 'But no one has seen him. Or at least those that have seen him are now dead.'

'My asset was on his trail ten years ago,' said Yokely. He held up his hand, thumb and first finger pressed together. 'And he was this close. Then it all turned to shit and my asset went off the grid.'

'What happened?'

'What do you mean?'

'Ten years ago? What happened and how did it turn to shit?'

Yokely sighed. 'I was caught up in a situation not too dissimilar to the one you find yourself in. The wife and son of the then Defense Secretary were on the flight that was shot down leaving JFK. He lost it and wanted revenge. I was brought in. I was told that what was happening had the approval of the President and that turned out not to be the case.' He shrugged. 'It almost cost me everything, Charlotte. But I managed to get back on the right track and here I am today, trying to stop you and Patsy Ellis making the same mistake I made.'

'I'm not admitting anything, Richard.'

'And this isn't on the record, it's just a chat between friends. Ten years ago Hakeem Khaled was behind the shooting down of that plane. We missed him then but we have a second chance now.'

Button frowned. 'Al-Qaeda claimed the credit for bringing down that plane.'

'Yes, they did. And they made a small fortune shorting aviation shares.'

'Then it can't be the same person because the stadium bombing was carried out by ISIS. Al-Qaeda and ISIS hate each other.'

'Hakeem Khaled doesn't care who he works for, he just hates the West,' said Yokely. 'Hates us with a vengeance. If eskimos ever turned to terrorising the West he'd be showing them how to blow up igloos. ISIS, Al-Qaeda, the Taliban, Al-Shabaab, he doesn't care. He'll work for anyone. It's definitely him, Charlotte. But I have to say up front that Hakeem Khaled might not be his real name. He's a Palestinian, and you Brits in your wisdom gave him citizenship about fifteen years ago. He claims that his family were killed by the Israelis and he fled to the UK. You clearly didn't do due diligence because I can tell you that he was a master bomb-maker even back then.'

'Why didn't the Americans say anything at the time?'

'You think you cross-check all your asylum claimants with the US? I wish you did, but that's not the way the world works. He gave your immigration people a sob story and they took it as read. And he repaid you by helping a team that was planning to shoot down planes in the UK ten years ago.'

Button's jaw dropped. 'And why am I only hearing about this now?'

'Your man Spider was on the case. He stopped the attack at Heathrow Airport, remember? A group of jihadists with a ground-to-air missile. Well, it was Khaled who arranged the financing for it. He was also financing a Brit soldier who went over to the dark side.'

'And again, you didn't share that information with us?'

Yokely sighed. 'They were difficult times, Charlotte. There was a lot going on. Khaled had also put together the team that shot the plane down at JFK. That was where my focus was. But my investigation crossed Spider's, out in Sarajevo.'

'And Khaled wasn't caught back then?'

'We were close. Damn close. But no, he got away.'

'And presumably came back to the UK? Hell, Richard, we should have been told.'

'Let's not start crying over spilt milk. Let's get the bastard now.'

'Easier said than done, Richard. As it happens, I do know where Saladin is. He's gone to ground on the Afghanistan–Pakistan border.'

'You have a location?'

'We're tracking his sat phone.'

'That's good news. That's very good news.' He nodded eagerly. 'You don't know what he looks like. I have an asset who has seen him face to face. We can get him, Charlotte. We can nail the bastard.'

'Ten years is a long time.'

'He got a good look at him. I don't think he has Spider's trick memory, but I don't think he'll have forgotten.'

'And you'll share this asset with me?'

He nodded. 'Happy to.'

Button frowned. 'If he's your asset, and if he has seen Hakeem Khaled, then why don't you use him?'

Yokely shrugged. 'There's a history there. I can't suddenly produce him like a rabbit from a hat.'

'Because?'

Yokely sighed. 'Because ten years ago I was supposed to have killed him. Happy now?'

Button shook her head in amazement. 'What a complicated life you lead, Richard.'

'I was told to get rid of the guy as he was regarded as a possible security risk, but I took a different view. It didn't seem to be the right thing to do to kill him. So he went off the grid. New name, new everything. I fixed him up with a Canadian passport and gave him enough money to get started. If he turns up now, alive and well, then it'll cause me all sorts of problems.'

'But if I produce him, all's well and good?'

'Give him a new identity and a decent backstory. If we get involved I can say that the intel has come from you and despite what happened at Five you're still highly regarded so you'll be taken in good faith. And the really good news is that there's a ten-million-dollar bounty on Khaled's head.'

'Which I split with you?'

Yokely chuckled and shook his head. 'Absolutely not,' he said. 'I just thought it might cover your expenses. So, are we good to go, Charlotte? Do we have a plan?'

'I suppose we do,' said Button. 'So, where is he? This asset?'

Yokely's smile widened. 'Paradise, I'm told.'

Chapter 68

Present Day, London

Patsy Ellis waited until her assistant had placed a cup of tea and two digestive biscuits in front of her before reaching for her office phone and calling Dan Shepherd. He answered almost immediately and from the background sound she could tell he was at his desk in the Super-Recogniser Unit.

'What happened last night?' said Ellis, brusquely.

'In what way?'

'Don't get coy with me, Shepherd,' Ellis snapped. 'You know what I'm talking about. First of all you tell me that Usman Yussuf is staying with Andrew Millen AKA Mohammed al-Britani and then a few hours later you tell me that the intel is wrong. How does that happen?'

'It was a flawed ID. Millen was there but Yussuf wasn't.'

'The whole point of that unit is that it doesn't make flawed IDs.'

'Mistakes happen,' said Shepherd. 'It didn't cause any problems, did it? I spotted the mistake pretty quickly.'

'You and I need to talk,' she said icily.

'We are talking.'

'We need a face to face, and soon.'

'I'm very busy here,' said Shepherd.

'You're getting very close to insubordination, Shepherd,' she said.

'I'm sorry if it seems that way, it's just that we are snowed under here and if all you're going to do is rebuke me for a mistaken ID then you can take it that I have been rebuked and we can move on.'

'There's more to talk about than that, Shepherd. And you know there is. There's someone else who needs to talk to you.' The mobile phone on her desk started to ring and she looked at the screen to see who was calling. She smiled thinly. 'Speak of the devil,' she said.

Chapter 69

Present Day, London

They met at a pub near Charing Cross station. It was eleven o'clock in the morning so it was almost empty. The lunchtime rush wouldn't start for an hour or so and when Shepherd walked in he had the pick of the tables. He chose one in the far corner that gave him a view of the toilets, the main entrance and the bar. He put his coat over the back of one of the chairs and went to buy himself a coffee. He was halfway through it when Charlotte Button arrived. She beamed when she saw him and hurried over. He stood up and they air-kissed but on the second pass her lips brushed his cheek.

'You're looking well,' she said. 'But are you putting on a bit of weight?'

'Bloody desk job,' he said. 'I still run but eight hours a day in front of a computer takes its toll.'

'Still with the Memory Men? How long's it now?'

Shepherd smiled. He knew that she knew exactly where he was and how long he'd been there. 'Almost a year,' he said. 'What can I get you?'

'White wine would be lovely,' she said. And she laughed when Shepherd glanced at his watch. 'It's never too early for wine, Dan.' She took off her coat and sat down as he went to order her drink.

The barman was pouring the wine when Patsy Ellis walked in. She was wearing dark glasses and had her hair tied back, which Shepherd assumed was an attempt at changing her appearance. She was wearing a dark blue trench coat with the collar turned up and had a large Dior bag over one shoulder.

Shepherd motioned that he was buying drinks and she nodded. 'I'll have what Charlie's having,' she said, and went over to join Button.

When Shepherd took the two glasses of wine over they were deep in conversation, but they stopped abruptly as he sat down. 'So, this is awkward, isn't it?' he said.

Ellis glared at him and Shepherd raised his hands. 'I'm trying to lighten the moment, that's all,' he said.

'Please don't,' said Ellis frostily. 'This is difficult enough as it is.' She sighed and sipped her drink, then raised her eyebrows. 'That's not bad,' she said. 'I'm pleasantly surprised.' She put down her glass. 'Well, I suppose I'd better kick this off.' She smiled at Button. 'Dan knows pretty much everything, obviously. There's no use crying over spilt milk or locking stable doors; all we can do is move forward from here. I'm hoping that this can be resolved without us all losing our careers, or worse.'

'How much does he know, exactly?' asked Button.

The two women looked at him. Shepherd knew the only way forward was to be completely honest and accept the consequences, no matter what. He leaned towards them and lowered his voice. 'It became clear to me fairly quickly that someone was killing those people connected to Ali Naveed, connected by birth or by association. Khuram Zaghba, Israr Farooqi, Imran Masood and his family. It was also clear that someone was making it look as if the killings were something they weren't. Clearly professionals at work. It was the sort of thing the Pool would usually be carrying out. I checked all the CCTV footage in the Farooqi case and I spotted Lex Harper, who works for the Pool. Charlie runs the Pool, so how was Charlie getting the intel because I sure as hell wasn't giving it to her.' He looked at Ellis. 'I personally gave you details of Zaghba and his van and within hours Harper had killed him. How is that possible?'

'How do you think it's possible, Dan?' asked Ellis quietly.

He smiled thinly. 'I think you passed the information on to Charlie and Charlie passed it on to Lex and within hours Khuram Zaghba was dead in a pool of blood. No pun intended.'

'Pun?' repeated Ellis.

'Pool,' said Shepherd.

Ellis frowned. 'That's not really a pun, is it? And please don't say you were trying to lighten the moment, I really hate it when you do that.'

Shepherd held up his hands and apologised. 'Can I just say that what I know stays with me. I haven't spoken to anybody about what I've learnt and I don't intend to.'

'Our secret is safe with you, is that what you're saying?' asked Ellis.

'I'm not sure I do know the real secret,' said Shepherd. 'Because, for the life of me, I can't understand why you are doing what you are doing. It makes no sense to me at all. There's something I don't know, isn't there?'

Ellis looked at Button and the two women locked eyes for a second. Button smiled the faintest of smiles and Ellis turned to Shepherd.

'My goddaughter was killed in the bombing. It's not generally known and hopefully never will be. But I wanted revenge. I didn't want them arrested, I didn't want them having their day in court and being behind bars with a choice of meals and a TV and a PlayStation. I wanted them dead and I wanted them dead quickly.'

Shepherd felt as if he had been slapped across the face. It was the last thing he had expected to hear. He looked at Ellis, then at Button, and then back at Ellis and it was clear from the looks on their faces that she was deadly serious. 'Wow,' was all he could think of saying.

Button smiled. 'Wow?'

Shepherd shrugged. 'I'm . . . wow.' He was still lost for words. Then he realised what Ellis had said and he leaned forward. 'Oh God, I'm so sorry. Sorry about your loss. I had no idea. Really, I'm so, so sorry.'

'Thank you,' said Ellis.

'You should have—' He stopped mid-sentence. He was going to say that she should have confided in him but there was no way she could have done that. He took a deep breath. 'What I'm saying is that where revenge is concerned, I'm not one to be throwing the first stone. Charlie knows that. I empathise and I sympathise. I was more concerned about the way your actions were affecting the investigation than I was about the morality or legality of what you were doing.' He looked into Ellis's eyes. 'And seriously, from the bottom of my heart. I am deeply, deeply sorry about your loss.'

Ellis forced a smile and nodded. 'Thank you.' She sipped her wine before continuing, more to steady herself than because she wanted a drink. 'Anyway, we need to decide how to take this forward. Charlie, fill us both in, will you?'

Button put down her glass. 'I was approached by Richard Yokely this morning. He's in London but unofficially. He came around to my house and we had a very interesting conversation. For a start, he's fully aware of what I've been doing, and while he almost certainly doesn't have any proof, he knows that I have been responsible for sanctioning the killings of Imran Masood, Khuram Zaghba and Israr Farooqi.'

'Sanctioning?' repeated Shepherd. 'Is that what you're calling it now?' He waved an apology as Ellis threw him a withering look.

'Now, Richard made it clear that he and only he is aware of what has been going on and that he has no intentions of sharing his, let's say, theories with anyone else. But he did drop something of a bombshell. The Americans are aware of Saladin, but that information has been classified at a level so stratospherically high that probably fewer than half a dozen people would be aware of him.'

'Do we know why that is?" asked Ellis. 'It would explain why my inquiries to the Americans came back negative.'

'Richard does love to play his cards close to his chest. But he said it was connected to that plane that was shot down leaving JFK ten years ago. Al-Qaeda claimed responsibility, though it was never ascertained what actually brought the plane down. If you recall, the Defense Secretary's wife and young son were killed in the crash. And a few days later he committed suicide. Media reports were that he was overcome with grief but Richard said there was more to it. In fact he told me the Defense Secretary had been involved in an operation very similar to what we have been carrying out.'

'Oh my God,' said Shepherd. 'Are you serious?'

'He didn't go into details but he said the Defense Secretary wanted revenge but the President found out what was going on and put a stop to it. Most of what happened will remain classified, there's no paper trail, it's all been swept well under the carpet and Richard is one of the very few people who knows what happened.'

'Probably because he was involved,' said Shepherd.

'I think there's no doubt about that,' said Button. She took a sip of her wine. 'But, moving forward. It was the man called Saladin who planned and organised the attack on the plane. Much of his planning involved the same email draft folder technique that we saw with the stadium bombing. But Richard, bless him, has a name. Hakeem Khaled. A British citizen, originally from Palestine.'

Shepherd swore. 'Why do so many of the world's terrorists turn out to have British passports?' He held up his hands. 'Because we'll give citizenship to pretty much anybody. When did he get his papers? During the Blair–Mandelson years?'

'Fifteen years ago.'

'When they were handing out passports like sweeties,' said Shepherd. 'And now that bloody chicken has come home to roost.'

'Dan, I already said this isn't about locking stable doors,' said Ellis. 'It's about moving forward.'

Ellis opened her bag and took out a folded sheet of paper. 'Charlie gave me the name and I ran a check,' she said. She unfolded the piece of paper. It was a printout of a photograph of a clean-shaven man wearing dark-framed glasses. 'This is the only photograph we have of Khaled.' She passed it to Shepherd. 'I'm guessing that it wouldn't be of much use, identification-wise?'

'It would be hard to get a match on CCTV if that's what you're asking. A head-and-shoulders shot is all well and good but we tend to be looking at the whole body to make an identification.'

'According to Richard, the last time he was seen he had a long grey beard, was considerably heavier than he looks in this photograph and wasn't wearing glasses,' said Button.

'Seen?' said Shepherd. 'There's a witness?'

Button nodded. 'A former Navy SEAL almost caught him just after the plane went down. Got very close to him.'

'There's no trace of Khaled entering or leaving the UK since the JFK jet incident,' said Ellis. 'In fact his original passport expired and he never applied for a replacement. That suggests he's now travelling using another identity.'

'And the Americans won't help?' asked Shepherd, handing back the printout.

'I think can't help is more appropriate,' said Ellis. 'Officially they know nothing about Khaled – it's only because of the information Richard gave you that I was able to get the details of his asylum application.' She turned to look at Shepherd. 'What you don't know is that we used the information on Farooqi's laptop to access the draft email folder he uses to make contact with Khaled.'

Shepherd raised his eyebrows. 'And Khaled bit?'

Ellis grinned. 'Yes, he did. He used a sat phone and was online long enough for GCHQ to pinpoint his location. He's close to the Afghan–Pakistan border in a network of caves that ISIS use for training.'

'Small world,' said Shepherd. 'When I was in the SAS I was on an operation to neutralise an al-Qaeda cave network near the border that they were using as a base and an opium storage facility.'

'Where was that?' asked Ellis.

'In the Registan Desert in Helmand Province, about four hundred kilometres south-west of Kandahar and fifteen from the border with Pakistan.'

'Different caves,' said Ellis. 'The ones we're looking at are across the border from the Pakistani village of Damadola.'

Shepherd nodded. 'I know of Damadola but I've never been there. Bloody inhospitable part of the world. So what's the plan? To go in after him?'

'One step at a time, Dan,' said Ellis. 'First things first. You need to go talk to our witness.'

'We know where he is?'

'Richard has been most helpful,' said Button. 'Though as always he almost certainly has his own agenda.'

Chapter 70

Present Day, Bali, Indonesia

Vic Malone was in his mid-thirties, bearded with skin burned dark brown from hours spent under the relentless Balinese sun. There was barely an ounce of fat on him and his six-pack glistened as he bent down and checked the air pressure of the cylinder he was going to use.

Shepherd was sitting at the rear of the dive boat, drinking from a plastic bottle of water. Like Malone he was only wearing a pair of shorts. His were black with blue dolphins on them.

They had already spent half an hour exploring the reef almost a hundred feet below the surface. The water was warm and clear and they had seen dozens of varieties of fish, crabs, shrimp, and even a couple of leopard sharks lying on the seabed. It was a myth that all sharks died if they stopped swimming. Some varieties did need to be constantly moving to keep oxygen-rich water flowing over their gills, but others, like the leopard shark, could send water through their respiratory system by pumping their pharynx. The leopard shark rested during the day and prowled the sea at night hunting crustaceans and small fish. Malone had found two lying on the seabed and pointed them out to Shepherd.

Shepherd had booked Malone and the boat for a private charter so that he could dive on a reef a couple of miles south of the island of Bali. It was a deep dive but Shepherd was an experienced diver and he had paid over the odds to be the only person on the boat. He'd used the name Gerry Hunter and had a PADI logbook that showed he'd done a dozen deep dives over the past year.

Malone had taken him down to the reef and kept pace with Shepherd as he explored it. Malone was totally at ease in the sea, using the merest flick of his fins to cut through the water. His breathing was slow and even and he seemed to be using his air at a much slower rate than Shepherd was going through his.

'So, Vic, there's something we need to talk about,' said Shepherd.

'Let me get my gear straight and then I'll go over the chart with you,' said Malone.

'It's not about the dive,' said Shepherd. 'I need to come clean with you. My name isn't Gerry. It's Dan.'

Malone straightened up, frowning. 'So the logbook's fake?'

Shepherd grinned. 'I can dive,' he said. 'No worries on that score.' He took a sip of water. 'Now that I've told you who I am, how about you return the favour.'

Malone's frown deepened. 'What do you mean?'

'I mean let's be straight with each other. Let's share.'

Malone put his hands on his hips. 'What the fuck is this? What's going on?'

Shepherd held up a hand. 'No need to get upset, we're just having a chat here,' he said. 'Look, I know who you are. Dean Martin. And not the singer, obviously, because he's, you know, dead.'

Martin's hand reached towards the knife in the scabbard on his right calf but Shepherd held up his water bottle and laughed. 'Dean, you need to chill. It's all good. This isn't a hit, it's a meet and greet.'

Martin let his hand relax. 'Are you here for the diving or not?'

'I'm here to chat away from prying ears,' said Shepherd. He waved his bottle at the dark-skinned Indonesian man at the wheel. 'I'm assuming you can trust him.'

'I can't trust anyone,' said Martin. He bent down, pulled the top off an icebox and took out a bottle of Heineken. 'But if we're not doing any more diving, I might as well have a beer.'

'I'll drink to that,' said Shepherd. He put down his water bottle and held out his hand.

Martin chuckled, popped the top of the bottle and gave it to him, then grabbed a Heineken for himself and sat down opposite Shepherd. 'So who the fuck are you?' he asked.

'I told you. It's Dan. Dan Shepherd.'

'Then what the fuck are you, Dan? I went to a lot of trouble to escape being Dean Martin.'

Shepherd grinned and raised his bottle in the air. 'A great singer, it has to be said. I'd put him above Sinatra, but then that's just me.'

'I've heard all the Dean Martin jokes, trust me,' said Martin.

'So was your father a fan of big band music?'

Martin's brow furrowed. 'What?'

'Your name. I figure only a fan of the Brat Pack would name their son after Dino.'

Martin grinned. 'He was a Led Zep and Black Sabbath fan. Heavy metal. Dean was my mother's father's name and she'd always promised him that her firstborn would be named after him. I guess she never figured on marrying a guy called Martin.'

'What did the SEALs call you?'

'Los Muertos.'

'Because that was Dean Martin's nickname, or was there something else?'

Martin's smile widened but his pale blue eyes were ice cold. 'Fifty-fifty,' he said. 'Is this a job interview we're having?'

'I think we're past that stage, Dean. Look, I'm a man on a mission, and you can help me.'

'And why the fuck would I do that?' Martin sipped his beer and wiped his mouth with the back of his hand.

'Because my mission is a bastard by the name of Hakeem Khaled.'

Martin shrugged. 'Never heard of him.'

'No, but I'm told you've seen him. He was the one who organised the shooting down of the plane at JFK ten years ago.'

Martin's eyes widened. 'You've found him?'

'We're close,' said Shepherd. 'I have the name. And I have a rough idea of where he is.'

Martin sipped his beer. 'And where would that be?'

'Somewhere hot and sunny,' said Shepherd. 'You were on his case ten years ago but he got away from you. He's still up to his old tricks, I'm afraid. You heard about the stadium bombing in London? The suicide bomber?'

Martin nodded.

'That was his work. He set it up, groomed the sad fuck who blew himself to smithereens. Probably built the vest or at least arranged for it to be built.'

'And who the hell are you, Dan, in the grand scheme of things?'

'Just a hired hand.'

'MI5? MI6? SAS?'

Martin sneered at Shepherd when he didn't answer. 'You remind me of the CIA guys we kept coming across in the Sandbox. Wouldn't tell you the time even if they had a watch on their wrist.'

'Sorry, force of habit,' said Shepherd. 'Fair enough, you deserve to know something about me. I was in the SAS but now I'm with MI5.'

'So you're James Bond?'

'Bond is MI6,' said Shepherd. 'And he's a fictional character.'

Martin laughed. 'So what's the difference between MI5 and MI6?'

'Five is domestic. Pretty much. Six is overseas. That's it in a nutshell but there is some overlap.'

'I met a few SAS guys in Afghanistan. Good soldiers.'

Shepherd grinned. 'You SEALs know what you're doing, too,' he said. 'I did my fair share of joint ops with you guys. But probably before you signed up. Look, Dean, I was in the stadium when the bomb went off. I saw what happened there and I'll never forget it.' He shuddered at the images that flashed through his mind and he could hear the injured father calling for his dead son. 'I want to get the bastard who did it. And I need your help.'

'Who told you about me?'

'I doubt you'd know my boss,' said Shepherd.

'But he's a Brit?'

'She,' said Shepherd. 'Yeah, as English as cream teas and croquet on the lawn.'

'How would the Brits know about me?'

'She's got her fingers in a lot of pies,' he said.

'I can think of only one man who would know where I was, that's all,' said Martin. 'I'm just surprised that he'd share that information. Why me? Why after all this time am I suddenly needed?'

'Because you're the only one who has seen Hakeem Khaled up close and personal. We have a passport photo from fifteen years ago but no one looks like their passport photo, right? You've seen him, you've seen his face and you've seen him move. You're the only one who can ID him. Am I right?'

Martin nodded. 'I'll never forget the bastard,' he said. 'The way he was congratulating the others, like they'd won some sort of award. Yes, I'd recognise him again.'

'That's why you have to step up, Dean.'

'I'm retired,' said Martin. 'And off the grid.'

'I think you'll find that's changed,' said Shepherd. 'Whatever happened in the past is the past. They want you back in harness.'

'I'm happy here,' said Martin. He waved his beer bottle at the cloudless sky. 'How could anyone not be happy here?'

'You've got unfinished business.'

'I left that life behind,' he said. 'And it wasn't by choice. I wanted to serve my country, Dan. But my country didn't want me. Fuck that. My country wanted me dead.'

'And now your country realises it made a mistake.'

'Does it? Or does it just want to use me?'

'I hear you. I really do. But if you don't want to do it for the US of A, do it for yourself. That bastard brought down an American plane. And so far he hasn't paid the price. He hasn't paid any price. He's still out there, killing innocents. You nearly caught him ten years ago. Now you get the chance to follow through. You need to do this, Dean. Without you, that bastard will carry on killing.'

Martin took a long pull on his beer and looked out over the

sea for several minutes, deep in thought. 'How are we going to get him?' he asked eventually, still staring off into the distance. 'Drones, or up close and personal?'

'We're going to try with drones first,' said Shepherd.

'I want to be there when he dies,' said Martin quietly, turning to look at him.

Shepherd raised his bottle in salute. 'I'm pretty sure that's the plan,' he said.

Chapter 71

Present Day, Bali, Indonesia

The plane was a Gulfstream jet and the pilots were definitely
civilians, so Shepherd figured the flight had been arranged
through the Pool. The pilots were both British, the captain in his
fifties and the co-pilot maybe half his age. The captain was friendly
enough, shaking their hands and introducing himself as Tom and
the co-pilot as Sean. He apologised for the fact that there were
no cabin staff but explained the bar was fully stocked and there
was food in the galley. The safety briefing consisted of Tom telling
them that seat belts were best worn all of the time. With that, the
two pilots locked themselves in the cockpit and a few minutes
later the engines burst into life.

Martin grabbed two beers from the bar and tossed one to
Shepherd. 'Might as well enjoy ourselves,' he said. He was wearing
a T-shirt advertising Bintang Beer and blue jeans. Shepherd was
only slightly less casual in a grey sweatshirt and black jeans and
he had carried on his leather jacket. They both had small holdalls
with a change of clothes and toiletries.

They chose seats on either side of the fuselage. Martin had a
footrest in front of his seat and Shepherd had a table. Martin
swung his feet up and fastened his seat belt. Ten minutes later
they were over the Indian Ocean, heading west.

The plane stopped to refuel twice, once in Cyprus and again
in Gibraltar. Shepherd slept most of the way. He woke up a few
times and when he did Martin was sitting staring out of the
window, deep in thought.

Their final destination was RAF Waddington, four miles south of the city of Lincoln. The plane landed smoothly and taxied towards one of several gunmetal grey hangars. The captain came out of the cockpit and opened the door and pulled a lever that unfolded a set of stairs. 'Pleasure having you both with us,' he said, though he had barely said a word to them throughout the flight.

Shepherd headed down the stairs, blinking in the bright sunlight. It was a cloudless day, the sky a perfect blue. Martin followed him. On the door leading into the hangar was a large 13th Squadron badge – a lynx's head in front of a dagger and the motto – ADJUVAMUS TUENDO, Latin for 'We Assist By Watching'. As the two men walked towards the hangar, the door opened and an officer in a blue uniform stepped out. He was in his early thirties with greying hair and carrying a few too many pounds around his waist. Shepherd grinned and held out his hand – he'd met Flight Lieutenant Sam Davies before.

'We can't keep you away, can we?' said Davies as they shook hands.

'You do serve excellent coffee,' said Shepherd. He introduced Martin to the lieutenant. 'This is Dean, he's our eyes on this one. Dean, this is Flight Lieutenant Sam Davies. He's a nice guy, just don't refer to his charges as drones. They're remotely piloted aircraft, or RPAs.'

Martin shook hands with the officer. 'Whatever you call them, they saved my life a few times when I was out in the Sandbox.'

'That's good to know,' said Davies.

He led them into the hangar. Inside were two large yellow metal containers with massive rubber wheels at either end. Large air-conditioning units were attached to the containers, without which the interiors would soon become unbearably hot. Davies took them inside the nearest container where two pilots were sitting in high-backed beige leather chairs facing a bank of screens. They both had control panels and joysticks in front of them and another panel between them on which there were two white telephones. They both twisted around in their seats.

'Alex Shaw you'll remember,' said Davies, nodding at the

man in the left-hand seat. Shaw waved a greeting. He was also in his early thirties, with a receding hairline and wire-framed spectacles.

The other seat was occupied by a blonde woman in her early twenties, also wearing glasses. 'Pilot Officer Anita Exley is a new addition to the team and she's been involved in the editing of the footage you'll be looking at.'

Exley smiled, nodded and then turned back to look at the screens. Shepherd was familiar with the equipment. The screens on the left showed satellite images and maps, and above them was the tracker screen that showed where the RPA was. Below that was the head-up display that showed a radar ground image. The biggest screen, in the centre of the display, was used to show a high-definition birds-eye image of the ground below the RPA.

The pilots of 13th Squadron operated ten Reapers, also known as Predator Bs. Each one cost a shade under twenty million dollars. With a twenty-metre wingspan and a take-off weight of just under five thousand kilos, the Reaper could fly fully loaded for the best part of fourteen hours up to a height of fifteen thousand metres with a maximum speed of close to three hundred miles an hour. Depending on the target, the Reaper could be fitted with up to four Hellfire air-to-ground missiles and two Paveway laser-guided bombs.

'We've been tasked with supplying you with any footage we have of a training camp on the Pakistan–Afghanistan border,' said Davies. 'I have to warn you, there isn't much that's usable. They've become a lot more savvy over the past year or so. They spend most of the daylight hours inside the network of caves there. From what we know there's a huge cave system and they have generators and a water supply so they don't actually have to come out if they don't want to. We see far more activity at night and we have night-vision cameras, but they're not much use for identification. From the way they manage to avoid our daytime surveillance, we're fairly sure they are monitoring our take-offs. There are Special Forces on the ground trying to stop them, but they've started using kids so there's not much our lads can do. They can't start shooting thirteen-year-olds just because they've got a sat phone.'

'The kids make a call whenever they see an RPA take off, is that it?' asked Shepherd.

Davies nodded. 'We try to fool them by flying away from our intended destination but they're not stupid. And if they know the take-off time they have a pretty good idea of when we'll be above them. They know exactly how high we can fly and for how long, and they have spotters in the area. We've fooled them a few times but generally by the time we get there they've taken cover inside the caves. But we've still got close to twenty hours of footage we can show you.'

'And we're okay to stay here until we've viewed it all?'

'Sure. It's night-time out there at the moment and we've nothing scheduled. I'm assuming you'll be done by this evening if you fast-forward through the boring bits. The mess is open all day and Anita can arrange for coffee and sandwiches if you need it. Alex and I will head off and leave you in Anita's capable hands.'

Shaw climbed out of his chair and followed the lieutenant out of the container.

'We had a flight over the area yesterday,' said Exley. 'There isn't much to see, but why don't we start with that?'

'Sounds good,' said Shepherd. 'Dean, why don't you take the seat?'

Martin squeezed past Shepherd and sat down as Exley tapped on her keyboard. The main screen flickered and then was filled with a rocky desert landscape.

'This is just after dawn,' she said. 'We launched at night and went into a holding pattern over the border until first light. But as you can see, the area is almost deserted. Early morning is pretty much the best time to get your training done, temperature-wise, but there's no one about. Except for the odd spotter.' On the screen they saw a man with his face covered with a black and white keffiyeh scarf at the entrance to one of the caves. He was holding a pair of high-powered binoculars. 'The spotters just sit there and watch until we fly off. Then presumably they all pile out and start their training.'

'How much damage could you do if you fired missiles at the cave entrance?' asked Shepherd.

'We could seriously damage the entrance but not beyond fifty feet or so, and the cave system goes right back into the hills,' said Exley. 'There are dozens of entrances and the systems are all linked. Plus, the spotters would see us making an attack run so they'd be able to warn the people inside. And we'd be firing blind, which is never a good idea. The Hellfires are best suited to specific targets out in the open. They're scalpels rather than chainsaws.'

'Got you,' said Shepherd. 'So how should we do this?'

'Despite their security measures we do have a lot of footage of jihadists out in the open,' said Exley. 'Sometimes we outfox them, sometimes we're just lucky. We caught them a blinder last week by sending out two Reapers, flying one low as a decoy and one much higher in the clouds. The low one circled for an hour and then headed back. After it had gone they came out to play and it was half an hour before they spotted the one at high altitude.'

Her fingers tapped on the keyboard and the main screen filled with a view from an RPA high in the sky. There was a coding along the bottom that gave the time, date, altitude and position.

There were wisps of cloud but it was easy to see the figures on the ground far below. The RPA was heading towards the cave complex, though it was too dark to see inside. Some distance away from the cave entrance there were a couple of dozen men exercising, doing a combination of press-ups, sit-ups and star jumps.

Another dozen or so men were lining up and being taught how to use an AK-47. Despite the fact that the RPA was at thirty thousand feet the images were crystal clear and Shepherd could even make out the curved magazines. Most of the men were wearing baggy trousers and long shirts, though several had the long thawb robes. Most used scarves to protect their heads from the fierce Afghan sun, which made identification difficult, as did the fact that most of the men had beards.

Martin's eyes narrowed as he scrutinised the men on the screen. Shepherd didn't say anything. There was no point – either Martin would recognise Khaled among the fighters and instructors or he wouldn't. Nothing he could say would make any difference to the process.

The RPA did a slow circuit. The camera zoomed in and out without Exley touching the keyboard or controls and Shepherd realised the changes had been made by the original pilot. He leaned towards Exley.

'Anita, what's the story with zooming in and panning? Can we do that with the recording?'

She shook her head. 'Unfortunately not,' she said. 'What we can do is freeze and then zoom in on the still. That produces quite good results. But other than that, what we see is what we get.'

Shepherd pulled up a small stool and watched the footage from behind the pilot and Martin. The resolution was awesome, way better than anything they had in the Super-Recogniser Unit.

'This pass is interesting. They were giving a demonstration of a suicide vest and we got a terrific view of it,' said Exley.

Shepherd leaned forward.

The RPA was on a different approach this time, heading towards the cave entrances from the side. The pilot who had made the run had spotted a gathering of half a dozen fighters standing around a portly man with a straggly beard. They were standing around another man but as the RPA approached the gathering Shepherd could see that it was a shop dummy, all white with a head that was featureless except for a nose. The older man was arranging a vest on the dummy, fastening straps and adjusting wiring. The camera zoomed in on the group.

'That's him,' said Martin.

Shepherd stood up. 'Are you sure?'

'No doubt. No fucking doubt in my mind.'

The camera pulled back as the older man led the young fighters away from the dummy. They walked maybe a hundred yards and then gathered behind an earth embankment. The older man was holding something, presumably a transmitter. The camera had pulled back so that they could see both the group of fighters and the dummy with the vest. The man pressed the transmitter and almost immediately the dummy exploded and a cloud of dust mushroomed above it. The fighters emerged from behind the embankment and began jumping up and down and hugging each other. The older man stood watching them.

'It's him,' said Martin. 'A bit heavier but I'd recognise him anywhere.'

'The resolution isn't that great,' said Shepherd. 'I don't think even I'd be able to recognise him from that picture.'

'It's him,' said Martin.

'Anita, can we get some stills?' asked Shepherd. 'Close-ups on the face and full body.'

'Sure,' said the pilot.

Martin twisted around in his seat. 'Now what? Can we use a drone to blow him to Kingdom Come?' he asked.

'They don't come out much,' said Exley. 'We were fortunate to get these pictures. We might get lucky again if we went on a kill mission, but it would be a matter of luck. A targeted drone strike isn't really an option. Not if you want to be sure.'

'So what do we do?' Martin asked Shepherd.

'That decision is above my pay grade,' said Shepherd. 'But I'll find out.' He looked over at Exley. 'That was a week ago, right? Is that guy in any of the more recent footage you have?'

'There are no suicide vest demonstrations but there are several tuition sessions going on outside. I can show you what we have.'

'Get started with Dean,' he said. 'I've got a call to make.'

Shepherd went outside and called Patsy Ellis on his mobile. Her assistant put him on hold for less than ten seconds before putting him through.

'What's the story, Dan?' she asked.

'Khaled is there,' said Shepherd. 'At least he was a week ago. We're going to start looking at more recent footage.'

'Can we carry out a drone strike?'

'I'd say not,' said Shepherd. 'He's in the caves most of the time. There's no guarantee that an RPA would be there at the time he comes out.'

'RPA?'

'Sorry, that's what they call drones. Remotely-piloted aircraft.'

'Why don't they call them drones?'

'I don't know. Maybe because they don't want us to lose sight of the fact that they are being piloted. But they are touchy about it.'

'Okay, so if we can't do it remotely, we're going to have to go in and get him, I suppose.'

'I don't think there's an alternative.'

'And we definitely need this American? Dean Martin?'

'The drone pictures aren't clear enough to make a positive ID,' said Shepherd. 'I could have a stab at it, but I'd never be a hundred per cent certain. But Martin remembers him. So the short answer is, yes. We need him.'

'What shape is he in?'

'Physically he's looking good. As fit as the proverbial butcher's dog. Are you thinking of sending him in to make an ID? He's been out of Special Forces for more than ten years.'

'He'd only be there as an observer,' said Ellis.

'I'm not sure an SAS hit-squad would want a passenger along,' said Shepherd.

'I hear what you're saying,' said Ellis. 'Why not take him up to Hereford and put him through his paces? I'll arrange transport and make sure they're expecting you.'

Shepherd opened his mouth to reply but the line went dead in his ear.

Chapter 72

Present Day, Hereford

The flight from RAF Waddington to the SAS's base in Hereford took just over thirty minutes with the Augusta A109E Power helicopter flying close to its maximum speed of two hundred miles an hour. The helicopter was part of the RAF's Command Support Air Transport unit at 32 Squadron, tasked with moving senior military commanders and government ministers around the UK and Europe. It was considerably more luxurious than the helicopters Shepherd had been ferried around in during his SAS days; the seats were padded with comfortable headrests and there was a cup holder close at hand, and pristine over-the-ear headphones allowed him and Martin to listen in to the radio traffic.

The helicopter circled the camp once and then landed. Shepherd grinned as he climbed out and saw a familiar face standing by the side of a sand-coloured Land Rover. It was Major Allan Gannon, his former CO and a long-standing friend. The major was wearing desert fatigues and had a Glock on his hip. He had grown a beard and his skin was tanned, which suggested he'd been in sunnier climes. Shepherd jogged over, bent low even though the still-spinning rotors of the Augusta were well above his head.

He straightened up as he reached the major and the two men shook hands.

'Good to see you, Spider,' said the major. He was a couple of inches taller than Shepherd, broad-shouldered with a square jaw and a nose that had been broken at least twice.

'And you, boss. Thanks for arranging this at such short notice.'

He turned and introduced Martin. 'This is Dean. Former Navy SEAL. We need to get him mission ready.'

The major shook hands with Martin. 'Well, you're in the right place,' he said. 'Let's get you some gear and get started.'

He climbed into the Land Rover. Shepherd got in next to him and Martin jumped into the back.

'You've been overseas, boss?'

'The suntan's a clue, is it?' laughed Gannon. 'The regiment is so stretched at the moment that even old war horses like me are seeing action,' he said. 'Purely in an advisory role, of course.'

Their first call was to pick up fatigues and webbing belts, and once Shepherd and Martin were suitably dressed the major drove them to the armoury. He parked and took them inside. Sergeant Peter Simpson was waiting for them behind his counter. He was grey-haired and stocky, wearing desert fatigues. Simpson was a Loggy, a member of the Royal Logistics Corps, and had been in charge of the armoury since before Shepherd had joined the regiment.

'Bloody hell, Spider Shepherd,' said Simpson in his gruff Geordie accent. 'Can't keep you away.'

'Spider?' repeated Martin.

'It's a long story,' said Shepherd.

'Which ends with our man here eating a live tarantula in the jungle for no other reason than to prove that he could,' laughed Simpson. 'So how can I help you gentlemen today?'

The major stepped forward. 'We're just going to put the guys through their paces,' he said. 'What do you want, Spider?'

When Spider had been with the SAS his weapon of choice had been the MP5 but the Heckler and Koch carbine was now dated and the regiment preferred to use the Belgium-made self-loading SCAR rifle or the Heckler and Koch 416 assault rifle.

'I'll take the HK416,' said Shepherd.

'A good choice,' said Simpson.

'It's a nice weapon,' agreed Martin. 'But me, I always preferred the 417.'

'Ah, a Yank,' said Simpson. 'You guys used 416s to take down Bin Laden, but I agree, you get more of a punch with the 417.'

The HK416 and HK417 had similar internal workings but the HK417 had an enlarged receiver to take the larger 7.62mm round.

The major wrinkled his nose. 'The 417 has a better range, greater accuracy and better penetration, but it has a lower rate of fire and you don't get as many cartridges in the magazine.' He shrugged. 'But horses for courses.'

'So you'd like a 417?' Simpson asked Martin.

Martin grinned. 'This might sound crazy, but I'd prefer an AK-47.'

The major raised an eyebrow. 'Old school. I like it.'

'Don't get me wrong, during training and on exercises I'd always take a 417, but as soon as I hit the Sandbox I'd pick up an AK-47. With a beard and a suntan and a Kalashnikov on my back I'd pass for a local. A 417 is a giveaway, every time. The AK-47s never jam, and there's ammunition and clips everywhere you look. Plus, if you fire the AK, anyone will think it's a local firing. If they hear a Heckler, they know it's us.'

Shepherd nodded in agreement. When he had been with the SAS in Afghanistan he'd often taken a Kalashnikov as his weapon of choice.

'Camouflage,' said the major. 'You're preaching to the converted.' He nodded at Simpson. 'So, a 416 for Spider and an AK-47 for our friend from America.'

Simpson took them down a corridor lined with wire-mesh cages. He unlocked one and took out an HK416, which he gave to Shepherd, then opened another cage filled with battle-scarred AK-47s. He waved for Martin to make his choice. Martin took one from the middle rack, checked the action, looked down the barrel and into the receiver, and nodded.

'Good choice,' said Simpson. 'The guys brought that one back from Sierra Leone. Used to belong to a child soldier. Thirteen years old and he had more than fifty kills to his name, they say.' He locked the cage. 'And for you, boss?'

The major shook his head. 'I'm good,' he said. 'I've fired more than enough rounds over the last month.'

They went outside and climbed into Gannon's Land Rover with their weapons and ammunition and he drove them the short distance to the outdoor firing range. He parked by the entrance. There was already a red flag fluttering from a flagpole, showing that the range was in use, and as they headed for the door there was the dull thud of a carbine being fired on full automatic.

There were two men on the range, both wearing desert camouflage trousers and T-shirts. Shepherd recognised one of the men – Chris 'Happy' Hawkins. He was in his early twenties with unkempt red hair and a sprinkle of freckles across his nose. His colouring and hair meant that he rarely worked undercover in the Middle East. His chances of passing himself off as an Arab were slim to none, with the emphasis on none.

Hawkins strode over, transferred an HK416 to his left hand and shook hands with Shepherd. 'How the hell are you, Spider?'

'All good,' he said.

'You putting on weight?'

'I'm flying a desk at the moment,' said Shepherd, patting his stomach. 'But it's only temporary. I hope.'

Hawkins looked over at Martin. 'He looks in good shape.'

Shepherd grinned. Hawkins was one of the few gay members of the regiment, at least one of the few who openly admitted their sexuality. While he came in for a lot of good-natured ribbing no one really cared what he did in his spare time or who he did it with. The soldiers of the SAS cared about only one thing and that was doing the job – everything else was secondary.

'Dean, Dean Martin, like the singer,' Shepherd said.

'With the same smouldering Italian looks,' said Hawkins, only half joking. He went over and introduced himself, and the two men shook hands. Hawkins looked at the Kalashnikov. 'You okay with that?'

'My weapon of choice,' said Martin.

The major strode over. 'We just need to put Dean through his paces here and then we'll do a couple of drills in the CGB room,' he said to Hawkins. 'Do me a favour and put up some fresh targets.'

'Will do, boss.'

The range was bog-standard and basic, with no frills at all. The ground was grass, the targets were pinned up on boards in front of a sandbag wall to absorb the rounds and it was open to the air. The SAS trained there in all weathers, for hours on end. The average infantryman might shoot a few hundred rounds in his entire career; the average SAS trooper expended that many in an hour. Hawkins pinned up four fresh targets and walked back.

'Want to go first, Spider?' asked the major with a sly grin. 'See if flying a desk has made you lose your edge.'

Shepherd grinned back but felt a lot less confident than he looked. He looked at the target on the far right, a jihadist in a headscarf sighting down the barrel of a Kalashnikov. The target was fifty yards away, not a difficult shot under non-combat conditions, but it had been more than a year since he had held a carbine and he hadn't been given a chance to check the sights. He raised the weapon to his shoulder, slipped his finger over the trigger, sighted and squeezed off two shots. He was aiming between the eyes but both shots went low, thudding into the neck. He raised his aim and fired two more shots. These were at the height of the nose but to the left, missing the head completely. He aimed to the right and the next two shots were in the forehead. He fired off three more double taps and then lowered his weapon.

'Not bad,' said the major, unenthusiastically.

Shepherd just nodded; there was no point in offering excuses. Everyone knew that he was firing the weapon for the first time, but he could see that the grouping wasn't great.

'Let's see what the new guy can do,' said Hawkins, patting Martin on the shoulder.

Shepherd moved back to the trestle tables at the rear of the range where there was a coffee urn and a stack of mugs. He poured himself a coffee. The major joined him and Shepherd gave him the mug and poured himself another.

Martin took up position opposite the target on the right side. He weighed the AK-47 in his hands. Shepherd wondered when he'd last held a weapon. Hawkins was talking softly to Martin and the American was listening intently and nodding.

'Former SEAL?'

'But he's been out for twelve years or so.'

'There are good SEALs and mediocre SEALs,' said Gannon. 'At any one time there are close to two thousand five hundred of the buggers. The regiment's full strength is six hundred so obviously their standards have to be lower. They want the regiment to double the size but we can't get enough men through Selection. And we're refusing to allow them to drop our standards. That would be the beginning of the end.'

Hawkins stepped behind Martin and the American shouldered the AK-47 and began firing quickly. Bang-bang-bang-bang-bang-bang. After six rapid shots he transferred the weapon to the opposite shoulder in a smooth movement and fired off another six shots.

Gannon looked at Shepherd and nodded appreciatively. 'Nice moves,' he said,.

Shepherd nodded in agreement. Firing from both shoulders was a necessary skill in Special Forces. When firing behind cover it was a big help to be able to shoot from either shoulder, but it was a skill that had to be learned through practice. Firing from the off shoulder felt awkward at first and it took dozens of hours before the movement would become automatic. Either Martin had been secretly practising or he was a natural.

Shepherd went over to join Martin and Hawkins, who were discussing the merits of the AK-47 as compared with the AK-74. Martin's aim was impressive; two tight groups either of which could have been covered with a teacup.

'Nice shooting, Dean,' said Shepherd.

'I don't think we need do any more work here,' said the major. 'Your eye is fine. Let's move on to some close quarter battle training.'

They left the range and piled back into the Land Rover. The

major drove them over to the Close Quarter Battle training facility. It was a single-storey building with an indoor firing range and a large room that had been fitted out as a practice area. The SAS had a high-tech two-storey complete killing house at a secret location a short drive from the Credenhill barracks, most of it underground so it wouldn't appear on Google Maps. It was a continuing source of annoyance to the Head Sheds of the regiment that anyone with access to the Internet could get high-resolution satellite images of every inch of the barracks and a perfect view of the entrance from the company's Street View program.

In charge of the facility was another Loggy, a lanky corporal with a receding hairline and jug-like ears. His name was Adam Hess and he was also a long-serving member of the regiment staff. The major explained what he wanted to do and Hess disappeared through a door.

'This is a simple enough scenario,' Gannon explained to Martin. 'You're going to be entering a cave system so the killing house won't be of much use to you. Caves tend not to have doors to kick down. So we'll run you through this CQB room. As soon as you go through that door you're in play. There are a number of rooms and I won't tell you how many. You move from room to room and in each room there'll be a scenario that you have to deal with. You'll be using live ammo – try to stay on target but there's rubber insulation around the walls that will absorb any stray rounds. Spider and I will be with you but we'll only be observing.'

Martin nodded. 'Got it,' he said.

Hess opened the door and stepped into the corridor. 'Ready when you are, sir,' he said.

'You okay, Dean?' asked the major. There was a line of dark green ear defenders on a bench and they each grabbed a set and pulled them on. Shepherd preferred not to train with ear defenders but in the confined area of the CQB area shots from the Kalashnikov would be loud enough to cause long-term hearing damage.

'Ready when you are, Dean,' Gannon said.

Martin nodded and turned to face the door, the barrel of his AK-47 pointing at the ground. As the major reached out for the handle, Martin flicked off the safety, and as the major pushed the door open his finger slipped over the trigger and he dropped into a crouch. He had the Kalashnikov up against his left shoulder, noticed Shepherd, so that he could look around the door without exposing himself.

The door opened further, revealing a cut-out of a terrorist holding a pistol. Martin fired smoothly, two shots to the chest and a third to the head. He did it on the move and immediately he had fired the third shot he was already scanning the room.

There was no furniture in the room and no decorations, none of the frills of the killing house, which used lots of props and projection screens to make the situations look as real as possible. The CQB area was as basic as it came, but it was a good test of judgement and reflexes and so far Martin was doing just fine.

The door to the next room was to the left and Martin kept the AK-47 against his left shoulder as he moved towards it, still in a half crouch. Gannon and Shepherd followed behind him.

Martin saw the two figures a fraction of a second before Shepherd and he was already firing. Both figures were holding automatic weapons but the one on the left had a flak jacket with SWAT printed across it and a baseball cap with POLICE above the peak. The figure on the right was wearing a leather jacket and aiming directly at them. Martin ignored the cop and fired three times at the villain, putting two rounds in the chest and one in the head.

They surveyed the room and as they did a third cut-out flipped up from the floor, another villain, this time with a sawn-off shotgun in his hands. The three shots from the AK-47 almost sounded like one.

Shepherd's eyes were watering from the cordite and he wiped them with the back of his hand. Martin was already moving to the next door and transferring the Kalashnikov to his right shoulder in a smooth action. He scanned the doorway from outside, then stepped through. Hess had been cunning; there were four figures this time, two obvious bad guys in the corners facing the door. The one to the left was holding a machete above his head, the one to the right an M16. Martin made the correct call and shot the villain with the gun – bang-bang-bang – and as he did he kept moving away from the figure with the machete. But as he moved he saw the other two figures. One was a hostage, a scared woman standing in front of a swarthy man holding a handgun. They were in the corner to Martin's right. It was a tough shot, though one that Shepherd had taken many times, but Shepherd was used to it and Martin was seeing it for the first time.

Martin turned his attention to the hostage-taker, sighted for a fraction of a second and fired once. The round smashed into the man's face, just six inches from the top of the hostage's head. Then he turned in a smooth, fluid movement, dropped down on to one knee and shot the guy with the machete, twice in the chest. The third shot, to the head, came a fraction of a second later.

The major took off his ear defenders and blew a loud whistle. 'Exercise over,' he said.

Martin clicked on the safety and stood up. He was breathing slowly and evenly and there was no sign of the pressure that he had been under.

'Nice shooting,' said Gannon. 'Very nice.'

He looked over at Shepherd and Shepherd nodded in agreement. 'Pretty much faultless,' he said.

'You always do the three shots?' asked Gannon. 'A double tap to the chest and one to the head?'

'I had a couple of close calls in Afghanistan,' said Martin. 'Fighters with bulletproof vests under their clothing. Happened to me twice. I put two shots to the heart and moved on to the next target and in both cases I knocked them to the ground but they were still able to get off a shot. I put the first one down to a fluke but after it happened again I decided to always make sure the guy was down before moving on.'

'To be honest, you're so quick it's not a problem,' said Gannon.

'What I would say is that if you're going up against multiple targets you might want to just do head shots. Your aim is good enough.'

Martin nodded. 'Sounds sensible.'

'And can I ask you, when was the last time you had a Kalashnikov in your hands?'

Martin grinned. 'Three weeks ago.'

The major and Shepherd exchanged confused looks and Martin laughed.

'I've a couple of diving buddies who live in Cambodia and I fly over to see them every now and again. They've got access to one of the army ranges near Phnom Penh and I get to play with whatever I want pretty much. Up to and including RPGs and hand grenades. You can play with anything there providing you've got the money.'

'Lucky for us,' said Gannon. 'I don't think we need to do anything with you. You've no bad habits, you make good decisions, you're fast and you're accurate. In fact, if you wanted to join us I could probably pull some strings.'

'I'll bear that in mind, thanks,' said Martin.

Shepherd's mobile phone buzzed in his pocket and he took it out. It was Patsy Ellis. He walked out into the corridor and took the call.

'How's it going?' asked Ellis.

'Martin is good to go,' said Shepherd. 'His eyes are sharp, he's combat-ready and like I said before, he's as fit as they come. Probably pass Selection if he went for it.'

'Good,' said Ellis. 'There's a team on hold in Gibraltar, waiting for you.'

'By "you" I assume you mean the two of us. Me and Dean?'

'Do you have a problem with that?' she asked.

'What's the mission? What's the objective?'

'To neutralise an enemy of the state.'

'So the team has been told to shoot to kill?'

'We're hardly going to go all that way to make an arrest, are we? This man is responsible for hundreds of deaths and if he isn't stopped will kill hundreds more. Your man Martin is the only one who knows what he looks like. He needs to be there and I need you there to keep an eye on him. The SAS will handle the neutralisation. You just have to point them in the right direction.'

Shepherd didn't say anything.

'What am I supposed to read into your silence?' said Ellis eventually.

'Nothing,' said Shepherd. 'I'm good.'

'This is your ticket back into operations, you realise that?'

'That's the carrot, is it? I do this and I get to walk away from the CCTV screens?'

'Do you want to stay on attachment with the Super-Recognisers? Because I can certainly make that happen.'

'No. I want to do what I do best.'

'Then you need to prove yourself. If you don't, the Willoughby-Brown business is always going to be hanging over you.'

'So I was being punished by being assigned to the Met? You admit that?'

'It's not about being punished, Dan. It just puts you in a less sensitive position. Jeremy had a lot of friends – you might find that hard to believe but it's true. Some of those friends would prefer it if you left the service, frankly. But you have a lot of friends, too. Now, if you were to be part of an operation that ended in the neutralisation of a terrorist of the stature of Hakeem Khaled, some of the former might be less inclined to keep you out in the cold.'

'I don't suppose I could have that in writing, could I?'

Ellis snorted softly. 'Charlotte did say you had the driest sense of humour,' she said. 'But it's time to put up or shut up. If you don't want to go on the mission, I can get someone from the SAS assigned to babysit Martin.'

'No, I'll do it,' said Shepherd.

'That's the spirit,' said Ellis.

The line went dead before Shepherd could reply.

Chapter 73

Present Day, Gibraltar

Shepherd and Martin arrived at Gibraltar Airport on a scheduled British Airways flight that left London at just after seven o'clock in the morning and arrived on the Rock at eleven o'clock local time. They were casually dressed in jackets and jeans. Two men in desert fatigues were waiting at the bottom of the steps and whisked them away to a sand-coloured Land Rover while the rest of the passengers filed their way into the terminal. The men were both in their late twenties with neatly trimmed beards and skin burned brown from the sun. They said nothing as they drove to a hangar at the far end of the airfield where a grey C-130 Hercules transport aircraft was waiting, its rear ramp down.

The Land Rover slowed and drove up the ramp into the hold, which was packed with equipment, including half a dozen Yamaha trail bikes and three stripped-down off-road vehicles, all painted the same sandy-brown as the Land Rover. The off-road vehicles were four-seaters, open at the sides and with no windscreens. There was a rack on the back for carrying equipment that could also be used for the evacuation of casualties, and more storage space on the roof. They had small wheels and high suspension and their engines had been muffled. Shepherd and Martin climbed out of the Land Rover. They were each carrying a small holdall containing boots and fatigues, courtesy of the major. There was no need for anything else – the operation would be over within a few hours of the Hercules touching down at Bagram Airbase, one way or another.

There were a dozen troopers already strapped into seats lining the fuselage. Two sergeants who Shepherd recognised were standing at the front of the hold and they both nodded at him. He nodded back.

A man in his mid-thirties wearing desert fatigues and a floppy hat, grey-haired and clean-shaven, walked towards Shepherd and Martin. 'Spider?' he asked.

'That's me,' said Shepherd. He held out his hand and the two men shook.

'Captain Wayne Gearie,' said the officer. 'I'll be running the show.'

'This is Dean,' said Shepherd. 'Dean is the one who'll be ID-ing our primary target.'

The captain shook hands with Martin. 'We'll be picking up extra gear once we're in Afghanistan,' he said. 'I'm told you want an HK416 and an AK-47? We've got both.' He looked at his watch, a black plastic Casio. 'Okay, we're ready to go, so strap yourselves in and I'll talk to the pilots. I'm sure you've been on enough of these birds to know that facilities are primitive so if you need to pee or worse we've got plastic bags available.'

Shepherd and Martin stashed their holdalls in nets lining the fuselage, and then pulled down two spare folding seats and fastened the harnesses. The two men who had collected them from the plane finished tying down the Land Rover and took their places.

The rear ramp slowly rose up and clicked into place, the engines burst into life and after a couple of minutes the Hercules began to move. Several of the troopers had already closed their eyes and stretched out their legs. Like soldiers the world over, they grabbed sleep and food whenever they could.

Captain Gearie had taken out an iPad and was studying it. Martin folded his arms and stared ahead, clearly deep in thought. Shepherd figured Martin had a lot to think about. One moment he was a diving instructor in Bali, living under an assumed name and thinking that his past was behind him, the next he was on a plane flying into a virtual war zone with a group of Special

Forces soldiers intent on killing a wanted terrorist. It was one
hell of a jump. It was a big jump for Shepherd, too. It had been
a long time since he'd been in action with the SAS and he just
hoped that he'd be able to get through it without making any
mistakes, because mistakes in combat tended to be fatal.

There were two young troopers to his right and he realised
they were staring at him. He smiled and nodded. 'How's it going?'
he asked.

'You're Spider Shepherd, right?' said the trooper nearest him.

'Last time I checked,' said Shepherd.

'Mate, you're a fucking legend.' The trooper shook his hand.
He was in his early twenties, tanned and with a long beard. 'I'm
Dave Hughes but everyone calls me Shaver. This is Creepshow.'

Creepshow was also in his twenties, short but stocky and well
muscled. He leaned around Shaver and shook Spider's hand.
'You ate a fucking giant spider on jungle phase, right?' asked
Creepshow.

'It was a long time ago,' said Shepherd.

'Those bastards are huge,' said Creepshow. He had a West
Country farmer's accent and piercing blue eyes. Shepherd knew
that the SAS men often wore brown contact lenses when on
operations in the Middle East, but this mission was at night so
changing eye colour was pretty low down the list of priorities.

'So you guys have been out here before?' asked Shepherd.

'Afghanistan?' said Shaver. 'Twice. It's usually Syria I get sent
to.' He jerked a thumb at Creepshow. 'This is his first time. But
he's been in Syria more times than me.'

'How is it over there?'

'It's a shithole,' said Shaver. 'They're all shitholes.'

Creepshow nodded enthusiastically. 'Fucking shitholes. The
last couple of missions we've been after British jihadists. Fuck
knows why they want to fight for ISIS out there.'

'It doesn't make sense, does it?' said Shepherd.

'Not if you're born in the UK, it doesn't. They're from good
families a lot of them. Better educated than me, some of them.
Fuck me, if they want to fire guns, join the fucking army. Why

sign up with a group of tossers who go around raping kids and throwing poofters off roofs?'

'And your mission was what?' asked Shepherd.

'To take the bastards out,' said Creepshow. 'Easier to deal with them out there. You just get them in the crosshairs and pull the trigger. If they go back to the UK they get Job Seeker's Allowance and a council house while they plan their attacks. If the authorities make any moves against them they start screaming about their human rights, don't they?'

'It's bloody madness,' said Shaver. 'I've seen two of the faces on our hit list in the papers back in the UK. One of them's been on bloody TV saying that he's realised the error of his ways. Fucking bullshit. That's one sort of leopard that never changes its fucking spots.' He shrugged. 'It's the politicians fucking it up for everyone. They should just let us do our job.'

'Well, they're letting us do it today, that's for sure,' said Shepherd.

'This raghead we're after, what's he done?' asked Shaver.

'What have you been told?'

'Just that he's a high-value target and it's shoot to kill.'

'That's about right,' said Shepherd.

'But who is he? He must be important to go to all this trouble.'

'Word is he did the football stadium bombing. Planned it, anyway. And he's been active for years.'

'Bastard,' said Shaver. He nodded at Martin. 'And what's the Yank's story?'

'He's seen the guy, up close. We need him for the ID.'

Shaver settled back in his seat and stretched out his legs. 'I hope I get the first shot,' he said. 'Who the fuck bombs a football match? If they want to attack the cops or the army, or the government, then I get that. When we're out in the desert and they attack us, that's fair. But blowing up civilians just out to watch a game of footie, that stinks.'

'Yeah,' agreed Creepshow. 'Fucking cowards.'

Shepherd didn't say anything. He wasn't sure that the SAS trooper was right. Cowards didn't blow themselves up. It took a very peculiar sort of bravery to end your life for a cause. Any cause. The attack was appalling and the victims were innocents, but there was nothing cowardly about strapping explosives to your body and blowing yourself up. Khaled was the coward. Khaled was the one who planned the attacks and used others to carry them out, then ran away to hide in the desert. Khaled probably thought he was safe, that he had all the time in the world to plan his next atrocity. But he was wrong.

The four-engine turboprop Hercules had a cruising speed of about three hundred and seventy miles an hour, so when it began to descend after just seven hours in the air, Shepherd knew they were still some distance from Afghanistan. The Hercules had no windows in the fuselage so he had no idea where they were landing, and after the plane had taxied to a halt and he'd walked down the rear ramp he was still none the wiser. They had parked close to a tented area, a few hundred yards from a basic terminal topped by a glass-sided control tower. There was a wire perimeter fence patrolled by armed men wearing desert fatigues and there was a low range of mountains in the distance. There were several dozen planes parked close to the terminal, none with any airline livery that he could see. His best guess would be that they were at a military airbase somewhere in Turkey.

The captain strode down the ramp and put on a pair of Oakleys. 'Right, we'll be refuelling here and picking up a new flight crew,' he said. 'There's a shower block here if anyone wants to use it and there's food and drink.'

'A beer would be nice!' shouted one of the troopers.

'A beer would be fucking marvellous,' agreed Gearie. 'But you'll have to settle for water or juice. I don't need to tell you guys to stay hydrated but please, stay the fuck hydrated.'

Several of the troopers had clearly been at the base before, as they strode purposefully towards one of the tents. Shepherd and Martin followed them inside. Two large fans supplied a much-needed breeze. Two trestle tables had been covered with white paper tablecloths and bulldog clips fixed to hold them in place. There was a stainless steel tea urn on one table with stacks of white mugs and cartons of milk and the two troopers headed straight for it. On the floor next to the tea urn was a large plastic bowl filled with bottles of water and ice. Martin grabbed a bottle, tossed it to Shepherd, then opened one for himself and drank greedily. Shepherd took several gulps of water but it was tea he really wanted so he went over to the urn and poured himself a mug.

'You Brits really love your tea,' said Martin.

'Our army marches on it,' said Shepherd, adding a splash of milk.

There were two large platters of sandwiches on one of the tables and Shepherd grabbed a couple. Martin followed suit and they carried their food over to a bench and sat down. A dozen or so troopers had followed them into the tent and were hoovering up the sandwiches.

'So do you know all these guys?' asked Martin.

'Some of them by sight and I've worked with a couple of them on the range, but they're mostly new faces,' said Shepherd.

'But you're SAS, right?'

'Former SAS,' said Shepherd. 'I left almost twenty years ago.'

Martin frowned. 'You quit early?'

'I was twenty-four. My wife didn't think it was a good idea for the father of her child to be in Special Forces.' He shrugged. 'She was probably right.'

Martin nodded. 'It's not a job for a married man,' he said. 'It's not fair on the wives and to be honest, you don't want warriors worrying about their loved ones in combat, you want them focused on the matter in hand.'

'I guess so,' said Shepherd.

'And are you still together? You and the wife?'

Shepherd shook his head. 'She died,' he said.

'I'm sorry.'

'It was a long time ago.'

'And the kid?'

'Liam?' Shepherd grinned. 'He's doing fine. He flies choppers for the Army Air Corps.'

'Chip off the old block?'

'Not really. I don't think he has any interest in combat, it's the flying he likes.' Shepherd took a bite of his sandwich. He wasn't used to being open about his family situation with people he barely knew. Usually when he was undercover everything he said was a lie, pretty much, but he figured that Martin deserved some degree of honesty. 'What about you?' he asked. 'Why did you leave the SEALs?'

'It wasn't by choice.'

Shepherd frowned. 'What happened?'

'Long story.' Martin took a long pull on his water bottle, then wiped his mouth with the back of his hand. 'Let's just say that towards the end I started to get a bit too enthusiastic about what I was doing.'

Shepherd nodded. 'It happens.'

'I thought I had it under control. And I don't think I was any different from the rest of my team. But an officer thought otherwise and the psych board agreed with him.'

'Officers can be twats sometimes.'

'They might have had a point. I was starting to take risks. We'd have a plan and we'd go in and I'd start doing my own thing. And you know as well as I do that SF ops are all about teamwork. You have to trust every member of your team and it's fair to say I became less of a team player.' He shrugged. 'Even though I knew what the problem was, I couldn't deal with it. So I was out. Tried to get into the FBI and the DEA and Homeland Security but my shitty psych evaluation followed me around.'

'This Hakeem Khaled. You were with the SEALs when you saw him?'

'You don't know?'

Shepherd chuckled. 'I'm pretty much a mushroom on this operation.'

Martin frowned, not understanding.

'A mushroom,' Shepherd explained. 'Kept in the dark and fed bullshit.'

Martin laughed. 'I get it. Need to know and you don't need to know.'

'They said you were a witness and that you were off the grid. They wanted me to get you back in harness and that's all I was told.'

Martin nodded and took a bite of his sandwich and swallowed it whole before continuing. 'I was working security at a shopping mall. It was the night that plane was shot down at JFK. I spotted a group of ragheads taking a MANPAD launcher out of a vehicle. Khaled was there. I came under fire and Khaled bolted. But I'll never forget what he looked like.'

'And that's when you went off the grid?'

'Another long story. And I'm pretty sure that it's still classified. Let's just say I was given a choice. A bullet in the head or stay off the grid for the rest of my life.'

'Hobson's choice,' said Shepherd.

'To be honest, it saved my life. If I'd stayed where I was I'd probably have swallowed a bullet. I'm much happier now. I get to dive, most of my clients are good people, the Indonesians are great. All the sunshine I can handle, and nightlife that's second to none. I can't wait to get back.'

Shepherd sipped his tea. 'You could have said no.'

'Not come?' Martin shook his head. 'I walked away from my old life but that doesn't mean I walked away from my country. That bastard killed hundreds of innocent people, he deserves to be hunted down and killed like a rabid dog. No, I'm happy to be here. And I'll happily pull the trigger if I have to.'

'Your role is to identify him, remember?' said Shepherd.

Martin grinned. 'And I'll have an AK-47 in my hand,' he said. 'Remember that.'

Chapter 74

Present Day, Incirlik Airbase, Turkey

S hepherd and Martin were finishing off their sandwiches when Captain Gearie walked over. He pulled up a folding chair and sat down.

'A little bird tells me you've been through something like this before,' he said to Shepherd.

'An attack on a cave complex?' He nodded. 'Yeah, but it was a long time ago.'

'Do you wanna talk me through the op?'

'Sure. We started with Air Troop carrying out a HALO jump into the desert to mark out a landing area for the Hercs that ferried on the rest of the equipment. We had two squadrons using twenty-eight Pinkies, eight scout motorbikes and two Acmat motherships. G Squadron set up a Fire Support Base and we had air support from the Yanks.'

'Fuck me,' said the captain, sitting back and folding his muscular arms.

'What's a Pinkie?' asked Martin.

The captain laughed. 'They were Land Rover 110 HCPUs. The regiment used them as Desert Patrol Vehicles from the mid-eighties. They had a wheelbase of 110 inches and a 3.5-litre V8 diesel engine and an array of mounts so they could take a range of weapons. Some boffin discovered that pink was the perfect camouflage colour in the desert so they were all painted pink. Hence Pinkies, or Pink Panthers.'

'No desert camo then?' asked Martin.

'Seriously, pink was just as effective. Though you did look a bit of a prat driving through urban areas. Even when they changed over to desert camo colours the nickname stuck, and they used them right up until 2014.'

Shepherd nodded. 'They were a bit cumbersome, it has to be said. You could only get one in a Chinook and up to four in a Hercules.'

'Sounds like you were geared up for a full-on war,' said Gearie. 'Why was that?'

'They wanted it to be spectacular,' said Shepherd. 'They flew in so much kit it was unreal. The Acmat motherships were just overkill.'

'Acmat?' repeated Martin.

'Acmat vehicles are basically supply trucks able to cross rough terrain and carry supplies and ammunition for smaller units,' said Shepherd. 'They in turn have to be protected from attack, which slows down any operation. But that was how the powers-that-be wanted it done back then and we had no choice other than to follow orders.'

'What weapons did you have?' the captain asked.

'The fire support team had Browning heavy machine guns and we had GPMGs on the Pinkies, plus eighty-one-millimetre mortars, Milan anti-tank missiles and MK-19 grenade launchers.'

'And a couple of kitchen sinks?'

'Yeah, the Head Sheds were in overdrive.'

'Why the eighty-one-mill mortars? They go up thousands of feet, so what good are they against caves?'

'Exactly what I said. Plus we had US aircraft overhead. Who the hell fires mortars in the air when you have air support?'

'What air support did the Yanks give you?'

'They had US Navy F-18 Hornets flying from an aircraft carrier in the Gulf, firing Maverick missiles.'

'Bloody hell,' said the captain. 'So this was no surprise attack, then?'

'Well, we went in under cover of darkness but we attacked at ten o'clock in the morning. They would have heard us coming anyway. They'd protected the cave entrances with reinforced sangars and the only way in was a dirt track between two huge boulders. As soon as they saw our dust they let loose with RPGs and G Squadron retaliated with machine-gun fire and we had snipers trying to pick off their guys from almost a kilometre away. As G Squadron put down suppressing fire we went in with the Pinkies, guns blazing.'

Gearie shook his head in amazement. 'Casualties?'

'Surprisingly few considering what we were asked to do,' he said. 'We took the caves, killed a lot of bad guys, and at the end of the day we had two dead and six injured.'

'Hopefully we'll do better than that,' said the captain. 'We'll have the full briefing when we get to Bagram but I can tell you now there'll be no full-frontal assault. We'll be going in at night with full night-vision gear and hopefully it'll all be over before they even know we're there.' He stood up. 'Right, next stop – Afghanistan,' he said. 'We'll be hitting the ground running so get your game faces on.'

The troopers filed on to the plane, several holding bags of sandwiches and fruit. Shepherd and Martin went up the ramp and strapped themselves in. Five minutes later they were in the air, heading east. Martin was back in his resting position, arms folded, staring straight ahead.

The second leg was just shy of six hours, then Shepherd's ears popped as the Hercules began its descent. The plane went into a steep dive, then performed a couple of tight turns before levelling off and landing, presumably to minimise the chances of being shot down on approach.

After a couple of minutes of taxiing, the Hercules came to a halt and the engines began to wind down. Captain Gearie was first to his feet.

'Right gentlemen, welcome to Camp Bagram. I need all the gear off within thirty minutes, we run our checks and then we're off. We need to get to the target before dawn otherwise we'll have to lie up throughout the day and none of us want that.'

The ramp came down and with it a blast of cold air. It was night and the sky was cloudless and peppered with stars. Shepherd and Martin headed down the ramp, breath feathering from their mouths.

'I forgot how cold it gets at night,' said Martin.

'Very different from Bali,' said Shepherd.

The Land Rover started up and began to reverse out. They moved out of its way. Troopers wheeled trail bikes down the ramp and the DVPs started up, filling the fuselage with foul fumes.

At its peak, Bagram Airfield was the busiest military airbase in the world, handling almost four hundred take-offs and landings every day. There was a town of forty thousand foreign inhabitants and almost ten thousand local workers built around two massive runways capable of dealing with any size of military aircraft, including the largest, the Russian-built Antonov transport plane. Once the coalition forces had pulled out of the country, the base had been handed over to the Afghan Armed Forces and the US-led Resolute Support Mission. The Resolute Support Mission was there to help and advise the Afghan troops, though there were almost three thousand US personnel involved in counter-terrorism missions and the SAS always had troops there.

Gearie strode over to Shepherd and Martin, accompanied by a squat bearded sergeant, one of the ones Shepherd had recognised on the plane.

'Jacko here will fix you up with your weapons, and he'll be shadowing you throughout the operation,' said the captain.

The sergeant grinned at Shepherd and the two men shook hands.

'Spider and me go back aways,' said Jacko.

'That we do,' said Shepherd.

Trevor Jackson was a Bristol-born paratrooper who had joined the regiment about three months before Shepherd had left and had done a mountain survival course with him. Jacko was just about the worst skier Shepherd had ever seen and after one of many tumbles Shepherd had had to carry him down a mountain with a sprained ankle.

'Nice that now it's me taking care of you and not the other way around,' said Jacko.

'I don't need babysitting,' said Martin.

'It's not about babysitting, it's about making sure that you reach the objective,' said Gearie. 'If we get there and you're not with us the whole operation will have been a waste of time. We don't know how much contact we'll have, if any, en route – all I'm saying is that your priority is to stay alive rather than to be shooting at hostiles.'

Martin nodded. 'Hoo-ya,' he said.

'Here's a bit of information for you that you might or might not know,' said the captain. 'You know how you Yanks love to say hoo-ya when you're all fired up?'

Martin grinned. 'Sure.'

'Do you know where it comes from? Why soldiers say it?'

Martin frowned. 'It's just a noise.'

'It's more than that,' said Gearie. 'It's the phonetic spelling of HUA – Heard, Understood, Acknowledge.'

'I did not know that,' said Martin.

'Then I bet you also don't know that it was we Brits that first used it. And it was first used here, in Afghanistan, back in the 1800s.' He patted Martin on the shoulder. 'History lesson over. You get yourself kitted up. We're moving out in about thirty minutes.'

Jacko grunted something and headed towards a tent. Shepherd and Martin followed. There were two troopers in desert camouflage inside the tent. Shepherd figured they were Loggys, there to provide logistical support. There was an HK416 on a table with half a dozen ammunition clips. Shepherd picked it up and checked the action.

One of the Loggys looked at Martin. 'You the one that wanted an AK-47?'

Martin nodded.

'We've got two. One with a folding stock.'

'I'll take the regular stock,' said Martin. 'I'm not planning on hiding it.'

The Loggy bent down and pulled a Kalashnikov from a metal trunk and handed it to Martin. 'What do you want in the way of magazines?' he asked. 'We actually have a 75-round drum magazine, but it's really only for the aficionados. We have all the 30-round magazines you can carry.'

'Four should do it,' said Martin. He looked at Shepherd.

'Four sounds about right,' said Shepherd. One hundred and twenty rounds should be more than enough. If he needed more than that then it meant they were hopelessly outgunned.

The Loggy looked over at Shepherd. 'I've got polymer tens, twenties and thirties for the HK416,' he said.

'Four clips of thirty'll be fine,' he said.

Martin took his four magazines and duct-taped them together in twos, nose to tail. It was an old trick that could save a second or two when changing magazines. All you had to do was pull out the empty one, flip the bundle around and slot in the fresh one without having to grope around for a replacement.

Jacko waited until Shepherd and Martin had checked their weapons and magazines before speaking, his voice barely above a whisper. 'Right, as the boss said, I'll be shadowing you. I know Spider knows what he's doing but former Navy SEAL or not you're a newbie to me so I'm going to have to take my captain's word for it that you're combat-ready. I won't be holding your hands, but when I say jump you guys need to jump. I won't be asking you twice.'

'All good,' said Shepherd.

Martin nodded.

'We'll be on one of the four by fours,' continued Jacko. 'You two will be in the rear seats and need to keep your eyes open for activity either side. We'll be in the middle of the convoy but that doesn't mean you can sit back and relax – we need all eyes looking for trouble. Once we arrive at the target, we'll be in the third wave going in, so hopefully it'll be under control by then. If it's still hot, you two are active members of the team.'

Shepherd and Martin nodded. Martin slung the AK-47 over his shoulder. Jacko gestured with his chin.

'On the four by four, you hold your weapon,' he said.

'Understood,' said Martin.

'Steve Garrett will be driving, and he'll be sticking with us during the rough and tumble. Any questions?'

Shepherd and Martin shook their heads.

Jacko looked over at the Loggys. 'They'll need night-vision goggles. And body armour.'

'I move better without armour,' said Martin.

'I don't care if you can run like Usain fucking Bolt,' said Jacko. 'My priority is to keep you alive so you will wear whatever I tell you to fucking wear.' His voice was still a whisper but there was no doubting how serious he was.

'Hoo-ya,' said Martin, and he grinned.

The two Loggys handed them body armour, which they strapped on, then the Loggys produced helmets with night-vision goggles and adjusted them to fit their heads. They were simple enough to operate – they were flicked down over the eyes when needed and there was a simple on–off button. Shepherd wasn't a fan of night-vision equipment – they did the job but they made moving difficult. They concentrated the vision directly ahead, which meant it was hard to see where your feet were. Looking up and down was awkward and tiring so the best technique was to simply remember where obstacles were and to tread carefully. Shepherd found them a nuisance but they were going into caves and the equipment would give them an edge over the enemy.

Once the Loggys were satisfied that the goggles were fully charged and working, they flipped them up and nodded at Jacko.

'Right, we've a briefing to go to,' said Jacko. He turned and walked out of the tent and Shepherd and Martin hurried after him.

Captain Gearie had commandeered a tent close by and had a laptop linked up to a projector that was flashing an image on to a whiteboard behind him. It was showing a satellite view of a rocky hill and from the time and date stamps it appeared to be a live feed. There was a map and several photographs stuck to the board.

All the men were gathered around, their night-vision goggles up and their weapons slung over their shoulders. The tent was lit with overhead fluorescent lights and in the distance was the hum of a generator.

'Right guys, listen up!' shouted Gearie to get everyone's attention. All conversation immediately stopped. 'I'm sure you all know I'm Captain Gearie and I'm running this show with the able assistance of Captain Frank Harrison, hiding over there at the back.'

A beefy man with a neatly trimmed beard raised his hand and there were several catcalls from the assembled men.

'So, we're attacking a cave complex, the entrance to which is on a slope at the base of mountains forming the border between Afghanistan, where we are, and Pakistan, where we're not. The main attack force will be troops six and seven from B squadron because, unfortunately, they were the only ones we could get at short notice.'

There were groans from the troopers and several muffled curses and Gearie grinned – troopers were always running down their officers but it could be a two-way street.

'Right, gratuitous insults out of the way, let's get down to business,' said Gearie. 'Two troops, Captain Harrison and myself, and two sergeants, Jacko Jackson and Phillip Smeed, both of whom have had experience in the area we're going to. Make yourself known, guys.'

Jacko raised a languid hand and at the back of the tent a short, stocky man wearing a webbed vest over his fatigues put his arm in the air.

'We'll be dropped by Chinooks about fifty miles from the target. A temporary landing zone has already been secured for us. All the vehicles have been muffled so we should be able to get to within two miles of the target without being heard. The terrain is rough but passable. I've allocated two hours for the drive but I'll be surprised if it takes us more than ninety minutes. We walk the rest of the way. There'll be four Chinooks and they'll wait for us at the TLZ but if by any chance the shit hits the fan they can be at the caves within minutes. We'll be using ten Desert Patrol Vehicles – we brought three with us and we'll be picking up seven more here. We'll take a Land Rover with us that's been fitted with a general purpose machine gun but that will stay behind at the TLZ. We'll also have six trail bikes. I'll be in the leading DPV, with a 2–3–4 formation behind me. The bikes will be three each side at the front. Now, you might have spotted the two strangers in our midst, though some of you might have recognised Spider Shepherd, who used to be one of us but who has now – he tells me – moved on to better things.'

Spider held up his hand.

'With him is Dean. He's a former Navy SEAL but don't hold that against him.'

Dean made himself known and there were assorted catcalls and jeers, though it was clearly good-natured. While there was a long-standing rivalry between the two Special Forces groups, they respected each other's skills and professionalism.

'Spider and Dean will be in the centre DPV in the third row, basically slap bang in the middle of the formation. Steve Garrett will be driving and Jacko will be in the front seat. Steve and Jacko will, if you forgive the pun, be shepherding our two guests. "Why", I hear you ask. Basically, we are going in to liquidate a nest of jihadist fighters who are being trained to cause mayhem back in the UK, so anyone in those caves is fair game. But we are especially interested in one particular high-value target, one Hakeem Khaled, who is believed to have organised a number of atrocities including the recent stadium bombing in London. The problem is, we have no usable photographs of Khaled. These are the best we have.' He pointed at three photographs on the whiteboard behind him. One was the head-and-shoulders picture from Khaled's asylum application. The two others were from the drone that had filmed Khaled demonstrating his suicide vest. 'The picture of his face is more than fifteen years old and isn't much help, and the detail on the two surveillance shots isn't great either. But Dean here has seen this Khaled up close and personal so we'll be using him to make a positive ID. Khaled does not leave that cave alive, gentlemen. Let's be absolutely clear about that. No matter what happens in there, he goes down.'

There were murmurings of agreement and nods from the troopers.

'We also have intel that says there are a number of British-born jihadists at the training camp, perhaps as many as ten. They're being trained, by this Khaled among others, to go back to the UK and carry out terrorist atrocities. Again, we're not looking to put them on trial and give them their day in court – they are enemy combatants in a war situation and will be treated as such. No one is going to be worrying about whether or not they were holding a weapon or if their hands were in the air. We're not looking to be taking any prisoners and I think it's fair to say that what happens in the cave, stays in the cave. There's no CCTV in there and no drones peering down on you so no Head Shed or politician back in the UK is going to be second-guessing you from the safety of his desk.'

He looked around, making eye contact with as many of the men as possible. 'Right, who'll be using the LiveScan equipment and the digital cameras?'

Three of the troopers raised their hands. LiveScan machines were small portable fingerprint readers used by most police forces in the UK. They allowed for fingerprints to be instantly compared with the national IDENT1 database, which held the fingerprints of more than seven million people. While the devices needed an Internet connection to access the database, they could store any fingerprints until they were back in the UK.

'Right, this is very much a seek-and-destroy mission, but once we have secured the area we need every body fingerprinted and photographed. These caves could be an intel goldmine so we'll be going through it looking for paperwork, computers, phones and ID carried by the hostiles. Anything that isn't nailed down, we take with us. Understood?'

He was faced with ranks of nodding heads.

'Now those of you who know Spider will know that among his many skills is a near-photographic memory. Spider's up to date on all the home-grown jihadists we believe are out of the UK so he's going to be taking a look at each and every casualty.

He's also been inside a cave complex not too dissimilar to this one so it might be helpful if he says a few words. Spider?' He waved over at Shepherd.

Shepherd nodded and looked around the tent at several dozen attentive faces. 'We were tasked with taking out an al-Qaeda base and major opium storage facility in the Registan Desert in Helmand Province, mainly because someone thought that Bin Laden might be there,' he said. 'Needless to say, he wasn't. Our attack was a full-front assault in daylight, so again not much in common with what we'll be doing tonight. About the only thing the two operations have in common is that they were both launched from Bagram. We were using torches in the caves . . .' He grinned when he heard the laughter from several of the troopers. 'I know, what can I say, it was almost twenty years ago.'

He waited for the laughter and catcalls to die down before continuing. 'They live in these caves so there's lots of stuff in there. We saw rugs and carpets on the floors and walls, furniture, desks, tables, lots of clutter, so watch where you're going. The caves we'd been in had been occupied for years and had been modified. Most of the big rooms were natural but they had carved out passages in the rock, usually quite narrow, perfect bottlenecks for an ambush. Back then they had electric lighting run from generators and there were wires everywhere. Because the caves are a natural formation there's no obvious logic to the layout, you have to take it as it is. The big danger is ricochets, and not being sure where your patrol mates are. Stray shots can be lethal; there are no rubber mats on the wall and no way of predicting where a ricochet is going to go. The caves twist and turn so at any one point you might not have your patrol mates in sight. You have to stay very aware of where everyone is.' He shrugged. 'That's all I can offer, I'm afraid. It was a long time ago.'

'Thanks, Spider,' said the captain. 'We'll be going in three waves. I'll be leading the first attack wave and Captain Harrison will lead the second. Bear in mind what Spider said – it could turn out to be a labyrinth in there and I don't want any friendly fire. Once we have the area locked down, Jacko will bring Dean and Spider in to make the IDs. While they're doing that, we'll spread out and liberate any intel we can, especially any electronics and paperwork. Right – on to the operation itself.' Gearie turned and pointed at the projected view on the whiteboard. There were six smudges of green, infrared images of figures on the ground. 'This is a live feed from a satellite that the Americans have kindly agreed to point at our target for the next hour or so,' said the captain. 'In a few hours we'll have two drones up with night-vision cameras and we'll be taking live feeds from them. At the moment all we have is the satellite view but it's proving very informative. What we have here are six guards in three groups of two. As you can see, they don't appear to be moving but that doesn't mean they're asleep. Our intel doesn't suggest that they have access to night-vision equipment but a lot of the fighters were born in the area and they're used to moving around the desert at night. Sniper teams Alpha, Bravo and Delta are to take out the sentries. They have been helicoptered into the area and will be making their way on foot. It's dark so they're going to have to get in relatively close but they'll be in position before we land. Once we've neutralised the sentries we move into the caves.' He pressed a button on the laptop and the satellite feed was replaced with a daytime view of the side of the hill. From the angle it appeared to have been taken from a drone.

'We don't have much in the way of intel about the interior of the caves, unfortunately. We do know that at any one time there are up to a hundred men in there. They come out for training when there are no drones around, but we also believe that the caves are large enough for them to train inside. They have generators for supplying electricity, and there's no evidence of water being taken in so it's assumed they have a well or an underground lake as a source of drinking water. We're going in about an hour before dawn so we're assuming that most of them will be asleep and we'll have the advantage of surprise.'

He tapped a large cave opening. 'This is the main way in,' he said. 'I'll be taking the main group in here.' He looked over at Jacko. 'This is where we'll bring in Spider and Dean, but only when the area is secure.'

Jacko nodded and grunted.

The captain then tapped a smaller entrance to the left of the picture. 'There's a secondary entrance here and jihadists are seen going in and out. The problem is, we have no way of knowing if it is connected to the main cave.' He looked over at Sergeant Smeed. 'Smeedy, you take your patrol in through here. If it's a separate cave, clear it and then move back to the main entrance. If it does connect to the main cave, we all need to be on full alert – I don't want any unpleasant surprises.'

The sergeant nodded.

'We'll stop the vehicles two miles from the cave and move in on foot. The terrain is rocky but fairly flat so if we don't hang around it should take us less than an hour. Any questions?' He was faced with a wall of shaking heads. 'Let's roll, then,' he said.

The SAS troopers filed out. Jacko appeared in front of Shepherd and Martin. 'Right, lads, grab your balls and let's be having you. Stay close – the captain'll have my guts for garters if I leave you behind.'

He headed out of the tent and Shepherd fell in step with him as Martin followed behind. 'So how many tours have you done here, Jacko?' asked Shepherd.

'Afghanistan? This is my sixth time here but I spend most of my time in Syria these days.'

'Syria's messy,' said Shepherd.

'It's all bloody messy,' said Jacko. 'Initially we were sent over to take out high-value ISIS targets but the last few times it's to track down the home-grown ones, the guys who were born in Birmingham and West London and think it's cool to sign up to fight with ISIS. They're the real dangerous ones and the government has only just woken up to it. They go over to Syria, get trained and bloodied, then they go back to the UK and set up their own terrorist cells.'

'So the plan is to take them out over there?'

'It's a war zone. If they get killed out there no one really cares. But if we started killing them in the UK all hell would break loose. But it's the same principle, right? Just a matter of geography.'

'I guess it is.'

'It's the same guys. The same end result. The difference is I have to fly three thousand miles to slot them. It'd be so much easier just to post me at Heathrow Airport. Give me ten minutes in a room with any young Asian male coming back from that part of the world and I'd know if they were naughty or nice.' He mimed firing a pistol. 'Job done.'

'There is something ridiculous about the way we allow them back into the UK without any repercussions,' said Shepherd.

'It's more than ridiculous,' said Jacko. 'They're putting our lives at risk. Here we are, on the other side of the world, about to storm a fortified cave with guns blazing to kill guys who not that long ago were on the streets of Bradford or London or wherever.' He grinned. 'Anyway, don't get me started on politics. If it was up to me I'd bring in the guillotine and chop the heads off every politician in the country.'

'To be fair, the French revolution was about killing the aristocracy, not the government.'

Jacko flashed him a sideways look. 'Aye, they said you were a smart arse, Spider.' He laughed and clapped him on the back.

Ahead of them troopers were heading over to a collection of hangars in front of which were four Chinook helicopters, their twin rotors still and drooping. Mechanics fussed around the helicopters carrying out last-minute checks, while Loggys were driving the DPVs up the loading ramps into the bellies of the massive machines.

The Chinook was a true military war horse – it could be used to insert troops, as an air-assault platform, as a supply vehicle and for casualty evacuation. It could be fitted with two M134 six-barrelled miniguns, one in each front side window, and an M60D machine gun. In the high altitudes of Afghanistan, the Chinook was far more effective on combat assault missions than any other helicopter as it could carry up to ten tons of cargo, or up to fifty-five troops, with a maximum range of just over two hundred and fifty miles. Extra fuel tanks had been fitted to the four Chinooks for this mission as there were no facilities for refuelling en route.

When it was in a combat role, the Chinooks were usually escorted by attack helicopters but no one was expecting any resistance that night so they were going in on their own. The Chinook carried a whole range of defensive measures, including infrared jammers, chaff and flare dispensers, a radar warning receiver and a doppler missile approach warning system. It had full night-time flying capabilities, with the crew of four wearing night-vision goggles. During his SAS years Shepherd had been on innumerable night-time missions using the Chinook. Each Boeing-manufactured helicopter cost almost forty million dollars and the RAF had acquired sixty of them over the years.

Jacko took Shepherd and Martin over to the Chinook on the far right and they followed him up the ramp. The Land Rover had been moved from the Hercules and had been tied down. Two DPVs were also lashed into place in the middle of the helicopter and half a dozen troopers were already sitting down, their weapons stashed next to them. A general purpose machine gun had been fitted to the Land Rover along with two grenade launchers. Shepherd figured the captain was leaving the Land Rover at the landing zone to provide some protection in case the helicopters were attacked while they were on the ground.

He fixed his carbine to the fuselage, sat down and strapped himself in. Jacko handed him a pair of ear defenders and he put them on. The helicopter's two Lycoming T55 turboshaft engines burst into life. The engines produced almost 5,000 horsepower. The rotors spun in different directions – one clockwise, the other anti-clockwise – which meant that a vertical rotor wasn't needed to counter torque and that allowed all the power to be used for lift and thrust and power, giving the Chinook a maximum speed of close to two hundred miles per hour.

Shepherd looked over at Martin. Martin grinned and gave him

a thumbs-up. The rear door rattled closed and the lights went out in preparation for take-off. Shepherd felt his heart begin to race. He took a deep breath to calm himself, but there was no doubt he was enjoying the adrenaline kick. He'd been sitting at a desk for too long – it was time to get back into action.

Chapter 75

Shepherd heard the engines power down a second or two before his stomach lurched and he realised they were coming in to land. The interior of the helicopter was bathed in a soft red light and he looked over at Jacko, who nodded. 'Won't be long now,' he mouthed.

There were no windows but Shepherd's stomach told him they were banking, then they went into a hover and after thirty seconds or so the helicopter settled on the ground. Almost immediately the lights went off and the ramp started to move down. The Loggys were on their feet immediately, hurrying over to get the DPV ready for offloading.

'Right guys, stay close to me,' said Jacko, unfastening his restraints. 'It's going to be organised chaos out there.'

Shepherd and Martin unbuckled their harnesses, grabbed their weapons and hurried down the ramp after the sergeant. Their Chinook had been the third to land and the fourth was in a hover a hundred yards away, its massive twin rotors kicking up a sandstorm below.

The first two helicopters were already unloading their cargo and the DPVs were being lined up in an arrow formation, pointing east.

The troopers who had set up the temporary landing zone had set up a perimeter and were facing outwards, weapons at the ready, scanning the surroundings with their night-vision goggles.

The Land Rover had been unloaded and moved away from the helicopters with a trooper manning the machine gun.

The final Chinook touched down and its engines were switched off. The rotors slowed from a blur but were still turning when the rear ramp came down.

Jacko took Shepherd and Martin over to the DPVs. The one they would be using was in the middle of the second row and the driver was already in his seat.

'This is Steve Garrett,' said Jacko. 'Garrett the Carrot, supposedly because of the shape of his dick.'

'That's such a lie,' said Garrett. He was in his thirties with an unkempt beard and his night-vision goggles in place. He raised a hand in greeting.

'I said supposedly,' said Jacko. 'If you want to argue that it's more like a Brussels sprout, that's your prerogative.' He climbed into the front passenger seat.

'Now where the fuck did a sergeant learn a four-syllable word like that?' said Garrett.

'I might ask you how a trooper with a single-digit IQ knew a word like syllable,' said Jacko. He motioned at Shepherd and Martin to climb in the back. 'Don't bother with the belts,' he said. 'You never know when you might have to bale at short notice.' Off to their right and left troopers were climbing on to their trail bikes and kicking their muffled two-stroke engines into life.

Shepherd and Martin took their places in the rear seats of the four-by-four and cradled their weapons. Their night-vision goggles gave them a greenish view of the desert around them.

The last of the DPVs were unloaded from the Chinook, their engines started and driven over to the formation.

Captain Gearie strode over to the lead DPV, looked around to make sure that everyone was ready, then climbed into the front passenger seat.

Shepherd heard a 'Tally-ho' over his headset and the lead DPV moved off. The rest of the convoy followed him and the trail bikes spread out right and left. Garrett eased down the accelerator and they sped off, the shock absorbers barely taking the edge off the rough desert terrain.

All the engines were muffled but they still throbbed as they powered across the desert, leaving behind plumes of whirling sand. Shepherd looked over at Martin and the American grinned.

'I can't believe I'm in the Sandbox again!' he shouted, the wind whipping away the words as soon as they left his mouth.

'Truth be told, neither can I!' Shepherd shouted back.

Chapter 76

Present Day, Afghanistan

The DPVs made good progress across the desert and covered the fifty miles in just under ninety minutes. It was one of the most uncomfortable journeys Shepherd had ever made, constant bone-jarring vibrations coupled with thick dust that had no problem working its way through the scarf he'd tied around his mouth, but it was still better than walking.

The convoy came to a halt close to a rocky outcrop, jutting up from the desert floor like a massive stone blade. The troopers dismounted with their kit and the drivers then lined the vehicles up at the base of the outcrop and covered them with camouflage netting.

Captain Gearie used his GPS to confirm their position and where they were headed. Sergeant Smeed used his comms to call up sniper teams Alpha, Bravo and Delta, who had been in position for hours waiting to take out the sentries.

'They're waiting for the green light, boss,' said Smeed.

'Let's give it a bit longer,' said the captain. 'We've still some way to go.'

Smeed relayed the information to the sniper teams.

Gearie held up his hand. 'Right, guys, in we go. I'll be taking point and I know how enthusiastic you all are but everyone stay behind me. You might not think so but I do know where I'm going.'

Jacko had appeared next to Martin. Steve Garrett was to Shepherd's right. Like Shepherd, they were both cradling HK416s. The captain was already moving off towards the mountain range in the distance, black against the night sky. One of the sergeants was keeping pace with him, but the rest of the troopers fanned out behind the captain.

Jacko waved for Shepherd and Martin to move forward, about fifty feet behind the captain. As Shepherd had feared, walking was difficult. He could see the ground about eight feet ahead of him but any closer than that and his view was restricted. The desert floor was littered with stones and rocks of all sizes and the soldiers were moving quickly. Shepherd's memory helped but it was still taking him time to get used to walking quickly across the rough ground. He looked over at Martin but the American didn't appear to be having any problems. Shepherd gritted his teeth and concentrated on following the captain.

After the first mile Shepherd's legs were aching but he ignored the discomfort. Most of the men around him were half his age and kept fit for a living, but Shepherd was a keen runner and he knew that he was more than capable of a two-mile forced march. It was nothing compared with the Fan Dance, a necessary requirement for anyone who wanted to join the SAS – a fifteen-mile timed hike up and down the 2,900-foot-high Pen Y Fan in the Brecon Beacons with a forty-five-pound Bergen backpack, a rifle, ten pounds of food and four one-litre water bottles.

Shepherd looked over at Jacko. The sergeant was moving with long, graceful strides, as sure-footed as a mountain goat, his carbine cradled in his arms. Shepherd's progress was less elegant but he had no problem keeping up the pace.

Captain Gearie had a compass on one wrist and he consulted it every few minutes. After fifteen minutes, Gearie called a halt, checked their progress with his GPS and had Sergeant Smeed give the sniper teams the go-ahead to take out the sentries. Within two minutes the sergeant was able to report that all six sentries were dead.

Gearie got the men moving again. The atmosphere had changed; the faces of the men had become more serious and all the banter had stopped. Contact was only minutes away.

The ground began to slope up and was now strewn with rocks

and boulders that meant it was no longer possible to move in a straight line.

The two cave mouths came into view, showing as grey patches in the night-vision goggles. Gearie raised a clenched fist to call a halt. He turned to Sergeant Smeed and pointed at the smaller cave entrance. Smeed flashed him an OK sign and then turned to wave at the four troopers who would be going in with him.

Shepherd looked over at Martin. Martin was gritting his teeth and staring at the main cave entrance. Shepherd knew that the American wanted to go in with the first wave. He knew exactly how Martin felt. He would have given anything just then to be allowed to go in, guns blazing. He missed combat, he missed the adrenaline rush that came from putting his life on the line, but no matter how much he missed it he knew that his job was to observe and report on the casualties, nothing more. He tapped Martin on the shoulder. 'You okay?'

Martin nodded. 'Sure.'

'We'll be in there soon enough,' said Shepherd.

'If we went in now, who would stop us?'

Shepherd chuckled. 'I'm guessing Gearie or one of his sergeants,' he said. 'Jacko would probably put a bullet in your leg. He'd be in deep, deep shit if anything happened to you.'

'Don't even think about it,' growled Jacko, off to their left.

'Nothing's going to happen to us tonight, Spider,' Martin said. 'I feel lucky.'

Chapter 77

Captain Gearie took a quick look over his shoulder, checked for the tenth time that the safety selector of his HK416 assault rifle was in the off position and moved forward towards the cave entrance. It was a strange feeling moving into a totally alien environment with absolutely no way of knowing what lay ahead. Usually they were well briefed and had studied maps or blueprints that would give them a reasonable guide as to what they were faced with, but the caves were a totally unknown situation. There could be one huge cavern or a dozen smaller interlinked caves. There might be one group of men all in one place or they could be scattered over a wide area. The one thing they knew for sure was that there were armed jihadists inside and they would meet any attack with lethal force.

He stepped across the threshold, scanning left and right. The night-vision goggles let him see in the darkness but they didn't allow him to use his peripheral vision, and peripheral vision was best at spotting movement. With the goggles he was restricted to viewing things according to their temperature. It was like hunting ghosts.

Two troopers moved to his right, three to his left.

Once they were through the entrance the cave opened up to maybe thirty feet in height, and was almost circular with a diameter of sixty feet or so. There were two pale green smudges off to the right, lying on the ground. Men sleeping.

To the left were four smudges, lined up like logs. More sleepers. Gearie mimed using a knife. Two troopers moved to the right, drawing their knives. Four went left. They moved silently, slitting the throats of the sleeping men before they even awoke.

'We're in the main cave,' said Gearie into his comms. 'Six hostiles dead.'

He scanned the far end of the cave. There were two tunnels, each about the height of a man and three times the width. The left one was in darkness but a light was leaching from the tunnel on the right, showing as a pale green smudge.

Chapter 78

Present Day, Afghanistan

As Captain Gearie led the first wave of troopers into the main cave entrance, Sergeant Smeed waved his patrol forward. He had Creepshow and Shaver with him, plus two veterans of the SAS, troopers Mark 'Pitchfork' Pitchford and Neil 'Wally' Walton, who were so alike they were often mistaken for brothers – big men with shaved heads and hands the size of small shovels. The five men moved quickly. The entrance was low and they had to duck to get in, but within a couple of paces the space opened up dramatically. The cave was four times the height of a man, long and narrow, and from the look of it was being used as an ammunition storage area, presumably to keep it away from the main area.

'Watch yourselves, lads,' whispered Smeed. 'Use your knives if you can; put a round in the wrong place and the whole place could go up.' There were boxes marked 'амуниция', which Smeed was pretty sure was Russian for ammunition, and others he recognised as the crates that Kalashnikovs were shipped in.

There were three hostiles in the cave, presumably guards, but they were sleeping on mats in one corner, the remains of a meal next to them on a low table. Smeed scanned the cave. There were two other men sleeping at the other side, either side of a narrow tunnel less than four feet high. Smeed pointed at Pitchfork and Wally and then pointed at the two men. They nodded and moved towards them, drawing their knives.

As they got within ten feet of the sleeping men, one of them snored loudly. The snore turned into a cough and then the man sat up. He started to shout when he saw the dark shapes moving towards him, and reached for a Kalashnikov that was leaning against the wall of the cave.

Pitchfork and Wally sheathed their knives and fired together, each putting two shots into the chest of their target. The jihadist fell back, dead before he hit the ground. Pitchfork took out the man next to the one they had already killed with a shot to the face.

The sound of the shots woke the other three men.

Over on the other side of the cave, one man sat up, blinking in confusion, but the other two were quicker off the mark. One had amazing reflexes and in a second had rolled over, grabbed an AK-47 and brought it up to point it at the troopers, but Smeed already had the man in his sights and put a round smack in the middle of his face. Blood and brain splattered across a stack of crates. The second jihadist was still groping for his weapon in the dark when Creepshow put two rounds in his chest. Shaver took care of the third and the man died, still blinking.

Smeed looked around to reassure himself that there were no other hostiles in the cave.

'Nice work, everyone,' he said, his ears ringing from the sound of the shots in the confined area. He nodded at the tunnel leading to the main cave. 'Let's join the lads.' He walked quickly over to the tunnel and ducked down to get through. As he emerged into the main cave two troopers swung their carbines in his direction and he immediately raised his weapon above his head to show that he wasn't a threat, but they had seen his uniform and helmet and turned away from him. Pitchfork and Wally were close behind him.

Captain Gearie turned to look in his direction and Smeed flashed him an OK sign. Gearie nodded and started to speak into his comms microphone.

'Frank, the main cave is clear. Two tunnels left and right. Lights on in the right. We're moving into both now so follow us in.'

'Following you in,' repeated Captain Harrison.

'Phil, you and your lads lead the way into the left tunnel.'

'Roger that,' said Smeed.

Gearie motioned with his hand for the team to split into two groups. He led the group to the right-hand tunnel, unclipping a flash-bang from his belt.

Creepshow and Shaver were now in the main cave and Smeed led them towards the left-hand tunnel, along with the rest of the troopers who weren't following Gearie.

Gearie moved into the tunnel but as he did a shot ricocheted off the cave wall just inches from his head. He ducked instinctively even though the round had already gone by. He pulled the pin from a stun grenade and tossed it through the tunnel, then turned his head away. The grenade exploded with a blinding flash of light and a bang of more than 180 decibels, guaranteed to stun anyone close by. Gearie turned back. The lights were still on at the end of the tunnel so he flicked his night-vision goggles up and brought his carbine to bear as he rushed through and into the cave. More troopers followed him and as soon as he was in the cave he moved to the side. There were two hostiles on their knees, holding their hands to their eyes, AK-47s on the ground in front of them. Gearie shot one in the face, by accident rather than by design – he had been aiming at the man's chest but his foot had slipped on the uneven ground at the moment he'd pulled the trigger. He took down the second man with two shots to the chest. A classic double tap. Shots were going off all around him.

Armed hostiles were firing at them from around a bend in the cave, half a dozen or so from the sound of it. A trooper shouted 'Fire In The Hole' before throwing a flash-bang around the bend. Everyone turned away as the grenade went off, then two troopers headed for the bend at a run, guns blazing.

Another half dozen jihadists had been sleeping on mats at the far end of the cave and they were shot dead as they scrambled for their weapons.

Gearie moved forward. The light came from bulbs hanging from metal spikes in the ceiling, and a wire ran along the roof of the cave, down the side and into a tunnel. Gearie followed the wire. Half a dozen troopers went after him.

Chapter 79

Captain Harrison led the second wave of troopers into the main cave mouth.

Martin looked across at Jacko. 'Come on, Sarge, let's go now.'

'We stay put until we're told to move in,' said the sergeant. 'It won't be long now.'

From where they were on the slope leading up to the cave, they had heard rapid fire from the Hecklers and return fire from pistols and AK-47s interspersed with flash-bangs going off.

Not long after Harrison's patrol had gone into the cave, the firing inside had become sporadic with gaps of up to ten seconds or so between shots. There was the occasional handgun being fired and bursts from AK-47s, but to Shepherd's ears the vast majority of the shots were from HK416 assault rifles similar to the one he was cradling. It sounded as if they were entering the mopping-up phase.

'Come on, let's go in,' begged Martin. 'It's all going to be over.'

'That's the idea,' said Jacko. 'My orders are to wait until we're told to go in.'

'We can at least see some action,' said Martin. He looked over at Shepherd, clearly hoping to have his support.

Shepherd shook his head. 'We're not here to see action, Dean,' he said. 'We're here to ID the bodies. The last thing we need is you in there tripping over a booby trap. We go in when it's safe, and not before.' As if to emphasise his words there was a sudden burst of intense firing from inside the cave that went on for almost thirty seconds.

There were several isolated shots, then shouts, then more shots.

Eventually it went quiet, then Captain Gearie spoke over the comms. 'We're clear,' he said. 'The area is secured.'

'Roger that,' said Jacko. 'I'm bringing them in now.'

He nodded at Shepherd and Martin. 'Here we go,' he said. 'But stay close.'

He headed for the cave entrance and Shepherd and Martin followed. Steve Garrett brought up the rear. Captain Gearie came out to meet them.

'More than ninety hostiles dead,' he said. 'We might have broken the ton.' He pointed to a small tunnel to his right. 'That leads to the smaller cave next door. It's being used as an ammunition store. There are five dead jihadists you'll need to check.'

'I'll do that first,' said Shepherd.

'I'll take Dean around, see if we can spot Khaled.' He turned and pointed at the far end of the cave. 'There are two tunnels there. The one to the left is effectively a barracks with camp beds and bunks and storage lockers. That was in darkness and we got most of them before they could return fire. To the right, that tunnel leads to a series of smaller caves. There are what look like training rooms there, more storage and a kitchen and basic bathroom facilities. There's a couple of generators and the lights were on. That was where most of the resistance was.'

'Anyone on our side hurt?' asked Shepherd.

'A few flesh wounds but nothing to write home about,' said the captain. 'We're trying to get the lights on in the barracks so I'll take Dean to the other side first.' He looked over at Jacko. 'You and the Carrot can start trawling for intel,' he said. 'We need to go through all the bodies checking for ID, any paperwork and any phones. We've found computers and a whole stack of filing cabinets so that's all got to be bagged and taken with us.'

'Right, boss,' said Jacko and he and Garrett headed off.

Gearie smiled at Shepherd. 'So far so good,' he said. 'So long as Khaled is among the dead, this has been pretty much the perfect op.'

'Fingers crossed,' said Shepherd. He headed for the tunnel as

Gearie took Martin across the main cave. Shepherd ducked his head down to shuffle along the tunnel and emerged to find Shaver Hughes holding a torch in his left hand and a digital camera in his right. Creepshow was checking the pockets of the dead and collecting their personal effects.

Shepherd had a Maglite torch in his pocket. He flicked his night-vision goggles away from his eyes and switched on the torch. He checked the two nearest corpses; they were both bearded Asians but he hadn't seen either of their faces before.

'What are you looking for?' asked Shaver.

'Hoping to cross a few names off the most-wanted list,' said Shepherd.

He went over to check three corpses splayed out over sleeping mats but again they were all new faces.

'Right, I'll leave you guys to it,' he said, and went back through to the tunnel to the main cave. There were a dozen bodies there, also being photographed and searched. Four of them had been shot in the face, which meant identification was impossible, seven he didn't recognise, but he knew the final one, an over-weight Asian with a short beard and bushy eyebrows who had been shot in the heart and probably died instantly. His name was Mohammed Arshad and he was from Leeds, where his parents were GPs. It was Arshad's father who had brought his son to the attention of the police after worrying that he was becoming radicalised at his local mosque. He had started to wear traditional Muslim clothing, grown his beard and pinned up inflammatory quotes from the Koran all over his room. The tipping point had come when the teenager had taken a hammer to his father's expensive wine collection. The parents were prac-tising Muslims but Mohammed's mother never covered her head and his father had always been partial to a good bottle of wine. As Mohammed's radicalisation deepened he had more and more arguments with his parents, which ended when he stormed out of the family home vowing never to return. MI5 had identified him as fighting with ISIS in Syria from various social media postings and as far as anyone knew that was where he still was. Shepherd had no sympathy for Arshad – he deserved his fate – but he was sorry for his parents, two people who had done their best for their son, giving him a life in a country where everyone was allowed to practise whatever religion they wanted free of persecution, only to have him betray them and take up arms in a fight that served only to terrorise and oppress. It made no sense to Shepherd that someone like Arshad, British-born and able to avail himself of all the advantages that the country offered, would end his days in a cave in Afghanistan learning how to kill and maim innocents.

He straightened up and went to the rear of the cave. As he approached the tunnel leading to the barracks, it filled with a soft yellow light. The tunnel was tall enough to walk through without bending his head and opened out into a cave some fifty feet long and almost as wide. There were a dozen or so camp beds and a line of four bunk beds, each sleeping three. More jihadists had been sleeping on mats on the ground. There was a line of metal lockers against one side of the cave, their owners identified by names scribbled on pieces of tape. A trooper was using a knife to pry the doors open.

There were two troopers going through the bodies, their assault rifles slung over their backs. There were half a dozen light bulbs hanging from wires that had been attached to the roof of the cave, giving more than enough light to see by. Shepherd switched off his torch and clipped it to his belt.

Most of the occupants of the room had obviously been asleep when the first wave of troopers had gone in and they had all died either in their beds or standing next to them. Shepherd was impressed by the accuracy of the shooting – each jihadist had been double-tapped twice in the chest and from the look of it not one had managed to get off a shot. He did a quick head count. Thirty-two dead. The fact that none of the jihadists was holding a weapon didn't worry him in the least. If they had, they would have had no hesitation in shooting at the SAS – they were in a war zone, a war zone where one side had no interest at all in abiding by the Geneva Convention, a war where it was considered acceptable to hack the heads off prisoners and to kill captives by burning them alive. Like Arshad, they deserved what they got.

He began checking the faces of the dead, looking for matches to the MI5 watch list.

Chapter 80

Present Day, Afghanistan

Captain Gearie took Dean Martin along a tunnel that looked as if it was man-made. Off to their right were a series of rooms, fronted by planks of roughly hewn wood.

'These were used as offices, probably,' said the captain. 'And at the far end there's a sleeping area and an area that was used for prayer. Most of the jihadists here were older, so they were probably the instructors and senior officers. They have their own washing area, too.' He grinned. 'Rank has its privileges the world over.'

There were scratches made by rounds and damage from flash-bangs and the air was still foul with cordite. Their feet crunched on cartridge cases as they walked.

'They heard us coming, obviously,' said Gearie. 'The fighting was fiercest here. But the flash-bangs did the trick.' He pointed at the room to the right. 'There's three in there.'

Martin stepped inside. There was one man slumped in a chair, his chest wet with blood. There was an AK-47 on the floor by his feet. If it wasn't for the blood, he could have been taking a nap. The man was overweight and bearded but it wasn't Khaled. Two other men were on the floor, a thin one wearing a white skullcap lying face down and a short stocky Asian with a moustache who was lying on his side with the back of his head missing.

'No,' said Martin.

Gearie took him along to the next room. There was a map of London taped to the wall of the cave with various markings on it and Arabic writing. A trooper was sitting at a wooden desk, going through the drawers. 'Don't forget that map,' said the captain and the trooper nodded. 'Got it, boss.'

There were two bodies on the floor, big men with bushy beards, one wearing a grubby salwar kameez, the other a pale blue thawb. Both had been shot five or six times in the chest. Neither was Khaled.

There were six dead jihadists in the sleeping area but all were in their seventies, old men with faces wrinkled from the sun, their beards grey and their fingernails yellowed and gnarled. Despite their age, all had been holding AK-47s or pistols when they died.

'Khaled is younger,' said Martin.

'How about him?' said the captain, pointing to a body in an area off to the side where there were six threadbare prayer mats, all pointing in the same direction, presumably towards Mecca. Sprawled across the mats was an obese man, a pistol still clutched in his right hand. He was wearing only baggy shalwar pants and there were several holes in his chest that from the look of the blood around the body were mainly through-and-throughs. The face was unmarked and Martin could tell straight away that it wasn't Khaled. He shook his head. 'Okay, let's check the other main prayer area,' said the captain. 'There are some older guys there.'

The prayer area was a circular sub-cave accessed through a wide entrance. The roof was about twenty feet high and domed. A single bulb had been fixed to the middle of the roof and the walls had been lined with prayer rugs and tapestries. There were more prayer rugs, several dozen in all, on the floor, all pointing in the same direction. There were seven dead jihadists on the ground, their clothing glistening with blood. Jacko was gathering up the weapons the hostiles had been using while Garrett was going through their clothing.

'Have they been LiveScanned yet?' asked the captain.

'No, boss,' said Jacko.

The captain muttered under his breath and headed off to the main cave.

Martin went over to the nearest body. It was a bearded Asian in his fifties but it wasn't Khaled. The second body he checked was too old and the third was the right build but it wasn't Khaled's face.

Jacko stacked the weapons against a tapestry on the wall and frowned when the tapestry bowed inwards. Figuring it might be hiding something, he grabbed it with both hands and pulled it away from the wall. It came away with a tearing sound and crumpled to the floor in a shower of dust. The dust got into Jacko's eyes and he turned away coughing.

Martin jumped back as he saw an Asian man standing in an alcove that had been hidden by the tapestry. Martin recognised him immediately. It was Khaled. And he was wearing a nylon vest covered with pockets of explosives linked by red and blue wires. Khaled was holding something in his left hand and a pistol in his right. Martin's AK-47 was hanging from its strap across his back and he grabbed for it.

Khaled lunged forward and grabbed Martin around the neck with his left arm and jabbed the gun into his throat.

'Drop your weapon!' screamed Khaled.

Martin did as he was told and his AK-47 clattered to the ground.

Jacko moved towards Khaled but Khaled screamed at him. 'Come near me and we all die!'

Several troopers heard the commotion and rushed forward but stopped short when they saw the suicide vest and the gun against Martin's throat.

Martin twisted his head and caught a glimpse of something metallic in Khaled's left hand. 'Stay back!' shouted Martin. 'Everybody stay back!'

Jacko aimed his weapon at Khaled but firing was out of the question, so long as Khaled was using Martin as a shield.

'You're Hakeem Khaled?' said Martin.

The man's eyes narrowed. 'Who are you?'

'We met a few years ago,' said Martin. 'In Queens.'

Khaled frowned. 'Queens?'

'New York,' said Martin.

'You are the officer in charge?'

Martin stared stonily ahead. 'No, I'm no officer.' His eyes focused on Jacko. 'Shoot him, Sarge,' he said. 'I don't care what happens to me, just shoot him.'

Chapter 81

Present Day, Afghanistan

Shepherd heard shouting echoing off the cave walls and he looked around, wondering where it was coming from. There was a rapid footfall in the distance and Shepherd headed towards it. Ahead of him was a group of troopers, standing with their carbines in their hands but looking at each other as if they weren't sure what to do.

He kept close to the cave wall as he approached the group, then peered around to see what they were looking at. His jaw tensed when he saw the large Asian man with a gun jammed against Martin's neck. He was facing more than a dozen troopers. They all had their guns levelled at the Arab but weren't pulling their triggers because Martin was in the line of fire.

The man was Khaled, and he was wearing a suicide vest. It looked as if the trigger was in his left hand and if he pressed it he would kill everyone in the vicinity. There was a chain of Muslim prayer beads wrapped around his right wrist.

'Where is the officer in charge?' shouted Khaled. 'I demand to see the officer in charge. If you do not step forward I will kill us all.'

Shepherd figured that Khaled had already decided to kill himself, and his hostage, but what he really wanted to do was to take an officer with him. SAS officers went into combat dressed the same as their men so that they couldn't be targeted on the battlefield, and the ranks never saluted. Khaled had no way of knowing who was in charge, and Shepherd hoped that Gearie would be savvy enough to realise what was going on. He didn't see the captain among the troopers but more men were turning up all the time.

'Stay back guys!' shouted Martin. 'He's ready to blow.'

'I mean it!' shouted Khaled. 'The officer in charge needs to step forward now.'

Shepherd squinted at the man's left hand, the one holding the trigger. The thumb was clearly visible, which suggested that it was an active trigger operated by pressing the thumb down. Suicide vests generally had one of two trigger systems, active or passive. With an active trigger the vest was detonated by pressing the trigger to complete the circuit. With a passive system the trigger was already pressed and it was releasing the pressure that completed the circuit. A passive system didn't usually involve the thumb; it was pressure from the hand that kept the trigger closed. Shepherd felt his heart pounding. If the trigger was passive then even if he killed Khaled with a single shot the vest would detonate and kill everyone in the cave. If it was an active trigger then there was a chance – albeit a slim one – that a killing shot would take out Khaled before he could press the switch and detonate.

Khaled took a step towards the troopers and tightened his grip around Martin's neck with his left hand, the gun pressed under Martin's chin. Shepherd got a better look at the trigger hand. The thumb was definitely pressing against something metallic. He let out a slow breath. It looked like an active trigger. But even if it wasn't he didn't really have a choice because Khaled was going to blow himself up whatever happened. If Shepherd was wrong and Khaled was using a passive system then it was just about possible that one of the troopers could reach the trigger and apply pressure to stop it from going off.

'Who is the officer?' Khaled screamed, clearly close to breaking point.

More troopers were coming into the prayer area. Now there were more than twenty, all pointing their carbines at Khaled. Creepshow was there. So was Shaver. Sergeant Smeed hurried in and then stopped when he saw Khaled and the gun jammed under Martin's chin.

'Guys, you need to back off!' shouted Martin. 'If that blows we're all dead! Sarge, shoot him through me. You have my permission, just do it.'

From where Shepherd was standing, pressed against the wall to his right, there was no way he could raise his gun, not without moving to the side and revealing himself. He lowered his weapon and slowly changed it so the butt was against his left shoulder. He took a long, slow breath to steady himself, then sighted along the barrel. It felt awkward but he knew he had no choice. He slid his finger on to the trigger.

Everyone else was facing Khaled; only Shepherd had the side view and he was pretty much hidden from Khaled by the curve of the cave wall. He had about three inches of Khaled's head to aim at but the face was obscured by Martin's head. In an ideal world he needed Martin to move his head forward, but shouting a warning was out of the question.

Shepherd's finger tightened on the trigger. It was a difficult shot but not an impossible one, though it would be a lot easier without the distractions of the Kevlar helmet and body armour.

Two more troopers walked in and stopped dead when they saw what was happening. They raised their weapons, fingers on the triggers, but it was clear from their faces they were as confused as everyone else. There was no way any of them could take a shot, not without hitting Martin. Shepherd was the only one with a chance of making a shot.

'Just fucking do it!' shouted Martin. 'If you don't, he'll kill us all!'

Shepherd was just about to squeeze the trigger when Khaled moved, taking half a step forward. Now he could see only a few square inches of the man's skull. Shepherd gritted his teeth, knowing that he was running out of time. He had no doubt that Khaled intended to kill himself, the only question was how many soldiers could he take with him. As soon as he calculated he would cause the maximum number of casualties he would detonate the vest. And that time was fast approaching.

'If your officer does not reveal himself, I will press the switch!' Khaled shouted.

Shepherd smiled to himself. At least he knew now that it was an active trigger and that if he could take out Khaled's brain there was a good chance the vest wouldn't go off. Small mercies.

Martin's head was now obscuring all of Khaled's. Shepherd did have another option, one that he hated himself for even considering. The Heckler and Koch 416 assault rifle he was holding would fire its 5.56 x 45mm NATO cartridge at something approaching 900 metres a second and because Shepherd was so close the round would almost certainly pass right through Martin's skull and still have enough momentum to kill Khaled. Two birds with one stone. Except that Martin was one of the good guys.

Shepherd's finger tightened on the trigger, knowing that he was fast running out of time. If Khaled pressed his trigger, more than thirty men would die. If Shepherd made the shot that he was trying not to think about, only two of them would die and one certainly deserved it.

His mouth had gone dry and it hurt when he tried to swallow. He forced himself to block out all feeling of discomfort. The only thing he could afford to think about was the shot. His finger. The round. The barrel. The target. All had to become one. He took a slow breath and then let half of it slowly escape between his pursed lips.

Khaled was shouting something but Shepherd was so focused on the shot that he didn't hear the words. Shepherd looked to his left. Captain Gearie had arrived, his Heckler clutched to his chest. He took in the situation with one glance and shouted at the top of his voice: 'Everyone out! Just get the hell out now!'

Khaled snarled in triumph as he turned to look at Gearie, realising that the officer had finally revealed himself.

'He's going to do it!' shouted Martin. 'Shoot the fucker now!'

Jacko took two steps forward, putting himself between Khaled and his hostage and the rest of the soldiers. Jacko spread out his arms, making himself as big a target as he could so that he would absorb the bulk of the blast and its deadly shrapnel and shield the rest of the men.

Shepherd knew that he had to take the shot now. He said a silent prayer for Martin but as he did Martin began to turn his head. Shepherd relaxed his trigger finger. Martin's head kept turning and he locked eyes with Shepherd. Then he smiled as if he knew what was coming. The turn of his head gave Shepherd an inch or two of Khaled's skull to aim at but it wasn't enough.

'You are in charge?' Khaled shouted at Gearie. Jacko took another step forward, his arms still stretched out to the sides. He was now just six feet from Khaled and Martin.

Shepherd's eyes were still locked on Martin's. Martin's eyes narrowed and the smile had become fixed as if he had already accepted his own death. Shepherd stared at the man hard, willing him to understand, and flicked his head, to the left. And again. Praying that Martin would understand.

He aimed through the sights, took a breath, steadied himself and tightened his finger on the trigger. He aimed at Martin's head, praying that the American had understood and knowing that even if he didn't he was still going to make the shot.

His finger eased the trigger back. He was totally motionless and every fibre of his being focused on the shot. That was when Martin moved, dropping his head forward and down at the exact moment the carbine fired.

Khaled's head blew apart in a shower of red and his body slumped to the ground. Troopers rushed forward, some to grab Martin, others to make the suicide vest safe.

Shepherd lowered the carbine and stepped out of the tunnel. Jacko was still standing with his arms outstretched, his face and chest splattered with Khaled's blood.

There were cheers from several of the troopers when they saw who had made the shot.

As Shepherd walked over to Captain Gearie, he was slapped on the back and punched on the arm and congratulated by pretty much everyone there.

'Fuck me, Spider, you were cutting that close,' said Gearie.

'Yeah, sorry about that, but, you know, Martin being in the way and all.'

They went over to Khaled's body. One of the troopers had pulled out the detonators from the packs of explosive. Martin joined them.

'That's him, right?' said Gearie, looking over at Martin. 'That's definitely Khaled?' he asked him again.

Martin wiped away blood that had splattered across his face and hair. 'Hard to tell now that Spider's blown half his skull away,' he said. He grinned at the way the captain's face fell. 'Joke,' said Martin. 'It's him. No doubt.'

One of the SAS troopers photographed the body while another knelt down with a LiveScan reader and took a copy of Khaled's fingerprints.

'We should take the vest back with us, minus the explosives,' said Shepherd. 'The forensic guys will learn a lot from it.'

Gearie nodded and told one of the troopers to remove the vest from Khaled's body.

'How many of the dead have you identified?' Gearie asked Shepherd.

'Three so far. I was about halfway through when we were so rudely interrupted. I did the barracks area, the main cave and the side cave where the ammunition is.'

Gearie looked at his watch. 'We need to be out of here in the next twenty minutes or so.'

'I'm on it,' said Shepherd.

Jacko came up behind him and looked down at Khaled's body, the head a broken mess of skull, brain matter and blood. The sergeant glanced at Shepherd and grinned. 'I think I'll forgive you for being a smart arse, Spider.'

Shepherd grinned back at the sergeant. 'You're welcome.'

Chapter 82

Shepherd climbed out of the Jaguar and slammed the door shut. He looked up at his apartment block as the car drove off, and smiled. He was dog-tired and glad to be back home. All he needed now was a good meal, and a long sleep.

It had taken the best part of forty-eight hours to get from the cave complex back to London. A two-mile walk from the caves with every man loaded up with equipment and paperwork, followed by a ninety-minute bone-jarring ride on the DPV, then a Chinook flight to Bagram Airbase, where there was a twelve-hour wait for a Hercules, which took him to Cyprus, Gibraltar and eventually to RAF Brize Norton, some sixty-five miles west of London. Dean Martin had left the plane at Cyprus. Two men in bomber jackets and jeans were there to meet him and take him over to a waiting Gulfstream jet. They didn't look military or even former military and the plane had civilian markings, so Shepherd assumed the flight back to Bali had been arranged by Charlotte Button.

A military helicopter was waiting to fly Shepherd into central London, where he was whisked away in a Jaguar with darkened windows to Thames House for a debriefing that took the best part of two hours. Patsy Ellis had a quick chat with him once he arrived. A handshake, a warm smile and a promise that he would be back on operational duties as soon as she had dealt with the paperwork.

'Everything Charlie ever said about you is true,' she had said, and while that could have been taken several ways he was left in no doubt that she meant it as a compliment.

The debriefing had taken place in a conference room over-looking Lambeth Bridge with a polished walnut table that sat twenty-four. Every seat was occupied, with extra chairs drafted in for another dozen. MI6 had sent along four grey-haired men in Savile Row suits and another three whose casual clothing and longer hair identified them as analysts rather than officers. The Met were also represented; they had sent half a dozen members of SO15, all of whom he recognised, and there were seven army officers in full uniform, ranging from two majors up to a three-star major general. The military men kept to themselves at the far end of the room and while Shepherd spoke and answered questions, the two majors took notes on iPads while the higher ranks stared impassively ahead. Shepherd got the distinct impression that they resented the fact that the SAS had been tasked with eliminating Khaled and the other jihadists. A lot of regular army officers felt the word 'Special' in Special Forces implied that the regular army was somehow less important, resented it and behaved accordingly. Shepherd simply ignored them.

The debriefing had started with a short speech from Ellis, basically thanking the SAS in their absence for a job well done. There was no one from the regiment at the debrief, they had all headed back to Hereford from Brize Norton. Two SAS Head Sheds had been waiting at Cyprus and they took Captains Gearie and Harrison off for a chat but expressed no interest in talking to either Shepherd or Martin, which suited them just fine.

Ellis had arranged to show the US satellite feed of the attack, though all that could be seen was greenish figures disappearing into the black hole of the cave mouth. A projector had been fixed up to a laptop that was being monitored by an earnest young woman in a dark blue suit, who when given the nod by Ellis started flashing up photographs of the home-grown jihadists who had been killed in the attack. There were cheers from some of the younger members of the audience but they died down when Ellis flashed them an icy look. Shepherd had identified seven as being on MI5's watch list at the scene and fingerprints and DNA samples had been taken and brought back to London for confirmation.

The tests hadn't yet been completed but Shepherd's near-faultless memory meant that the ID wasn't in question. Three of the young men were from Bradford, one from Birmingham, one from Leeds and two from London. All had been out of the country for at least three months and had been spotted in Syria fighting for ISIS.

'There's no doubt that each and every one of these men were being trained to carry out terrorist atrocities here in the UK and that what our people did out there in Afghanistan saved countless lives,' said Ellis. 'We also had spectacular success on the intel front. We seized laptops, phones, sat phones and paperwork that will be a goldmine for our analysts. We believe that we have in our possession the computer that Hakeem Khaled used and once we have cracked the password and encryption we believe it will help us identify the sleepers that he has been in contact with in the UK. It is currently being discussed in Cabinet what action we should take once they have been identified. Obviously my hope is that action won't involve trials and prison sentences. But we shall see.'

There were knowing chuckles from around the room and this time Ellis did not try to silence them. Everyone knew what she meant: there was no point in sending trained jihadists to prison for a year or two, all that did was harden their resolve. Far better to use the SAS or the Pool.

Shepherd sat back and listened to Ellis as she went on to outline MI5's strategy over the coming months and how that would impact on MI6, the military and the police. He knew exactly what Ellis was doing: she was making sure that everyone appreciated what a success the operation had been and that the credit belonged to MI5. Yes, the SAS had done the hard work, but it had all been based on intel provided by MI5 and Ellis wanted to make sure that everyone understood and appreciated the fact. Once she had finished she offered those present the chance to ask questions and for half an hour Shepherd was gently interrogated, with those who didn't know him being especially interested in how his eidetic memory functioned. The general had several questions about what actually happened inside the cave but Ellis cut him short each time, explaining that the SAS didn't want operational tactics revealed but that she was sure the regiment would arrange a private briefing for him down the line.

Once the debriefing was over, Shepherd was ushered out of the building to the waiting Jaguar. And that was that. Job done.

He groped in his pocket for his door key.

'So all's well that ends well,' said a voice behind him, jolting him out of his reverie, and Shepherd whirled around to see Charlotte Button standing with a sly smile on her face.

'How the hell did you creep up on me like that?' said Shepherd.

Her smile widened. 'Give me some credit for my years with Five,' she said. 'I did pick up the odd bit of tradecraft. How did it go?'

'The mission? The flight? The debriefing?'

'All of the above.'

'The mission was a complete success. The flight was a pain in the arse. Ditto the debriefing.'

'Patsy just wanted her moment of glory,' said Button. 'She wants it known by all and sundry that it was driven by Five.'

Shepherd flashed her a tight smile. 'Presumably so that no one will think to look too closely at what happened to Ali Naveed, Israr Farooqi and Imran Masood and his family.'

'It was a spectacular success, Dan. We took out the terrorist responsible for killing dozens and maiming hundreds in London and killing God-knows how many others in the past. We took out seven British-born jihadists who would have caused untold havoc when they got back. Plus we killed close to a hundred ISIS fighters and snapped up a plethora of intelligence that will set them back years.'

Shepherd grinned. 'You keep saying "we", Charlie.'

She shrugged. 'I like to think I played a small part in it, yes. But I won't be getting a medal. Unlike Captain Gearie, who I hear on the grapevine might be getting put up for a Military Cross or perhaps even a DSO.'

'You are joking,' said Shepherd. The Distinguished Service Order was second only to the Victoria Cross as an award for bravery during a military operation. 'Please tell me you are joking.'

'It was a success and credit where credit is due. Captain Gearie was in charge of the operation.'

'Right up until the point where Khaled was going to blow them all to Kingdom Come with one of his suicide vests.'

'Well, you have a point, but that was resolved and there were no casualties on our side so we come out of it as clear winners in the fight against terrorism.'

'And Gearie gets his medal even though I saved his life?'

Button grinned. 'But you were never there,' she said. 'And nor was Dean Martin.'

'Funny that.'

'It has to be that way, and you know it. Explaining Martin's involvement would open up a whole can of worms that is best left unopened.'

'I suppose so.' He shrugged. 'I was never a fan of medals, anyway. They need too much polishing. So what's going to happen regarding Dean?'

'He's back in Bali and he tells me he's going to stay under the radar. Says he's happy being a diving instructor but we'll see how long he feels that way once he gets his share of the reward money.'

'Reward money?' repeated Shepherd.

'Didn't I mention that? The Americans had a ten-million-dollar bounty on Khaled's head.'

'That would be the head that I blew apart, right?'

She chuckled. 'But you were never there.'

'The money would have been nice, Charlie.'

'You're a civil servant carrying out his civil servant duties, so you wouldn't be eligible anyway,' said Button. 'But I'm very much in the private sector these days, as you know, so the Americans are quite happy to pay me and I'll be splitting it with Mr Martin.'

'So Dean gets five million dollars? Nice.'

'I said I was splitting it with him, I didn't say he was getting half. I had expenses. A lot of expenses. He'll be getting a million dollars and good luck to him. And you, you get what you've always wanted, a return to active operations.'

'You've spoken to Ellis?'

'Of course. Patsy and I have no secrets. She's very grateful to you. We both are. The operation couldn't have been more successful. You took out one of the world's most prolific terrorists, and you nailed home-grown jihadists who would have been back here before too long.'

'Go me,' said Shepherd.

'Indeed. And now MI5 will start using you the way you should be used. Your desk days are behind you.'

'I hope so.'

'You have Patsy's word on that. Just be careful what you wish for.'

Shepherd frowned. 'What do you mean?'

'Your love for the adrenaline rush could be the death of you one day. Just be careful.'

'I'm always careful.'

'Yes, and you're lucky. But one day your luck might run out. You've got a son and a girlfriend. It can't be easy for them when you put your life on the line.'

Shepherd laughed. 'This from the woman who was instrumental in sending me to a bloody war zone.'

Button smiled. 'You're right, of course. Listen to me pontificating about how you should live your life and yes, I had no qualms about putting you in harm's way.' She reached out and touched his arm. 'My heart was in my mouth all the time you were out there. I would really miss you, if anything ever happened to you.'

'I'd miss you too, Charlie.'

She took her hand away. 'I'm being serious.'

He could see from her eyes that his flippancy had offended her so he stepped forward and hugged her, then planted a light kiss on her cheek. 'I'd miss you, too, Charlie. You're devious and cunning and sometimes you take risks that you shouldn't but the world would be a much more boring place without you.' He released his grip on her and grinned as she blushed and re-arranged her hair. 'Now, next time phone, don't come up behind me like that. I might be carrying a gun.'

She laughed. 'I'll bear that in mind.' She turned and walked away.

Shepherd watched her go for a few seconds and then went inside the apartment block. He rode up in the lift and let himself into the flat. He called out for Katra but there was no reply. He took his bag into the sitting room and saw her standing by the window.

'Who was that?' she asked.

He dropped his bag on the floor and went over to her. 'What do you mean?' He tried to put his arms around her but she flinched and moved away.

'That woman, outside. You were talking to her.'

Shepherd realised she had seen him with Button through the window. He laughed and reached for her again and this time she let him hold her. 'That was work,' he said.

'It didn't look like work,' he said. 'And since when do you meet people from work in the street?'

'You'd be surprised how often that happens,' he said. 'That was Charlie Button, my old boss. She left MI5 under a cloud so she can't come around to my office.'

'What did she want?'

'It's complicated.'

She put her hands on his shoulders and pushed him away. 'I'm not stupid, Dan.'

'I never said you were. It's just that most of what I do is covered by the Official Secrets Act, you know that. I'm not even supposed to tell you where I've been.'

'But I'm your girlfriend!'

'Friends, family, it makes no difference.' He pretended to look around and lowered his voice. 'But I can tell you I was in Afghanistan, okay? But you mustn't tell anyone.'

Her eyes widened. 'Was it dangerous?'

Shepherd shook his head. 'No, I was there in an advisory

capacity. And the job's done now so I can spend some time with you.'

Her face brightened. Then just as quickly she frowned. 'You kissed her.'

Shepherd laughed. 'A peck on the cheek. Katra, I swear, there's nothing there you have to worry about?'

'Cross your heart?'

He laughed again and made a play of drawing a cross on his chest. 'I swear. She's a work colleague, that's all.'

'Not a friend?'

It was a good question and Shepherd wasn't immediately sure how to answer it. Shepherd had worked for Button, and alongside her, but he had always felt that there had been more to the relationship than just work. But friendship implied trust and the simple fact was that he didn't think he could ever trust her, not one hundred per cent. He smiled and shook his head slowly. 'No, she's not a friend.'

Katra hugged him and buried her face in his neck. 'I'm glad you're home,' she said. 'And you can go back to working regular hours and I can take care of you and we can eat together every night.'

Shepherd kissed her lightly on the top of the head. He figured it probably wasn't the right time to tell her that he was going back to operational work and while that meant he would be doing the job he loved, it also meant he'd be back to irregular hours and long periods away.

'What's for dinner?' he asked.

THRILLINGLY GOOD BOOKS
FROM CRIMINALLY
GOOD WRITERS

CRIME FILES BRINGS YOU THE LATEST RELEASES FROM TOP CRIME AND THRILLER AUTHORS.

SIGN UP ONLINE FOR OUR MONTHLY NEWSLETTER AND BE THE FIRST TO KNOW ABOUT OUR COMPETITIONS, NEW BOOKS AND MORE.